32,984

NORTH DALLAS FORTY

PETER GENT

NORTH DALLAS FORTY

WILLIAM MORROW & COMPANY, INC.
New York 1973

Grateful acknowledgment is made for permission to quote from the following songs:

"Sympathy for the Devil" and "Jigsaw Puzzle," both by Mick Jagger and Keith Richards, both © 1968 by ABKCO Music, Inc. All rights reserved.

"One of Us Must Know (Sooner or Later)" Copyright © 1966 by Dwarf Music.

"You Ain't Goin' Nowhere" Copyright © 1967 by Dwarf Music.

"Tell Me that It Isn't True" Copyright © 1969 by Big Sky Music.

"She Even Woke Me Up to Say Goodbye" Copyright © 1969 by Acuff-Rose Publications, Inc. All rights reserved.

"Love Minus Zero" © 1965 by M. Witmark & Sons. All rights reserved. Used by permission of Warner Bros. Music.

"At the Crossroads" and "Dallas Alice" both by Doug Sahm. Copyright © by Southern Love Music Co.

Printed in the United States of America.

Library of Congress Catalog Card Number 73-5815

2 3 4 5 75 74 73

For Jodi and Holly

With thanks to Bud and Marvin
And remembering Freddy who died
in vain in Beverly Hills

You can teach me life's lesson
You can bring a lot to know
But you just can't live in Texas
If you don't have a lot of soul . . .

—Doug Sahm

NORTH DALLAS FORTY

MONDAY

I was freezing my ass in the back of the pickup when O.W. Meadows finally turned off the blacktop and pulled to a stop alongside an oat field. We had been driving west about forty-five minutes from Fort Worth on the old Weatherford Highway. Meadows, Seth Maxwell, and Jo Bob Williams were crowded in the cab. I had been elected to ride in the back, owing more to my smaller size, milder demeanor, and lesser status than to my desire to do so. Occasionally Seth passed me the bottle of Wild Turkey bourbon and it helped cut the cold some, but mostly I just huddled behind the back of the cab against the damp wind.

As the truck bounced to a halt, Jo Bob stumbled out laughing and fell in the ditch. He was clutching the bottle of Wild Turkey. There was about an inch of the amber fluid left. He tossed it at me.

"Here, motherfucker," he growled. "Finish off the bird-bigger and let's unload them guns."

I complied, grimacing as the heat burned my throat and boiled up into my sinuses.

It was a drizzling, cold autumn day. Everything was either gray or yellow brown. It was the kind of day I like to watch from the warmth and security of my bed. Instead, I was with three drunken madmen on a Texas dove hunt. I told myself it was for the good of the team.

"Goddam, lookit that." O.W. Meadows had scrambled from behind the wheel. He was standing in the road pissing and pointing at several mourning doves coasting lazily into the oat patch. "Jeeeeesus. Gimme my gun."

"They're out of range," I protested.

"Gimme my gun!" he screamed.

I handed him his square-backed Browning 12-gauge automatic with the gold trigger. He blazed away, the shot raining into the oats about halfway between the pickup and the doves.

"Jesus Christ," I yelled. "That fucking gun was loaded!"

Several more doves flew out of the field and away from us. The three men scrambled to the back of the truck for their shotguns and shells and then headed into the low brown oats. I grabbed my Sears 20-gauge and followed a few yards behind, trying to load and walk at the same time.

"The wet'll keep 'em down," Jo Bob said. "All we gotta do is put the phantom stalk on 'em and they'll start comin' in with their hands up."

"As soon as they know we're here," Meadows added, "I 'spect they'll just surrender."

A field lark jumped about ten yards in front and headed away from us. Meadow's Browning and Jo Bob's Winchester over-and-under roared simultaneously, and the tiny speckled bird exploded into feathers.

"Still got the ol' eye," Jo Bob laughed. Meadows slid another shell into the bottom of the Browning.

Seth Maxwell looked back at me and grinned. I had come on the hunt at Maxwell's insistence. He thought it would be good therapy. I had been on the same football team with Jo Bob and Meadows for several years and, at best, we had reached an uneasy truce. They disliked me and I was terrified of them. Naked in the locker room they were awesome enough, but drunk and armed, walking through a Parker County oat field, they were specters. I was depending on Maxwell to protect me from severe physical harm. There was no protection against emotional damage. That was an occupational hazard.

Jo Bob and Meadows moved a few yards ahead of Maxwell. Jo Bob picked up the shambles that had been the field lark and threw it back in my direction. I ducked; the gore fell several feet short. The two giant linemen, walking side by side, shotguns over their arms, were an anxious sight and I wanted only to please them. The problem was to figure out how. Maxwell dropped back and fell in step with me.

"Hey poot," he asked, "what's the trouble?"

I eyed him curiously. "This is like a long weekend in the DMZ."

"Relax." Maxwell soothed with the manner that made him one of professional football's better leaders. "Ain't nobody gonna get hurt."

"Mention that to the scalp hunters," I suggested.

"Just stay behind 'em," he instructed. "That's what I always do."

"That's comforting."

Our conversation was cut off by the roar of shotguns. Jo Bob and Meadows had brought down three doves between them.

"I got a double," Jo Bob hollered.

"Double my ass," Meadows argued. "I shot two of them birds myself. That leaves you only one. And I think he died of fright." Meadows howled with laughter.

"Bullshit," Jo Bob argued, breaking his gun and jamming in two more shells. He reached down and picked up the first bird, which was still flopping, its wing shattered. Jo Bob caught the bird's head between his thumb and forefinger and jerked it off. The wings flapped spasmodically and then the beheaded dove went limp. Jo Bob tossed the head back at me. I caught it and threw it back at him; it left my hand covered with blood. I wiped my palm on my Levi's but the blood had quickly coagulated and I couldn't rub it all off. When I clenched my fist the skin stuck together.

Meadows moved ahead and picked up another of the birds. It too was still alive.

"Here," Meadows said, tossing the cripple at Jo Bob. "Pop its head. I'll find the other." The wounded bird sailed through the air like a baseball. At the top of the arc it suddenly came alive and began to fly toward us.

"Son of a bitch," Meadows screamed, raising his gun, aiming at the bird.

"Hold it, O.W.," Maxwell yelled, already ducking.

We hit the ground as the Browning roared twice more and the bird fell out of the sky, dropping next to me. I pounced on the dove like a loose fumble for fear it would start to crawl toward me and Meadows would open up again.

We continued on through the oat field, getting five doves. Maxwell and I scored one apiece. Jo Bob shot two more doves and demolished an owl asleep in a tree along the fence line. Meadows hit two doves, finding only one, and produced another bottle of Wild Turkey. When we reached the opposite edge of the field we stood around taking pulls out of the bottle and considering our next move. Finally we decided to hike about a mile to a cattle tank, where Meadows said there were some duck blinds. At least we could sit and drink out of the wind.

At the tank, we slipped up on five careless mallards. Jo Bob and Meadows killed four before the ducks got off the water. Maxwell brought down the fifth when it circled back over the tank, looking for its pals.

"Did you see that?" Meadows laughed. "I got two with one shot."

"Shit," Maxwell argued. "You shot 'em on the water."

"Did not," Meadows said, grinning and holding his arms askew, his left foot off the ground. "They had one foot up." He broke into peals of laughter.

"How do we get 'em?" I asked.

"You can swim after 'em for all I care," Jo Bob said. "I don't want 'em. Just have to clean 'em. Besides, I don't have a duck stamp."

The pond was about five acres in all, with small blinds on each side. Maxwell and I positioned on one side, Jo Bob and Meadows on the other.

"What am I doing here?" I said, after a cold, silent wait. The lonesome sounds of the wind picking up and the water lapping against the side of the blind were depressing.

"Calm down," Maxwell said. "It'll do you good."

I watched a hawk drift overhead, its wings outstretched, soaring on the currents of the barren west Texas sky.

The two shotguns on the other side roared. I scanned the sky. It was empty. The guns boomed again and something rattled on the outside of our blind.

"Jesus Christ," I yelled. "They're shooting at us."

We dropped to the floor of the blind as the two men blazed away from the other side of the tank. Pellets rained off the side of the blind. After every shot, I could hear Jo Bob laughing like a loon.

"Goddammit, Jo Bob," Maxwell screamed. "You two cocksuckers better cut the shit or I swear to God I'll have your asses." The shooting stopped, but Meadows and Jo Bob continued to giggle.

I peered over the side of the blind. The ambushed mallards floated limply in the water. A dying green head flapped weakly. Jo Bob and Meadows both shot it again. After a half hour of empty sky, we moved back through the oat field to the truck. I got two more doves as we reached the road. Maxwell had bagged one just as we left the tank. That made a total of eleven.

The second bottle of Wild Turkey was dead. We stood at the truck again trying to decide what to do next.

"Look out, Jo Bob." Meadows had slipped two dead doves from his pocket and had thrown them into the air. "Shoot 'em quick. . . . shoot 'em."

Jo Bob quickly shouldered his gun and fired twice, hitting one of the birds. When they struck the ground Meadows emptied his shotgun into them, blowing the birds to shreds. Jo Bob and Meadows left them where they fell and clambered onto the fenders of the truck.

The decision was made to road hunt. I was elected to drive. Maxwell sat next to me. The two assassins remained on the fenders.

As we drove slowly along the gravel road, Maxwell ferreted another bottle of bourbon from beneath the seat. We passed it back and forth. The warmth of the liquor was relaxing me. I tried to settle back and enjoy the day. It was Monday, our day off. The day before we had beaten St. Louis—through no small effort on my part. There was no reason why I shouldn't be having fun.

As I reached for the hundred-proof bourbon the booming shotguns turned my attention back to the road.

"You got him, O.W.," Jo Bob laughed, barely keeping his balance on the fender. "Right in the ass."

"Goddammit," Meadows howled, "I spoiled the meat." They both laughed insanely, beating their thighs with open hands.

A gray-striped cat was trying to pull itself off the road with its forepaws, its hindquarters shredded by a double load of number six shot. I stopped the truck and Maxwell grabbed his shotgun.

"Jesus Christ, you two." Maxwell was angry. He raised his gun and shot the tortured animal again. The force of the shot slammed the cat limply into the ground and made it skid several feet. A hind foot kicked out twice, stiffly. The animal twisted its head up and died. Maxwell looked at the dead cat, then back at his smirking teammates. He shook his head and crawled back into the cab.

"They're fucking crazy," I said.

"Naw," Maxwell disagreed. "Just tryin' to relax and have a good time."

I grabbed the bottle and took a long, stinging swig.

"Well, I can't relax as long as they got the guns."

"We'll head back to Fort Worth in a bit."

"Do I have to ride in the back again?"

Maxwell looked at me and shrugged.

I had to and by the time we reached the Big Boy Restaurant where we had left our cars, I was numb. We returned cold, tired, drunk, and empty-handed. Jo Bob had thrown the remaining doves at passing cars.

"Jo Bob, you take my car," Maxwell ordered. "I'll ride with Phil. We'll catch you at Crawford's place."

Jo Bob and Meadows looked quizzically at each other. They didn't understand Maxwell's desire to hunt or drink with me. His riding all the way back to Dallas in my car was pure bedevilment. I enjoyed their confusion.

It was late afternoon. In a last gasp the sun had burned away the gray sky and had disappeared into the Panhandle. The air had warmed some and the best part of the day remained. Being in Texas is a skin feeling, strongest this time of day. There is a softness to the twilight. The days could be overpowering in their sun-soaked brightness, not so much now since the smog, but still incredibly vibrant. This afternoon, it was the predark peace that I needed, a quiet power I had never felt in the changing gray of the Midwest or the choking paranoia of New York.

I love Texas, but she drives her people crazy. I've wondered whether it's the heat, or the money, or maybe both. A republic of outlaws loosely allied with the United States, Texas survives, and survives quite well by breaking the rules. Now there is a new generation of Texans who want to do away with the rules. The old resist violently, unable to conceive of that dream of wealth, devoid of any rules to break.

I took out my keys and bent to unlock my car, a brand-new honey-beige Buick Riviera with all the extras, an embarrassing car. Maxwell had sent me to the Buick dealer who sponsors his television show. He swore the guy would give me a great deal. I had wanted a used Opel.

In one hour, the sales manager (the dealer had been too busy to talk to me) showed me how "for practically the same money" I could own a new Riviera and all the accompanying good feelings.

A good salesman knows the purchaser is totally without

sense—why else would anyone ask a salesman anything? Once you speak to a salesman you have shown your hole card. I not only spoke, but shook his hand and hoped deeply that we could become friends.

On the other side of the lot Jo Bob was getting into Maxwell's blue-on-blue Cadillac convertible.

"Say er ah babee." Maxwell fell into a black dialect, which he often did when asking for or talking about drugs. "Ah, let's have some of what you call your grassss." He hissed out the last word purposely.

"Hey man, just say grass."

"Can't, babee. Gots to get in de mood. Now where's dat killer weed?"

"There's some in the glove compartment."

I picked through the cartridge tapes scattered on the floor beneath my feet. I pushed the Sir Douglas Quintet *Together After Five* into the deck, adjusted the eight-position steering wheel, and pulled out of the lot. Doug Sahm sang about the ill-fated love of two kids in Dallas.

"Seems her father didn't approve
Of his long hair and far-out groove . . ."

Maxwell lit the joint and took a long drag, making the familiar hissing sound that could only come from someone inhaling cannabis.

"So . . . that there is what you call yer killer weed." Maxwell held the joint up for inspection. "Well, it ain't Cutty and water, but it'll do." He passed me the joint, and I sucked on it in short soft puffs, a habit acquired from turning on in airplanes, public restrooms, and dark back yards at straight parties. All getting pretty risky what with the current dope publicity and universal vigilance for peculiar smells.

Three years ago, on the team plane from Washington, Maxwell and I had kept sneaking to the john to smoke dope. The stewardess noticed the smell and thought the galley wiring was smoldering. There was a five-minute panic, both for those who were scared the plane was afire, and for Maxwell and me, who were terrified that it wasn't. We weren't caught but we swore a blood oath to never smoke on the team plane again. It was a promise we kept until the next road game.

The lights from the toll plaza appeared up ahead. I eased off the gas and rolled down my window. A fat man, about forty-five, in a sweat-stained gray uniform, stood at the door of the booth. One hand held out the toll ticket, the other was stuffing what appeared to be a peanut butter and lizard sandwich into his face. I slowly coasted the car through the gate, neatly picking the ticket from the outstretched hand. A name tag stenciled BILLY WAYNE ROBINSON hung from his shirt-pocket flap.

"Hey, Billy Wayne." Maxwell leaned toward the open window. "How's yer mom and them?"

The attendant looked startled, then confused, then, recognized the famous smiling face. Like a true Texas football fan he went completely berserk. Waving and trying to speak as we glided through, he spat half his sandwich on the trunk.

"Did you know that guy?"

"Naw, just a little of the ol' instant humble. I shoulda offered him some of this here maryjawana."

"Show 'em you can straddle the old generation gap," I said.

I accelerated into the main lanes of the Dallas-Fort Worth Turnpike, heading for Dallas at about ninety miles an hour, a high-speed island of increased awareness and stereophonic sound heading back to the future. The turnpike was twenty-eight straight miles of concrete laid on rolling hills, connecting the two cities for anyone with sixty cents and a Class A automobile. Factories, warehouses, and two medium cities smother the land the length of the highway. Back in the early sixties, five minutes past the toll gate, heading for either end, you were out in the West. That was when Braniff's planes were gray. Jack Ruby ran a burlesque house. And the School Book Depository was a place they kept schoolbooks.

"Smoke will rise
In the Dallas skies
Comin' back to you
Dallas Alice . . ."

"Here."

"Huh?"

"Here!" Maxwell was thrusting the joint at me. His eyes and cheeks and neck were bulging. He was trying to stifle a cough. His face was crimson. I took the joint. Maxwell exhaled, coughing and clearing his throat. He looked and sounded like a four-pack-a-day man getting out of bed in the morning.

"B.A. wants me in his office at ten tomorrow morning," I said, remembering.

"He's probably gonna tell you you're starting Sunday."

"I doubt it." I frowned. "If he was gonna do that he'd just call in Gill and tell him he wasn't starting. No, I think B.A. just wants to make certain I understand the nonprejudicial, technically flawless way he arrived at the opinion I should sit on the bench."

"I dunno." Maxwell gazed out the windshield. "That was a big catch you made yesterday. It put us ahead to stay."

"Yeah maybe, but it was the only pass I caught."

"You only played the last quarter. Besides, it was the only one I threw at you."

"He'll want to know why you don't throw at me more." It frustrated me to use the coach's logic. I paused. "By the way," I turned my face from the windshield and frowned at Maxwell, "why don't you throw to me more?"

"Cause you ain't been playing that much, asshole."

"I suppose. After that truly amazing catch, you'll surely want me as the special guest on your television show. Gimme the opportunity to snuggle my way into the heart of Dallas-Fort Worth. It's the least you could do."

"It's also the most," Maxwell said. "Besides, I'm having Jo Bob on the show this week."

"How about a remote interview?" I suggested, smiling widely. "I could tell how I overcame a truly Middlewest upbringing and a childhood case of paralytic ringworm. Maybe they could do some closeup shots of my hands doing something—like picking my nose."

"Listen, man," Maxwell interrupted, "it's a family show."

I shook my head. "Why can't there be a football show for the hard-core pervert?"

There was no response from Maxwell. He seemed lost in thought.

"What do you think of the SCA?" Maxwell said finally.

"What?"

"The Society of Christian Athletes." His voice was deep and halting as he tried to keep the marijuana smoke down in his lungs. "B.A. asked me to make an appearance at the national rally they're having in May. At the Cotton Bowl."

"You don't believe that shit, do you?"

"Sort of." Maxwell's voice became submissive. "I mean, when you have a chance to influence people you oughta do some good."

"Who says that's good?" I asked. "Besides B.A."

"What's wrong with him? For God's sake, the man's a Christian. That's a helluva lot more than you are."

"Sure, our coach has money, success, his life planned down to the minutest detail. Everything going off like clockwork. He must have God on his side."

"You sure are bitter," Maxwell said. "What harm can it do?"

"I don't care, man. Go ahead, influence people." I deepened my voice to affect an imitation. "Hi, kids. Seth Maxwell here to give you a little good influence. Don't get your kicks doping. Get out on the ol' gridiron and hurt somebody. It's cleaner and more fun."

Maxwell stared silently through the windshield. I turned my attention back to the road.

Six Flags Amusement Park flashed by on the right. In all the years I'd lived in Dallas, I'd been to this "Disneyland of the Southwest" only once. I'd spent the entire time, stoned on mescaline, in the Petting Zoo caressing a baby llama. I considered screwing the furry little bugger as a protest against captivity, his and mine. But I decided even if the llama understood, the guards wouldn't, so I chalked up another sexual and sociological frustration and went home.

Flailing arms and loud coughing brought me out of my thoughts.

"Goddam. Goddam." Maxwell's voice was raspy and he was gagging. "Goddam. I swallowed the roach." He shook his head. "It burned the livin' shit outta me."

"I warned you about suckin' so hard."

"Fuck," he said. He leaned over and spit on my floor. "You got another?"

"In the glove compartment."

Maxwell pulled out a joint rolled in a replica of a one-hundred-dollar bill.

"Shit." He held the joint out in front of him. "I'll bet the guy that came up with that made a killing."

Sir Douglas started into "Seguin." I pushed the reject button and replaced the tape with the Rolling Stones. They started somewhere in the middle of "Honky Tonk Women."

"You know," Maxwell said, staring vacantly at the road, "I've always wanted to take about six months and just travel around Texas, going from one honky-tonk to another. Find the best jukeboxes and the women with the saddest stories."

"The people in honky-tonks," he continued, "are just like a good country-music jukebox. Full of stories about people who just lost somethin', or never had anything to start with." He clasped his hands behind his head and leaned back in the seat. The joint dropped from his lips. "We'd go to a different one ever' night. Just drink, fuck, eat pussy, and listen to country music. You could learn a lot, podnah."

"Maybe. But we could get the shit beat outta us in a lotta those places. Like the Jacksboro Highway."

The Jacksboro Highway was a honky-tonk-lined road leading from Fort Worth to Jacksboro. The Old West still lived in the bars along this particular stretch and there were shootings and knifings every night.

Maxwell thought for a moment, then turned slowly to look at me. "What are you so scared of?" he asked.

"Pain, man. Nothing flashy or existential. Just plain old pain. I don't like it, never have. I can't even stand the thought of my skin splitting open and my bodily fluids spilling onto the Astroturf in front of millions of screaming fans—for money. Do you think I wanna do it for free? Alone? And in the dark?"

"But it's all part of being alive, man. The pleasure and the pain. You can't have one without the other."

"It's an age of specialists."

We were both silent. I was reminded of another car trip we had made back in the early spring. On a dull Wednesday in March we had gotten high, filled the car with gasoline, whiskey, speed, and grass and driven to Sante Fe nonstop. We spent two nights at an old hotel, until at 3 A.M. the second morning Maxwell finally seduced the night clerk on a brown leather couch in the lobby. I alternated between standing guard and watching them fuck. She was a heavyset woman, about forty-five, and all the time Maxwell humped away at her, she babbled endlessly about him being her son's favorite football star, and how pleased the boy would be to learn she and Maxwell had met and become friends.

The return took eighteen hours. All the way back we took speed, smoked dope, drank Pepsi, and ate pork rinds. Beginning ten minutes outside of Sante Fe and continuing to the outskirts of Dallas, Maxwell described in detail every sex act he had ever committed. Except for gas and piss, we stopped only once, in Odessa, to see the World's Largest Statue of a Jackrabbit.

"You know," Maxwell began talking, "I'm actually getting to where I don't think I mind pain. You know what I mean? Remember when I dislocated my elbow? For a minute there it hurt so bad I thought I'd go crazy. There was no way I could stand it. Then all of a sudden . . . Well, I can't explain it." His face screwed up in an attempt to find words. "Except that it hurt. And it didn't hurt. I mean, it still really hurt bad, but I could stand it and actually sort of liked it, in a different sort of way."

"I'm not sure I get it," I said, nonetheless feeling a nebulous sense of identity with the feelings he was trying to describe.

"Well, it's sorta like pain makes me think I'm doin' something. Nothing occupies my mind but the pain, it's all I care about. I feel secure in it. When the pain is the worst I'm the most relaxed. Weird, isn't it?"

"I don't know if *weird* is a strong enough word."

I gripped the wheel tighter and looked ahead to the approaching Dallas toll plaza. The Dallas skyline was directly ahead. I paid the toll and headed for the Trinity River Bridge and I35 beyond. Crossing Commerce, Main, and Elm of the I35 overpass, I read the giant Hertz sign atop the Schoolbook Depository. I looked to the spot on Elm Street where Kennedy was shot. I had seen the historic place hundreds of times, but I still couldn't actually picture it happening. Now the country had another President who liked guys like me and football and attended the Washington practices to call screen passes. What was more perfect? A President who liked deceptive plays. He was B.A.'s favorite.

I turned into the Motor Street exit, followed Motor past the hospital that had received the mangled Kennedy and onto Maple, then right again to The Apartments. The parking lot was jammed. The only open spot was adjacent to a fire hydrant. I parked there.

"Lock your door, Seth," I said. "If they can't take a joke, fuck 'em."

Maxwell stepped out, leaned over and took the last drag on the joint. Taking long, slow strides and throwing his arms and head back, he broke into song.

"Turn out the lights, the party's over."

He walked around the hedge into the passageway that led down a flight of stairs to the pool. The song faded off.

I leaned back, hands on my hips, and stretched, looking up at the sky, wishing I would witness a supernova. No such luck.

As I walked around the pool and toward Andy Crawford's apartment, I watched Maxwell make his entrance to the party. Standing bowlegged in the doorway, his knees flexed, Maxwell hopped from one foot to another, fingers held over his head in peace signs.

"Peace God Bless. Peace God Bless," he cried. "Peace God Bless."

"Peace on you," someone yelled from inside.

Everyone laughed.

I waited outside until the crowd greeting Seth moved away from the door. Then I slipped unnoticed into the kitchen. I hopped my butt up onto the drainboard and sat watching the party through a hole in the kitchen-dining room wall that served as a bar. There were about thirty people milling around. I recognized most of them from other parties. Except for the other players, however, I didn't know the names of more than a half-dozen.

Jo Bob and Meadows had already arrived and were sitting on either side of a big redhead with huge breasts. Both were grabbing at her giant tits, laughing and calling her Booger Red. Vainly her outnumbered hands tried to keep the grinning men from becoming too obscene.

Thomas Richardson, the handsome black running back from Hattiesburg, Mississippi, was squatting Indian-style against the far wall, observing his teammates in action. He was an incredible athlete, but he was considered peculiar and unapproachable by management, the coaches, and most of his teammates. His attitude stemmed in part from an intensely personal contract dispute. As a result he seldom played. The club seemed reluctant to trade or release him. Instead they buried him, hoping he would fade from memory. He was always outstanding when he played, but he refused to deal in anything but profoundly relevant and personal terms. He insisted that management meet him on a man-to-man basis. Not even the most confident of football general managers or head coaches is willing to meet an angry 225-pound black on a man-to-man basis.

Probably sometime soon *Richardson* would appear in six-point type on the waiver list and few, if any, would notice.

I was alone in the kitchen, except for a couple standing

near the refrigerator. The man was wearing wide-stripe bell bottoms and a hot-pink silk shirt open to the waist. He was sporting a tan, the kind you get from executive sunlamps. The girl was cute, blonde, about twenty, and crying.

"Come on, relax, honey, he's not such a bad guy," the man was saying, trying to calm her.

"He shouldn't have done that," she cried. "I don't like him at all."

"Come on now."

"That bastard, who does he think he is?" She was angry. "No more of this blind-date shit, Steve. I mean it." She looked at me and noticed I was staring. He followed her eyes.

"Hey." He moved in my direction. "Phil, how ya' doin' man?" He extended his hand. "Steve Peterson, we met at Andy's last party."

I took his hand but continued to watch the girl, who was further infuriated. I nodded a greeting at the man and said nothing.

"Oh, that's Brenda." He had noticed my gaze. "She's pissed off at Andy about something."

Hearing her name, Brenda turned her back to us and faced the refrigerator.

"Hey man, you played a fantastic game." Steve Peterson slapped me on the shoulder and left his hand there, rubbing my collarbone gently. "That was a great catch. You have got to be my favorite receiver, man. You can have Billy Gill and Delma Huddle."

I nodded and looked at the floor.

"Listen," he said, still rubbing my clavicle. "I gotta get back to her." He stopped rubbing my neck, and fumbled in his back pocket for his wallet. "Gimme a call when you come to town. We'll go to lunch. I've got some things you might be interested in." He handed me his card and I set it on the drainboard without looking at it.

"I'll be seein' you." He turned to Brenda, then back to me. "Don't forget to call, we'll get some dollies."

I looked out of the kitchen without acknowledging his good-bye.

The host, last year's Rookie of the Year, Andy Crawford, was leaning against the wrought-iron lattice that separated the living room from the dining room. He was talking to a rookie defensive back from Texas named Alan Claridge. Both were powerful, good-looking men, weighing around two twenty and standing well over six foot three. They were well tanned and muscular and often mistaken for brothers. Crawford was pointing to the front of Claridge's shirt. When Claridge looked down, Crawford brought his hand up into Claridge's nose. Crawford doubled up with laughter while his victim jumped back.

When Crawford straightened up, Claridge pounced and grabbed him by his biceps. Soon they were reeling around in a friendly pushing match, each gripping the other's arms. Laughter and groans punctuated the contest as both men strained mightily against each other. From the color of their faces and the cords standing out on their necks, I could see they were exerting fiercely. Crawford suddenly lost his footing and Claridge stumbled forward on top of him, both of them crashing through the dining room table and chairs. Crawford had ripped off Claridge's shirt, and they lay gasping. I leaned across the bar and looked at them lying directly below. They were sweating profusely, looking at each other and laughing. Claridge whispered something to Crawford, then carefully held Crawford's face with both hands and planted an open-mouthed kiss full on the lips. Crawford responded and their tongues strained against each other. The embrace lasted about ten seconds.

Steve Peterson and Brenda had come to the door at the sound of the crash and seemed to be the only others who witnessed the kiss.

"God, I'm getting out of here." Brenda's eyes had widened. She ran out the back door to the alley.

Steve Peterson looked at me and shrugged. "She's from SMU," he said.

"Hey Phil," Andy Crawford said. He had regained his feet when he saw me leaning across the bar. "Glad you could make it." We shook hands.

Claridge headed back toward Andy's bedroom to get a new shirt.

"Hey, podnah," Crawford was addressing me, "you got a dolly with you?"

I shook my head.

"Well, I'll go find you one." He headed into the mass of people in the living room.

The party had been on for some time, possibly early afternoon, and was still picking up speed. It wouldn't be as awesome as a postgame party, but it looked interesting enough for a man with a slow time in the forty-yard dash and a glove box full of grass.

Postgame parties were outrageous. Players bottle up a lot of fear and frustration trying to maintain a tone during a week's practice and a Sunday afternoon. It all comes spilling out after the game. Compound that with amphetamines, taken to maintain a pitch before and during the game. The effect of the speed didn't end with the gun. Mix liquor and adrenaline with the aforementioned ingredients in a two-hundred-sixty-pound container, multiply it by about twenty and you have a POSTGAME TEAM PARTY. Mix only liquor and fear and you had tonight's party. The results promised to be awesome.

Postgame parties had another special catalyst—wives. The public displays of mutual disaffection were always intriguing. They constantly renewed my belief in divorce as the only sane American Institution. At times like those, I considered my divorce as my only true success. There were more punches thrown between player and wife than there ever were between player and player. Few football teams could withstand the disharmony that several of my teammates incorporated into their marriages with the utmost of ease. The amount of bodily harm these marriage partners inflicted on each other was amazing. Physical violence was a daily component of their marital give-and-take. The real offenders were the women. They took to violence much quicker than their husbands. The favorite weapons are usually heavy cut-glass articles like vases and ash trays. Makes for a gory wound.

During my short, violent marriage, the wives had attempted several times to organize against the unbridled insanity of postgame parties. They were tired of their husbands acting like animals in public, even if the public was only other teammates.

There was a curious, subtle homosexual bond that united the wives in their battles against the husbands and vice versa. The men shared the dark secrets of locker rooms, training camps, and road games. No matter the cost, these secrets were never to be shared with the wives. The women used baby showers and bridge games as strategy sessions for counterattacks against this chauvinistic secret society. The wives swapped rumors, suspicions, facts and fantasies for later use on unsuspecting spouses. Favorite times for wifely sapper raids were just before coitus or while packing for a road trip. "Judith Ann said Seth was with her Thursday. So, where were you?"

Like most wives, ours aspired for better, more genteel lives and began to plan the team parties like debutante balls. Power plays would be carried out in full dress.

One Sunday in late October, I had struggled home after a disappointing loss to Baltimore. My wife met me at the door dressed in a bunny suit. The wives had planned a Halloween party. I realized the worst of my day was yet to come.

"Hurry up and put this on." She held out an identical hollow rabbit for me. (Now, I must explain, so our behavior doesn't seem aberrant but merely intense, that social status was distributed among the wives according to the husband's current status with the team. This shaky dependence on their husbands for identity made wives hypersensitive to any deviant behavior. My wife was constantly concerned that I might fuck up, and I did.)

I refused to put on the costume.

After spending the afternoon sweating, bleeding, and baring my soul in a losing cause, I wasn't going to dress in a fluffy white tail and long pink ears and meet my teammates for a drink.

"You don't care about me," she cried. "You don't care about anybody but yourself. I'm in charge of the refreshments. You have to wear a costume."

"Oh, for Christ sake, I refuse to go to the Sheraton ballroom looking like the Easter bunny."

"It's not Easter. It's Halloween." She wiped her nose with a little white paw.

"Look, I've already made a fool of myself in front of seventy-six thousand people." (I had dropped the one pass that might have broken the game open.) "I'm not going to compound it by going out in public looking like Uncle Wiggily. Leave me alone. I'm tired."

"You're always tired when I'm around. But you're never too tired to go out drinking and screwing those little whores that hang around Rock City." She pulled nervously at one pink ear. "I want to do things that other people do."

"We're not like other people. Can't we discuss this some other time?"

"You never want to do anything I like." She was starting to sweat. The bunny suit was getting hot. "You never wanted to get married. Did you?" This was a word game we had started playing shortly after her marriage-inducing pregnancy ended in miscarriage. I would deny the accusation immediately. My denial wouldn't stop the argument or even slow it, but it served as a landmark while our anger broke new trails.

Looking back now, I realize the importance of the little procedures in maintaining a relationship. You can obliterate the emotions in a marriage and it will plod on into eternity. But if you tamper with the rhythm, it'll tumble around your ears.

Maybe I was just tired or distracted, or maybe I meant to do it. Whatever my reasons, that day I denied too slowly.

Her eyes widened when the right moment for pledging fidelity had passed. They turned wild as the second stretched into eternity.

"No. No. Of course, I wanted to get married." It was too late.

"You son of a bitch," she screamed. "I'll show you." She ran into the kitchen and began rummaging through drawers. It was to be a suicide attempt, her fourth in as many weeks. Her first fraudulent attempt had been with a knife. It left no marks. Subsequent headlong rushes to the big sleep had involved less deadly implements. Her last attempt had been with a potato peeler.

I walked upstairs. I was tired. It had been such an easy pass.

"You bastard," she screamed, as I reached the top of the stairs. "You don't even care. Goddam you, I hope you die." I hoped I did too . . . and soon. The ball had been right on my fingertips. I stumbled or something. It just seemed to float away. I couldn't hold it.

I washed my face and pissed to the sound of breaking glass and slamming doors. It irritated my wife much more when I ignored her, but I didn't want to fight with her. She was a hell of a scratcher.

When I returned downstairs, Tony Bennett was singing about the heart he had left in San Francisco.

It had been our song in college.

She was sitting on the living room floor looking through an album of our wedding pictures. Her face was tearstained and red. One of the pink ears was bent double. She looked up at me.

"I love you." A teardrop trickled down a fake whisker and hung, bobbing, on the end.

I laughed. I couldn't help it.

The laugh was the final insult. Tearing off her costume and grabbing mine from the table, she ran onto the patio and threw them in a pile. She soaked them with charcoal starter and set them afire. Chest heaving and eyes blazing, clothed only in her bra and panties, she watched the bunny suits go up in smoke.

I was going mad.

The fire seemed to burn everything out and shortly we were on our way to the party, casually dressed and observing a shaky armistice.

"Are you all right?" I had been driving about ten minutes.

There was no answer. "Look, I'm sorry. I was tired and depressed."

"You're always tired and depressed. You just come home and stare at television. And whenever B.A. does something you don't like, you don't come home at all. Well, I'm sick of it. I want to be tired and depressed sometime."

She leaned against the passenger door and pulled her neck down into the fur collar of her coat. I couldn't blame her for being disappointed. She wanted to join a country club and I wanted to watch television.

"I want to have a baby."

"We can't afford a baby, you know that."

"Why not? You make plenty of money."

"Sixteen thousand dollars isn't plenty of money, particularly when we have a three-hundred-dollar-a-month house payment and a maid. After today, I may be out of work." Jesus, it had been right in my hands. The defensive back had fallen down. Son of a bitch!

"All you do is worry about your precious football."

"It's our precious football, unless you'd like to get another job." I had been all alone, nothing but open field. Goddammit! How did I miss that fucking ball?

"I might as well if I can't have a baby. Staying home is really boring." She had held a job as a nurse's aide for three days. Our closet was full of pink-and-white-striped aprons.

"We wouldn't be worrying about money if you hadn't quit your job with Brooks."

"I didn't quit. I was fired." I had worked two off-seasons for Brooks Harris "usin' the ol' name to make contacts and tell the folks our good news about real estate." There was one problem, "inability to close" Brooks had called it. I just didn't seem to be able to make that demand that would "push the customer from confusion to conviction to close." All the customer's reasons for refusing to buy seemed perfectly rational to me. Dammit, I know I didn't take my eyes off it. B.A. could bench me.

"Darlene Meadows said O.W.'s thinking about taking that job and . . ." she turned to face me, ". . . Judith Maxwell told me she thought you and Seth were smoking marijuana again. Are you?"

"No, we aren't." Maxwell and I had both tried to get our wives to turn on with us. They were horrified and screamed of brain damage and perversion. Seth and I had been under close scrutiny since. I must have been off balance when I made my break. It was right in my hands.

We were the only people not in costume at the party. I said we had come as a famous flankerback and his wife. It didn't help. My wife left me and sat with Darlene Meadows, who had come as Scarlett O'Hara, and Judith Ann Maxwell, who appeared to be Jacqueline Kennedy Onassis. Judith Ann was Seth's third wife. I sat at the bar and thought about how much I would like to screw Darlene Meadows. O.W. Meadows had come as the Grand Dragon of the Ku Klux Klan; several of the black players left in frightened indignation. Judith Ann had dressed Seth in a solid-black gunfighter's rig. He seemed a little embarrassed by it but rode it out to the bitter end. Maxwell even had a mock shootout with Jo Bob Williams, who, crisscrossed with bandoliers, had come as Pancho Villa. Both of them fell in a writhing heap on the dance floor. Shortly after midnight, Alan Claridge arrived in drag and claimed he was the real Gloria Steinem. The party broke up about forty-five minutes later. All the men had gotten hopelessly drunk.

During the ride home, I slept in the back seat of the car. I awoke when I felt the car stop. My wife shut off the engine, leaned over the seat and punched me in the nose.

"Lousy drunk son of a bitch." She slammed the car door and I could hear her high heels clicking up the sidewalk to our house. My nose began to bleed.

Thinking about wives brought me down and I headed back to Andy's bedroom to smoke a joint. The bedroom was off limits to all but a select few, of which I considered myself a member, quite without any encouragement from Crawford.

I immediately sat down on the bed and lit a joint, inhaling deeply, letting it seep through me.

"Better than booze," I thought, to assuage my conscience.

The bed was unmade. On the bedside table was a half-eaten peanut butter and jelly sandwich and a bowl that in the distant past had contained soup. The red bedspread matched the carpeting and wallpaper. The sheets and pillowcases were silk. There was a small Sony color television lying on one of the pillows. On the other pillow was a vibrator and a set of Vise Grips.

At the foot of the bed lay three checkbooks, all on different banks, and a stack of bills months old. Andy frequently mentioned that he handled his finances so badly he would often be overdrawn a couple of thousand dollars, a figure not far from my overdrafts.

Bankers were amazing. They would lend any amount of money, and as long as the debtor remained on the active playing list, renewals were always forthcoming. It was hard to believe they were just football fans.

On the dresser, stuck in the corner of a jewel box, were five telegrams. Each bore a different date, one for each of our five previous games.

The message and signature were the same on all. SOCK IT TO 'EM, signed Susan B.

Susan Brinkerman was Andy Crawford's girl. Currently studying to be a portrait painter, she had been a cheerleader at SMU and maintained, in the face of a rapidly disintegrating universe, a nineteenth-century morality with options. She still fucked, but seldom admitted it, even to her partner. Postcoitus was fraught with remorse. The result was the standard amount of guilt with the heavy advantage of more orgasms. Andy loved her for it and made a great show of trying to respect her chastity but they usually lost control about twice a week and went "all the way." The next day was reserved for penitence and the throes of self-chastisement.

Susan wasn't coming to tonight's party. It was the mutually agreed upon night for Andy to sow his wild oats. They planned to get married after he got it all out of his system.

The roach was burning my fingers, so I crushed it out and ate it. I lay down across the bed, my eyes fixed on the ceiling. I tried to relax. Sometimes, grass worked like a perfect tranquilizer and I would just float. Tonight, I couldn't keep my mind still. My thoughts raced from yesterday's game to B.A. to tomorrow. I was desperate to regain the starting position. I couldn't stop thinking about it.

I had recovered, miraculously, from three serious injuries, but the recovery couldn't erase the fact of the injuries. I was damaged, and if I didn't make myself an integral part of the offense quickly, management would be shopping for a new piece of equipment. Time was my competition and, if I let down for a moment, it would just go on increasing its already considerable edge on me.

When B.A. replaced me with Billy Gill because of my injured leg, I thought I would go crazy.

At first I rationalized it as a temporary thing and prepared each game to return to action to show what I could do with a football in free fall. As my leg healed, I had difficulty restraining myself from just running onto the field and joining the huddle uninvited. I was ready to play. I would pace the sideline, staying close to B.A., waiting for the order, watching his eyes expectantly. By halftime the fear of not getting to play would begin to creep in, but I would sit in the dressing room and watch B.A. diagram adjustments or I would nervously walk over to Maxwell to inquire how the game was going. His distant reply reminded me I wasn't a part of it. I knew I could help if they would just let me.

By the end of the third quarter I had stopped pacing and would sit despondent and angered to the point of tears, all that unused energy tearing my insides out, watching and listening to a crowd that just a few weeks before had loved me like their own. Didn't they know I wasn't out there?

By the middle of the fourth period, the depression had turned to embarrassment. I didn't want to play and would hide at the end of the bench, waiting for the agony to end so I could cut off the unused tape, hand in my spotless uniform, take an unnecessary shower, and get so drunk I wouldn't remember the pain of abscessed excitement.

The team won the next two games after my demotion and I never left the bench. The third game was in Chicago and we were losing at the half and B.A. substituted me for Gill. I caught two long passes in the two-minute period, helping to set up the tying field goal. The next week the team beat Atlanta, 36-6, scoring on the opening kickoff. I never set foot on the field.

A curious pattern began to emerge. I found myself used only when the team was losing, or in danger of losing. Soon I was sitting tensely on the bench pulling for the other team, elated at my teammates' miscues, profoundly distressed by their good performances. Several times I accidently cheered out loud when the opposition took the advantage.

What good is team success if the individual doesn't survive to share in it?

When an athlete, no matter what color jersey he wears, finally realizes that opponents and teammate alike are his adversaries, and he must deal and dispense with them all, he is on his way to understanding the spirit that underlies the business of competitive sport. There is no team, no loyalty, no camaraderie; there is only him, alone.

The team itself is a fiction and playing for B.A. made it all the more obvious to me. Team success to B.A. meant personal success. But it wasn't winning that B.A. cared about, or football, or God; it was how those things combined to make him successful.

That is why I know, even though Maxwell and B.A. seem to share a strong mutual respect, that one day B.A. will destroy Maxwell. Maxwell is an individual and will eventually compete with his coach for the real prize—personal success.

My body ached; I rolled back to my feet and headed out the door back down the hall. The Supremes were doing "Baby Love." Thomas Richardson was still squatting on the living room floor. I slid down next to him.

He didn't look at me. His eyes drifted aimlessly around the party, taking it in with a stoic amazement. "That was a nice catch yesterday."

"Thanks." I blushed. Richardson's praise always had an authentic ring and immediately made me feel less than worthy.

"I'm meeting with B.A. in the morning," I added. "Another chapter in my struggle for grace and glory against rapidly increasing odds."

"Good luck." Richardson laughed and turned to look at me for the first time. "I met with him in St. Louis to ask if he'd sign my antiwar letter. He told me that it was none of my business and I should keep my mind on the game." The black man snorted and dropped his eyes to the floor. "The goddam Vietnam War is none of my business. Can you dig it? He just sat there staring blankly at me, you know, that sort of superior preoccupied look. Like I couldn't possibly understand what was going on in his mind, me bein' a colored boy and all. Jesus, I could have strangled him."

Richardson was an activist and I respected him for it. But all I needed to know about the war had been babbled to me years ago by a drunken political science professor I had met at the Michigan State Varsity Club Chicken Fry. After several stiff drinks he confided to me that not only did he work for the CIA, but he had been in on the final planning of Diem's assassination. I pointed out that Diem was still alive.

"I'll tell you this," the professor had spit, his eyes blazing from my rebuff, "the son of a bitch'll be dead in six weeks."

The "son of a bitch" was killed three weeks later. Since that time I have tried to ignore politics; if a man with no innate political interests at all could find out such things because he was a football player, I didn't want to know the real secrets. Thomas Richardson was finding out that the hero status of professional football merely allowed him to become privy to the bigger lies.

Last year, Richardson had filed an unfair-housing suit against a north Dallas realtor who had refused to rent him an apartment. Up until that time, all black players had been forced to live in south Dallas and commute to the north Dallas practice field. Several times, Richardson had gone to the team officials and asked for help in securing housing near the practice field. Each time he was politely refused with an explanation that the club shouldn't interfere in community matters.

When he filed his suit, Richardson was severely reprimanded by B.A. for doing something that might distract from the team's preparation for the coming Sunday.

"Don't let it get you down, Thomas. Remember, God's got his hands full figuring out how to stop the safety blitz."

Pushing myself upright I punched Richardson lightly on the shoulder and staggered into the kitchen. Through the open front door, I could see people dancing by the pool.

Jo Bob was in the middle of the living room, wearing a Hutch Brand Children's Football Helmet. It was so small on his giant head that it squashed his face together in a grotesque pucker. He had taken his pants off. The general reaction was favorable though nervous. If Jo Bob was true to form, he might start molesting the women.

Most of the men tried to look at Jo Bob's antics in the spirit of good fun, the alternative being a beating and no further invitations to the parties. But it is extremely difficult to overlook physical insults aimed at one's date when the antagonist is six foot seven, naked from the waist down, and in a state of semierection. Knowing these people by their presence at the party, I was sure they could adapt. It was probably their outstanding personal trait, excessive adaptability.

I pulled myself back onto the drainboard and watched the party surge on into the night, while my eyes slowly searched out the single girls. There seemed to be five. The three sitting on the couch, knees tight, were most likely stewardesses who hadn't been apart since they left Lubbock together to go to flight school. Separating them would require an elaborate intellectual and emotional surgery, to convince them that all the pride and personal integrity that Delta Airlines had just spent thousands to instill was bullshit and could best be overcome, for everyone's benefit, by some outrageously deviant sex act. I had enough strength for the deviancy but not the surgical process. A thin girl in Levi's, with long, straight, brown hair and wire-rim glasses, was now talking to Thomas Richardson. She looked the most interesting, but from her animation it was obvious she dug on spades, Richardson in particular. That left Bob Beaudreau's girl. She was sitting alone, behind the rubble of the dining room suite.

The son of a wealthy Texas oil family, Beaudreau had become a successful young insurance agent who started his own firm before his twenty-fifth birthday. Recently he had taken a well-deserved "rest" at Fairhaven, the hundred-dollars-per-day shelter for those Dallas wealthy who have been so careless as to get themselves officially catalogued as "in need of rest." Beaudreau had been picked up twice in the early morning hours at Main Place Mall naked—shooting off a pistol, and loudly claiming personal responsibility for the murders of Martin Luther King and Medgar Evers. He was quickly diagnosed as "extremely exhausted," hustled out to Fairhaven, and pumped full of thorazine.

Beaudreau and Crawford were friends. They spent hours riding around in Beaudreau's new Mark III, drinking, talking on the car phone, and shooting Beaudreau's .357 Magnum out the window. It was one of several guns the paranoic insurance agent carried. Although his current phobia was a certainty that someone was trying to slip him LSD, he remained a friend of Andy's and came to most of the parties.

Like Steve Peterson, Beaudreau often brought extra women for the use of his favorite players. He also had, like Peterson, a disconcerting habit of always touching the person he was talking to, rubbing and patting while he babbled on about everything from twenty pay life to niggers taking over sports. Right now, Beaudreau was standing at the front door, a drink in one hand and his other pudgy mitt clamped tightly on Seth Maxwell's shoulder. Seth seemed offended and bored, but he postured just enough, out of respect for Beaudreau's wealth.

I decided to talk to Beaudreau's date. She had long brown hair and perfect teeth. What else mattered?

"Can I get you a drink?" I asked her.

She looked up startled, then smiled and handed me her glass.

"Yes. Please. A Pepsi."

"A Pepsi?" I frowned.

"Yes, please, with lots of ice, and pour it down the side of the glass so you don't lose all the fizz."

"Right." I headed back toward the kitchen, wondering how someone like that had gotten in here.

Alan Claridge was standing at the drainboard beating his hand against the wooden cupboard door. His knuckles were gouged and bleeding, and the shirt he had borrowed from Crawford was spotted with blood.

"Alan?" I said. "You're certainly being hard on yourself tonight."

"Yeah, I know," he answered. "But that little honey in there," he pointed to one of the three stewardesses on the couch, "really gets her rocks off over football." He held his hand up and inspected the blood oozing down the back of it to his wrist, then resumed pounding the skin to pulp against the natural-grain door.

"I got some tit—" he continued, staring at the dark smudges his blood was leaving on the cupboard, "—just by showin' her this bruise on my calf." He pulled up his pants leg to reveal a purplish-yellow blotch the size of a softball. "So, I figure if I show her a little blood she'll let me pound her peehole."

His eyes were set. There was a wry smile on his tight lips. It was rumored that Alan took a lot of pills. I never doubted it.

"That's pretty primitive," I observed.

"Yeah, but it's also effective."

"I guess so." I nodded absently. Alan screwed more women than I knew. "Well, don't lose so much blood you're too weak to fuck."

"Naw, man, I can hardly feel this." He looked at his mutilated knuckles, nodded approvingly, and wandered out.

Elaborate intellectual and emotional surgical process, my ass.

I spotted a twenty-eight-ounce bottle sitting in the sink. I poured two glasses full, careful to conserve as much carbonation as possible, holding the glasses in exactly the manner

Beaudreau's girl had prescribed. When I'm stoned, things like this become immense matters of pride.

The trick would be to get her to leave with me. It was obvious she wasn't one of Beaudreau's regulars, someone who might ultimately end up on loan to his favorite defensive tackle. She seemed too much in control, too confident. If there was a relationship, she controlled it and more than likely she was sitting alone now because she preferred it.

When I got back to her, I noticed the party had picked up intensity. Those who weren't drunk or outrageously stoned had already been driven off. The terror was escaping each individual's personal limits to flood the room with energy.

"It looks like the direction is set," I said, handing her a perfectly poured Pepsi. "Now to await the obscenities."

"Thanks." She took the Pepsi, then looked quizzically at me. "You mean it gets worse?"

"I don't know if I'd call it worse. It definitely gets different."

"Far out." She smiled and leaned back, relaxing.

"Yeah," I said. "Say, I'm sorry, but I don't know your name."

She extended a thin white hand. "I'm Charlotte Caulder. Charlotte Ann Caulder."

"Charlotte Ann Caulder, it's very nice to meet you." As I gripped her soft, warm fingers, a chill went through me. I find good-looking women almost uncontrollably exciting. "I'm Phillip Elliott. Phillip J. Elliott."

"What's the J. for?"

"Jurisprudence. I'm very together."

I looked into her brown eyes. The lines at the corners pulled slightly when she realized I was staring, trying to penetrate. The smile faded and she looked away.

"Let's go someplace other than here," I said, keeping my eyes on her face.

"No. I'm here with someone."

"I know. But you don't have to leave with him just because you came with him."

She raised her eyes to meet mine. They were set, angry. "I don't have to leave with you either. Just because you're here and have shiny eyes."

"I'm a lot more fun and fully skilled in the art of acupuncture," I said, figuring retreat now would bring disaster, if it hadn't already arrived.

"I'll bet you are," she sneered.

In a few short seconds I had made a fool of myself. I started again. "I'm sorry, I fail miserably at small talk. If you're interested, we could try and have a conversation."

"It's worth a try." Her face and voice betrayed little enthusiasm.

"Great," I said, and was immediately lost in her eyes again. I could think of nothing to say. The silence was awkward. Her eyes kept getting larger.

"You have fantastic eyes." It was all I could think to say.

"Tinted contact lenses." She frowned and cocked a look up at me. "Your style is pretty lame."

"I don't get much practice."

"Ah." She held up one finger. "A man of status much sought after by the ladies, I assume."

I nodded. "Who knows? Someday I may be a bubble-gum card."

"You can read to me from it. But till then what have you got to recommend you?"

"Well," I paused and thought a moment, "I graduated summa cum laude from a land-grant college and have never to my knowledge fathered any syphilitic children. I have all my own teeth, except for these front ones. They're always the first to go. I have never beaten up a woman even though my first wife tried to murder me in my sleep—on two separate occasions. How about you?"

Charlotte smiled up at me.

"Well, I'm self-sufficient and only have two fillings in my whole head. In my early teens I considered silicone but now seldom think of it. I consider no sex act repulsive although there are several I would classify as sick. I'm from California and own a Mercedes Benz."

"Mother!!" I cried, reaching for her. She knocked my hands away.

"I also find professional football players boring egomaniacs."

I stepped back sheepishly. Then all hell broke loose in the front of the apartment.

"Goddam you, Jo Bob, you don't own the world." I recognized the hot-pink shirt and executive tan of Steve Peterson.

Jo Bob had appropriated Peterson's current fiancée, Janet Gilroy, the reigning Miss Texas. Standing behind her, he was holding her breasts in his large, knobby hands and grinding his naked pelvis into her cute little bottom. The scene was rather erotic but this was not the kind of treatment Miss Texas or Peterson had expected. The shock had reduced Peterson to a confused rage and Janet Gilroy to tears. The girl's frantic squirming to escape served only to increase Jo Bob's delightfully carnal movements. I felt the sexual stirrings of constricting blood vessels.

Peterson grabbed one of Jo Bob's offending hands and tried to yank it from the lovely breast. Jo Bob instantly stopped moving and looked, shocked, at the pink little fingers wrapped around his thick, hairy wrist. He furrowed his brow and raised his eyes to Peterson's cherubic face, trying to decide who this man was and why he was interfering with the fun. Jo Bob's eyes fixed on the stockbroker. He gave the girl's breasts a farewell squeeze, turned them loose, and grabbed the front of Peterson's hot-pink shirt. The executive tan vanished and the tiny man blanched with fear.

Tightening his grip on the front of Peterson, Jo Bob began slapping him on the top of his prematurely balding blond head. The slaps weren't too hard, just enough to hurt and humiliate. Simultaneously jerking Peterson up and down by the front of his shirt and slapping him on top of his head, Jo Bob appeared to be dribbling him like a basketball. There was a ripple of nervous laughter. Some people were scared Jo Bob would replace Peterson with one of them.

"Can't you stop him?" Charlotte said.

"Are you kidding?"

"Yeah. I guess I am."

"Jo Bob's not hurting him too bad, although Peterson's

pride'll be sore for a while. I'm sure he thought he and Jo Bob were good friends, what with him supplying dollies and all."

"Dollies?" Charlotte frowned. "What an awful word."

"Not mine," I said, pointing at the bouncing stockbroker. "His. Poor guy figured that supplying girls and slapping backs would keep him pretty tight with the ballplayers. Shit, we don't even like each other. Why should we like him?"

"You don't like each other?" She seemed surprised.

"I don't think so."

"That's strange. Why not?"

"Scared, I guess. At least I am."

Jo Bob finally turned the crestfallen man loose. He and the thoroughly molested Miss Texas fled out the door.

"What happens now?" Charlotte asked. It seemed like a fair question.

"Nothing, tomorrow he'll go to his office, one of Dallas's young financial wizards, like your friend Beaudreau. Exactly like him." She gave me an indignant stare but said nothing. "He'll buy and sell shares of America—help determine her economic destiny. He'll come to the next party, claiming to have been so drunk tonight he barely remembers. He'll be there sans Miss Texas, but will have another equally pretty fiancée and probably, if he's smart, one for Jo Bob."

Jo Bob reeled drunkenly around the room. "Motherfuckers! You're all motherfuckers!" he screamed. His eyes lit for an agonizing moment on Charlotte. I stiffened, my mind racing to determine a sane, but quixotic position.

"Seth," I yelled across the room, "find Jo Bob something to do with his hands."

Maxwell, grateful to escape Beaudreau's grasp, grabbed Jo Bob by the arm and they headed outside to the pool. Beaudreau, shaken from his communion with eminence, walked back toward the dining room, grinning fatly. Bob Beaudreau was flatulent and puslike. I would ask Charlotte Caulder sometime how she had hooked up with him. Right now I didn't want to talk to him, so I excused myself.

"Don't leave early," I pleaded with Charlotte, and moved out toward the pool, nodding at Beaudreau as we passed.

"Good game, man." Beaudreau slapped me on the shoulder; I didn't break stride.

He called after me, "We need you and Gill out wide—instead of that fucking spook."

He was referring to Delma Huddle and I should have turned around and jammed my fist down his throat. I didn't.

I reached the pool and looked around for Maxwell. A hand closed tightly on the back of my neck. Pain shot into my head and shoulders and down both arms. I continued to stand upright, but was paralyzed.

"Hey motherfucker, when did you start givin' orders?"

"Goddammit, Jo Bob, let go of my neck." I tried for the right mixture of anger and mollification.

Jo Bob squeezed harder.

"Turn loose, Jo Bob," I cried.

"Come on, Jo Bob." It was Maxwell.

The grip eased into a rough massaging motion, and finally he turned me loose.

"Jesus Christ. That hurt." I rubbed my neck and rolled my head. The pain had brought tears to my eyes. I closed them tightly.

"Jo Bob don't seem to like you," Maxwell said, as we watched the giant step into his undershorts and walk back inside.

"Who does?" I asked, distracted by the peculiar popping noises my neck was making.

"He thinks you're a smart ass."

"Who doesn't?" I rubbed my neck thoughtfully and considered the outcome had Jo Bob refused to turn loose. In a fight with Jo Bob I would have stood a slightly better chance than Peterson and Miss Texas combined. I recalled my rookie year when Jo Bob and Meadows had held me down and taped my head. I had refused a hazing and they had covered my head with five rolls of one-inch tape. It took almost an hour and two cans of adhesive solvent to free me. I lost my sideburns, eyebrows, eyelashes, several great hanks of head hair, and almost all my pride.

"And," Maxwell continued, listing my popular faults, "he thinks you smoke marijuana, and he's pretty certain you're queer."

"And he thinks Crawford and Claridge are the Katzenjammer Kids, right?" Before I'd finished the sentence I was sorry I'd said it.

"What?" Maxwell had never considered their behavior peculiar.

"Nothing."

"What about Crawford and Claridge?"

"Nothing, forget it." That seemed to satisfy Maxwell, and we stood quietly watching the people moving around us. They were all drunk on something.

"That Beaudreau is a cocksucker." Maxwell was angry. "He wanted me to come see him the first of the week. He has a letter stock to sell. Shit."

"I'd like to grudge-fuck his girl," I said. "That'd teach his ass."

Maxwell suggested going to the other side of the pool "to inhale a little more of that killer weed. Maybe I'll be able to relax."

"I'll have to go to the car. I'll meet you at the cabanas." I pointed across the pool.

I wondered what it was I liked about Maxwell. Admittedly, he was the most selfish man I had ever met. He looked at everything and everyone as pieces in his great game of chance. He had told me once, after an evening of copious doping and drinking, that he maintained our friendship "against the advice of a lotta people" only because he had not yet figured out what I wanted out of life. I didn't seem to have any goals. At the time I didn't know I was supposed to have any. I still don't have them, but he doesn't know that.

Our friendship was based on a mutual respect and envy of each other's particular football skills and would end when either of us left the game. Competition needs an arena or it just degenerates into unbridled hatred.

"You think you're something special, don't you?" he had said without much conviction. "All them books an' shit you read. Well, somebody had to write those books an' you ain't no different for readin' em." He had glared at me as though he was angry about something.

Since that time I've tried to maintain an outward show of direction during all my chaos. Confusion is not dangerous in itself but can be fatal if interpreted as a lack of destiny. Fortunately, I am suffering from a form of incompetence that is not easily recognizable. It adds to my inscrutability.

I have to admit, on Maxwell's behalf, that I have never met a more inspiring and competent individual on a playing field. He is a flawless, confident quarterback who plays the game with his whole being, holding nothing back, ready to sacrifice life and limb, yours and his, to win. Opponents fear him; his teammates worship him. He shames his lineman to tears over missed blocks, and distracts linebackers with reprisals for late hits. Two years ago in the snow in Pittsburgh, he threw two touchdowns in the fourth period to win by a single point. That night he checked into the hospital with a fractured jaw. There wasn't a pass he couldn't throw, a team he couldn't beat, a pain he couldn't endure, or a woman he couldn't fuck, given the right time and combination of pieces. That was how he lived. Time took care of itself; he collected the pieces.

I was one of the pieces.

I knew friendlier players, but most had families and lived in three-bedroom ranch houses in Richardson. Incredibly dull, they spent every spare minute studying the stock market or the real estate business. They ignored their wives and filled them with kids to keep them busy; they paid three hundred dollars a month for brick veneer, central heat, and air, and bought a nine-passenger station wagon to cart the whole mess to Highland Shopping Center.

"You only play ball a short time," they would tell me. "You gotta cash in while your name means something." I always wondered about that something.

When they were through playing and became full-time stockbrokers or insurance agents, they suddenly realized they had always been brokers or agents. Intent on getting ready to live, they never noticed where they were. So tenaciously middle class, they had torpidly worked their way through their days of majesty on toward the American Dream.

No, whatever Maxwell was, he was certainly the most unique, and in a world striving for similitude, there has to be value in that. So while he was busy manipulating me, I was busy manipulating him. It was a good match.

I retrieved a couple of joints from the glove box and returned to the pool.

As I approached the cabanas I could see the red glow of Maxwell's cigarette. It was a good safe place to turn on. The fear of getting busted was always present, though the blanket amnesty for contemporary folk heroes provided a certain protection for most crimes, as long as we were slightly discreet and never forgot who had the pocketbook. The real dangers were nondoping teammates, who might easily turn me in "for my own good" or "for the good of the team," and for corrupting Maxwell. So we tried with as much solicitude as is possible to keep our doping a relative secret. It had become our private ritual. I enjoyed it and so did he.

"Look at those people," Maxwell said, pointing toward the party.

"What about them?"

"They're all crazy."

"So what? You is too."

"Yeah, but I know it."

"I might argue that point with you."

"They all think," Maxwell said, gesturing at the crowd dancing madly inside and outside the apartment, "that all this is normal."

"You mean it ain't?" I tried to sound shocked.

"Life is just one big ball game," he said, ignoring me. "Superstars knowing exactly what we're doin' and where we're goin'."

"Well," I said confidently. "I dunno about you, but this superstar here is right on course. Life is just one big driver's test to this kid."

Maxwell frowned with disgust. "I dunno." He sighed, looking across the glittering water of the pool. "Sometimes I think I know exactly what I want and head for it. But I don't know by the time I reach it. After I've worked my ass off, I don't seem to care much about it. It's like it's all changed or moved . . . or I don't know maybe . . ." He was groping for the thought.

"The problem, man," I suggested, with the tone of having made a major intellectual breakthrough, "is that life is dodging you."

Maxwell gave me a full-face look of disgust. We were silent. Some faceless girl flew out the door of the apartment and landed, fully clothed, in the pool. Jo Bob followed her through the door and stood at the edge of the pool. He was laughing and wearing only his undershorts.

"That's why they love football, man," I said, nodding toward Andy's apartment. "Easy to understand. Win or lose. Simple. Direct. Not nearly so confusing as their lives. Have you noticed that nothing is quite so aggravating to a football fan as a tie?"

Jo Bob helped the girl from the pool, picked her up, held her over his head and dropped her into the pool again. A small crowd had gathered, watching approvingly. Jo Bob called the swimming pool a motherfucker.

"Why do people think we're so clever?" I asked Maxwell, who was staring unseeing into the deep end of the pool. "We make our living getting hit in the head."

The girl hit the water for the third time. The crowd laughed politely and began to wander back inside. I scanned the sky for the cause of a peculiar yellow flash I was sure I had just seen.

"We're just hybrid freaks hired to do a specific job of putting more numbers on a scoreboard. We're like those chickens they shoot full of hormones so they'll be all white meat."

"What are you talkin' about?" Maxwell growled.

"I was wonderin' how I got so high and . . ." I pointed to the waterlogged girl climbing out of the pool, ". . . if Jo Bob is gonna kill that woman."

The girl snuck up and hit Jo Bob with a piece of lawn furniture. He grabbed her, slapped her twice, and tried to push her face into his crotch. Then he threw her back into the pool. Maxwell hadn't taken his eyes off me.

"What is botherin' you?" Maxwell pressed.

I turned to see if he wanted a serious answer. He did.

"Wonderin' how I'm gonna make tomorrow, I guess. You know, the usual paranoid shit."

"What are you afraid of now?" He was more incredulous than inquisitive.

"The same thing you are, Seth. I don't buy that high school varsity confidence-in-the-face-of-all-things. This goddam incredible competition frightens me."

"Shit, man. I thrive on competition."

"So do I, but that don't mean I like it."

Maxwell frowned but remained silent.

"Fear, man," I continued. "It's fear and hatred that supply us with our energy. They're what keep us up."

He shook his head, stretched out in the chair, and stared at his feet. After a long while he said, "I'm not afraid."

"Not afraid of what?"

"Just . . . not afraid."

"Bullshit. You're so scared of losing . . ." I couldn't think of how to end the sentence. I started again. "The hopelessness of it all, man, having to win. It's just a flashy treadmill with no way off but failure. I know guys who are still trying to explain why they didn't make it in high school. Telling me how the hand of God intervened to keep them from fulfilling a sixth grade potential that would have impressed the great Red Grange himself. It all finally boils down to circumstance and a matter of opinion. Ten thousand degrees of failure and only one champion."

"What are you complainin' about? You're doin' okay."

"Things could be a lot better."

"They could be a helluva lot worse."

"My point exactly. They could be a helluva lot worse."

Maxwell slid down in his chair, rested his neck against the seat back, and stared at the canvas roof. I assumed approximately the same pose and we didn't speak.

"I wonder why we do it?" I sighed absently, tired of silence.

"The only way to find that out is to stop."

He was right. But I wasn't prepared to stop. I gazed vacantly across the water. The girl was gone. She either had escaped from Jo Bob or was at the bottom of the pool.

I was trying to decide whether Seth Maxwell had fallen asleep or was just waiting for my eyes to close so he could strangle me. Judging by the stiffness in my back and legs, I had drifted confused for some time.

I looked over at Maxwell; he looked asleep.

"Seth." There was no answer.

I got up, walked around the pool and back into the apartment. Inside, Bob Dylan was finishing up Side 1 of *Blonde on Blonde* on the unattended stereo. Everyone had vanished. I was sorry I had missed Charlotte Caulder. Muffled sounds indicated something was in progress in Andy's sleeping quarters. I shuffled down the hall, trying to clear my narcotized mind.

"Shhh," Crawford signaled, as I stuck my head in the door.

He was wearing red silk boxer shorts with a large A.C. embroidered in white on the right thigh. A long, nude blonde lay on the bed to Andy's right. At the foot of the bed two of the three stewardesses from Lubbock sat cross-legged. Everyone was facing across the room, to my left, where Alan Claridge perched atop the dresser, clothed only in a baseball hat. Standing between his legs was a girl I had not seen before. She was sucking him off.

"We're timing him," Crawford said, holding up a stopwatch.

I recognized the watch as the same one B.A. used, to time quarterback setups.

"He's been going three minutes and forty seconds," the long blonde said, without taking her eyes from Claridge's face, which was beginning to contort.

"I think he's hitting the tape," I offered.

The cocksucker turned her head slightly and strained out of the corners of her eyes to see who I was. I held up my hand, palm out.

"Don't let me interrupt," I said.

"Hon't horry hou hon't," she replied, in perfect cadence.

"Says she's gonna suck off every guy in professional football," Crawford volunteered. "Claims she's already done all the important Rams and 49ers."

"She seems to be moving east," I observed.

"Looks like it." Crawford nodded. "Come on, help her realize her dream." He pointed to the slumped shoulders and erotically bobbing head. "Send this girl to camp."

It all seemed rather bizarre and tempting. I looked back to the blonde on the bed for a little encouragement, but she looked right through me.

"No thanks," I decided. "I guess I'll go on home and jack off. I'll send in Seth, he's sleeping by the pool." The girl increased her pace on Claridge. I could hear him as I closed the door.

"How long has it been," he groaned, "not counting the next second?"

I was considering going back when Maxwell came in, stumbling and coughing.

"Where's the party?" he moaned sleepily.

"The survivors are in the bedroom, trying for a league record."

"Guess I'll go back and show 'em what made me a star. You comin'?"

"No, but that's what it's all about."

He eyed me curiously.

"I'm afraid I'd end up with a guy and like it," I explained.

"Well," he said, "different strokes for different folks."

"Yeah," I said, already sorry I had declined.

I locked the front door behind me and hummed along with Dylan, who was doomed to spin the night through on Andy's turntable.

"*. . . and then you told me later*
As I apologized
That you were just kiddin' me
You weren't really from the farm . . ."

TUESDAY

The sun woke me. It was 8:30 A.M. and I felt like shit. My legs ached, my back was so stiff I couldn't roll over, and my sinuses were full of plaster of paris. I slid out of bed slowly, hobbled bent over to the bathroom, and sat down on the commode. The only advice from my father that I ever followed was to shit first thing every morning. It was supposed to improve my health. I wondered what kind of shape I would be in if I weren't regular.

Trying to blow a breathing hole through my shattered nose resulted in lots of blood but not much relief. My nose had been broken several times and the cartilage was now lodged at peculiar angles across the nasal passages. It made breathing difficult and uncomfortable.

I shoved a Q-TIP deeply into the recesses of my sinus and dislodged several hunks of bloody effluence; breathing was easier for a while. The first hours of the morning were always the most miserable. Getting arthritic joints, torn muscles, and traumatized ligaments warm took at least an hour. In addition, large quantities of blood and mucus had to be emptied from my head.

The shower was hot, and I let it pound my neck and lower back. The chills signaled some easing of the general tightness.

The phone rang.

My knees were unusually sore this morning, and it made stepping out of the tub awkward. Wrapped in a towel, I shuffled on my heels, careful not to bend the knees.

"Hello."

"Hello, Phillip." It was Joanne. "I missed you last night."

"I missed me last night, too. I'm sorry, I got hung up with Maxwell and ended up at Andy's until about five."

"Did I wake you?"

"I was already up."

"Oh. Will I see you tonight?"

"Yes," I promised. "Is he in town?"

"No, still in Chicago. He just called to say he can't get back until tomorrow."

"Then I'll see you about eight."

"Great!"

The kitchen was the usual mess. The sink was full of dirty dishes and the smell from the unemptied garbage was sickening. I could hear the distinctive scratching of cockroaches scurrying into hiding along the countertop. The wall above the stove was spotted brown from overperked coffee.

A bottle of Number Four codeine pills sat on the windowsill over the sink. I took a couple to temper my suffering. Codeine helped deaden the pain in my back and legs and allowed me the larger range of movements I needed to loosen my body for football. Codeine was sufficient for practice and most games, but frequently I needed stronger medication—Novocain or Demerol. And I noticed, recently, that even my doses of codeine were increasing markedly. It had become a heavy, daily medication.

If I left now I would have just enough time to make my ten o'clock meeting with B.A. I decided to smoke a joint. Puffing on it slowly, I got dressed, left the front door unlocked for Johnny my maid, jumped in the car, and headed for the North Dallas Towers and the team offices on the tenth floor.

The week before, B.A. had called me in because I had attended the week's practice sessions in a false beard, a wig, and a top hat. By the end of the week several other players were attending practice in costume.

Jim Johnson, the defensive coach, went nuts. Johnson had cornered me at the weight stations while I was wearing the beard. "I don't know who you think you are, but if I was the head coach here, your ass would be gone!"

"You ain't the head coach." I had stroked the beard thoughtfully.

"You son of a bitch!" Johnson choked and reached for my throat.

Just then the whistle blew, signaling the start of exercises. I dodged his outstretched hands and raced to the other end of the field, the beard trailing over my shoulder.

The steel and black-glass building, housing the team offices, loomed up on my right. I turned off the expressway, pulled in front, and parked in the fire lane. My brain was short-circuited by the day's first joint and my body was beginning to feel the delicious numbing effects of the full grain of codeine.

The elevator doors opened at the tenth floor. The walls were covered with giant action photos, larger than life, halftone screens of fear and pain, stained brilliant magentas and cyans. I had been delivered to football land, where your wildest dreams had an option clause.

"Tell the coach I'm here." I was standing at the reception desk.

The receptionist dialed B.A.'s office. "Phil Elliott is here to see the coach." There was a pause. "Ruth wants to know," the receptionist looked at me, "do you have an appointment?"

"No," I lied. "But tell her I have an item in my briefcase no American home should be without."

It was marvelous how they ran the front office. Forty men on the team, and at least one secretary and a receptionist stood between you and the head coach.

I danced a clumsy soft-shoe to the Muzak from the overhead

speaker, my boots rasping against the short-pile blue carpeting. The codeine numbness had flooded my body, and my mind, released from pain, darted gleefully from thought to thought.

Bill Needham, the business manager, came out of the back offices.

"Hey, Phil," he said, holding up a finger as he waddled toward me. "I need to talk to you. I got a bill from the hotel in Philly. You charged fifteen beers and ten chicken salad sandwiches to your room."

"I know," I said, frowning.

"You can't do that."

"I already did."

"You get per diem. You're supposed to eat off that and besides," Needham paused for a breath, his huge stomach heaving with excitement, "fifteen beers and ten sandwiches. Did you eat that much?"

"Gotta keep my weight up." I smiled and did a short dance.

"Clinton will have your ass."

Clinton Foote was the general manager and director of player personnel.

"Tell Clinton," I said, "that the chicken salad tasted like shit and not to pay the bill. Goddam city slickers, figured a hick like me couldn't tell good chicken salad."

Actually, Maxwell had ordered the food for a card game he had organized in our room and had forged my name on the bill. No sense telling management the truth. Ultimately, they would deduct the charge from my pay check.

The reception phone rang.

"You can go in now, Phil."

"Thanks."

"You'd better get this straightened–" the door closed, cutting off Needham in midsentence.

I walked past the square little offices, full of razor-cut executives and action pictures of NFL stars on the walls. Each office was identically furnished, with stainless steel and an outside window. Business. Public relations. Player personnel. Assistant general manager. General manager. The next office was B.A.'s.

Beyond, the hall opened into a large bullpen with small cubicles for the assistant coaches. At the back was the film room.

"Hi, Ruth. Should I just go in?" I did a quick tap step, ending on one knee with my arms extended toward her.

"Just have a seat."

I sat in one of the two straight-back chairs. On the low table there was reading material to ease the wait. *The Care and Treatment of the Outside Sprain, Vol. 1, No. 11* and *The History of the Forward Pass.*

"Fantastic," I said.

"What?" Ruth looked up.

"The reading material." I held up the piece about ankle nerves and ligaments. "It's fascinating."

"I wouldn't know."

The door to B.A.'s office opened and out walked Clinton Foote, general manager and director of player personnel.

"B.A. said to go on in," Foote said, without looking at me.

Clinton Foote was an incredibly ugly man. His face, corrupted with pimples, pits, and blackheads, was indicative of his pride in his personal appearance. Clinton's whole countenance looked rotted and it was a point of continuous conjecture why he seemingly cultivated his gruesomeness. The popular theory held that he didn't want anyone looking in his eyes when he made contract promises.

Part of Clinton Foote's job was to oversee the scouting and signing of draft choices and free agents. He was totally without honor or integrity, and stories comparing what Clinton promised with what he actually delivered rivaled fuck stories as training-camp time passers. He supplied the one true rallying point of the club. He was unanimously hated.

A former accountant, Clinton was a wizard at negotiating contracts—players' and television. He was the most successful general manager in the game. After my first encounter with Clinton I learned one of pro football's elementary corollaries—reading a contract is vastly more important than reading a blitz. A great negotiator makes much more money than a great running back.

B.A. had his back to the door, writing on the blackboard. Hearing me enter, he turned, pulled a movie screen across the board, brushed the chalk from his hands, and indicated I should take a seat.

His eyes were cold, half-lidded, and his face, deeply tanned, was expressionless. A former quarterback, B.A.'s six-foot frame was still in superb condition. The coach prided himself in never neglecting his daily calisthenics. There was just a slight bulge at the waist of his form-fitting blue polo shirt. "Dallas Coaching Staff" was embroidered on his heart.

He began shuffling through a pile of Personnel Grading Sheets. The assistant coaches compiled the Grading Sheets by watching the game films and scoring each individual's performance. A running total was banked in a computer downtown. Complete printouts of any individual's performance for any game or combination of games were available instantly, no tendency overlooked. B.A. selected a sheet and studied it for a full minute.

"Well, Phil," he said, not taking his eyes from the sheet, "what do you think?"

I considered the question, running my thumb and forefinger nervously down my upper lip as if I still had a moustache to smooth. I sensed a trap.

"What do you mean, what do I think?" I said, finally. "You called me up here."

"About things in general, I mean." He leaned forward, rested his elbows on the desk and clasped his hands in front of him. He smiled warmly.

I fought off the urge to tell him and leaned back, my eyes down, looking into my lap. "Well, B.A.," I said, "what can I say? I hate sitting on the bench and don't think I should be there. But it's what you want. So," I shrugged elaborately, "I'll wait my turn."

"Phil, I know you don't like the bench." He narrowed his eyes. "I wouldn't want a man that did." He paused. "But a man has to learn to adjust. I've had lots of players in here in the same position. Why, look at Larry Costello." He pointed off to his left at nothing. "He didn't want to sit on the bench when I first put him there. Just like you. But when I explained to him what was best for the team, he adjusted. Why, I'd even say he likes to sit on the bench now, if that's possible."

"Well," I said, slowly, "I don't think I'll ever get used to sitting on the bench, but I'll accept it now and wait my chance. I think I can help the team by starting."

"Remember," B.A. held one finger up, "we can't all be stars. I know you like to consider yourself special, but if I was in your place, I'd try and humble myself a bit."

There was a long pause as B.A. attempted a deep stare into my eyes. He failed and the gaze ricocheted off my cheekbone.

"Do you ever pray?" he asked.

"Not very often." I was confused. I frowned and shook my head.

"None of us are so big that we can't humble ourselves before the Lord." He tried another warm glance and I ducked my eyes, letting it hit my forehead. "I often find the answers to a lot of my problems in the Scriptures. Aren't you a Catholic?"

"No, my wife was. I was kicked out of Sunday School in the sixth grade." Why did I say that?

B.A. was angered by my flippancy. His face flushed slightly.

"Okay, let's put all the cards on the table, shall we?"

"By all means," I said, reminded of Seth Maxwell's constant comparisons of life with a giant card game.

"Now Phil." B.A.'s tone told me that, like it or not, I was in a card game right now. "You've had your share of trouble. Your wife, the divorce. Now, I don't hold it against you. It's the setbacks of life that make us strong. But last week I had you in here for playing Halloween." He paused and stared hard at me. "In training camp you kept writing 'Clinton Foote is a transvestite' on the bulletin board."

I started to protest that they had never proved I had written that line.

"Let me finish," B.A. insisted. "There's a theme that runs through all of this—and it's immaturity. You just don't take life seriously enough. I would have thought that your divorce would have settled you down."

I considered questioning the logic of the last sentence, but instead sat silent.

"Your teammates," he continued, "come to me complaining that you laugh in the locker room before games and tell jokes in the huddle. This has got to stop. You can't continue to clown through life."

"You've got the Grading Sheets in front of you," I said. "Check and see how I compare with Gill, or anybody."

"I know how you compare. I told you three weeks ago you grade higher statistically than anyone. But . . ."

I exhaled loudly, causing B.A. to stop in midsentence.

"I won't stand for that," he yelled. "Now, it's like I was saying, you grade higher, but, and I mean *but,* Gill has that ungradable something that makes a seasoned professional. And part of that something, Mr. Elliott, is maturity. Looking at the shambles you've made of your life so far, I think it is something you need. I know you're gonna need it to continue to play for me."

There was a long pause as I stared down at my hands and nervously picked at my fingernails. I exhaled slowly, trying to relieve some of the tension.

"B.A.," I said finally, sitting thoughtfully still, "if my immaturity has offended you, I'm sorry. I'll honestly try to do better. I don't like to sit on the bench, but I'll gladly wait my chance and when it comes you'll be glad I was around." I stopped and looked at him. "Is there anything else?"

He seemed confused by my apologetic manner and picked up my Grading Sheet to disguise his loss for words.

"Well," he said, scanning the sheet, "I think you're losing a little speed. You need to lose about five pounds."

I nodded.

"I appreciate what you just said," B.A. continued. "Keep playing like you have the past weeks and you could really help us. And remember, you don't have to be a star to help the team. On the field at one today."

I turned and walked out. He was right. I am immature. I

am also crippled and growing rapidly older. And there is nothing I can do about any of it.

Driving to the practice field, I thought about the meeting with B.A. and my future in football.

My attitude was definitely a problem—the meeting had illustrated that—but my real problem was injuries: five major operations, plus numerous muscle tears, breaks, and dislocations. I could see the computer printing me out now. I had already taken precautions to jam the diagnostic machinery by faking minor injuries to cover more severe, chronic problems. The less truth the computer knew about me the better.

The clubhouse parking lot was about half full. It was 10:45 A.M. The films were scheduled for 11:30. I had enough time to get into the whirlpool, loosen up, and convince the trainers and coaches I was in the prime of my life. The pain shooting through my back and legs as I slid out of the car convinced me differently. I stopped at the bulletin board and read the ancient message.

NOTICE

ALL PLAYERS WILL KEEP THEIR COATS AND TIES ON IN HOTEL LOBBIES AND AIRPORTS. THIS IS A TEAM, LET'S LOOK LIKE ONE.

CLINTON FOOTE
General Manager and
Director of Player Personnel

Five blacks, in jocks and T-shirts, sat on the blue-carpeted locker room floor. They were playing cards, as they did almost every day. No money changed hands but, slapping palms and laughing a lot, they seemed to have great fun. The blacks always seemed to have more fun.

I had to walk through their circle to reach my locker.

"Hey, man, whatcha doin'?"

"Sorry," I apologized for disrupting their game.

"That's okay, man, you can stomp them hearts and clubs,

but don't you lay your sole on no spades." Their howling and laughing was punctuated by the fleshy slap of palm against palm. They sure had a good time. Natural rhythm, and all that.

I sat down in front of my locker and undressed, picking at ingrown hairs and scratching my testicles. I stared into the bottom of my locker at the pile of soiled and damp equipment, several discarded game plans and a few pieces of old fan mail. I had lived in front of this locker for years. I grabbed a clean supporter and T-shirt, pulled them on, and walked out the opposite end of the locker room into the training room.

The dull roar of the whirlpools, the crackling blare of the trainer's radio, the voices straining to be heard, and the constant motion of people gave the room a surreal quality. It was a room that starved some senses and overloaded others. It was a violent, tactile room full of carnal feelings. The physical body was distracted by analgesics, soothed by narcotics, and emotions seeped out through pores opened by warmth and massage. The air literally surged with unrestrained energy.

Both whirlpools were full. I waited my turn, reading the wall signs.

WHAT YOU SEE IN HERE
WHAT YOU HEAR IN HERE
LET IT STAY HERE
WHEN YOU LEAVE HERE

Nothing, except an occasional case of clap, or crabs, seemed worth mentioning.

REQUIRED TRAINING ROOM DRESS:
CLEAN JOCK AND T-SHIRT
THIS MEANS YOU!

I walked to the medicine cabinet. The pill drawer was locked.

"Hey, Eddie," I called to the head trainer, Eddie Rand.

"Yeah?" Rand looked up from a half-taped ankle.

"I need some pills," I said. "Codeine Number Four."

"Just a minute." He turned back and quickly finished the ankle.

"You can just throw me the keys," I offered.

"I did that last week and had to have all the prescriptions refilled."

"Oh." I smiled sheepishly and began dancing to a static-filled Loretta Lynn coming from the radio.

"Great artist," I said, still dancing as Rand approached.

"Who?" Rand had his keys out, fumbling for the right one.

I nodded toward the radio. The trainer frowned and shook his head.

"I've met some strange people in this game, Phillip," Rand said, turning the lock and pulling the drawer open, "but, undoubtedly, you have to be the—goddammit, quit dancing—how many do you need?"

"Enough to get me through Saturday. I'll get more from you for the game." I held out my hand. He dropped a sterile gauze wrapper into my open palm. Inside were twenty Codeine Number Four.

One of the whirlpools ejected a cumulation of pink flesh. I set the pills on the tape counter, pulled off my jock and T-shirt, and stepped into the hot, swirling water. It took a minute for my balls to crawl to the back of my throat, but soon I was up to my neck in tonic heat, taking a long, relaxing piss. The hot water began to distract agitated nerve endings, to thaw numberless minor knots. The dull ache in my lower back remained, untouched.

"Hi, men." Conrad Hunter issued a blanket salutation from the doorway. He came by daily to check the stock, pat butts, and shake hands.

The football club was owned by Conrad Hunter. Ten years ago Hunter had paid a half million dollars for the franchise, now valued in excess of fourteen million dollars. The corporate offices of his CRH Holding, Incorporated were on the thirteenth floor of the CRH building downtown. A big "13" painted on the outer-office doors testified that Conrad wasn't superstitious. With two hundred million dollars, who needs to be?

Conrad Hunter viewed his team as family. During training camp his five children lived on the same floor with veteran players. Conrad lived one floor below. He considered the dormitory a family residence and admonished children and players alike in matters of personal behavior, dress, and hygiene.

A two-year veteran of the squad automatically qualified for membership in the family; no player personally disagreeable to Conrad or to any of his children ever lasted more than two years. I had passed quietly into the family several years back, but avoided its privileges whenever possible. I preferred climbing an extra flight of stairs and rooming with rookies to living near his megalomaniac children. I often saw them in the hallways, listening at someone's door for something to tell their father.

I played football where, and when, Conrad Hunter desired. It was all I knew to do, and it was terrifying to be owned by a fifty-year-old, devout Roman Catholic millionaire, whose only pleasure was hanging out in locker rooms.

"Phil." Conrad approached my whirlpool. He was dressed in spotless sweats and new Adidas flats. "How's the back?"

"Good, Con," I answered. "Feels real good."

Conrad nodded, then bounced up and down several times on the balls of his feet.

"Ever tried these?" he asked, pointing down at the new Adidas.

I shook my head.

"Bill Roberts from Adidas gave 'em to me." He made little jabs to the side with his feet, testing the traction of the green-and-white striped shoes. "Light. Real good support. You oughta try 'em."

I nodded.

"You played a great game Sunday. I was proud of you. The kids were still talking about that catch this morning on the way to church." Conrad and his nuclear family were daily communicants.

"Emmett called from Chicago this morning," Conrad continued. "I think he's planning to get married."

"Good," I said. "Good."

Emmett John Hunter was fifteen years his brother's junior and, as a result, Conrad treated him more like a son, smiling at his monumental fuckups, never really expecting him to be successful. Emmett was oily and unpleasant. He had been bounced from every Southwest Conference campus except one before he finally got a night school degree in business administration. As a graduation present, Conrad elected Emmett president of the football club.

"Emmett likes you," Hunter said. "So do the kids, and so do I! I'd like you to give some serious consideration to settling down and becoming a permanent member of our family."

"You want me to marry Emmett?"

"No," he laughed. "I'm afraid Joanne has him hooked." Conrad liked Emmett's girl and was proud of him for finding her.

"She's a great gal," Conrad continued. "You know her, don't you?"

I nodded.

"She's just what Emmett needs to settle him down," he said thoughtfully. "Then maybe I can quit sending him all over the country to those stupid league meetings and keep him here to help me run the club."

I shifted my weight on the metal bench and lifted my right leg to let the water pound on the chronically sore hamstring.

"You ought to think about getting married again," Hunter said, absently reaching down and running a finger along the zipperlike scar on the inside of my right knee.

"I don't know, Con," I stalled, not wanting to pursue the subject.

"Nobody blames you."

We both fell silent, drowned in the roar of the room.

"She was a Catholic, wasn't she?" Conrad said.

"Yes, but that's not . . ." I protested.

"It's hard to believe she could have so little respect for the sacred vows." Hunter frowned. "You were married in the Church?"

"Yes, but it wasn't just her fault. This isn't an easy life, you know," I said, aware he didn't know at all.

"That's no excuse. If she was a Catholic, she knew the vows were eternal. It was all pretty messy."

Conrad's eyes wandered to the white puckered line running from my right calf over my ankle to my instep. "How's the ankle?"

"Great," I lied. "Better than before. It's amazing, but I feel better now than I did my rookie year."

"Maybe so." His reply was slow, his eyes traveling carefully across my naked body. "But you really ought to give some thought to what I say. I'm not promising anything, but there's always room for the right kind of boy."

I moved again, sliding my leg back under the swirling water, away from his inquisitive gaze.

"Well." He stepped away from the whirlpool and stretched. "I guesss I'd better get out and do my exergenie." He slapped his stomach with both hands, turned, and walked back into the locker room, heading for the practice field beyond.

The air rushing from my lungs made a whooshing sound as I relaxed my posture and sighed with relief. After all my years in Dallas, Hunter still had no idea who, or what, I was.

Conrad Hunter came to almost every practice session, running laps, lifting weights, and doing exergenie during the first part of workout. Then, standing on the sidelines, surrounded by assistant coaches and lesser club officials, he watched pass drills and scrimmage. Discussing the team and individual players, he pointed out mistakes and broken plays, often yelling encouragement or criticism to players and coaches alike. Conrad Hunter and his brother Emmett owned 90 percent of the club stock. B.A. and Clinton Foote split the other 10 percent.

A deeply religious man, Hunter spent a part of every day

at the Sacred Heart Catholic Church, two blocks from the practice field, discussing with Monsignor Twill everything from salvation to the acquisition of a good white running back. Twill was an affable, heavyset priest in his late fifties whose only previous connection with football had been attending undergraduate school at Notre Dame. The Monsignor traveled with the team to every game and was often called upon by Hunter to "say a few nondenominational words of inspiration" before particularly important contests.

During our lean years, it was rumored Father Twill was having difficulty explaining the nuances of multiple-formation offense to God.

I looked beneath the foaming water at the legs Hunter just scrutinized. The thin white scars were barely visible. Beside the long knee scar, commemorating extensive ligament damage, were three smaller incisions arranged strategically around the kneecap to facilitate removal of pieces of articular cartilage that unaccountably kept breaking loose from beneath the kneecap. It was quite a shock to be running full speed and have a quarter-sized chip of cartilage lock in the joint. Fortunately, it had happened only twice in games and both times I was able to grind them free before anyone noticed.

The scar across my ankle marked a compound fracture and dislocation suffered in a freak collision with a New York free safety and a Yankee Stadium goalpost. Neither the safety nor the post got a mark on them.

A roll of fat around my waist floated fallow in the water. Professional athletes don't need healthy bodies, they do it all with their minds. That is why experience is such an important commodity. The body wears out quickly, but with training and chemicals the mind is conditioned not to notice.

Sweat rolled off my scalp onto my face, making my head itch. I reached up and scratched just above the hairline, my nails running roughly over the dry, scabby scalp. Several strands of my already thinning hair came away in my fingers. I reached back and scraped at the acne and boils that began to dot my shoulders about this time every season.

Standing up, I grabbed a towel from the stack next to the tub. My legs still ached. And the spot along my spine where the linebacker's knee had smashed through the big muscle and knocked off the short ribs was acutely sore. I would need more codeine. I had my head in the sink, washing down the pill directly from the faucet, when Jo Bob Williams slapped me on the back. I almost choked to death. It was going to be a long day.

The meeting lasted over two hours.

Tuesday was reserved for reviewing the films of the previous Sunday's game. The whir of the projector and the drone of B.A.'s voice were accompanied by the sound of forty stomachs churning in fear. It was bad enough to miscue in the heat and fury of a Sunday afternoon, but it was pure agony to sit alone in the dark on a cold steel folding chair while your mistake flickered forward, backward, in slow motion, and in stop action on a six-foot screen. Every misstep, stumble, and drop was carefully dissected and analyzed with a bovine detachment. B.A.'s dispassionate tones cut through the darkness to reduce the strongest men to cowards.

"Now, look at this here." B.A. reversed the film and men flew backward through the air to their feet, until our offensive team was realigned at scrimmage.

"Richardson, what were you thinking about here?" B.A. stopped the projector with the team one step into the play.

Thomas Richardson was at a running back spot. The recalcitrant black had been substituted for Andy Crawford on the previous play.

"I'm not sure," Richardson answered.

"You're not sure?" B.A.'s voice modulated slightly. "There's no room for uncertainty in this business, boy."

Nervous laughter rippled through the darkness.

"Yessir."

B.A. ran the film. Richardson had failed to read a blitz and pick up a shooting outside linebacker. The head coach reran the play five times, without saying another word. The silence was excruciating.

I could relax through the first reel and a half, because I had remained on the bench until the fourth quarter.

It was B.A.'s philosophy to point out only mistakes, as we were "paid to make great plays." He also felt the team "deserved to know who was letting them down" in the course of a game.

My leaping catch went officially unnoticed, although several murmurs of praise escaped my teammates. I was floating on a cloud of self-confidence, the reel almost ended, when B.A.'s voice knotted my stomach.

"Elliott. Look at this!"

We were lined up in a tight wing. I was split out about two yards from the right end. My job was to block the outside linebacker to allow Andy Crawford to skirt the end, cutting inside the lead guard's block on the force man.

"You're tryin' to position him!" B.A. described my attempts to get upfield of the gigantic linebacker and make him come through me to get to Andy. I was standing almost upright. It was a dangerous technique.

"You see what happens when you think you're better than the diagrams," B.A. said coldly.

I let the linebacker get too close before I tried to block him, and he grabbed my shoulder pads. He held me off balance, shoving me in front of him, waiting. When Crawford tried to get by, the linebacker literally clubbed him to the ground with me. It was humiliating. The whole room rocked with laughter at the sight of the opponent using me as a baseball bat.

"I fail to see the humor." B.A. phlegmatically stilled the room. "Stupidity like that can cost you guys the championship. If you don't want the twenty-five thousand dollars, it's no skin off my nose. My contract is longer than any of yours."

He ran the play over five times. It began to take on the appearance of a Punch-and-Judy show.

The film ended and the lights came on.

"Okay." B.A. was walking to the front of the room. "Everybody on the field in shorts and helmets. Exergenie and weights in ten minutes. Stallmon, you wait, I want to see you."

Everyone headed for his locker except David Stallmon, a third-year safety, who waited in his chair for the room to clear.

Inside the locker room the equipment manager was cleaning out Stallmon's locker. Several silent looks flashed between players. "Sandwich and a road map," somebody said softly. When we came back inside from workout Stallmon would be gone.

"Ready . . . Go! . . . One . . . two . . . three . . ."

Twenty faces flushed red in isometric strain (nineteen to be exact; I was faking) as the team worked through the exergenie stations. The procedure was ten seconds of push or pull against an immovable force, to exhaust specific muscles, then ten more seconds of isotonic motion as a muscle builder. There were fifteen different stations, each with exercises designed to exhaust and strengthen specific muscle groups. It was a prepractice conditioner that many of the NFL teams used. Working in two-man teams, one man supplying the resistance, the other doing the exercise, the drill was designed to condition, as well as loosen, the body for practice.

". . . eight . . . nine . . . ten . . . release!"

Maxwell released the rope at the other end of my exergenie, and I, slowly faking intense effort, went through the specified range of motion. Neither Maxwell nor I did the exercises correctly. The two of us were partners, each allowing the other to loaf through the stations.

Before instituting the exergenie, B.A. had used another conditioning program involving weights and a complex of vitamin and body-building pills. He had discontinued it when two players developed kidney stones and a third began to pass blood in his urine.

"Next stations. Ready . . . go! One . . . two . . . three . . ."

Slowly, we moved through the complete drill. Maxwell and I held our breath to flush our faces and simulate extreme effort. When the drill ended, we were completely rested.

After exergenie, we had ten minutes of calisthenics, and

then covered punts. Everyone would get in some running. It was a short Tuesday practice, lasting over an hour and was designed to start loosening the kinks from Sunday. B.A. finished with pass skeleton for receivers and backs and defensive secondary, while all the linemen worked on the blocking sled. I truly enjoyed pass skeleton and totally exhausted myself running routes.

"Red right. Freeze. Wing down and in. On two." Maxwell nodded at me as we broke the huddle.

The ever-present butterflies tired me slightly as I jogged to a fifteen-yard split on the right and tried not to look at the spot where the ball and I would soon meet. My stomach churned as everything but Maxwell's voice and the cornerback's face faded from my mind.

"Four, three, set," Maxwell called an imaginary defensive line alignment.

I remained upright, preferring the advantage of better vision to the slightly faster start of a three-point stance. I was boiling with excitement.

"Hut one . . . hut two."

I drove off the line, looking right into the back's eyes, moving slightly to the outside, trying to make him protect his position. He did, sliding two or three steps toward the sideline.

Three, four, five strides. I kept easing to the outside. He kept backing up and out.

I planted my right foot hard and, without any fake, slanted inside at a forty-five degree angle. The outside linebacker, dropping to his coverage zone, flashed underneath me. Four more steps and I would be to the middle linebacker. I looked back for the ball. Maxwell had already released it. It thumped into my chest, a full step before I reached the middle linebacker, his hand waving uselessly in the air. Goddam, I loved to catch a football.

"Okay." Maxwell's eyes gleamed. "Let's get six and go on home. Red right. Freeze. Wing zig out. On one."

The butterflies were bouncing off the roof of my mouth by the time I had taken my split and Maxwell had set us. There is something to be said for the thrill of constant pressure. Fear can be an incredible high.

"Hut one."

I kept my head down as I drove off the line, conscious of nothing but the sound of air rushing through the earholes in my headgear. One . . . two . . . three strides, again I moved slightly outside. This time the back moved straight back, protecting his inside, giving up the sideline.

Two more strides and I made a slight fake to telegraph my inside move. The back picked it up, eased slightly inside, and bunched himself to begin his drive for the ball.

I planted my right foot hard and angled across the middle. On my third stride I swiveled my head and looked back for the ball. Maxwell raised it high over his head and made a pump fake at me. I planted my left foot hard and drove back to the sideline, passing underneath the back, who had bitten and was charging to stop the down and in.

I dug hard for three strides toward the outside before looking back for the ball. It was in the air, floating softly toward me. Reaching out, I took it on my fingertips, held it to my side with one hand and trotted casually into the end zone. It took control to keep from jumping gleefully up and down. I had been doing this kind of thing every day for years and was still not used to it.

Back in the training room, a mood of well-being washed over me. It was a combination of the thrill of competition and a full grain of codeine. I would feel like shit when the codeine wore off, and I remembered that I was still second string. I milled around the medicine cabinet, trying to get some more pills, but the drawer was locked. Eddie Rand was filling the tub he had just disinfected.

"Just your legs?"

"Yeah, and my nose."

"Can't do anything for your looks. Get in here for twenty minutes, then contrast for another twenty and, if we got time, I'll put some ultrasound on that hamstring."

"Eddie, my wrist hurts when I move it like this." I demonstrated a circular motion. "What can I do?"

Rand watched me manipulate the sore wrist, his face screwed up in a frown. He shook his head. "Don't move it like that. Get in the tub."

An hour and a half later I left the training room. I had been parboiled in the whirlpool, quick frozen in ice-water contrast, and sterilized by the ultrasound. I had also pissed again in Rand's newly disinfected tub.

I walked around the corner and stepped into the sauna. Inside the one-hundred-twenty-degree cedar-lined room were three benches raised in tandem like choir risers. All the benches were occupied by large whitish-pink perspiring men.

The benches faced the entrance. I stepped inside, looked around slowly, raised my hands grandly and, on the downbeat, began singing "God Rest Ye, Merry Gentlemen," waving my arms wildly in the manner of Fred Waring.

Nobody even smiled. I cleared my throat and sat down on the floor by the door. I leaned back against the cedar wall and felt the stinging dry heat open my waste-clogged pores and allow all the poison to pour out. The heat burned through my sinuses with every breath, opening a ragged breathing passage. I took several deep gulps of the hot air, trying to suppress the feeling that I was suffocating. It felt as if the air was going into my lungs and immediately escaping through my distended pores. No quantity of oxygen was enough. I bit on my towel. The first few minutes in the sauna were always the toughest.

"I've got a theory," O.W. Meadows, the leviathan defensive tackle, said. He had a new theory every week, depending both on the outcome of the previous game and on his own performance. "I don't think we get enough work during the week," he continued, "and by the third quarter we start to fade."

The week before his theory had been almost the exact opposite: We worked too hard and, consequently, were exhausted near the end of the game.

"Goddammit, Meadows, you always got some fuckin' theory." Tony Douglas, the middle linebacker, spoke up from the top bench.

"We oughta do at least ten windsprints and run the ropes at the end of each practice," Meadows said.

"Bullshit!" Douglas was irritated. The discussion ended.

There was a long pause while everyone sweated and thought.

Larry Costello, the man B.A. thought "liked to sit on the bench," was sitting at the front. He was bent over, his head in his hands, staring at the floor.

"What's the matter, Larry, didn't you make your weight?" There was malevolence in Douglas's voice. He enjoyed other people's misery.

"No, I didn't make the fucking weight." Costello was a second-string defensive tackle, thirty-one years old, with bad knees. Because he seldom played on Sunday, the three days without work made it difficult for him to stay down to his assigned weight.

"How much over?"

"Four fucking pounds." Costello was depressed. He had a wife and three kids and no prospects outside of football.

"Goddam, two hundred dollars."

Costello spent every day in the sauna. At fifty dollars a pound, he had to or go broke.

"I've got it figgered out," Costello said, talking into the floor, his head still in his hands. "I count the drops falling off the end of my nose. One hundred drops equals one pound. I just sit here and count."

I escaped to the showers. I had barely broken a sweat. The shower cooled me down, and as I dressed I enjoyed the empty spent feeling that a good physical workout gives.

By the time I had crossed the parking lot, started my car, and pulled out of the lot, the sweat from the afternoon heat was soaking through my shirt.

I pushed a tape into the deck and fished in the glove box for a joint.

The car was heading south on Central Expressway, the tape deck was at full volume, the windows were rolled up, and the air conditioner was on Maximum Cold. Two joints, combined with the exhaustion of the workout, had smashed me sufficiently and I floated toward downtown Dallas, insulated from the world by modern technology and good dope. It was the afternoon rush hour and I was going against the grain of the traffic escaping north to the suburbs. I passed miles of glazed eyes, tight jaws, and hands tensely gripped on steering wheels, people rushing home, dazedly thankful that the world had held together for another day. Race home, drink martinis, barbecue in the back yard, scream at the kids, try and get a hard on, give up and fall asleep, trying not to think about tomorrow.

I nodded my head in time with Mick Jagger.

"I'm a man of wealth and fame . . ."

I was headed downtown to the fifty-second floor of the CRH Building and the Royal Knight Club.

Floor-to-ceiling windows behind the bar made the club the finest place in town to sit stoned and drink. I would look out over Dallas and in on the business community's afternoon cocktail hour.

The CRH Building bore the initials of its owner, Conrad R. Hunter, and housed the corporate headquarters of CRH Systems, Incorporated, Hunter's original electronics firm and the source of most of his wealth. Systems Incorporated manufactured aircraft and missile-guidance systems for the Defense Department, supplying the largest portion of systems in use in Southeast Asia.

I stepped aboard the express elevator and interrupted a conversation between two men in identical gray glen-plaid suits. The men remained silent and motionless the entire ride, while I hummed to myself and otherwise tried to ease the strange tension that filled the elevator. The doors opened to the darkness of the club's foyer and the two men stepped out and resumed their conversation in midsyllable.

"What'll it be?" A bartender in gartered sleeves, a plaid vest, and a Sebring haircut put a napkin on the bar.

"Beer."

"Coors?"

"No, Budweiser." I thought about ordering Pearl out of a vague, confused loyalty, but stuck with Budweiser.

I looked out the windows, north across Dallas. The landscape was slightly rolling, with no outstanding topographical features with the exception of a couple of small bodies of water, presumptuously called lakes. It was a clear day, but the rush-hour ground haze and smog robbed the view of much of its sharpness. It was growing dark and I could see the lines of headlights still heading north on the expressway.

The club was dotted with groups of neatly dressed, immaculately groomed men. There was an undertone of motion as intense conversations were punctuated with pointed fingers or whole bodies leaning forward aggressively to accent a conviction.

"I told the little bastard if I ever found him with any, I'd turn his hairy little ass over to the police." A man with gray muttonchop sideburns stood, with three other men, behind me and to my right. "I'll do the same thing John Gauthier did with his kid."

John Gauthier, an eminent Dallas stockbroker, had recently discovered his fifteen-year-old daughter in a carnal embrace and in possession of marijuana. He immediately had her committed to a mental institution, where, in the course of her internment, she was administered electroshock treatments. The successful stockbroker was recently quoted in the local Sunday magazine as saying how wonderful the institution's care of his child had been and that since returning home his daughter had been "quite calm."

"Did you see what they're doing in Spain?"

I turned completely around at the sound of a familiar voice, and instantly wished I hadn't.

"Phil Elliott!" The voice belonged to Louis Lafler, a wealthy realtor and close friend of Conrad Hunter. I had met him at several quarterback club luncheons. "Come on over and join us," he said. He was standing with Muttonchops.

I turned on the stool and the four opened their circle and moved to the bar to surround me.

Lafler quickly went through the introductions. I half-rose and gave firm grips to disguise my confusion and terror at having to communicate. The names went right through my head. I nodded a lot.

I sat back down. Sitting, I was as tall or taller than all four men.

"As I was saying," Lafler continued, "Martha and I were in Madrid a month ago, and they were sentencing hippies to six years and one day in prison for possession of pot."

"I'd heard that." A fat man with the ruddy complexion that comes from broken blood vessels spoke up. "They know how to handle 'em."

"They can say what they want about Franco," the fat man continued, "but I was over there last year and it's a great place. Prices are cheap. The streets are clean and the trains run on time. He knows how to run a country, I tell you."

"That's what they said about Hitler." It jumped out of my mouth before I could stop it.

"Huh?" The fat man looked at me, momentarily confused. "Oh, yeah, he sure did. Yes, he did." His eyes brightened, pleased with Hitler for supporting his philosophy. He bore on. "Yessir, you can say what you want about a dictatorship, but there's no crime in the streets."

"You can say that again," I nodded, smiling wryly at Louis Lafler.

When I was still married, Louis Lafler had invited my wife and me to his house for drinks one afternoon. I had smoked a couple of joints on the way over and was completely loaded. My wife didn't dope and was furious. About twenty-five other married couples were already there and I parked our car behind the Lincolns and Cadillacs that lined the street in front of Lafler's palatial north Dallas address. Once inside, Louis quickly hustled us a couple of drinks, introduced us, and then called the room to order for the Pledge of Allegiance to the flag. It was a John Birch Society meeting.

At the end of the meeting they passed around pencils and paper and asked everyone to list people they thought might be Communists, use drugs, or otherwise act suspicious. I was afraid to hand in a blank sheet of paper, so I listed my wife.

"What do you think about that, Phil?" Muttonchops stared quizzically into my face. He looked like a hip Porky Pig.

"About what?" I noticed my glass was empty and turned to the bartender. "I'd like another beer, please."

"The death penalty," Muttonchops pressed. "What do you think about the death penalty?"

"The what?" I had heard him distinctly, but was shocked by the question. I needed more time to collect my cannabis-dazed mind.

"Death penalty . . . to guys who sell dope."

Oh, beautiful. The death penalty. I wished I had another beer so I would have something to do with my hands and mouth.

"Well, I wouldn't lump heroin and marijuana together. . . ." That was a pretty stupid thing to say.

I heard the distinctive clunk of my fresh beer hitting the bar beside me. I whirled and picked it up. I drank half the glass in long, terrified gulps. I focused intently on the beer and everything fell back into place. I took another long drink.

"I think the death penalty is pretty extreme," I said, "no matter what the crime." Nice safe middle-of-the-road humanitarian statement. I was proud of myself.

"Yeah, that's true," somebody agreed with me.

"Enough of this. Let's hear about that football team," the red-faced man interrupted. "How you guys gonna do in New York this weekend?"

"Okay, I guess. They don't have much, but you never know."

"On any given Sunday . . ." Muttonchops said, nodding his head, his lips in a tight line. He sounded like *Sports Illustrated*.

"Boy, I'll never forget the time you hit the goalpost against New York. I thought you were dead."

"I thought I was dead, too."

They all laughed heartily.

It was always surprising to me to see respected businessmen who deal in millions of dollars and thousands of lives giggling like pubescent schoolgirls around a football player. I could never figure out if it was worship or fear. Probably just confusion.

"Boy, you sure took some lumps last year."

"I took some this year, too."

They all laughed again. Apparently, we were having a good time.

People always like to discuss my injuries in great detail. I wondered if this happened to all players.

"Which injury hurt the most?"

"Well, one year I had hemorrhoids."

"Hemorrhoids? Oh . . . no . . . no . . ."

They all laughed again. Here I was, having a big time with the cream of the Dallas business world.

"No, really, which one?"

"Did you ever have hemorrhoids?" I asked.

"I've got 'em now."

"Well, that explains the expression on your face."

They all laughed again.

"Well, then." The laughter had subsided. "What after hemorrhoids?"

"Back, I guess."

"That time against Cleveland?"

"Yeah, smashed the big muscle along the spine and broke off some short ribs. Hurt pretty bad."

"Yeah, I know," Muttonchops offered. "Can't do a thing when your back is hurt. Stand up, lay down, screw. I know." He didn't elaborate on how he knew.

"Who do you like better, Unitas or Starr?" People always asked me to compare players. I didn't know how they compared. To me it was a stupid question.

"I dunno, they're both pretty good."

"I think Unitas is better," Louis Lafler concluded. He told me once he loved Unitas because he wore high-top shoes. Louis had worn high tops when he played in high school. The shoes were the only thing he remembered about the game. They were the only things about the game to which he could relate.

"Yessir, he is a good, steady quarterback. He'll get those key third downs," Louis continued confidently. "He wears those high tops and he means business." The inference was obvious all those guys in low cuts didn't mean business.

"That's the trouble with America today." Louis's voice softened and his eyes became distant.

"High-top shoes?" I asked.

"No. Not enough people mean business."

I noticed my glass was empty again. I was drinking fast, a sign of heavy tension. I signaled the bartender and asked the four if they needed a refill. They were all fine, so I just ordered a beer.

"Coors?" It was a new bartender.

"No." I started to order a Budweiser, then changed my mind. "Bring me a Pearl." I nodded and smiled, pleased with my order.

"We ain't got it," the bartender replied unsmiling. "How 'bout a Coors?"

"No. Bring me a Budweiser." I felt a twinge of nostalgic remorse over the passing of the West and the end of Texas beer sovereignty. It was a rotten shame.

"Do you like these slacks?" Louis said suddenly and stepped into the middle of our circle to do a half-turn. They were madras slacks, the kind that were popular in East Lansing in the late fifties. "They cost forty-five dollars a pair here at Jack's," he continued. "But I get 'em for fifteen dollars a pair whenever I'm in Hong Kong. The guy's got my measurements and everything."

"Next time you're over there, get me two pair." Muttonchops seemed interested.

"Two pair?"

"Yeah." Muttonchops smiled. "One pair to shit on and the other to cover it up with."

They all laughed again.

"I saw Conrad at Windwood Hills, Saturday," said Muttonchops, changing the subject.

Windwood Hills was the newest, richest Dallas country club. Conrad R. Hunter was *the member*, as he was in all Dallas business and social circles of any consequence.

"He was hitting a few shots, waiting for the rest of his foursome."

"Yeah, we were in the same foursome last weekend," Louis interrupted. "Charlie Stafford was along. He goosed ol' Con on the fifth tee and made him hit one in the water."

They all laughed again.

I excused myself and went to the bathroom. I stood in front of a black urinal with gold fixtures, feeling guilty about the intense pleasure I felt. My eyes wandered around the room. It was a palatial toilet with gold-plated fixtures, hand-carved floor-to-ceiling doors, and walnut paneling.

A tiny black man crept up behind me and began brushing my back rapidly with a whisk broom. I ignored him and continued to survey the walls. A small mark on the paneling, just above the urinal, caught my eye. Leaning closer, I could make out four words etched deeply into the walnut:

CONRAD HUNTER SUCKS COCKS

It was 7:15 P.M. as I drove back north on the expressway, heading for Joanne's high-rise apartment. I had just turned off the radio after the seven o'clock report of death and violence in the Southwest: A Dallas property owner had been acquitted of the murder of a sixteen-year-old boy who was stealing tools from his garage. He had shot the boy twice in the back and left him to bleed to death in the alley. The police chief came on the radio to warn the citizenry that shotgun-wielding officers would be lying in ambush in high-crime areas. He was reminding the public to avoid suspicious behavior that might result in an innocent person getting blown in half. There had been twelve armed robberies in the last twenty-four hours.

I passed the North Dallas Towers. The tenth floor was brightly lit. They would be watching the New York films, designing the game plan for Sunday.

The light was on in Clinton Foote's office. The general manager was working late too. I was reminded of one particular meeting in that office. Late one March I had been notified (a form letter addressed "Dear Player") that my option had been picked up. I had answered by form letter and was quickly summoned by phone to the North Dallas Towers. Clinton's was a corner office that smelled of fresh paint. One wall was covered by a full-color superstat of a fifty-yard-line ticket from Super Bowl I. The furniture was stainless steel and there was a complete selection of last year's game programs on the glass coffee table.

Clinton was on the phone when his secretary ushered me inside. He waved me to take a seat and continued his conversation.

"No. No. Absolutely not." His foot tapped loudly under the desk. Clinton worked long hours and often relied on Dexamyls from the trainers to keep going. The way his foot was working was a sure sign that time pills were going off somewhere. "No. Absolutely not, you can't have it." He hung up and picked a piece of paper off the desk. It was my letter to him. "Before we go any further, why did you send me this smart-assed letter?"

The letter had been mimeographed and addressed "Dear General Manager."

"You sent me one. You could have just picked up the phone."

"I got more than one contract to negotiate and more important things to do than concern myself with your delicate sensitivities." He wadded up the letter and tossed it away.

"Sorry, it seemed like a good idea at the time. I apologize." I hadn't expected him to get quite so mad. It had seemed funny while I was doing it. I didn't need to be putting obstacles in my own path.

Negotiating with Clinton Foote was extremely difficult for three reasons. First, Clinton owned a small part of the club and had an override on profits. Thus, a percentage of any money Clinton saved in overhead (i.e., player's salaries) came back into his own pocket. Second, Clinton tried never to let a player know the whole truth about his status with the club. It kept the players off balance and easier to control. A player didn't need to know any more than was necessary to play on Sunday. Third, Clinton Foote was one smart son of a bitch.

Contract negotiations were honorless, distasteful, and totally frightening experiences. There were no fixed rules and behavior varied radically, depending on the individuals involved.

"Well, Phil," he had been gazing at a yellow note pad. He set it down and looked directly into my eyes. The man who extracted millions from the television networks was about to extort a measly few thousand from a fool. "How much do you want?"

I shifted uneasily in my seat. My head was crammed with facts: number of catches, number of touchdowns, yards per reception, and so on. My head was also crammed with considerations: I was the starting flanker, I was younger than Gill—he was healthier but that could change—and more. The contest would be between my head, jammed full of assumptions, facts, and fear, and Clinton Foote's note pad, a neat outline of undisputable truth.

"Well, Clinton, I . . ." My voice cracked. I cleared my throat and started again. "I was the starter last season and we won the division and I caught thirty passes, so . . ."

"Only two of those passes were for touchdowns." (I had known he was going to say that.) His eyes were on the pad.

"That's right," I came right back, "but, twenty of those thirty were key third downs and . . ."

"I see you've been studying your own statistics." Disgust edged his voice. Nothing is more despicable than an athlete who keeps his own score. He glanced at me and then dropped his eyes to the pad. He wrote something. I could hear his foot still tapping. It seemed slightly louder. My stomach churned nervously.

"Well . . ." Clinton always spoke in a firm, measured voice. Every word was carefully selected and clearly and loudly pronounced. "How much do you want?" He boomed it out.

I wanted $20,000. The Player's Association survey listed the average starting flanker's salary at $25,000. I would start there, knock off $5,000 for my unpopularity and Clinton's tightfistedness, and arrive at $20,000. It seemed fair to me. Billy Gill was getting $24,500 and I had already beaten him out before I got my knee fixed.

"Twenty-five thousand."

Clinton laughed in my face. "I'm sure we'd all like twenty-five thousand, but it's out of the question."

I had expected to be refused but there was a note of disrespect I hadn't anticipated. It left me shaken and feeling foolish.

"What do you mean?" I was scrambling and trying to reorganize.

"Just what I said. You're not worth it." He ran his finger down the margin of the yellow pad. The finger stopped and a smile turned the corners of his mouth.

There was something I didn't know. I dove back into my head: Griffith Lee, a spade from Grambling, was the only other possible threat to my starting job, but with Delma Huddle at split end and Freeman Washington starting at tight end, they wouldn't give another black a shot unless he was awful good. Griffith Lee wasn't that good. I was safe there. Where was my weakness?

"You paid that kid from New Mexico thirty-five thousand and he didn't even make the team." I knew that was a bad argument. In the early years of the club, Clinton had ordered the players not to discuss their salaries with anybody, including other players. The rule lost much of its effectiveness with the increased press coverage that came with winning, but a vestige of it still hung on in Clinton's mind. He shot me an angry glance.

"What other players earn is not the concern here." His foot started tapping louder. Christ, it would be just my luck if the damn trainers had given him a fifteen-milligram Benzedrine. I discarded my argument about Billy Gill making $24,500. "Besides, that's one reason why we can't pay you twenty-five thousand. I only have so much budget allotted for salaries. Mistakes like that have to be made up somewhere."

I didn't know how to argue with that kind of logic. It was based on the spirit of competition and free enterprise. Teammates have to fight each other for their piece of the pie. My confidence vanished. I sat dumbfounded and scared.

"Well, Clinton . . . how much then?" When he started whittling he wouldn't stop at any $20,000.

The general manager and director of player personnel took a long, slow look at his yellow note pad. His eyes ran up and down the page. He made a great show of figuring. Finally, he straightened up and cleared his throat.

"Thirteen thousand for one year."

My heart stopped.

"Thirteen thousand! Christ, you paid me eleven thousand to sit on the bench. You mean, you're only going to give me two thousand more for starting on a championship team?"

"It's all you're worth. Besides, when you add in playoff and championship money, it comes to quite a bit."

"But, Clinton, the average starter's salary is over twenty-five thousand."

"Don't believe everything you read. And even if it was true, and it's not, the players who are making that much signed for a lot more as rookies than you did."

"You mean what you pay me now depends on how I signed out of college."

"Of course, I've got a budget to balance. It wouldn't be fair to your teammates if I gave you a bigger raise just because you didn't have the foresight to sign for more money as a rookie."

My rookie negotiations had been carried out over the phone. I was an eighteenth-round draft choice and signed for $11,000, after receiving Clinton's personal promise that Dallas was signing only three other rookie receivers. Nineteen flankers showed for rookie camp but Clinton was quick to point out that only three were white.

"Goddammit, Clinton, I'm worth more than thirteen thousand. I'm the starter."

"That remains to be seen." His eyes were back on the note pad. What did he mean? I had beaten Gill out. They couldn't possibly be thinking of Griffith Lee. That would mean three blacks catching passes. "B.A. is considering Gill the starter until we see how your leg responds."

My intestines fell out on the floor. I was the starter. I had started all the games. They couldn't bench me in the off season. Could they? My face collapsed. I could maintain no pretenses.

"My knee is fine. Ask the doc." My voice was small. "I won't play for that. Trade me."

"I doubt if we could get much for you . . . coming off surgery and all."

"All right." I had begun to control the panic. "What if I

don't sign and come to camp and if my leg is fit then we'll talk contract." I knew I could beat out Gill. They wouldn't move Lee to flanker. I was a sure bet by league season.

"Doesn't matter. You're still only worth thirteen thousand." He took a long look at his yellow pad. "I could give you a little more if you signed for three years."

"No cut?"

"I don't give no-cut contracts." That was a lie. At least nine men, including Maxwell and Billy Gill, had no-cut contracts.

"How much money?"

Clinton took another long look at the note pad. He looked at me and frowned. "I shouldn't do it. Conrad'll be on my ass, but I'll give you sixteen thousand for three years."

"That's not enough Clinton, and you know it. It's nine thousand dollars under the average."

He shrugged. "Take it or leave it and hurry up, I've got other appointments." He looked at his watch and started tidying up his desk.

"I'm not signing. Gill can have the flanker spot. I won't come to camp."

"Then you'll be fined one hundred dollars a day until you do. You're still under option to us. I could make you play for ninety percent of what you got last year, but instead I've made a fair offer. And don't go out of here thinking you'll get an agent to do your talking. I won't deal with one." He picked up the yellow note pad and tapped it against the desk. "I've already discussed your contract with B.A. and he thinks it's fair. You just overrate yourself."

"I won't sign." I got up and started out. Clinton stopped me at the door.

"Phil," he called, smiling and sliding the yellow note pad into the desk drawer, "this is nothing personal, you know."

"I guess not," I answered, "if you can separate what you do in your job from what you are as a person. I can't." I slammed the door.

Clinton never called me back.

The day before camp opened Bill Needham, the team business manager, phoned me.

"I have to know if you need a plane ticket to training camp," he said.

"I'm not coming."

"Hold on a minute."

A moment later B.A. came on the line.

"Phil, this is B.A. I don't care about your contract squabbles with Clinton. That's between you and him. I make it a point to never get involved. If you can get more money, more power to you. But I expect you in camp tomorrow, or I'll fine you a hundred dollars a day for every day you miss. If I was in your position, I would have come out early."

I arrived in camp the next day. That night I signed a three-year contract calling for $15,000 base salary per year plus a $1,000 incentive clause if I started. I took it all very personally.

I drove in silence for a while, dividing my time between worrying about regaining the starting job and the feeling I had forgotten something. By the time I pulled up in front of the Twin Towers Apartments my face was twisted into a scowl, trying to remember if what I thought I forgot was important or just casual anxiety.

"I thought I would dress later," Joanne said as she opened her door. "I was hoping we might fuck right now."

"Are you sure there's no good TV?" I walked past her to the wrought-iron stairs that lead to the bedroom loft.

Screwing Joanne was no easy matter. Being an even six foot, and big-boned, she wasn't easy to maneuver around the bed. She had a good shape but there was just so much of it. Also, she had long, dark brown hair that fell below her hips. We were constantly getting tangled up in it. Frequently I would be shaken from some minor perversion by her screams as, in a move to gain some sensual advantage, I would accidentally kneel on her hair. The violence resulting when bodies of our respective sizes engaged in the sex act often totally distracted me. I was reminded of the team doctor who said the increased size and speed of professional football players had outdistanced the ability of the body joints to withstand the strain. The same theory seemed to apply to screwing Joanne. Part of my consciousness remained detached, watching, lest the sex play get too spirited and I suffer a dislocation or serious sprain. On the night we met she had separated one of my rib cartilages.

Once up in the loft, she stepped out of her gown and lay back on the bed. The covers had already been thrown back; the sheets were bright yellow with huge white flowers, the pillowcases white with yellow flowers. She laid her head in the middle of a daisy; her face, outlined in the bright yellow petals, was flawless. Her nose, jaw, and cheekbones were sharply defined by a prominent but surprisingly delicate bone structure. Her eyes were like dark shadows, hidden under full brows. Making up her eyes was a daily sacrament and I was glad she went to the trouble.

"Don't hurt me," I whined as I crawled into bed. "I've been hurt so much lately."

"Poor baby."

"Congratulate me." Joanne was smoking a cigarette while I rubbed a spot on my right calf that had somehow gotten bruised. "I'm officially engaged."

"I already heard," I said, wincing as my fingers dug, trying to loosen the muscle. "You hurt me. I asked you not to hurt me."

She ignored me and held her left hand at arm's length, gazing at the empty ring finger. "We're going to pick out the ring at Neiman's Thursday."

Joanne had been dating Emmett Hunter for the past two years. Marriage wasn't necessarily her goal, but it would suffice.

Three years before, Joanne had moved to Dallas from Denton, where she had attended North Texas State after escaping a stultifying secondary school experience in Childress. Childress was a small town on the west Texas plains, known for its cotton and lack of water. It had rained only twice during Joanne Remington's four years in high school and her father had gone broke in a bait shop and boat landing on Lake Childress. The lake dried up in 1967.

Joanne had decided to leave Childress her sophomore year in high school, after relinquishing her virginity to keep the starting left halfback of the Fightin' Bobcats from having sore nuts. After the season he admitted that she had been his second sexual relationship. Her predecessor was his 4-H calf, Muffin. She began to make plans to attend college.

I hadn't been surprised when Conrad told me about the engagement. Emmett supported her already, though she still kept her job with the airlines, and banked her entire pay check each month. "Well, congratulations," I said. "When?"

"Oh, not for several months. I told him I wanted to keep the apartment afterward to maintain some independence. He agreed."

"Foolish man," I said. I cleared my throat, stretched, and sat back against the headboard. "Got any dope?"

"In the drawer."

I reached across her stomach to the bedside table. In the drawer a small plastic baggie lay atop the Fightin' Bobcats Yearbook. I had thumbed through the book before. Joanne had gone through and had neatly snipped out every picture of herself. "Any good?" I nodded toward the baggie that was now on the sheet spread across my lap.

"Emmett got it in L.A. He calls it, and I quote, Dynamite Shit."

Although Joanne had smoked dope when we first met, she was not what I would call a heavy doper. Nor was Emmett. He smoked to please Joanne and she did it seemingly, to please me. She seldom turned on alone.

The first joint fell to pieces in my hands. I held them out in front of me and turned them over. "These are considered by some," I said, "the finest hands in the league. God, the irony of it all."

I finally rolled a bowling-pin-shaped joint. "They burn better this way," I insisted, lighting up, taking a long drag, and passing to Joanne. We smoked in silence.

The bedroom loft faced out over the two-story living room and its floor-to-ceiling picture window. The view of downtown Dallas, although not awe inspiring (no view of Dallas could inspire awe), was still impressive. I read the lighted message on the north side of the CRH Building. The entire north and south sides of the building contained banks of lights used to spell out messages to the city. Tonight letters twenty stories high spelled out POW, part of a communitywide campaign to get involved in the Southeast Asia war. The war ranked third in community importance behind the Texas-Oklahoma Football Weekend and Conrad Hunter's acquisition of one more good white running back.

I laughed out loud.

"What is it?" Joanne asked.

"The CRH Building. Look at the message."

"POW?"

"No. P. O. W."

"So?"

"Well," I elaborated, "most of the P. O. W.'s are pilots, right?"

"I guess so."

"Well, don't you think it's weird? I mean, if Conrad didn't make guidance systems those P.O.W.'s wouldn't be P.O.W.'s. Other guys might be, but not those particular ones."

"So?"

"I can see you don't recognize the cosmic values in all this."

She gave me a noncomprehensive smile and shook her head.

"I mean, now Conrad and that other guy are trying to fly gifts and food to the same P.O.W.'s. Doesn't it all strike you as strange?" I looked at her more for effect than response and then continued, undaunted. "Can you imagine some ricksha magnate trying to fly fish heads and rice to captured North Vietnamese pilots who had just bombed Dallas and Fort Worth?"

"The mind reels." She yawned, got up, and padded nude to the cabinet that held her stereo and records. She put on the Byrds' *Sweetheart of the Rodeo* and the apartment filled with strains of an old Bob Dylan song.

Emmett had had the stereo cabinet specially made. It ran

the width of the loft and served double duty as a railing to keep from falling into the living room. There was another stereo downstairs. Joanne always bought records in pairs, an upstairs and a downstairs copy. She had a ten-record-a-week habit.

Getting back into bed, she kissed the head of my shriveled cock.

"Poor baby," she said.

It always amused me the way she thought of my sex organ as a person. I often wished I could master ventriloquism, just to see the look on her face. I grinned broadly at the thought and suddenly it struck me how good I felt.

"Dynamite Shit," I said, shaking my head.

"How was practice?" Joanne's greatest asset was her ability as a confessor.

"The same," I said. "B.A. called me in again today. We had another one of our classics. He told me I should learn to adjust to sitting on the bench. Can you believe that?"

At a time in life when most men were just beginning to build careers, mine seemed to be coming to a screeching halt. Football was rapidly becoming a dead end.

But everything's dead end, isn't it? I realized that one Sunday, lying near the endline with my right foot twisted backward and flopping uselessly, the broken bones poking through the skin. I watched my sock staining red and understood that success comes by accident, and that the same process brings failure. Success is only a matter of opinion. Failure is a cold hard fact. I have had my successes; they were empty and short-lived. But, from all early indications, my failure will be awesome and eternal.

"Why don't you quit?" Her voice was so matter-of-fact it was irritating.

"What could I do that wouldn't be the same or worse? Besides, it's the only thing I'm good at, and goddammit, I'm proud of myself for being good at it." I looked down at my right knee and picked at the scars. "And shit, Gill isn't any better than me, just healthier."

"Let's get something to drink." Joanne was up, putting on

a pale-blue terrycloth robe that just barely covered her round bottom.

"I'll be down in a minute," I said. "I'm gonna roll another joint."

The second joint resembled a snake that had swallowed a volleyball. I held out my hands again and looked them over slowly. Then I glanced back over my shoulder, reached up deliberately and gathered in an imaginary pass. I turned upfield and outraced Adderly to the end zone, all in ultraslow motion. Flipping the ball behind my back to the official, I headed for the bench. The crowd was still roaring in my ears as I lit the joint, pulled on my Levi's, and limped down the stairs. My calf was still tender.

WEDNESDAY

". . . that was that ol' rascal, Johnny Rivers." The clock radio had clicked on. The "Uncle Billy Bunk Show" was in progress. The show's format featured an imaginary ninety-year-old rancher named Uncle Billy Bunk and his nephew Carl. Carl Jones, a local disc jockey, did both characters.

"Uncle Billy, tell me, how is your new car running?"

"Muffler trouble. Ol' Billy's having muffler trouble."

"What are you gonna do?"

"Do? Why I'm gonna take it down to them boys at Dickie Don's Muffler Repair at Lemmon and Cedar Springs. Those fellas'll fix ever' thing."

"Fuck you, Billy." I reached under the bed where Joanne hid the radio and turned it off. I had met Carl Jones about a year ago. He was an avid football fan and had heaped such praise on me it had felt like a homosexual experience. Jones and his wife Donna Mae had come into Casa Dominguez where Thomas Richardson and I and our dates were eating Mexican food. Introductions led to the Joneses' joining our party. It was a disaster.

Donna Mae Jones was from Jackson, Mississippi, and was delighted to meet Thomas, who was from Hattiesburg.

"Imagine, comin' all the way from Jackson tah Dallas," she had said. Her accent was high-pitched but syrupy. "An' sittin' down tah dinnah with ah nigrah from mah own home state."

I immediately ordered more wine, which I poured quickly down on top of two marijuana cookies I had eaten earlier. I hurriedly raced the evening to oblivion. The clearest memory of the night was Richardson's eyes filled with vacant despair as Donna Mae loudly denied ever being prejudiced against "nigrahs."

"Why I don't even mind sittin' next tah one at dinnah," she had confided. "Although I sure hope mah po' granmommah don' find out."

"You know, Donna Mae," Richardson's date, a tall blonde stewardess who flew back and forth to Houston, finally said, "I don't like eatin' with nigras at all." She leaned forward into Donna Mae's face. "But I sure do like to suck their cocks."

Donna Mae turned red and lurched backward as if hands had grabbed her throat and were slowly throttling her. She tried to leap to her feet but hit her knee solidly against the table. Carl had to carry her screaming out of the restaurant.

"Fuck you, Billy," I repeated. "Fuck you and the horse you rode in on."

I moved to get out of bed. The pain in my legs and back brought me sharply awake.

"Motherfucker," I groaned.

Usually I woke up five or ten times during the night in response to various aches and pains, but last night I had been so stoned I slept in the same position all night. I was like leather dried in the sun. My head felt like someone had been squeezing it all night. Rolling off the bed, I limped, bent over, into the bathroom and started filling the tub.

When I stepped into the full tub I noticed my right foot had gone to sleep. All up the back of my leg and into my ass I felt the needles and pins. I made a mental note to find out what it was, but even if I remembered, which was doubtful, it wasn't the kind of symptom that elicited much response from the trainers or team doctor.

Joanne walked into the bathroom with a cup of coffee and the morning paper.

"There's an article about you in the paper," she said. "They call you the team funnyman."

"I wonder if they have a special room for that in Canton? Pro Football's Greatest Funnymen. Me and Dick Butkus. It's probably down the hall from the Pete Rozelle Humanitarianism Awards."

I took the paper and scanned the article, eyes acutely sensitive to the peculiar shape of my name. It was all very silly and seeing myself quoted incorrectly in print embarrassed me. Sportswriters were such assholes. They didn't know shit and acted as if they understood a game far more complex in emotion and technical skills than they had the ability to comprehend. They couldn't even transcribe my jokes correctly. That is why they were sportswriters, because they didn't know shit about anything.

The front page of the paper was much more interesting and enlightening. There were incredible satirical chronicles of the rather frightening direction of the technomilitary complex that was trying to be America. The Dallas newspapers had become almost camp. The banner headline read: CIA BELIEVES VIET CONG TRYING TO EMBARRASS U.S. It seemed a safe assumption. Two other stories dealt with Texas justice handed down scant feet from the main settings of the Kennedy-Oswald-Ruby drama. The first headline announced a several-hundred-year prison sentence for possession of marijuana. The other concerned a seven-year probation handed to a narcotics agent for the kidnapping, sodomy assault, and murder with malice of his twenty-two-year-old airline stewardess girlfriend. In front of witnesses. Airline stewardesses always seemed to get the short end of the stick. On the other hand, narcotics agents didn't seem to have it as good anymore. Either way, the doper would be eligible for parole sometime around the turn of the century. So the picture really wasn't as black as my early morning depression and paranoia tended to paint it. Besides, it was a price one had to pay to live in Dallas at the apex of the American social evolutionary cycle.

I threw down the paper and stared blankly at the wall.

"It's pretty freaky all right." Joanne was sitting on the commode, sipping from a glass of iced root beer, her favorite morning drink. She was bent forward, reading the paper I had tossed to the floor. "Pretty freaky. Did you read about this Mexican family the police shot up accidentally?"

I nodded.

"It says here they didn't even speak English."

"Who?"

"The Mexicans. Musta really scared 'em. The police bustin' in their door and shooting 'em with shotguns like that."

"I'll bet it stung some, too," I said, leaning back and sliding under the water until just my nose and eyes peeked out. The hot water on my head eased the throbbing ache, but it still felt like my skull was being crushed. A sharp pang behind my left eye brought me upright quickly. Water sloshed out of the tub.

"Hey!" Joanne jumped.

"Sorry." I pulled my wet hair off my forehead and out of my eyes.

"Why don't you cut your hair?"

"My head hurts too much. You didn't hit me with anything last night, did you?" I rubbed a spot on my forehead. The bone underneath felt cancerous.

"The paper said they booked the whole family as dope pushers. Three of the kids are under ten."

"Can't trust them greasers," I said, standing up and dripping more water onto the floor.

"Poor baby." Joanne leaned over and kissed the head of my red, wrinkly, dripping little penis. "What do you want for breakfast?" She straightened up into an elaborate yawn then handed me a towel.

"He'll have a live mouse and I'll have what you're having." I rubbed myself vigorously, trying to convince myself I was healthy.

"I'm having chocolate pudding."

"How about bacon and eggs?"

"No bacon."

"How about eggs?"

"Nope."

"Toast?"

"No butter."

"Okay," I said, giving up. "I'll have some of that pudding."

"Only one serving, but I'll share it with you."

"No . . . no . . . I'll just drink the coffee. Why'd you ask?"

"I couldn't send you out on a day like this on an empty stomach." Her voice made a three-octave jump and she began to laugh her delightful little laugh. She turned and walked out and clomped back down the stairs.

"Fuck." I laughed at Joanne in spite of my blood oath never to smile before noon and not at all on a rainy day.

It was 9:15. I had time to go by my house to pick up a heavier coat. Another cup of coffee and a joint would revive me enough to get out the door.

The morning was gray, cold, and rainy. The wind was blowing in bone-penetrating gusts. It was the kind of day to ride fence in a plaid mackinaw, astride a buckskin Appaloosa, hat pulled over squinted eyes and tied tightly with a wool scarf, face scrunched into the collar of the red plaid coat.

Traveling west on Loop 12 to the North Dallas Tollway, I flicked on the radio.

"I told Con," Uncle Billy crackled, "let me talk to them boys . . . they'll win for Ol' Billy. I'll take 'em to the Superbowl . . ." I turned the radio off and shoved a tape into the deck.

The car topped a rise and I could see the western horizon; billowing gray clouds rolled overhead. Behind them, probably over Fort Worth, a black mass followed. A hell of a storm was coming.

I pushed the car up to seventy-five as soon as I pulled onto the toll road. It was a risk because of the radar and late morning traffic. I was more scared of the traffic than the radar.

Dallas drivers are a peculiar sort. Spoiled by wide flat highways and convinced the ability to drive an automobile comes automatically with the money to buy one, they smash into each other at a phenomenal rate. Despite all my fears the sound of the tape deck and wet tires on wet pavement hypnotized me and I almost ran through the tollgate. The marijuana had relaxed me, had increased my headache, and had made me tired all at the same time.

When I reached home my front door was open. I assumed it was the maid—or the wind. It was neither. The house was a shambles. Furniture was overturned and drawers had been emptied onto the floor. I dug through the mess, trying to assess the loss. But it was a difficult accounting, as I didn't know what I had had in the first place. The bedroom was worse. All the big things, television, stereo, cameras, and shotguns, were still intact. Twenty dollars was missing from the top of the dresser. I had been burgled for twenty bucks. It would cost me more than that to get the place cleaned up. I decided against calling the police, lest a carelessly discarded marijuana cigarette turn this into the crime of the century. I could see the headlines:

DOPE FIEND GRIDDER GETS CHAIR!!

I left the mess and clawed my way to the back of the walk-in closet for my sheepskin coat. I pulled on the coat, stepped back into the bedroom, and scared the shit out of Johnny, my maid.

"EEEEEEEEEEE!!!" She had just walked into the room and my sudden materialization from the closet reduced her to stark terror. She looked a caricature, fear-gorged white eyes against a purple-black face, fingertips pressed to a brilliant magenta grimace.

"Goddammit, Johnny, don't ever scream like that," I said.

"Oh, Mistah Phil, you scared poor Johnny into da middle a next week." She dropped her hand to her heart and patted her breast. "I seen this here mess an' didn't know what to think."

"I was burgled."

"You was what?"

"Burgled. Burgled. You know, robbed."

She nodded her head slowly, still disoriented with fright.

"I was afraid this had sumthin' to do with Mr. John David."

"What about John David?"

"He's dead."

John David was my crow. He had been given to me by Don Willie Dimmitt of the legendary University of Texas Dimmitts. Johnny, in some bizarre interpretation of social propriety, always referred to him as "Mr. John David."

"Dead!" I had always considered John David indestructible. One night, after a disastrous day and a bout at the Royal Knight with five bottles of cheap sauterne, I had come home in a fit of depressed rage and had emptied a thirty-shot, banana-clipped, M-1 carbine into my darkened back yard, accidentally blowing John David's wooden cage to shreds. He had somehow miraculously escaped and sat cawing fatly at me from the garage roof while I reloaded. I emptied the gun again, indiscriminately into the neighborhood. I fired at shadows and passing airplanes. It was a nonspecific, multidirectional rage.

I figured I had seen the last of John David that night, but early the next morning he avenged himself with loud waking calls against my blinding hangover. I quit feeding him that day for his own good, in hopes that he would return to the wild. But, like all crows, he was an amazing scrounge and, most nights, when I opened the back door he would just walk in, holding in his beak a whole chicken leg or a sourdough biscuit or several french fries. It was beyond me where he got them.

"How'd it happen?" I asked Johnny.

"I swears, Mistah Phil, I don't know." She talked rapidly, her eyes wide. "I was in here straightenin' your bed when I hears this awful squawk. I runs outside an' Mr. John David is laying dead in the driveway." She stopped momentarily and pursed her lips. "I thinks he fell off the garage and bust his neck. The rev'ren' thinks he committed suicide. Animals do that, ya know."

"It was probably suicide," I agreed. It probably was.

"Anyways, we buried him in the flower bed."

I walked to my window and peered into the back yard. Stuck in the freshly spaded earth, next to the unpainted stockade fence, was a small cross made from a coat hanger. I was ashamed of my past transgressions against John David.

Turning back to Johnny, I noticed for the first time that she was lugging a huge Wollensak tape recorder.

"What's that, Johnny?"

"Oh—I did some recodin'. Me an' mah sistah an' the rev'ren' made a record. She plays the piano."

The reverend was idling in the driveway in a 1963 Cadillac just as he did every day Johnny cleaned my house. I always suspected Johnny wasn't as meticulous as some domestics I had known.

Johnny was active in a south Dallas evangelical church and often extorted money and time off from me for alleged church functions and family tragedies. She had worked for me a little over a year and had already gone through most of her immediate family and had created some religious holidays I had never heard of. She had also convinced me to supply her with photos of myself and my teammates. Forging the autographs, she sold the pictures for a dollar apiece in the ladies room of a local nightclub. I got none of the receipts.

"Come on. Sit down an' listen, Mistah Phil." She waved me back into the living room.

"Well now, Johnny, I've got to . . ." I obediently followed into the front of the house, trying to protest.

"It'll only take a second." Her eyes at once became sad and insistent.

"Okay, but only a few minutes. I've got to get this place cleaned up and get to practice."

"Don't you worry yo' head none—Johnny'll take care of her boy."

I replaced the cushions on the couch and lay down. Out the window I could see the reverend, a big man around two hundred fifty pounds. He was smoking a cigar. All the windows in the Cadillac were rolled up and the engine was running. The sky was getting darker.

The first couple of songs were nondescript pieces about God, salvation, and hell. They were Johnny's own compositions, and she sang them at full volume, only slightly flat. Every now and then a high-pitched wail would accent a verse or repeat a phrase. Johnny would smile and nod her head.

"Dat's my sistah. She sings reeeal good high . . . real good."

I nodded my head slowly and stared at the ceiling. A song ended.

"This here's the one I sent to Uncle Billy." I resolved it would be the last I would hear.

"Mistah Phil Elliott is a good man!
He nevah do no wrong . . ."

"Johnny, what in the hell is that?" I sat straight up. I could hear the reverend's deep bass.

"He nevah do no wrong."

"Shhh . . ." Johnny held her finger to her lips and scowled at me.

"Mistah Phil Elliott is a fine man
He nevah go downtown . . ."

"He nevah go downtown." A high-pitched scream identified Johnny's sister.

"She sure do sing reeeeal good high."

"Goddammit, Johnny, you can't—" I started to get up from the couch.

"Shhh . . ."

"Yessir, he's a good man
And nevah fool with God.
He . . . nevah . . . fool . . . with . . . God."

The sister began to beat hell out of the piano.

"Goddammit, Johnny, shut that thing off." I was heading for the recorder. "You can't send that to a radio station."

"I already done it." She beat me to the Wollensak. "I sent

a copy to Uncle Billy Bunk . . . he's always talkin' 'bout ya'll."

The futility dawned on me and I stopped in the middle of the living room. With my hands on my hips I stood, staring at the floor. I stifled a smile.

"Okay, Johnny," I said finally. "I gotta go. Clean this place up, will you? I'll pay you extra." Maxwell said I overpaid Johnny, but she was the only maid I had. If God had wanted me to have a real maid, he wouldn't have sent me Johnny. And after all, I never fool with God. "And Johnny, thanks for burying John David."

I turned and started out the front door, my mind already moving toward the practice field.

"If'n I don' finish today—I'll come back," she called after me. "We got this doin's at the church an' I—"

"All right, Johnny." I waved my hand over my head without breaking stride, my mind already in the training room.

"Hi, Reverend," I called out as I passed the rusting car.

The reverend grinned and waved, the cigar clamped firmly between his teeth.

The sky was black. Big drops of rain started. By the time I got back to the toll road and headed north again the rain was falling in sheets.

I kept my speed under fifty, pushed in a tape and began to think over the peculiar events of the morning. John David was dead. I regretted more than ever that insane night when I had almost killed him and everything else. It scared me to know that person, but I guess John David understood. He had come back. I quit feeding him for his own protection, figuring the wilds of Texas safer than living with a madman. That evening had been a culmination in rage of a week that had begun with my demotion to the bench and had ended with my tax accountant disappearing with three years' income records and eight thousand dollars of my money. Poor John David, he had stayed with me through the hardest of times.

I made a concerted effort to stop thinking of deceased friends and began to consider the burglary. Things had disappeared from the garage before. It was not surprising; the neighborhood was not the best. An old residential district, it was making the difficult transition to an apartment-commercial area. The change would take years to complete. Until then, with the resultant higher taxes and better security, transients could move through undetected. In the twelve-block square that surrounds my house there were scores of new apartment buildings and an incredible number of attendant crimes of violence. I considered myself lucky that I hadn't been raped.

The flashing red lights brought my attention back to the rain-slicked highway. The storm had slackened some, but the rain was still coming down cold and hard. Traffic in the southbound lanes was backed up, but not stopped. An ancient black Chevrolet pickup truck was turned sideways in the two outside lanes. Its rear axle had broken in half. Police cars were stationed in front of and behind the immobile truck, their flashing lights reflected eerily in the rain. A gray-headed black man in striped bib overalls stood, soaking wet, by the tailgate of the Chevrolet. He was talking to a policeman. Two other officers were directing traffic past the scene. The black man looked desolate. A truck farmer on his way to farmer's market, his corn, okra, and tomatoes were scattered across three lanes of traffic. Grim-faced men in business suits smiled slightly as they navigated their machines through the overturned baskets. Once they reached clear pavement they roared away toward town, trying to make up lost minutes.

"Okay, first we'll pass out the kicking sheets. You guys on special teams listen up. Buddy will go over the assignments." B.A. had started talking the instant he stepped into the meeting room.

"All rat, you guys." Buddy Wilks walked to the front of the room. "I want some asses kicked this week." He started to write on the blackboard. The chalk broke and made a bone-grinding screech. Buddy held the chalk to his face and inspected it, then tried to write again. The noise made me think of dental drills and surgical saws.

"Goddammit." Buddy threw the chalk on the floor. Silent

grins flashed around the room. The angry man turned and pointed his finger. It was shaking. "Write this down!" he demanded. "Those returns against us last week were five point four yards per carry over our reasonable goal and nine point six yards from our outstanding. You can't win a championship with a return defense like that."

Buddy was an ambitious former All-Pro running back who saw a head coaching job as the fitting conclusion to a life well spent in sports. He had started five years ago as our backfield coach and since then had been steadily demoted. Now he was in charge of specialty teams and statistics. Three years ago B.A. had designed a questionnaire to unearth the reasons for a recent team slump. Buddy was named as a major factor in thirty of the thirty-five returned questionnaires. Several players, myself included, didn't believe B.A.'s promise of anonymity and had refused to return the mailing. That off season saw three unexpected trades and Buddy's first demotion. It seems the enclosed return envelopes had been coded with pinholes.

"You'll see," Buddy continued, his hands clenching and unclenching the front edge of the podium. "I've listed their punt return tendencies first, rather than to start with their kickoff return tendencies like we normally do. There's a reason for that. Their punt return team is one of the best in the league. If you guys ain't ready they'll run right down yer throats and out yer assholes." He raised his voice slightly and slammed a hand down on the podium top. The boom startled even Buddy.

A loud murmur went through the room as players oohed and aahed in mock fear.

"Okay, you guys." Buddy's face was crimson. He couldn't stand to be taken casually. "You better know this stuff," he warned. "'cause we're havin' a written test on it, Friday."

More moans and several distinct snickers floated up to the front. Buddy stared at the papers in front of him as he fought to control his anger. His hands shook noticeably.

"I guess that's all, B.A." Buddy's voice trembled. "These guys don't wanna win." He retreated from the front of the room. Several players put their heads down to hide grins and to stifle laughs.

"You fellows better know this stuff," B.A. said, returning to the front of the room, knowing Buddy was too enraged to finish. "Okay, let's break up."

The defensive team shuffled out to another meeting room. The offense stayed. We would get our tendencies where we sat.

B.A. handed a sheaf of papers to the first man in every row, instructing him to take one and pass the rest to the men behind.

"I want to read this to you, so you all know what it says," B.A.'s voice was grave. "I think it's pretty important."

"If you think that you can't win . . . you won't." His voice modulated rhythmically. "If you think that you're losing . . . you're lost."

It was a poem designed to remind us that winning could be assured and losing made an improbable accident by a positive state of mind. B.A. had clipped it out of some athletic-equipment catalog back when times were leaner and had it reprinted and stuck in the front of every playbook. Apparently he thought it was time to get back to some basic transcendental values.

I looked around the room. Several players frowned to disguise grins. Most of the assembly stared vacantly into their playbooks or drummed their pencils on desk tops, keeping time to some personal rhythm. Alan Claridge sat curled two seats away. The poem was devastating him. He saw me looking at him and put his hands out toward B.A. in a gesture of defense. Ducking his head, he tried to retreat into his chair. My face collapsed into a grin and I immediately put my head down lest I be accused of resisting acculturation.

". . . it's all in a positive mind." B.A. ground through the fifth and final verse and stopped. He fell silent, looking down at the podium.

"I guess you guys understand what this poem means," he said finally, looking into our faces. His eyes were strangely blank.

"It means you've lost your fuckin' mind," Seth Maxwell

whispered from directly behind me. I coughed to keep from laughing.

"You guys are all great football players, that's why you're here," B.A. continued. "The difference between good and great is only that much." He had held up his thumb and forefinger; they were pressed together. "And, it comes from right up here." He tapped his head above his right ear.

"I thought it came from all those little pills we took," Maxwell continued to mock in a small voice. I cleared my throat. If I cracked under the incredible tension that filled the room, it might be several minutes before I stopped laughing. It would be disastrous. I coughed again and tried to collect myself.

"You got a cold or somethin', Elliott?" B.A.'s voice sent a shiver through me. Although terrified, I still wasn't safe from a laughing fit.

"No sir," I said, nostrils flaring. I rubbed a hand across my face, trying to stem the ear-to-ear grin. "Something in my throat. Sorry." I cleared my throat and kept my eyes averted.

"I can't think of anybody who could use this advice more than you." B.A. sensed he was being sent up.

"I listened to the poem. I know the goddam thing by heart."

"We don't need that kind of language, young man."

"Yessir." I dropped my eyes to the desk and doodled nervously.

I kept my head down the remainder of the meeting, intensely studying every sheet of paper in front of me. Several times I could feel B.A. glaring at me, but I never looked up.

When the meeting ended, it was still raining. We climbed aboard a waiting city bus and drove to a nearby recreation-center basketball court to practice. The size of the facility limited the workout to three-quarter speed and ruled out any contact drills.

The pass patterns for the New York game were standard sidelines, turn ins and down and ins with the exception of one sideline and go and a fire pass wing zig out, the only deep routes the flanker had. I was anxious to try them, but the limited space ruled it out.

Pass scrimmage consisted of short routes run against a skeleton defense of linebackers and deep backs. In the confusion of the surroundings, I lost sight of a quick slant in and took the ball on the end of my fingers. There was a loud, hollow thunk and my hand went numb. I could tell by the sound I had dislocated some fingers. I looked down at my right hand. My ring and little finger were perpendicular to the rest. The hand started to throb.

"Goddam . . . goddam," I yelled to John Wilson, who was playing the strong safety. "Pull em out, Jesus . . . pull em."

My face was twisted in pain and there were tears in my eyes. Wilson reached out, grabbed the fingers, and pulled as hard as he could. There was a loud pop, the sharp pain eased, and a dull throb set in.

"Goddam . . . shit." I shook the hand vigorously, walking toward the huddle.

The trainer intercepted me and grabbed the aching hand. "Which one?" he asked.

"Which do you think?"

The two fingers were already twice the size of any of the others. The trainer took two strips of flesh-colored tape and splintered the sausage-looking fingers to the middle finger.

"How's that?"

I flexed the fingers a couple of times; the pain was bearable. I nodded and headed back to the huddle.

"That comes from not concentrating, Phil," B.A. yelled from the bleachers. I waved the two fat fingers at him and shrugged. He smiled and then turned and said something to Buddy Wilks.

"Tell 'em you want a new ball," Andy Crawford greeted me with a smile as I stepped into the huddle. "And then try the palms of your hands instead of the ends of your fingers."

"Fuck you." I made an obscene gesture with my middle finger. The splinted fingers made it look more like a boy scout hello.

"Teflon," Crawford addressed the huddle and nodded toward

me. "His hands are like fryin' pans and nothin' ever sticks to 'em."

"Okay. Okay," Maxwell said, glancing over to the bleachers and B.A. "Red right. Fire wing down and in on two." He looked up at me from his one-knee position. "You feel up to it?"

I nodded.

"Well, then, hold onto it this time."

I set up my break at about three-quarter speed and rounded my cut, weaving by the outside linebacker who was perfunctorily going to his coverage zone. Space was too limited for all-out effort. I looked back for the ball. Maxwell had slipped on his setup and was late on delivery. He lofted the ball gently over the middle. In a game, or on the practice field, it would have been intercepted. The cornerback drove for the ball, pulling back at the last second to allow me to catch it. I was reaching out when the middle linebacker Tony Douglas smacked me in the throat with his forearm. The first thing to hit the floor was the back of my head. Everything went red. I was choking. I felt like I had swallowed an alphabet block. I didn't want to open my eyes until I was certain my eyeballs wouldn't fall out. When I finally rolled my eyelids back the trainer was standing over me. B.A. had moved the drill to another part of the floor.

"You okay?" Eddie Rand asked, holding out a hand.

"I guess so," I answered, swallowing hard. The lump in my throat had shrunk to the size of a domino, nothing felt broken, and there really wasn't much pain. I was embarrassed and angry. I reached up, took Rand's hand, pulled myself to my feet, and limped to the bleachers to sit down.

"Phil," B.A. called from several rows behind me. I turned my head, wincing from a stiffness in my neck. He broke into a big smile and nodded his head. "Now, that's concentration." I had to laugh.

I sat out the final twenty minutes of practice. Little was accomplished. It was always that way when practice location changed. Discipline broke down and most of the time was spent just trying to organize drills.

Back at the clubhouse, I was pleased with the way my legs felt, although I had a pretty good headache. The workout had been short and the codeine I had taken before the meeting had been more than sufficient. As I walked by the locker occupied by Monroe White, a black rookie defensive lineman, I noticed Jo Bob Williams putting a live toad in the webbing of Monroe's helmet. Monroe hated scaly, slimy, crawly things at least as much as I hated spiders.

I got into the whirlpool and, at the same time, soaked my hand in ice water. Although the dull ache traveled clear to my shoulder, it was a minor injury, nothing to worry about. It still hurt.

A half hour later I went to the showers.

"Hey, tripod," O.W. Meadows pointed out the obvious endowment of a black rookie named Sledge. "If that thing gets hard, there ain't gonna be room in here for the rest of us."

"There'll always be room for you, O.W." Sledge pointed at the tiny white knob peeking out of Meadows's pubic hair. Everybody laughed.

"It ain't my dick they love, it's my pile-drivin' ass." Meadows tried to rally his own defense.

I butted in. "I'll bet fucking you is like getting mugged." I rinsed myself and walked into the locker room.

"Fuck you, Elliott," Meadows growled. "Fuckin' queer."

I was dressed and walking toward the outside door when Monroe White threw his headgear at Jo Bob.

"Goddam you, Williams," Monroe raged. "I tol' you, you muthahfuckah, to cut the jive." He was standing dressed only in a jock, his six-foot-six, two-hundred-sixty-pound frame gleaming black with sweat. One hand on his hip, he was pointing the other at Jo Bob's face. Jo Bob looked strangely uncertain. The men silently faced each other. The toad was squashed on the floor.

"Sheeit," Monroe said finally. He spit and turned back to his locker. Jo Bob walked into the training room. I continued on outside.

It had stopping raining. Several players, black and white, were gathered around John Wilson's Corvette, drinking beer from the ice chest he kept in the trunk. Everyone was laughing and slapping palms. The conversation was pointless and friendly. I was warmed by the camaraderie and disappointed when the beer ran out. Besides myself there was Maxwell, Crawford, Richardson, the rookie Sledge, and Wilson; we made plans to meet later that evening at Rock City, a discotheque in east Dallas.

Maxwell had to speak at a YMCA football banquet and asked me for a joint before he left.

"I can't spend two hours with those kids and their overachieving parents, straight," he said as I handed him two joints. "I'll see you later," he called out as he headed for the blue Cadillac convertible.

"Give 'em hell," I yelled back.

The stash in my glove compartment was running dangerously low, so I decided to head to Harvey's to buy some dope and catch up on the counterculture.

Harvey Le Roi Belding was a psychology instructor at Southern Methodist. He had been suspended about six months back for participating in unauthorized demonstrations. The ACLU was pursuing his reinstatement; Harvey had confided to me that he wasn't interested in securing his job, but hoped to get some of his back pay.

Since the suspension, Harvey's house in a bohemian part of Dallas had become a gathering place for the disgruntled children and dilettante revolutionaries of Southern Methodist University and wealthy north Dallas.

A lot of dope came through the house. More recently the heavier stuff—coke, liquid amphetamine, and meth crystals—had found its way inside. I had known Harvey for years and since I scored directly from him it was the safest place I knew to get grass.

When I first met Harvey, I was the only man on the team, with the possible exception of some blacks, who turned on. But each year a larger percentage of the rookies came into the league with several years of drug experience, often dating back to high school. Marijuana use had become so widespread in professional football that league officials had retreated from their position of antimarijuana enforcement. An internal security division of the league hired ex-FBI agents to work with federal, state, and local authorities to protect the league from scandal. Even so, a careless or unlucky player could find himself in the wrong place at the wrong time and get arrested for possession. The league would then categorically deny any knowledge of the player's felonious habits. Our team was violently split over marijuana. Everybody used drugs of some sort, but players like Jo Bob and Meadows, heavy amphetamine users, were violently opposed to grass. Their main objection was that it was illegal. Their after-the-fact rationalization about brain damage and marijuana leading to harder drugs fell by the wayside the summer I brought a gross of amyl nitrite to training camp. Since Amys could be purchased quite easily and legally without prescription, Jo Bob, Douglas, and several others began carrying loaded Benzedrex inhalers everywhere. It was not unusual to be watching B.A. diagram a play in the nightly meeting and hear a loud gasp and a heavy thump at the back of the room. B.A. seemingly did not notice while everyone else would be acutely aware of Jo Bob or Meadows sprawled face down over his desk, immobilized by a hefty dose of amyl nitrite. Their necks and ears would turn a brilliant crimson while the giant bodies heaved and shook uncontrollably in laughter stimulated by an oxygen overdose. It was great fun.

But grass was another matter, and as soon as amyl nitrite became a prescription drug it was too. So, those who really doped kept the secret from those who didn't. Twice in training camp O.W. Meadows barged into my room while I was rolling a joint. Both times the light was dim and my posture such (hunched over rolling in my lap) that he thought he had caught me jacking off. An impression I was obliged to foster for obvious reasons. The danger was that a nonsmoker like Meadows would go to management. B.A. and Conrad would be extremely hard on any player suspected of using marijuana. Punishment, of course, depended on the player's value to the club.

The radio news occupied me during the drive to Harvey's.

Three quick-stop markets had been held up the night before. A four-year-old girl was accidentally shot to death by a man who emptied his deer rifle at a suspected prowler. A plainclothes police detective shot and killed a long-hair who made "obscene and suspicious gestures" at the officer. The victim turned out to be a garage mechanic on his way home from work. And the manager of a supermarket stabbed and critically wounded a customer in an argument over the price of a case of beer. The customer managed to shoot and kill the outraged manager. I didn't bother to listen to the sports and weather.

It was after five when I pulled up in front of the old two-story gabled frame house Harvey occupied with two students—an English major who had recently moved from a wealthy home in north Dallas, and a female art major who fucked almost everyone that set foot in the house, something to do with her recent commitment to women's lib. The music student usually sat around writing poetry complaining of the injustice in his parents' threat to cut off his allowance because of his long hair and his five-year probated sentence for possession. Judy, the art major, had moved to Dallas five months before from Odessa, where her mother belonged to the Junior League and her father owned several chemical patents that the oil companies found indispensable. She spent most of her time berating the Dallas art community (whatever that was) for being too commercial. All her canvases seemed unfinished. The only one I ever liked pictured herds of armadillos, sexually violating all the Republican Presidents since Lincoln. It turned out to be the creation of a bearded madman from Austin who had traded it to her for several vintage Captain Marvel and Wonder Woman comics.

Harvey was alone in the front room, reading *Rolling Stone* and listening to Leon Russell. The television flickered soundless in the corner. Mr. Spock and Captain Kirk facing some indefinable danger that resembled a living fruit salad.

"Hello, Harvey."

"How yew, Phillip." Harvey's eyes shone as he got up from the couch. We perfunctorily shook hands. "Want some mescaline?" Three white capsules lay in his open left palm. He held them up to my face.

"How much?" I asked.

"Nothin'. You can have 'em."

"I'll take two for later."

"Take 'em all." He dropped the pills into my hand.

"Thanks, Harvey. I need to use your phone."

"Go ahead, I'll turn down the stereo." He turned the volume knob to the left, cutting off the opening strains of "Delta Lady."

I dialed Joanne's number. After three rings, she answered.

"Hi," I said.

"Oh hi, how was your day?"

"All right, somebody tore the shit outta my house last night and stole twenty dollars, nothing special." I held up my injured fingers and flexed them. They were still taped together. "How about you?"

"Emmett called, he's taking a late flight from Chicago tonight. He'll be in about midnight. Do you want to come by till then?"

"I'm at Harvey's now. Better not, he might take an earlier flight. No sense taking chances. I'll call you tomorrow."

"Joanne?" Harvey asked. He was one of the few acquainted with the situation and had hosted Joanne and me earlier in our relationship before paranoia forced us into greater seclusion.

"Yeah." I was still standing by the phone, staring at the floor and trying to organize my mind. I was disappointed that I couldn't see Joanne but strangely relieved that I wasn't expected to be somewhere tonight. Now I could meet Maxwell and the rest later, if I chose, or I could do something else. I was without commitment. My spirits suddenly picked up at the freedom.

"Well, Harvey, what's on in the revolution tonight?"

"I dunno . . . assassinations . . . a couple of fire bombings. Nothing much, it's a weekday. I'm sure some kids from the campus will stop by and give vent to their dope-crazed fantasies of correcting the social ills of the great Southwest.

It gives 'em somethin' to do while they look for a nice uncompromising job with a big salary and an expense account." Harvey smiled and shook his head. "Whew. Myself, I took two of them mescalines and I'm waitin' to go up . . . after which I'll wait to see if I can get laid." He grinned evilly and sauntered into the kitchen.

I recalled a statement Harvey once made:

"The only difference between these kids," he had said, referring to the native Dallas hippies, misfits, and pseudo revolutionaries who streamed through his house, "and their parents, whom they profess to despise, is their choice of mind-altering agents. They need success as deeply as mom and dad. And when they start selling grass and acid at the Royal Knight Club, these kids will be down there eating steak sandwiches and smoking dope and manipulating purchasing agents. It may be rock shows and gas masks instead of guidance systems, but it's gonna be the same old game."

"Man," he had continued, "this is where America is headed. A combination of Richard Nixon and B. F. Skinner, operating inside a Charles Manson morality. Everything is all right as long as it feels good and doesn't pollute the environment. And I'm just along for the ride."

Harvey had joined the university counterculture to irritate his department head and had not planned to become a martyr. But since he had, he found himself surrounded by lots of dope and lots of neurotic young girls anxious for real experiences. Harvey believed the majority of what he mouthed about the revolution, the sickness inherent in the land of the free; but he was by no means committed to it.

Harvey Belding's commitments were to dope, rock music, young girls, and anything else that would bring him intense if transitory pleasure.

"Want some?" Harvey was at the stove, stirring a pan of dark brown gruel. He took the spoon out and tasted it.

"What is it?" I moved closer to the stove, trying to catch the scent, but stayed back far enough to lessen the risk of overdose. Harvey ate some incredible shit.

"It's supposed to be chili, but it tastes like fish."

Harvey, like most dopeheads, ate all day long—things like canned chili, beans, spaghetti, and all kinds of sweets. His teeth were starting to go, a consequence of his insatiable appetite for sweets and the slipshod oral hygiene peculiar to dopers.

The front door banged open and shut. It was Judy, Harvey's recently liberated roommate. She was just twenty-one, with a pretty little-girl face and long blonde hair. She had a slight weight problem that made her too heavy in the ass and thighs. Her big tits swung free under a cotton T-shirt, the nipples stuck out like thimbles.

"Harvey?" She walked into the kitchen. "Oh, hi, Phillip." Her eyes darted from Harvey to me and down to the floor.

"Hello, Judy," I said. "How is everything?" I smiled pleasantly and without intent.

I was always carefully formal with Judy. It was a defense against her sexual liberation, in which she continually wanted me to participate. My reluctance to accept her invitations stemmed from my belief that she wasn't nearly as liberated as she thought. My suspicions were confirmed when Maxwell accompanied me to the house one evening and immediately took her up on her blanket offer to ball. The next day in the sauna Maxwell compared the experience with "fucking a dead fish" and complained she would neither perform fellatio, nor let him eat her pussy. He added that in the morning she had accused him of high conceit and showing her no respect. Then she broke down and cried, holding onto his leg as he tried to leave. "I finally had to give her a light boot in the short ribs or I'd still be there," Maxwell confided.

"Harvey, can I borrow your car?" Judy was hopping anxiously from one foot to the other. "Please. I've got some friends coming in from Austin. I have to pick them up at the bus."

"The keys are on my dresser." Harvey never raised his eyes from his stirring.

"Luv ya, Harv." She wheeled and raced out.

"Harv? . . . Harv? Who the fuck calls me Harv?" He was shaking his head looking after her. "Goddam. I wonder if I was that stupid when I was twenty-one? I hope so. I know I'm being punished for some transgression in my impetuous youth."

"Harvey," I said, "you're being punished because you're an evil man with perverse desires and instincts. And you like being punished."

Harvey looked up from the pan and squinted an eye in my direction.

"You, on the other hand, me boy . . ." Harvey pointed the spoon at me. Some chili ran down onto his fingers. ". . . are being praised, and if I have my choice, I'd rather take my punishment." He wiped his fingers on the seat of his pants.

"In fact," Harvey rolled his eyes and opened them wide, "I think I feel the very first rushes of my punishment, and I can tell you at the outset, I deserve it." The mescaline was beginning to work. A smile broke across his face and his eyes gleamed wetly.

"If this is made from cactus," he continued, waving the spoon and splattering chili on the wall, "I'm gonna eat my way across south Texas."

I reached into my watch pocket and felt the three capsules, briefly weighing the advantages of insanity. I decided, and quickly popped all three into my mouth and, drinking directly from the faucet, washed them into my empty stomach.

"We'll see what kind of reality comes in gelatin-encased white crystals," I said, wiping my lips on my sleeve.

Whether it was watching Harvey eat the diarrhetic chili, or the bits of strychnine in my empty stomach, I soon felt nauseated, and went to the back of the house to lie down. I was very tired and my mouth was watering.

As I passed the bathroom, I choked down the urge to vomit and continued on to the small room at the end of the hall. I stretched out on an old-fashioned high-backed couch. I stared, unseeing, at the ceiling. I felt awful, my body ached and bile kept irrupting up my throat into the back of my mouth.

Several more times, I fought back the desire to vomit. My

head started to ache and when I closed my eyes, bright flashes of vivid colors made me dizzy. The cords and leaders in the back of my neck began to stiffen. I rolled my head on my shoulders and my neck popped and cracked loudly in my ears.

A bitter taste flooded my mouth and I decided to throw it all up. Once I made the decision, it was a race to the bathroom. Standing up was no mean accomplishment. My whole body was sore and my movements felt leaden and disconnected. I felt my way blindly down the hall. I didn't even think to open my eyes until I reached the bathroom. The new-found vision guided me to the commode amidst multicolored spots that were filling the room.

It was slow motion. The small amount of bitter effluence didn't seem capable of producing the misery I had just suffered. But as soon as it surged up my throat into my sinus cavities and out my mouth and nose, I felt fantastic. I forced myself to vomit twice more, it felt so good. Finally, I straightened up, blew my nose, and rinsed out my mouth.

I retraced my steps along the hall to the couch and lay down. As I stretched out, my legs quivered violently and relaxed. Then the chronic pain left my legs and back; my body felt strong. The feeling of renewal and relaxation rushed through my lungs and chest, roaring up my neck and blowing out the top of my head. The tightness left the back of my neck and the muscles relaxed. The skin on my face sagged, I could feel the weight of it. I felt brand-new.

I held my hands out in front of my face, turning them over, inspecting each finger with great interest. The sight of my hands filled me with an inexplicable joy, a sense of well-being and oneness. They seemed to radiate, I could feel their energy. They were my hands. They were part of me. They had always seemed as strangers, like my feet: they were tools whose purpose was to take care of my head. I was in my head, all wrapped up in a tight little black ball. I had retreated up there years ago from the broken bones, torn muscles, and ruptured pride. It wasn't near as much fun, hiding in my head, but it was a lot safer.

Now I wanted to move back down my neck, through my shoulders and arms, to those hands and farther to my distant feet. I felt strong, and I started slipping through my neck, into my back and shoulders, arms, hands, fingers, hips, thighs, knees, ankles, and finally my feet. It had been years since I had been in my feet, they were still a little sore. I took off my boots so I could breathe easier.

The light from the hall seemed unusually bright and clear, everything seemed so crisp. Energy surged through me; I shuddered and chills ran up my spine and exploded in my head. My jaws became tight.

I was immersed in a rushing river, something roaring by me on all sides, a sort of limitless flow. An incredible flow of motion forward as if forward wasn't a direction but a state of being. I was feeling the earth rush through space—186,000 miles a second. I was light.

The sound of someone approaching brought me to a sitting position. It was Harvey.

"Hey, I thought you'd gone," he said, a heavy white coffee mug tightly gripped in his right hand.

"I have." I pulled my boots back around me.

"Judy's back," Harvey said. "And you gotta meet the girls."

"Huh?" I had been sidetracked by the remark about Judy's back and was picturing her spine and shoulder blades from various angles, in various colors.

"The girls she picked up," he elaborated.

"Who picked up?"

"Judy. The three girls from Austin, she picked them up at the bus station."

"Huh . . . oh yeah . . . whew!" I was totally confused but signaled comprehension, in hopes of a new subject.

"They're into revolutions and women's lib," Harvey continued.

I just nodded, transfixed by the glow in Harvey's eyes.

"They ran me outta my own kitchen with stern looks and vengeful remarks about dudes," he complained.

"Dudes? . . . what?" I only heard *dudes* but the word seemed such a strange shape to come out of Harvey's mouth.

I repeated it out loud as I watched it tumble to the floor at Harvey's feet.

"Yeah, I know." Harvey looked down at his feet. ". . . It's a strange word, isn't it?"

I burst into laughter, Harvey joined in, and we both laughed uncontrollably, gasping for air, tears rolling down our cheeks.

Harvey suddenly stopped laughing and started out the door back toward the kitchen. I followed automatically.

The four girls were huddled around the giant cable spool that served as the kitchen table. They took no notice of us.

"This is Phillip." Harvey spoke in a lower tone than normal, slumped his shoulders, and hung his head. I recognized the submission and followed suit, just smiling and raising a hand, palm out, shoulder high, in a short wave.

Judy, sitting across the spool, looked up and smiled. The girl next to her, with a squarish face, wearing a fatigue jacket with *Rhinehart* on the pocket, frowned and nodded, not bothering to look up. The other two kept their backs to us and nodded absently. They continued their conversation.

I shivered again as more energy surged through me. A flash of movement by the stove startled me and I turned quickly to investigate. The hard lines of the stove started to waver as I stared. It seemed to move, a rippling motion that blurred the distinct edges. I tried to petrify the stove with my gaze, but the harder I stared the more violent the motion became.

I glanced over to the four girls Rhinehart was rolling a joint. I walked over to join the caucus.

"Could I smoke some of that with you?" I asked, trying to sound as neutral as possible.

"That's what it's for, ain't it?" Rhinehart said.

The *ain't it* confused me, as I wasn't sure if she expected an answer, and if she did, what the correct answer was, there being so many popular opinions as to what dope was truly for. The confusion served its purpose. During the pause she finished the joint and passed it to me first.

I dragged deeply and, sitting down in the only empty chair, I passed the joint to Judy on my left.

"What do you do?"

I knew the question was for me, but it seemed so out of place. In the alternate culture you weren't supposed to ask people what they did.

I made a palms-up gesture of unknowing. Mixed in somewhere were feelings of modesty.

"Do? . . . What do you do?" It was Rhinehart and she seemed impatient.

"I'm a folk hero . . . contemporary folk hero." I set my jaw, surprised but satisfied with my answer.

"You a singer?" Her tone was cautious, not wanting to be discourteous if I was a folk hero, but she was most definitely not to be put on.

"No. I'm an athlete. Professional athlete." I liked the ring of it.

"You play for SMU?" She seemed interested.

"No . . . ah . . . I'm professional. I play professional football." I was embarrassed at having to repeat it. I was sorry I hadn't said I was an electrical contractor.

"For who?"

"Dallas—the team here in Dallas."

"Oh." Rhinehart's interest vanished.

Suddenly the girl in the poncho burst out laughing.

"Folk hero—I get it . . ." She continued to laugh. "All those square little people in their square little houses watching you on their square little picture tubes. . . ."

I wasn't sure I had meant it like that, or for that matter how I had meant it, but it really pleased her, so I smiled and nodded. I felt calm and very much in control.

The phone rang several times in the next room. It was Maxwell for me.

"Phil, listen. I've gotten hung up with some of the people from the YMCA." Maxwell's voice sounded urgent. "Anyway, I'm gonna pass on Rock City."

"Ah. All right, okay." I nodded at the phone.

"But listen, meet me at the locker room around eight-thirty tomorrow. We'll take a sauna." He lowered his voice. "I've got a story you ain't gonna believe."

"Okay." I immediately hung up. It makes me nervous to

talk to people I can't see. I reseated myself at the table. Harvey wandered out of the kitchen.

". . . well, anyway . . ." Rhinehart was in the middle of a story, ". . . I tol' the motherfucker, he'd better have a goddam warrant."

I wanted to listen to the story, but the harder I tried, the less I heard. I couldn't follow a thought pattern. Everything seemed to be rushing into the past like a train into a tunnel.

". . . we were afraid he'd been given shock treatments." Rhinehart pierced my confusion.

"Had he?" Judy flinched expecting the worse.

"I dunno . . . he didn't say."

The conversation ended, leaving everyone in confusion as to what to do next. I waited a moment, then walked head down out the kitchen door through the dining room and up the stairs to Harvey's bedroom. I took a baggie of grass from the six in the nightstand and left a ten-dollar bill in the drawer. I returned downstairs and walked to the front of the house.

In the living room the stereo was on full volume. Harvey was lying on the floor, eyes closed, with the huge KLH speakers on either side of his head, pressed against his ears. George Harrison was singing "My Sweet Lord." I waved at the unseeing man and left.

As soon as I opened my car door, I saw that the glove compartment had been rifled. I quickly looked in. Nothing seemed to be missing. I placed the new baggie next to my last two joints and closed the glove box.

I started the Buick, pushed a tape into the deck, pulled into the street, and steered indirectly toward Rock City. I turned off Mockingbird onto Airline Road and wound my way through the sprawling campus of Southern Methodist University. Lovely rich girls in Levi's, long hair, and moccasins, strolled purposefully across the wide lawns that divided the military-looking brick dormitories. Young bursting women, looking riper and naturally more beautiful than anything I could remember at 1960 Michigan State. I would never have believed it could seem so long ago; the old times and faces flashed yellowed through my memory.

But she came clearly back to mind. Her madras pleated skirt, white tennis shoes, and blue cardigan sweater thrown casually over her shoulders. A white round-collared blouse that often wrinkled open to reveal a small, firm breast tightly guarded by a stiff white 32B. She had dressed exactly like every other girl in the Kappa Kappa Gamma house. I loved her for her consistency.

I took great confidence from her exactness and conformity and began to dress myself in a blue blazer, gray slacks, and white Keds.

My outfit lacked the fraternity patch and it concerned her that I never resembled an intense Greek quite as much as I looked like a refugee from the big-band era.

I never joined a fraternity; I once pledged but refused to go through Hell Week. It seemed senseless to let accounting majors from Detroit or aspiring coaches from Kalamazoo perform comradely perversities on me just so I could live in a dirty little room in the bowels of a twenty-room house full of people I barely knew.

The act of pledging had given me a Big Brother, who was responsible for my emotional and physical development into a full-fledged Sigma Chi. He called every night during Hell Week and pleaded with me to come join in the fun. I refused politely, more out of laziness than conviction. I was touched by the man's desire to have me as a lifelong fraternal friend and felt considerable guilt over "all the great contacts" I was going to miss.

A week later, I was in the center of the student union grill, sitting in the green circular booth reserved for athletes of distinction, when Big Brother, along with several other Sigma Chis and their dates, entered and took a booth in the Greek section at the opposite side of the cafeteria. I was delighted to have a chance to say hello and quickly excused myself from two black sprinters and a strangely deformed hockey player. I ambled across the crowded room in the half-limp, half-stumble perfected by college letter winners.

They all turned and watched my approach. The girls were dressed in madras skirts, white round-collared blouses, tennis shoes, and blue cardigan sweaters. I walked up and extended my hand to Big Brother, who was sitting inside next to a pretty girl. Before I could speak, he lunged past the girl, his hands clawing for my throat. I stepped back and pushed his hands away. He kept coming, swinging his fists wildly at my face.

It wasn't much of a fight, the tiny Sigma Chi stood barely five feet six inches off the ground. He had to jump to try and land a blow above my shoulders. I held my arms in front of me and just let the blows rain off my chest and forearms. I was shocked and thoroughly embarrassed. I thought about getting mad but didn't know how, or why.

Finally the infuriated man fell to his knees.

"You son of a bitch," he sobbed. "I was the only man in the house with a depledge."

I tried to tell the man it wasn't his fault and also explain it wasn't my fault, all the time wondering whose fault it was.

Now, crazed on mescaline, driving across another college campus twelve hundred miles and several light-years removed, I was beginning to understand. If a man is lonely enough, he will eat raw eggs, carry olives in his asshole, and let homosexual history majors from Flint beat his butt bloody with a paddle. He does it all in the belief that with the new morning they will have learned to love him by brutalizing him.

But when the ritualized humiliation ends, how can he admit to himself that it had no meaning and he is still alone, only momentarily distracted from the fear and loneliness and hatred that consumes us all?

Three girls passed in front of my Riviera and crossed the street to the art center. The girls were dressed, properly shabby, in Levi's and work shirts. One, a pretty blonde, wore wire-rimmed glasses. They all had long straight hair that showed signs of bleaching at a point down their backs maybe two years ago.

I stared down the hood as they passed, the mescaline playing tricks with their faces. The girl in the wire rims looked into the car. I smiled into the eyes behind the glasses. Instinctively she turned back to her companions, offended that I would try to join her, even for an instant, a stranger uninvited.

I wondered if I had been younger, and driving a Volkswagen that towed a motorcycle: then would she have waved? It was hard to admit that I was passing to the back side of the generation gap and the future belonged to those people who called me mister. But I knew I would never try to join anything again, even youth.

I reached Lovers Lane and turned east, passing the house my wife and I occupied during our brief and stormy life together. Blind luck and laziness had saved me from Sigma Chi, but raw passion drew me to the Kappa parking lot and the steamy back seat of her car. Not long after we had moved into the house I came home early from a twenty-five-dollar speaking engagement and found her on the living room couch hidden beneath the naked mass of Jo Bob Williams. It was the only nice feeling I held for Jo Bob—he supplied the inescapable reason for ending the marriage.

The ensuing divorce proceedings were quite sticky, Jo Bob apparently only one of several teammates, mostly married, who had streamed through my house. A lopsided settlement leaving me broke and deeply in debt headed off a jury trial and Clinton Foote's plan to trade me to Los Angeles before my court hearing exploded the always uneasy family situations of a good part of his team.

Later, I came to suspect even Maxwell, but I avoided the subject, as further repercussions would send me at least to Los Angeles and very possibly to Pittsburgh. She told the court I was a homosexual. I probably am, nothing would surprise me anymore.

The first rushes of the mescaline had smoothed out and I was sitting in the car watching the landscape zoom by when I suddenly realized Rock City was approaching me from the north. I had no idea how I had gotten there.

The marquee advertised Little Richard, currently promoted as "The Redman of Rock." If it were true, Wounded Knee was more disastrous than currently believed.

"They're inside, Mr. Elliott." A black man held the outer door for me. I stepped into the foyer.

A large man with slick black hair and flaccid white skin swung his arms wide open in a grand gesture of embrace. A flesh-colored Band-Aid did a poor job of covering a huge boil on his chin.

"Phil—Phil baby." He moved toward me. "Tony . . ." he continued. "Tony Perelli. I met you in Vegas. . . . I'm the maître d' here."

I flinched and shrank back. I tried to smile but only one side of my face responded.

"They're all inside," he said, grabbing my hand and pumping it furiously. "How many points you givin' against New York?"

I pulled my hand free, still smiling lopsidedly, and moved past him through the double doors into the dark.

"How many. . ." His voice trailed after me.

The show hadn't started yet. The stage and house lights were off, and except for candles flickering on tables, the darkness was impenetrable. I recognized some laughter down close to the small raised stage and moved toward it. Shortly, I sat down next to Andy Crawford and his "Sock it to 'em" sweetheart, Susan Brinkerman.

The other faces at the table were familiar. Claridge and a redheaded Texas International stewardess named Fran that he dated often. John Wilson, the safety, had left his wife and kids at home and was in the company of a pumpkin-headed girl who resembled the classic Texas cocktail waitress. The black running back Thomas Richardson and his girl, the one who so horrified Donna Mae Jones at Casa Dominguez; and Sledge, the black rookie with the intimidatingly large penis. Steve Peterson, the stockbroker Jo Bob had harassed so unmercifully at Andy's party, was at the far end of the table flanked by two very pretty girls. I just smiled, lowered my eyes, and didn't say a word until the excitement and confusion of my entrance faded.

I leaned back in my chair and tried to comprehend what was going on at this particular table out of all the other nightclub tables in time and space. Most of the female faces around the table, with the exception of Richardson's blonde girlfriend, registered varying amounts of fear. Claridge was obviously on the pills, his spasmodic movements and insane chatter seemed almost manic; in addition, he was drinking heavily. Andy appeared irrevocably drunk, while Susan kept glancing nervously at him from the corners of her eyes. Peterson just seemed crazy.

Richardson and his girl and Sledge huddled together and observed the group with an amused awe. Sledge's mouth hung slightly open.

"Drink for my friends." Claridge was on his feet screaming toward the bar. "And water for their horses." A waitress hurried to the table to take orders. I asked for a Coke.

"A Coke? A Coke?" Claridge yelled at me. A grin broke across his face. He pointed at me and looked at the other faces around the table. "This guy is doin' dope—dope—do you understand? He's crazed."

I squirmed down in my seat.

"Look out." Claridge dove under the table. "He's got an ax. He's a ritual killer." The sound of his voice from under the table seemed incredibly funny and I broke into a giggle. Everyone at the table looked horrified.

Fortunately the stage lights came up and an anonymous Texas twang announced, "Rock and roll's only full-blooded Blackfoot, Little Richard." To the sound of "Good Golly, Miss Molly" the tiny curtain zipped open and behind a solid-white baby grand piano sat Harlem's Hiawatha. He was magnificent, dressed in a beaded white buckskin suit with twelve-inch fringe. He wore a leather headband and a solitary feather. His eyes and lips were outlined with eyebrow pencil, grotesquely exaggerating his facial expressions.

Claridge peeked over the top of the table at the stage. He moved his eyes back and forth surveying the assembly of friends. Suddenly, he leaped to his feet and broke into a long high-pitched howl that first startled, then flattered the grinning singer.

Little Richard drew his face into an eye-rolling grin and

waved limply at Claridge, who howled again. Everyone, with the exception of Fran, Claridge's date, laughed. Fran slid down in her seat and tugged at Claridge's sleeve.

Little Richard was starting into a new arrangement of an old Hank Williams song when the double doors opened, admitting Bob Beaudreau and Charlotte Ann Caulder. My eyes followed them to a small table in the back. I watched her for several minutes before my brain waves overwhelmed her. I could see her eyes clearly across the dark expanse as she looked at me and smiled.

Little Richard finished the set. Everyone at the table screamed, stomped, and whistled while Claridge kept up a piercing howl. As soon as the curtain closed, Steve Peterson abandoned the two girls at the table end and moved next to Claridge. Draping his stubby arm over Alan's shoulder, he began whispering in his ear. While they huddled, Crawford ordered another round of drinks and began to suck on his little finger. When his finger was sufficiently soaked, Crawford held it up and inspected the saliva dripping down, then leaned across the table and shoved it into Peterson's ear.

"Wet Willy," Crawford cried. He and Claridge both broke into cackling laughs. The women all seemed disgusted by the spittle running out of Peterson's ear. Peterson seemed disgusted too.

"Goddammit, Andy," Peterson yelled, flinching away. He quickly yanked out his shirttail and dug into the violated ear. "Don't do that." He appeared ready to cry.

Richardson, his date, and Sledge got up, said they were going to a club in south Dallas and quickly left. "Wet Willy," Claridge screamed gleefully as his spit-soaked finger seemed to penetrate at least to Crawford's midbrain.

Crawford had been turned talking to someone at the table behind him, and he vainly tried to turn away from the invasion. In the process he spilled his drink all over his date, Susan Brinkerman.

"Ooh." Susan jumped up and brushed off her skirt. "Andy, look what you've done."

"Fuck it." Crawford tilted his head and screwed a finger

into the canal, wiping out the saliva. His face was strangely contorted.

"What did you say?" she asked, her eyes wide and her voice trembling.

"I said," he pronounced the words slowly, carefully forming each with his lips; he looked directly into her face, "fuck it."

She jumped slightly as the words hit her in the forehead.

". . . and . . ." he continued, leaning closer to her twitching face, ". . . fuck you too."

A short cry escaped through her nose. She had her hand clamped tightly across her mouth. The daughter of a well-to-do Dallas family and last year's Southern Methodist Homecoming Queen, Susan just wasn't ready for unbridled insanity. She turned to run out, but Crawford's thick fingers closed on the back of her neck, caught her in midstride, and yanked her back to her seat.

Susan sat down meekly, her head down and her eyes tightly closed. Crawford's fingers were still digging into the cords of her neck. She seemed in great pain but remained silent. As soon as Andy released his grip, she doubled up and began to sob.

Poor Susan, I thought, she finally got to see Andy "Sock it to 'em."

I waited for somebody to console the sobbing girl. Nobody moved.

Claridge raised his empty glass and began to howl, Crawford raised his glass in response.

"Fucking cunts," Claridge screamed. They both laughed.

The waitress arrived with more drinks, and everyone, except the quietly whimpering girl and me, continued as if nothing had happened. I frowned and slumped in my chair, saddened by the inconsolable girl caught in her own time warp.

As I pushed up from my chair, I noticed Crawford had his finger in his mouth and was eyeing Claridge. I didn't even break stride when the commotion behind me signaled the third, but by no means the last, Wet Willy of the evening.

The table Charlotte Caulder shared with Beaudreau was against the wall. There was an extra chair on the aisle; I turned it around and straddled it, my arms resting on the back. Beaudreau was delighted.

"Hey Phil, how's ever' lattle thang?" His fat face lighted up.

"Fine, thanks," I said calmly, not betraying the tricks the mescaline played with his face.

"Honey," Beaudreau said, gesturing toward me with his open hand, "this here's Phil Evans."

"Elliott." I raised two fingers and waved. "Elliott."

"Huh?" He was startled. "Oh yeah. What am I thinkin'—Phil Elliott, he plays football."

Charlotte smiled slightly. "We've met."

"We were wondering if you all might join our party?" I lied, gesturing toward the increasing confusion in front of the stage.

"Great idea." Beaudreau scooped up his drink and was out of his chair in one movement. "I been wantin' to talk to ol' Andy about this letter stock I got." He started toward the front, hesitated and turned back to Charlotte. "You comin'?"

"I'll be along."

"Yeah . . . yeah," I said. "I'll bring her."

"All right." He headed toward the stage. His coat swung open and I glimpsed the blue flash of a revolver stuck in the waistband of his red Sansabelt slacks.

"Why do you date that creep?" I knew my eyes were shiny from the mescaline.

"You're hardly in the company of the royal family." Her expression remained unchanged.

"I know. I know." I watched Beaudreau being greeted. "But at least they're unarmed. Does he have a permit to carry that gun?"

"Yes. His father's a big financial backer of the sheriff. The sheriff made Bob a deputy."

A burst of laughter and the sounds of breaking glass came from the table.

"What's going on?"

"Wet Willy."

"What?"

"Wet Willy," I explained. "They lick their fingers and stick 'em in each other's ears. It's a test. Not unlike jousting."

Charlotte wrinkled her nose and opened her mouth in a mock expression of vomiting.

"Puke," was all she said.

"Twentieth-century man," I said, shrugging.

I looked up from the ash tray I was spinning, directly into her eyes. Ever so slight movements at the corners betrayed an ambivalence toward me.

"Are you afraid of me?" I asked, continuing to watch her eyes for clues.

"No," she said quickly. Her eyes couldn't agree and she dropped them from my gaze. There was an uneasy pause. Finally she began again.

"Yes, I am," she said. "You'll think this is silly." Her eyes came up to meet mine. "But I've had this strange feeling ever since I first saw you."

"At Andy's party?"

"No, no, long before that—over six months ago—in here."

My mind raced backward, but as usual I could barely remember this morning. I needed a clue.

"You were with Janet Simons," she continued. "Chuck Berry was here and you were on crutches."

Janet Simons came flooding back with painful clarity. I turned my eyes back to the ash tray and unconsciously spoke out loud.

"She was a Lesbian." The sound of my voice surprised me.

"Yes, I know."

"Well, why didn't somebody tell me? I thought she was having her period for six weeks.

"What a scene that was," I added. "If I hadn't been in a cast, I think she would have kicked the livin' shit outta me. I never knew whether it was sympathy or fear that I'd beat her with the crutches." I laughed again and then fell silent. There was another long expectant pause.

A loud crash carried our attention to the group by the stage. Alan Claridge had jumped onto the stage, knocking over a microphone, and was hurriedly taking off his pants. Fran, his date, and several waiters seemed to be the only people upset by the scene. As the waiters raced toward the undulating man,

Crawford intercepted the closest with a stiff arm to the chest. The blow hurled the waiter back several feet. He landed with a thump and skidded crazily, ending tangled in a patron's legs beneath a table. The others slowed their approach as Andy stepped between them and the bizarre strip show on the stage.

Claridge by this time had removed his pants, undershorts, and jacket, and was working on the buttons of his shirt. As each article came free, he was wadding it up and throwing it at Fran. She remained motionless as the wads bounced against her. The shirt came off. He twisted it into a ball and hit her full in the face. She never moved.

Grabbing his cock, Claridge began the motions of masturbation, pointing the limp organ indiscriminately around the room. People ducked and dodged, as if they were afraid of being hit. A few women screamed politely and one couple got up to leave, but the rest remained, watching intently.

The naked man was laughing and pointing his penis at Fran, who had put her face into her hands.

"Goddam you, Fran," he yelled. "Look at me, you fucking whore."

He jumped from the stage, grabbed her chair, and jerked it from under her. She fell to the floor.

The meaty sound of openhanded slaps roused the paralyzed waiters and they tried to move to the girl's assistance. Crawford intercepted the first one and pushed him over a table. The waiter leg-whipped a middle-aged woman in the face, knocking her in a heap on the floor.

"My God," Charlotte gasped, standing up.

I grabbed her and headed toward the door. We were in my car heading north on Greenville Avenue before either of us said another word.

Charlotte broke the silence. "I have to go back. Bob will be wondering."

"Don't worry. The police will give him something to think about."

"Will they arrest them?"

"No," I said, thoughtfully, half my brain still caught in the swirl of bodies and emotions at Rock City. "Unless your boyfriend tries to shoot his way out, they'll probably take 'em out to pacify the crowd and then turn 'em loose. If that woman wasn't hurt too bad." I could still see her head bouncing off the dance floor.

"Well, then," she asked, turning to look at me, "why did we run out?"

"'Cause I'm stoned and holding," I said. "It's one thing to strip naked and beat up women in public. It's two to life for taking dope. Besides it was a way to get you alone."

"Oh." She was silent for a moment. I could feel her mind dealing with the alternatives. "Well, then I must go home."

"Where's home?"

"Lacota."

"Lacota? Goddam, that's fifty miles from here."

"Do you want to take me back to Rock City?"

In twenty minutes, we were heading south and east toward Lacota, a square little Texas county seat built around the proverbial red-brick courthouse.

"Are you from Lacota?" I was leaning over the steering wheel, searching the sky for the source of a bright blue flash I was sure I had just seen.

"No. My husband."

The thought of her being married was shocking and I was immediately lost in a hallucinogenic swirl of moral ramifications. The mescaline would make compromise difficult but not impossible.

"He was killed two years ago near Da Nang," she answered the question she knew I was asking.

"I'm sorry," was all I could muster.

"No, you're not. You're just trying to be polite." She was right. She could read my thoughts. All sorts of perverse and diabolical feelings and ideas spilled from my head onto the seat between us. She didn't seem to notice. "But nothing's wrong with being polite. I appreciate the effort. He didn't like the war, but he didn't know how to quit."

"Who does? Quitters never win and winners never quit. It doesn't matter what you do as long as you're the best at it." I steered deftly around a large furry creature sitting in the middle of the road. "It's not whether you live or die but if you win the game. You know, the old you-gotta-decide-which-sized-frog-you-wanna-be-in-what-sized-pond-and-then-win-win-win syndrome." Jesus, I was high. Charlotte looked at me in amazement. I shrugged my shoulders. "Don't look at me. I just say it. I don't know what it means."

She continued her story. "Well, when he finally decided to quit he was already over there. He was a career officer and it really confused him to be on the wrong side. He kept trying to decide what his duty was and finally resigned his commission. It made him feel terribly guilty. He was killed while his resignation was being processed."

"It's a shitty war." I hadn't meant to say that. It just jumped from my mouth. It sounded trite and foolish. I was too stoned to deal with the emotions she was skirting. Life, death, and foreign policy were a little heavy for a mescaline tripper behind the wheel of a six-thousand-dollar, stereophonic, and temperature-controlled automobile. Waves of cold chills made me feel as if my skin were shrinking, squeezing me smaller. Paranoia pulled at the corners of my eyes and my mouth turned dry. My lips stuck to my teeth in a maniacal grin. I mashed down on the accelerator and the car leaped ahead. The sound and response of the engine reassured me. I was in control. Everything fell back into place. Bob Dylan was crying from the rear speakers.

> "*. . . All of these awful things that I have heard.*
> *I don't want to believe them.*
> *All I want is your word . . .*"

"Listen, there's no reason to get nervous." She noticed my panic. "I'm not in mourning or anything. He was a nice guy and we might have been happy together. But, I mean, how do you know? He was a soldier when I met him and the war was hanging over our heads all the time. I knew him three months before he went over and everything we did and felt was related to the war. He wanted to get it out of the way and settle down. It was a business decision. But when he got over there it really brought him down. It was tragic and I cried a lot. But it's not to be done over, is it, and whether I'm happy or sad right now depends on me, not something that happened ten thousand miles away and two years ago." She smiled at me. "I choose to be happy."

"Good." I smiled back at her. "Life is choice. I heard that somewhere. Or I made it up. I don't remember which." A row of mailboxes transformed into a marauding motorcycle gang and back to a row of mailboxes. I concentrated on the road. The faster we went, the better I felt. I was overtaking my speeding brain. Loaded on mescaline is no time to be faint-hearted. I gave the Buick a little more gas and resumed the conversation. "I guess I heard it somewhere. Probably from a coach. The major guiding forces in my life have been coaches. Can you imagine what little tidbits of insanity I've got tucked away up here?"

"I can't imagine how you've lived this long. Slow down, will you?"

"Sure." I eased off the gas and turned up the tape deck. "The first major choice in my life was deciding how successful I wanted to be." I flinched slightly as a huge hole suddenly opened in the road and, just as suddenly, closed again. Charlotte didn't seem to notice. "The old frog-in-the-pond paradox I mentioned earlier. I did mention it earlier, didn't I?"

"I'm certain you did. Please keep your eyes on the road."

"Sure. Sure." I turned back to the road in time to catch a glimpse of a large spotted bird disappearing over the top of the car. I flinched again. "I learned in high school that once a man chooses a goal he must never quit or be satisfied with less. Similar situation to your late husband's—no offense intended. There is great social value to stubbornness; it implies character and a sense of destiny."

"I don't know about destiny—" Charlotte shifted uneasily in her seat, "—but riding with you gives me a real sense of fate."

"That's good enough." I lifted my foot and watched the needle drop below seventy. "As long as you're moving. You don't really have to know where. Just act like you do."

"Turn the wipers off."

"What?"

"The windshield wipers. Turn them off."

The rubber blades were squeaking across the windshield glass, spreading the smashed bugs into greasy yellow streaks.

"How did that happen?"

"I'm not sure, but I hope this car is enchanted. It's my only chance to get home alive."

"Sorry." I slowed way down and kept my eyes on the road. "Now like I was saying it may seem presumptuous for a seventeen-year-old boy to decide never to fail but I should point out that optimism abounded in those times. My braces had just been removed after six long years, I had beaten back the ravages of acne, a girl had jacked me off on the beach, I had scored in the ninety-seventh percentile on the SAT tests. And I had received scholarship offers from five Big Ten schools. Besides it was the late fifties, everybody had decided to succeed at everything."

"Not everybody."

"Oh? What were you doing while the rest of us fought for our chances to make fools of ourselves?"

"I was a long-haired fourteen-year-old sneaking around the San Fernando Valley trying to have fun without getting busted."

"Did you?"

"Yes and no. Yes, I got busted and no I didn't have any fun. I got pregnant." She turned to look at me. "Are you shocked?"

"Naw. I used to jack off to Betty Furness Westinghouse commercials. Are you shocked?"

"Not as long as you don't do it while I'm in the room."

"Same here. In fact I sorta wish you were fourteen now."

"I was more fun then. Getting pregnant calmed me down a little. You learn a lot about yourself lying awake all night trying to stop the unstoppable. I don't know why I'm telling you all this."

" 'Cause I'm the kind of man that can look with compassion upon your incredibly degenerate childhood. C'mon, tell me about it."

"Well, I went through all the fights with my parents and

his parents and him. They all wanted me to have an abortion. I didn't want to have the baby particularly, but I sure as shit didn't want to have any abortion. I finally decided to keep the baby and told them all to fuck off; it was a great feeling. A month later I miscarried."

"I'm sorry." I turned and smiled at her. "And I'm not just being polite. I'm being cunningly obsequious."

"It's refreshing to meet someone so openly devious. I hope my confessions haven't upset you."

"Sounds like a normal childhood to me. I guess it was inevitable that you should end up with a professional football star racing across Texas and listening to Bob Dylan."

The road suddenly ended at the edge of a cliff. There was no time to stop. The general alarm reaction flooded my bloodstream with adrenaline; I felt as though I'd been electrocuted. My body stiffened in panic. My mind clung to one hope: in the long history of monumental fuckups in Texas there was no known case of the highway department's building a farm-to-market road over a cliff. I held my breath as the car bore on.

"It could be worse, I guess." Charlotte smiled. "You could be drunk."

"You mean I'm not." The cliff mysteriously vanished and the road stretched out long and straight toward a bridge that looked about half the width of the car.

> "*. . . Why wait any longer for the world to begin*
> *You can have your cake and eat it too . . .*"

About six miles past Lacota, Charlotte spoke. "Turn right at the next gravel road."

It was her driveway and I followed it to a white wooden gate. A small frame bungalow stood outside the gate.

A young black man in a western shirt and Levi's and a battered brown Resistol had come out of the bungalow.

"Is that you, Charlotte?"

"Yes," she called out the window. "I have a friend with me. Do you want to come to the house with us?"

"Sure."

Charlotte slid over. The black man opened the gate and

then got into the car, reaching in front of Charlotte to shake my hand.

"Hello. I'm David Clarke."

"Phillip Elliott," I said, grasping his hand firmly. It was a warm greeting and it surprised me.

"The football player?" The inquiry was enthusiastic.

"It's becoming a matter of opinion."

"I enjoy watching you play."

"You must have long stretches between thrills."

He laughed. I was flattered.

The lights of the Buick caught the outline of a two-story frame house and several large outbuildings. It was a big farm. Two white Alsatians trotted out of one side of a two-car garage. The other side housed a white Mercedes 220 SL with blue California plates. The plates were two years old. An old red Chevrolet pickup was parked next to the garage. The white gravel road continued past the house, through another white wooden gate, and into the darkness of a back pasture. I stopped next to the house.

"Lemme get the dogs," David said, jumping from the car and calling them to him.

I shut off the engine and got out. Charlotte slid out behind me and I followed her through a back door into the kitchen. David entered a few seconds later.

"David, take Phillip into the den, I'll fix some coffee."

The den was gigantic. The far wall was an expanse of glass spreading some twenty feet across and reaching from the rough-beamed ceiling to the stone floor. The inside walls were covered with books. Two large sofas flanked a massive stone fireplace and a large Indian rug was spread on the floor between them.

David walked to the gigantic hearth and began building a fire.

He held a long fireplace match against the wood and turned a small key in the hearth. The fire exploded to life with a roar. "Have you lived here long?"

"A little over two years. I knew Charlotte in college and moved here with her when John went over. She didn't want to live alone and he didn't have any family worth knowing. They showed up the first week we were here, took one look at me and split. We ain't heard from 'em since. They didn't even come to the funeral." David shook his head and smiled into the fire. "I told 'em I was Mexican. It didn't seem to help."

"Terrific. Next time tell 'em you're a Reconstruction Republican. They'll love that."

"No thanks." David's voice was deep and resonant and he pronounced his words distinctly. "If they ever show up again, I'm hiding in the woodpile." He tossed another log on the fire.

I stared at the hypnotic ripple of the flames. The mescaline was still working and the changing shapes and colors of the fire painted pictures from the past and future on my brain. I felt incredibly alive. I wanted to stick my hand into the fire and feel the flames wash against my skin like water.

"How do you like playing football? Professionally, I mean?" David turned from the fire to face me. His heavy brow was dotted with perspiration. A moderate Afro surrounded his face, making it seem small. A broad flat nose dominated his features.

"It's hard to say. It's better than selling life insurance but not as good as being born rich. You know, like just about everything."

"I played some in high school, but just didn't have the size or temperament for college." David was six feet and well muscled. "I'm glad I'm out of it. High school and college sports are the hypocrisies. Pro ball admits that it's for money, but high schools and college still talk all that character-building bullshit. Hell, when I was trying to make it in football, I thought people were supposed to treat me like shit. You know, earn my way to equality, be a credit to my race and crap like that.

"Well, the brothers and sisters are coming together." David turned the small key in the hearth again and the roaring fire immediately died to an orange glow. Small tongues of flame clung to the charred logs. "Things are changing."

"What makes you say that?"

"I've seen it, man. I spent a lot of time on the street before I came here and I've talked with a lot of people who believe like I do. There has to be more to this system than achievement games set up by the people in power. Look at your man Richardson, he won a court case and rented an apartment in north Dallas."

"I wouldn't consider Richardson an overwhelming victory. He wanted that apartment so he could be close to the practice field and I would imagine Thomas'll be gone before his lease is up. His pride outweighs his usefulness to the club."

"I dunno, man." David straightened up and stepped away from the hearth. "That all sounds pretty bigoted and diabolical. If they're that way, why haven't they just cut him before this?"

"Because they're businessmen and he was a relatively valuable piece of property. After all, you wouldn't shoot a pedigreed bull for shitting in the yard. But Richardson is reaching a point of diminishing returns, where his demands on discipline and order outweigh his value. Andy Crawford is already a great running back and watch how many running backs they draft this year."

David shook his head. "I don't believe it man. If he was getting fucked around like you say, how come the other blacks aren't screaming about it?"

"Fear. They all got too much to lose. To them being a second-class citizen on a football team is a hell of a lot better than being a first-class citizen in south Dallas. The ones that did speak up are gone."

David stabbed at the glowing wood. He seemed irritated.

"Well, man. What you say about the team may be all well and good. But I don't see where you possibly got the knowledge to think you know what motivates a black man." He pointed his finger directly in my face. "Cause you don't." He wasn't actually angry, but I had apparently excited him some.

"Listen," I said in subdued tones, "what I'm telling you is only my opinion and I'm pretty high besides. But I've been in pretty close to both sides and commitment to anything other than one's own survival is pretty pointless."

I stared into the fire and we fell silent. The mescaline drew me into the coals. Survival: that was what Jerry Ragen had told us at the strike committee meeting. Representatives from all the teams were there and we were about to call for professional sports' first labor walkout. The negotiations were being held in Los Angeles at the Beverly Wilshire. Maxwell had been elected a representative by the team and had chosen me to accompany him. I was to be a part of history.

"Survival. That's what this strike is all about," Ragen had said. "The survival of the players association is more important than the survival of any one player. That's why I am proud as the president of the association to take these demands to the owners."

Jerry Ragen had been a middle linebacker for Pittsburgh for nine years and had been president of the association for the past two years. "I'm glad to see everyone here. The guys from Detroit will be in on United at noon. I think it's very important that the champions Detroit and Dallas are very prominent in our display of strength and unity of purpose. Seth. Why don't you give us a few words on how the boys in Dallas feel?" Ragen had peered to the back of the room to where Seth and I sat, disheveled and hung over. We had gotten in the night before and had gone out drinking with a *Life* reporter who was doing a feature on Maxwell. We had gotten incredibly stoned and then met the reporter for dinner at an old converted warehouse called The Factory. The night had ended at five thirty A.M. We had passed out for four hours, then had taken some Dexamyl and made the ten A.M. meeting. My Dexamyl was just beginning to work when Maxwell got to his feet to address the strike committee "on how the boys in Dallas" felt.

"Well . . . sure . . . Jerry, Ah . . ." His eyes were bloodshot and he nervously scratched at the heart-shaped mole on his unshaven chin.

"Excuse me, Seth," Ragen had interrupted. "I don't see O.W. Didn't he come?" Ragen had sent Maxwell the ticket money and letter instructing him to "bring another representative, preferably O.W. Meadows." Meadows didn't come because Maxwell had asked me instead. I was more fun.

"No . . . ah . . . Jerry," Maxwell stammered. "O.W. couldn't make it. But you all know Phil Elliott, our flankerback."

They didn't know, but I smiled and waved anyway.

"Oh—uh—sure. Hiya doin', Phil." Now we had Ragen going. I nodded at the president. Maxwell took confidence from Ragen's confusion.

"Yes, well, the guys back in Dallas are ready to see this thing through to the end. That's what a team's about, ain't it?" There was a bit more Texas twang in his voice than normal. "We unanimously voted to strike with the other teams in the association." Actually it had been a bitter, split vote. "We're behind the association one hunert percent." Maxwell sat down to thunderous applause from the small group of players and advisors.

"Thanks, Seth." Jerry Ragen stood at the front of the room beside a large flip chart. In a blue pinstripe suit and solid blue tie he looked not unlike a young politician. "Okay. Before we go any farther, I wanna say something about those cocksuckers in the other league. That fucking gimp-legged Miami running back McGregor promised me that they wouldn't sign until we signed." The league merger had recently been agreed upon but it was still not in effect. Both players associations had to negotiate their collective bargaining agreements separately. "Well that little motherfucker signed and I ain't forgetting it." Ragen's face began to turn red and he paced nervously across the front of the room. "We play those assholes in exhibition season." Beads of sweat popped out on his face and the angry Pittsburgh linebacker kept slamming his fist into the palm of his hand. "And I tell you one thing, I'm gonna kill that little motherfucker. He'll be so fuckin' sorry he double-crossed us." Ragen whirled around and slammed his fist against the wall. There was a stunned moment while the blow echoed around the room and then Ragen turned to the flip chart. "Okay. Let's take a look at these numbers and see if we can't cut ourselves a deal." He smiled and turned the first page of the chart to reveal a breakout of the total dollar revenue from bubble-gum-card sales.

The rest of the meeting had been pretty dull with lawyers

and accountants telling us how much money we had coming to us and how to go about getting it. I hadn't understood the numbers and the straight businesslike tactics had seemed pretty stupid to me. Clinton Foote headed the owners negotiating committee and I knew what he would do with businesslike tactics.

That night Maxwell went out with Ragen and the quarterback from Green Bay. I had been sitting alone in the bar when a waiter plugged a telephone into my booth. He handed me the phone.

"Hello?"

"Phil. Is that you? Where's Seth?"

"He's gone. Who's this?"

"This is Schmidt. I need to talk to Seth." Bill Schmidt was the twelve-year veteran center of our team and one of Conrad Hunter's favorites. He worked for Conrad several off seasons and was the godfather of Conrad's youngest boy. On the Sunday the boy was born Schmidt won the game ball.

"Seth ain't here. What's the trouble?"

"It's Conrad, that's the goddam trouble. Tonight's paper quoted Seth as saying that our strike vote had been unanimous. Did he say that?"

"Yep. I watched him do it."

"Goddammit. Fuck. Why did he do that?" Schmidt's deep voice had turned into a whine. "Conrad came down to my office and fired me this afternoon. I told him I voted against the strike but he showed me the paper. My God, what am I gonna do?"

"Don't ask me, Bill. If he didn't believe you over the newspaper I'd say you were in serious trouble to begin with."

"I don't need any goddam advice, you stupid asshole. All this is your fault. You're not supposed to be out there anyway."

"Goddammit, Schmidt, I don't have to listen to this shit." I hung up. A few moments later the waiter returned and told me to pick up the phone again.

"Elliott, you hang up on me again and I'll kill you."

I hung up again.

The waiter returned and I picked up the receiver for the third time. There was no response.

"Hello?" I said cautiously.

"Phil?"

"Yes."

"Now don't hang up on me. This is costing me money. Listen, man, you gotta help me. You gotta call Conrad and tell him what really happened. I want my job back. I been there twelve years. I can't get another job like that one." He began to sob. "I won't have anything when I retire."

"Jesus, Bill." I was embarrassed and shifted nervously in my seat. "I don't know what to do. Conrad won't listen to me."

"You gotta call him," Schmidt pleaded. "I want my job back. Tell him I voted against the strike, please."

"Okay, okay. Jesus, stop crying."

Schmidt gave me Conrad's private number and I tried to reach him during the remainder of the night but he wouldn't accept my calls. When Maxwell came in I told him the story but he wasn't too interested. After a good night's sleep I had forgotten the incident.

The next day's meeting was canceled. The association's negotiation files had disappeared. On a hunch Ragen stormed into Clinton Foote's hotel room and found Clinton and the commissioner reading the files. Ragen had to be dragged screaming from the room by a defensive tackle from San Francisco. The furious association president threatened to kill Clinton if he ever caught him alone. The commissioner issued a statement that an unidentified third party had brought the files to Clinton's room and they were merely going over them to establish ownership.

Several days later, a select committee of players' representatives reached an agreement with the owners' group. A document was drawn up and Clinton asked permission to take it to his superiors for their signatures. The next day he returned with the signed agreement and announced that the owners were pleased the strike was over. While Clinton was making his speech, Jerry Ragen thumbed through the twenty-five-page agreement and found that the owners had substituted fourteen new pages.

"You lousy cocksucker." Ragen had leaped over the conference table and grabbed at Clinton's throat. The startled general manager had fallen over backward and scrambled for the door. Ragen hit Clinton on the back as the terrified man dove out onto the mezzanine. The same defensive tackle from San Francisco subdued Ragen again.

Another agreement was reached three days later and the owners' signatures were witnessed by the select committee.

It had all seemed pretty pointless. The owners refused to honor several portions of the agreement, preferring long court hassles to compliance. The San Francisco defensive tackle who had twice saved Clinton's life and another player who attended the negotiations were released outright the first day of camp. Bill Schmidt had gotten his job back after Maxwell had convinced Conrad Hunter the strike vote had been a narrow majority.

Six months later, it was discovered that Ragen and one of the association lawyers had been diverting funds for personal use. And McGregor, the Miami running back Ragen had threatened to kill for double-crossing the association, retired from football and went into politics. It all had to do with survival.

"Survival," I said aloud. The sound of my own voice jerked me back to the present. I was still staring into the fire.

"What?" David Clarke was looking at me.

"Just remembering." I was having difficulty pulling myself from the fire.

"Well, I think you're wrong, man. I got more faith in people than that."

I nodded, still lost in the fire and trying to decide who did win the strike. Me, I guess, I got a free trip to Los Angeles.

David walked to the picture window and flipped a switch. Instantly the outside was illuminated. It was a rolling pasture of thick coastal Bermuda grass; the shadows of live oaks filled the landscape. I immediately pictured Brahma and Black Angus grazing lazily through the trees.

"Is this a working ranch?"

"Sort of. John owned several large oil leases and left them to her, so she doesn't need the money. But working keeps us busy and she seems to like it. Mostly we just bottle-raise calves and sell 'em at about five to seven months."

"Who's in charge of your cow placement?" I inquired. "I'd like to apply for the job."

"Cow what?" Charlotte asked, stepping into the den from the hallway. She was carrying a tray with a coffeepot and three heavy brown mugs with bridles and saddles hand painted on the sides.

"Cow placement," I said. "Placing the cows in just the right spots in the pasture for an overall aesthetic effect. You know, so they blend just right with the trees and sky and clouds. It's a job most dopeheads in this part of the country dream about. My favorite is to place them in small clumps, sitting and standing, on the tops of the low rolling hills, so they stand out against the horizon. It's called the Edge of the World Technique."

"Are there many job openings?" Charlotte asked, smiling.

"I've never seen one. It's sort of like a royal patronage and if a guy gets a job like that he don't quit. It becomes a legacy. That's the trouble with this world today, power and privilege." I winked at David. "They never give a truly creative man a chance. I mean, how many people really care how the sun hits a Brahma's hump?"

"Not me, that's for sure." Charlotte smiled. "How about some coffee, maybe it'll bring you down."

"Is it that noticeable?"

She just raised one eyebrow and poured the coffee.

"I guess I should apologize to you," I said to David. "I have a tendency to rave"

"No need to apologize. I just don't agree with you."

"Cream or sugar?" Charlotte was looking at me.

"Sugar. One."

Outside, the dogs started barking. David got up and started out of the room. "I might as well check the gate and lock it for the night."

"David's a writer," Charlotte said, gazing absently at the doorway he had just passed through.

"He seems like a very nice guy."

"He is a very nice man." She accented the *man.*

"That's what I meant."

"All his brothers married white girls. It confused him terribly."

"That's strange, all mine did the same thing. It didn't bother me a bit."

Charlotte ignored the remark and crossed the room to the bookcase. She dug through the record trunk and put a Willie Nelson album on the turntable.

We stared silently at each other. I made a stab at mental telepathy but I couldn't hold one thought long enough. Her face softened and seemed to glow. She was beautiful and sad. I knew by her eyes that she liked me; I just knew. Madness crept from behind my eyes and I dropped them from her gaze. Panic bubbled at the back of my throat. I walked to the bookcase and watched the record spin. Then I walked back and sat down again.

The kitchen door slammed and the sound rescued me from my spiraling mind. Suddenly, I felt better, the tightening stopped, my thoughts slowed and the fear vanished. Shortly David stood in the doorway.

"There was a car down by the gate, but they drove off. Probably high school kids. I locked up. I think I'll go to bed. Good night." He tossed a ring of keys on the table and then continued down the hallway to the bedrooms.

"Good night," we called out in unison after him.

"Does David live in the foreman's house?" I asked after what I thought was a proper interval.

"Only when he's working on something." Her eyes narrowed slightly. "He writes down there and when I'm out he stays there until I get back."

"He sounds like a good friend."

"He is."

We fell to staring at each other again. She licked her lips and they seemed to sparkle in the firelight. Her fingers played in the long brown hair that rolled over her shoulders.

"What about Beaudreau?"

"What about him?"

"Isn't he your friend?"

"Hardly."

"Well, why do you date him?"

"I don't date him," she answered, a touch of venom in her voice. I didn't know whether it was for me or Beaudreau. "He owns some land near here and runs cattle. He came by to ask if I was interested in leasing him some of my land. He called and asked me out several times after that."

"Oh."

"I can't hide here forever," she flared.

"I didn't mean anything."

"Anyway, I'm not going out with him anymore." Her tone quieted. "He said some pretty shitty things about David tonight on the way to Rock City."

"I think he's nuts."

"He talks like you and he are old army buddies."

"I barely know the son of a bitch. He's a hard-core football groupie and energy thief who comes to all the parties whether he's invited or not."

The music ended and Charlotte got up and turned the record player off. As she stood by the stereo, she was outlined in the light from outside. I could see her body clearly through the thin material of the dress. She walked to the window and turned off the floodlights. The room was filled with the changing shadows of the fire. She slipped back to the couch.

"Are you married?"

"Divorced." I went to the hearth and tossed in a log. "The same old story. College star from wrong side of tracks pulls himself up by his jockstrap and marries wealthy debutante. Star brings office woes home with him and turns to bottle, while wife looks for consolation elsewhere and finds it . . . in the offensive line . . . defensive backfield . . . specialty teams . . . and so on. All rather sordidly funny but highly expensive."

I pulled and rubbed on my nose, a nervous tic I had picked up in high school basketball when I thought every eye in the gymnasium was on me and waiting for me to fuck up. I usually did.

"Would you like to turn on?"

"Yes." I answered too fast.

Charlotte got up and left the room. She was gone a good while and when she returned, carrying a red Prince Albert can, she had changed her dress for a pair of faded Levi bell bottoms and a loose-fitting Mexican peasant blouse.

"My dope smoking uniform."

I eased myself awkwardly to the floor at her feet; I stretched out my legs and moaned, partly from pain and partly for pity, as the kinks came out. A lighted joint appeared from the sky, I took it, dragged deeply, and passed it back. After two or three drags, I noticed a definite effect.

"Goddam," I said, trying to hold in the smoke that burned my lungs. "To . . . quote . . . absent friends . . . that is . . . dynamite shit." My voice was a rasp.

"John sent a duffel bag full back from Nam with a friend," she said. "Don't smoke too much—it'll make you sick." She took a long drag off the cigarette and passed it back to me.

Smoking a dead man's dope was creepy enough, but to think of a whole duffel bag full was frightening.

"It ought to last a long time."

I walked to the end of the room and stared out the window. The shadows of the trees changed into Viet Cong and moved quietly toward the house.

"What do you do besides working your calves?" I asked, without turning from the window. The VC were almost to the house, little yellow bastards with drum-type submachine guns like those the Red Chinese carried in all the GI Joe comics. At least they weren't wearing those quilted suits. Jesus, I hated those quilted suits.

"Not a whole lot. I like to read and ride my horse."

Charlie disappeared around the side of the house and the dogs started barking again. I turned from the window.

"Sounds like a nice life."

"It is. I've got almost a section here and I love to just wander around it."

I walked over to the couch and bent down. She held the joint to my lips. I took a deep drag and then pressed my mouth to hers; I blew the smoke deeply into her lungs.

I ran my hands beneath the blouse. She started to pull away and then relaxed. I stripped the blouse off over her head. The levis had slipped down and rested on her hips, revealing a strip of pale white skin. I bent to kiss her. She kissed me softly, then turned and left the room. A moment later she returned trailing a quilted comforter, which she spread on the floor in front of the fire. I pulled off my shirt and boots and crawled onto the quilt.

We made love for a long time. The mescaline turned it to a pornographic hallucination. My whole body had sight. When we finished I didn't know what was real and what was imagined.

The fire had burned down to embers. I crawled to the hearth and threw more wood onto the coals. I felt calm and peaceful. Charlotte was curled up on her side staring into the fire; her eyes seemed sightless. I lay back next to her.

As I floated I dreamed I was following a cattle truck on the highway. The cattle were jammed in and crashing against each other and the sides of the trailer as the driver weaved through the traffic trying to make the packing plant a few minutes sooner.

I wondered if these dumb beasts knew where they were headed, where this man with his hairy, tattooed arm hanging out the cab window was hurrying them. They couldn't know. Maybe they felt anxious, sensed something strange, but how could they know that in a short time, a very short time, they would face a sweat-soaked black man, who, while talking in low soothing tones, would, with the precision of a sculptor, strike them down with a single blow between the eyes. As I pulled around the truck a pair of brown eyes looked out from between the wooden slats. The eyes were mine and I was on the truck watching Charlotte ride by in my car. She was crying. B.A. was driving and Maxwell was in the back waving and holding up a can of beer. I jerked awake.

My head was throbbing. The wall clock said it was almost 5 A.M. I tried to clear the buzzing from my thoughts. The aches and pains were slowly creeping back as the old reality returned.

Charlotte was curled on her side clinging to my arm. Her smooth face was peaceful and expressionless in sleep. I stared at her for a long time wondering what she thought of me. Did she know me at all? What did she want from me? Nothing, I hoped. There was nothing to give. I looked around the room. It all seemed unreal, like a fantastic dream. The fire was dead and the room was cold. There was no trace of the excitement and energy I had felt last night. Had I actually been close to this woman? Did I have feelings for her? Or was I just high? Out of my mind and wishing for people and emotions that didn't exist.

I am a man who has learned that survival is the reason of life and that fear and hatred are the emotions. What you cannot overcome by hatred you must fear. And every day it is getting harder to hate and easier to fear. I wrapped the quilt around Charlotte; she moaned and stirred. She didn't look frightening and I certainly didn't hate her. I found a tablet and wrote a note saying I would call.

I left the note next to her, picked David's keys off the table, made my way down the hall through the kitchen, and stepped outside.

The predawn silence was only slightly broken by the intermittent noises of the morning birds. I stood beside my car and stared at the purple-pink glow that was to be Thursday, countless things below the horizon waiting to happen. Well let them come, Wednesday had been one for the book.

THURSDAY

It still wasn't light when I reached south Dallas and found a truck stop.

I ordered breakfast and bought a paper from the rack. Browsing the jukebox, I selected Jerry Lee Lewis's "She Even Woke Me Up to Say Goodbye." I particularly liked Jerry Lee's first line. "Mornin's come . . . and Lord . . . my mind is achin'. . ." I drank six cups of coffee and read the paper. A government scientist was found murdered in a downtown hotel, a situation that had homosexual overtones. A young housewife was found dead with her throat slashed. She had been sexually assaulted. It was the third such case in as many weeks. A city councilman had been connected with Mafia figures in a stock scandal. I read the entertainment section, checking movie and television listings. I seldom read the sports.

The three scrambled eggs, hash-brown potatoes, a side order of ham and two greasy slices of Texas toast were enough to get me moving again.

I went rather awkwardly to the car; the sun and the Dallas

air turned the purple-pink daybreak to a fluorescent orange. The morning smelled like diesel fuel.

If I was speeding I didn't know it and wasn't aware of the squad car until it turned on its siren. The siren scared the shit out of me and I pulled over, digging for my wallet at the same time. By the time the officer reached the car, I was holding my driver's license out the window. He ignored it.

"Step out of the car, please," he said, his eyes hidden behind wire aviator sunglasses.

Fantastic, I thought, a brand-new lid of grass in the glove compartment. I followed the officer back between the cars, where we stood while the early morning traffic whizzed by. He studied my license, comparing my face with the photograph. It was an old license and the hair length threw him off.

"When were you born?" he asked stiffly, his right hand resting on the butt of a chromium .45 automatic that hung at his side.

"Are you gonna do my chart?" I asked, irritated by his posture.

He pulled down his sunglasses and looked over them at my face.

"August 12, 1942. I'm a Leo."

"You were clocked going sixty miles an hour in a forty-five-mile zone, Bertrand."

Bertrand Phillip Elliott is my full Christian name, but I am not quick to admit it.

"I didn't know. I'm sorry," I said, trying to appear remorseful but not cowardly.

The officer looked me over from head to foot. I was slightly disheveled. He tried to peer past me into the car.

"You been drinkin'?"

"No," I shook my head. "I wish I had." I rubbed my eyes and scratched my head. "I been drivin' all night from New Orleans. I had to go down there for a boys' club football banquet."

The policeman pulled off his glasses and squinted at me, then at my license again. A slow smile broke across his face.

"Well, Phil," he said, handing me back my license, "don't

be drivin' when you're too tired to pay attention. We need you out there."

"I'm sorry, I'll be more careful next time." I would be too.

"You guys gonna do all right in New York?"

I nodded, putting my license back in my wallet.

"Let's get to the Superbowl this year, huh? I promised my wife I'd take her if we went." He smiled widely. "Would you be able to get me any tickets?"

"Sure. Just call me about ten days before the game, I'll get you a couple." I reached out and shook his hand. "Thanks."

"That's okay," he said. "You be careful drivin' now; I hate to see people splattered all over the highway. Makes me feel like I'm not doin' my job. If you had an accident now I'd take it real personal."

By the time I reached north Dallas and the practice field, the sun was up, the ground haze turning it into an orange Day-Glo ball. Maxwell's convertible, the top down and the seats wet with dew, was already in the lot. It wasn't much past eight.

The front door to the clubhouse was locked. I walked around to the back and found a broken window. I looked inside. Asleep on a meeting-room couch was last year's Top Pro Athlete and winner of the Atlanta Minutemen's Outstanding American Award.

I clumsily climbed through the window. The noise woke Maxwell. He sat bolt upright.

"Who is it?" he mumbled, rubbing his eyes.

"The tooth fairy." I dangled from the window, my feet searching for the floor.

"Fuck you," he said and fell back on the couch.

I dusted myself off and looked at the exhausted man.

"Shit, I hope I don't look that bad."

Maxwell lifted his arm from across his face, squeezing open a reddish-blue eye against the light.

"You do." He replaced the arm.

"I was afraid so. I have been on a long journey to the dark recesses of my psyche."

"Recess was always my favorite time," Maxwell said without moving.

"Come on, let's us bust into the ol' medicine cabinet." I stepped into the hall and headed for the training room. "First aid is the best aid . . . physician heal thyself . . . a stitch in . . ." I stopped at the sauna to switch it on, then continued to the training room. When Seth stumbled, moaning, into the room, I was already at work on the drawer with a pair of tape scissors.

"The trainers are really gonna be pissed," he said, with an uncharacteristic urgency.

"They won't do anything to you." I jammed the scissors into the catch.

"What do you mean me?" Maxwell cried. "You're the one that's doin' it."

"Yeah. But, you'll share in the take and that makes you an accomplice. If they turn me in, they got to turn you in, and they won't do that."

The drawer slid open with a crack.

"Goddam," Maxwell groaned. "You broke it."

"Not so's you could notice. The trainers'll know, but they won't say anything. Look at this stuff." I rummaged through the drawer. "As ol' MJ says, only take what you need, not what you want, loose translation."

"Who the fuck is MJ?"

"Mick Jagger."

"That little fairy."

"He always speaks highly of you." I held up two pill vials. "Dexamyl and Compazine. Spansules. That'll do it."

I poured out four pills of each kind into my hand. I passed two of each to Maxwell and kept the remaining four. I swallowed two. Maxwell took all four of his at once. I shook several Codeine Number Four out of the white plastic bottle, took two and put the rest in my pocket.

Ten minutes later we were both under cold pounding showers, waiting for the sauna to heat up and the drugs to start doing battle in our shattered brains.

"Last night was an all-time show stopper," Maxwell said.

If one was to believe the descriptive phrases used by Maxwell in the course of a fuck story, not since the Marquis de

Sade has anyone touched him, either as a practitioner or raconteur.

Once during training camp, Maxwell and I rented a house near the practice field. Our first exhibition game was against San Francisco, and after the game we returned directly to camp. After bed check we sneaked out and met two girls at the house. It had been a tough hot game and, although I had only played the first half, I was exhausted. My companion was peculiarly cooperative. Although refusing to remove her panties, she did a commendable job of fellatio, pulling her mouth away at the crucial moment to take the spray in her face and hair. It was bizarre and pleasing and I was soon sleeping peacefully. Sometime later, I awoke with a throbbing pain in my right arm. The bed was rocking and bouncing violently. Maxwell was screwing the daylights out of my bedmate. They were both lying on my arm and my hand had gone to sleep. The girl's panties were shredded and lying across my chest. The bed was soaked with blood. It seems she was in the middle of a rather abundant menstrual period. Seeing that I was awake, Maxwell leaned over and whispered in my ear.

"I tol' her," his voice was a rasp, "that I'd wade in the Red River anytime, jus' wouldn't drink from it."

I extracted my arm and crawled to the other twin bed and fell back to sleep. It was only one of several instances that pointed to Maxwell's insatiable desire and incredible stamina.

"An all-timer," Maxwell groaned.

The nice thing about Seth as a teller of pornography, an art he had perfected to its quintessence, was that the listener only had to make infrequent one-syllable guttural responses to keep a conversation going for several hours.

"An all-timer," he repeated, shaking his head and walking from the showers to the sauna, grabbing a handful of towels on the way.

The water felt good beating on the back of my neck, which was beginning to stiffen from the aftereffects of the mescaline and the general strain of the night.

Leaving the showers, I detoured to the equipment manager's cage, tuned his FM intercom to the Fort Worth country music station, then joined Maxwell in the sauna. The sound of "Sunday Mornin' Comin' Down" convinced me that my life had a soundtrack.

Maxwell jumped up and left the smothering heat, returning seconds later with two cans of Coors.

"The trainers had a six-pack in their refrigerator. It seemed like a good idea."

I was already despairing that the Dexamyl and Compazine had fallen through the big, black holes burned in my brain. I was willing to try anything to change the way I felt. The beer tasted cold but not particularly good. I rubbed my neck vigorously, trying to relieve the tightness that was sending hammering pains into my head.

"Why do I punish my body like this?" Maxwell asked, his fingers lightly tracing the thin white surgical scars that made a road map of his torso. Two long zippers, starting behind and coming up over the point of his right elbow, ended at his forearm. He had a white puckered hole on the back of his left hand, the result of playing half a season with an unrepaired break. A calcium sheath had formed around the fractured bones and the breaks never healed. Periodically, the unmended hand would abscess and swell to the size of a volley ball. The team physician would puncture him like a bloated cow and pus would shoot all over the room. The white puckered scar was where he stuck the knife. Three other red welts commemorated two shoulder dislocations and a compound fracture of his collarbone.

Although Maxwell's upper body took an incredible beating, he had good strong legs and had been a running back in college. Only specific orders from B.A. kept him from running out of the pocket. On occasion he would disregard those orders and turn a certain loss into a good gain. He liked to run and hit.

"You're the only man I know with an older body than mine," Maxwell said, looking at the large knot sticking out from the side of my ankle, the vestige of a compound fracture and dislocation.

The doctor told me the knot had developed because I had taken several steps after the injury, but I got the feeling it was just too much trouble to put everything exactly back in place. And besides, as the doctor said, it was functional and would only bother me if I wore Oxfords. To me the ankle seemed minor compared to my back injury and it seldom bothered me, except for occasional jokes about having the head of my dick stuffed in my sock.

I often felt that this brotherhood of mutilation was a very large part of the strange friendship Maxwell and I shared. Each bore his particular pain in front of the other with a stoic humor. When one went down, the other was always among the first to his side, unless he had already gone down, which happened more than once. The intimacy of our doping ritual had begun, with codeine and Demerol, long before marijuana had become the sacrament. At first the pills were used just to bear the pain of shredded and smashed muscles and ligaments. Then later we combined them with alcohol to shorten the long, anxious return trips to Dallas. We would sit, strapped in our seats, packed in ice or wrapped in elastic, in lengthy discussions of the sounds and feelings of excruciating injuries. Enjoying the communion of pain thresholds and recovery times, we developed a bond not unlike a Prussian Saber Club. To mention it at the time would have seemed ridiculous. After all, it was just a day's work. But as the years wore on in meetings like this, we would sit in naked silence and marvel at each other's ability to withstand pain and wonder how much longer the misshapen limbs would last. This morning, from the look of us, even money said the end of the day. But somehow, we would make another day, as we had so many days in the past, each taking strength from the other's agony. It was all we knew how to do.

It was a peculiar, maybe even a homosexual bond, but it was strong, and in a life of continual change, I took my solace in its intransigence.

"An all-time show stopper," Maxwell said, lying on his back on the uppermost of the bleacherlike sauna seats. He was staring at the ceiling, absently fingering his testicles, a towel spread across his chest.

"Uh-huh," I said, hoping the story would finally move past the opening expletive.

"Do you know Jerry Drake?" Maxwell swung his chicken legs off the bench and sat on the edge, staring down to where I was stretched out on the floor. The name sounded familiar, but it was Maxwell's story and best to let him tell it all.

"He owns Big Tex Automotive and Electrical Supply."

"Oh, yeah." I nodded.

"Well," Maxwell lay back down, "it was his YMCA team that I spoke to last night." He paused to towel the sweat off his face. "I smoked both those joints you gave me on the way over so I was really high and really paranoid. They'd already eaten when I got there so I just got up and told 'em that football wasn't everything in their lives, that it was just a passing phase, that they should spend more time on other things—"

I burst out laughing. "I'll bet all those dads loved that."

"They didn't seem too pleased. But what the hell, I'm a star. Drake got up and told 'em not to take what I said literally—whatever that meant—and that the YMCA Championship was one of the most important things in their young lives. You know, discipline, will to win, building character—all that."

"Amazing."

"Oh yeah." Maxwell smiled. "And when I first walked in he took me off to the side and asked me not to smoke in front of his boys. I nearly shit. He meant cigarettes."

Maxwell hobbled out to the showers. I waited on the floor for his return.

"Afterward," he said, stepping over me. "Afterward, he invites me to his house for a drink. Since the talk took less than an hour, I figured for three hundred dollars, why not? We go to his house and I meet his wife. That's when I called you. He wanted you to come over and fuck her too."

"What?" I straightened up in a combination of shock and sexual stirrings.

"I know . . . I know," Maxwell continued, his hands over

his head in surrender, his face the picture of mock remorse. "I shouldn't have done it." He frowned and bobbed his head. "I know how you feel about group fucking, that's why you weren't invited, but shit, she was in great shape for her age."

"How old?" I asked. I was sitting upright on the floor with my legs pulled up, wrapped in my arms, my chin resting on my knees. I was in a state of semierection.

"About thirty-five."

"A regular Methuselah."

"It was incredible. I had a hard on a cat couldn't scratch. He sat at the foot of the bed watching and telling her what to do, pointing and telling her to lick this and suck that. It was like being in surgery. I ate her pussy for a solid hour."

"Did Drake just watch?" I pressed. Maxwell seemed confused by my question. He eyed me curiously, then continued.

"Oh he crawled in and rubbed against both of us for a while. But most of the time he would sit and watch, or pop amyl nitrite in our noses.

"After we'd fucked for hours, we took a shower and then she got out some of those fake dicks—"

"Dildoes." I smiled at Seth's unfamiliarity with the vocabulary of perversion. Maxwell was a master of execution, not abstract theory; he had no need for the jargon except when recounting a particular adventure, at which time I would supply the technical gaps with a knowledge gleaned of much vicarious research and little actual practice.

"Yeah—whatever." Maxwell was anxious to get on with the story. It was as if the experience hadn't really happened and he couldn't really feel it until he recounted it to someone and watched and listened to their reaction. Until he talked about it, it wasn't real. He did it and I enjoyed it, another aspect of this peculiar symbiotic-parasitic relationship we called friendship.

"Well," he continued, "one was about this big." He held his hands a foot apart and then made a circle with his index fingers and thumbs. They just barely touched. "It had all sorts of teeth and bumps on it. The end of the other one looked like a miniature pickax. She went totally crazy when I fucked her with that one." He smiled and squeezed down his eyes. His voice slipped again into the whiskey rasp. "I give her a real good fuckin' . . . she won't forget ol' John Henry for a long time." He wrapped his fingers around his cock and shook it gently.

"Then," Maxwell said, his excitement showing, "she sucked me off 'til John Henry was achin', while Jerry fucked her with the fake dick. God what a night! She passed out with ol' John Henry in her mouth." He pointed his penis toward his face, dropped his head, and stared into the solitary eye. "Didn't she, boy?"

Maxwell pulled John Henry's foreskin back and inspected the little red, raw patches on the underside of the head.

"Shit. The son of a bitch is really sore."

"What time did you leave?"

"That is chapter two. Why do I punish myself like this?" A note of exhaustion crept into his voice.

The heat and excitement of the story, combined with the sauna, were a little too much. I got up to go to the showers and cool down. In the shower, I began to feel the effects of my earlier prescriptions; I would make it through another day.

Rufus Brown, the forty-year-old black "clubhouse boy," walked to the entrance of the showers.

"How'd you get in?"

"Hey, Rufus, how you doin'?"

"Fine, Phil, how'd you get in?"

"Maxwell broke a window in the back. Cover for us, will you?"

"Okay," he said, frowning. "But if I have to pay for the window you'll have to give me the money. They don't give me nothin' without reason."

That was certainly true. The team scouts spilled more in liquor than Rufus got in salary, but Clinton Foote, in true general-manager style, bitched at him for every extra dime he needed to run the clubhouse. Last year, after winning the division, we voted Rufus a $2,100 share of the purse, but

Clinton overruled it and reduced it to $500 because "the vote was not unanimous and we can't give that colored boy a larger share than the office personnel."

"Okay, Rufus," I said. "Thanks."

"Sure." He smiled and returned to the locker room to finish picking up yesterday's dirty socks and jockstraps. I picked up some Q-TIPS and tried to force a breathing canal through my omnidirectional nose. I got a lot of blood from the left nostril and a clear, watery fluid from the right. My left ear had been plugged for several days and ached violently when I worked my jaw. As a result, I hadn't eaten much in the past few days. The speed was activating my mind, but the stiffness continued returning to my legs and back; the codeine seemed to be working slower or not at all. The skin on my lower back and left hip burned, referred pain from the nerves and muscles crushed by the linebacker's knee in the back. I rubbed my hip absently, noticing the alternating areas of deadness and extreme sensitivity.

"It was about midnight," Maxwell said, diving right back into the story as soon as I opened the door to the sauna. He was obviously feeling his medication, too. "When his wife passed out, we went to the kitchen to get a beer and he made a phone call to some doctor's wife in Lakewood. She told us to come on over. The doc was out of town. Jerry said she was a nymphomaniac and was in therapy. Her husband didn't care who she fucked as long as he met them." His lips curled into a wicked sneer and he fell into the obscene rasp. "She made an exception in my case . . . me bein' a star and all."

"Amazing." It was all I could think to say.

"It was the same shit all over again. Although Drake did eat her pussy after I'd fucked her."

"Puke," I said. "Do you think the guy's a football fan or what?"

"I dunno, man. But she was great-lookin'—in her twenties."

"Please," I said, holding up my hands, "no more."

"Lemme tell you the weird part." He was pleading.

"Weird part?" I yelled. "Weird part?"

Maxwell just raised his eyebrows and shrugged, holding his open palms out in front, in a gesture of noncommitment.

"Anyway," Maxwell proceeded, "after we'd fucked me and John Henry 'bout to death, she opens the drawer by her bed and shows me a syringe full of morphine—"

"Morphine?"

"That's what she said." Maxwell's face was blank. "She said her husband left it for her. It scared the shit outta me. Man, she was perverted. I left a little later."

"What makes you think she was perverted?" I asked, smiling slightly, clasping my hands behind my head and leaning back against the hot cedar wall. "Maybe she's just precocious."

"Whatever." Maxwell lay back down and after a few minutes silence he began to hum the verses of "The Mansion You Stole."

The door jerked open and Eddie Rand, the trainer, stuck his head inside, glaring down at me on the floor.

"Okay," he yelled, "who did it?"

I immediately pointed at Maxwell.

"He did," I said.

"That right, Seth?" Rand asked, his tone softening noticeably.

"Do what?" Maxwell asked calmly, making no outward movement, his eyes fixed on the ceiling.

"The medicine cabinet," Rand answered. "If B.A. finds out, it's somebody's ass."

"Don't tell him then," I said. "Give the kid a break, man. I was there. I saw it all. The man was desperate. Think of it as an emergency."

"I suppose you just stood there and watched?" Rand shot back.

"He held me down and massaged my throat to make me swallow 'em." I was lying on my back on the floor, my hands behind my head. "But I don't hold a grudge, so why should you?"

"No more of that shit," Rand said, feebly. "You guys understand?"

"Sure, Eddie, you bet," I said, rolling onto my side and

turning my back to the angry man in white duck pants. "I suppose you're gonna be pissed about the beer, too."

"You cocksuckers," Rand screamed. "You took my beer?"

His crepe-soled foot kicked me hard in the ass. The door slammed shut.

"Goddam," I said, rubbing the bruised cheek, "that hurt."

"What did you do last night?"

I jumped at the sound of Maxwell's voice; I had fallen asleep.

"Huh?"

"What did you do last night?" he asked again. He was on his back pushing his toes against the wall, making the whole room shake. The tiny time pills were going off like time bombs.

I moaned, turning over to sit up. "Nothing. Got pulled over and raped by a girls' basketball team from Corsicana. You know, the usual Wednesday night shit."

Actually, the evening had slipped from my mind and I was having difficulty recalling the details. It seemed years ago.

"I was really high. Took a shitpot full of Harvey's Grade A cactus and got a good look at the real me. I'm a real asshole, as near as I can tell." I sighed and tried to relax, realizing that what I had just said was mainly truth.

"You better cut that shit out, man," Maxwell warned. "It can fuck up your mind. You're getting a little too far out."

"Oh, Christ," I said. The evening began to trickle back. "I forgot. Crawford and Claridge had another fight."

"With each other?"

"No. Everybody else. Claridge took his clothes off again, this time on stage at Rock City. Then he and Crawford beat up their dates. When the fight started, I grabbed Bob Beaudreau's girl and split."

"Same old Fightin' Phil Elliott," Maxwell said, a slight touch of disgust edging his voice. The nickname was a reference to a game in the distant past when a fight had broken out and our bench had emptied into the field to join in the fray. The following Tuesday, viewing the game films, the camera panned the deserted bench, where only two figures remained: standing at the sidelines shaking his fist toward the field was B.A. and huddled near the phone table, wrapped in a parka, was me.

"I wonder if they got arrested?" I had been so intent on escaping with Charlotte, I hadn't fully considered my teammates' possible fate.

"Probably not, unless they hurt somebody."

"Some woman got kicked in the head."

"That could mean trouble, unless she was a fan. Then she'd probably like it."

We both laughed.

The door to the sauna opened and Art Hartman, our number two quarterback, stepped inside.

"Hey, guys," Art grimaced against the heat. "Foot guys, how hot is it in here?"

"How ya doin', Art?" Maxwell greeted him.

"Tired as shit," Hartman answered, gingerly stepping over me and reaching up to shake hands with Maxwell. "The kid kept me up half the night. How 'bout yourself?"

"Never felt better."

Art Hartman was in his second year, having graduated as the top NCAA passer from Maryland. He was Seth's heir apparent, physically outstripping Maxwell in every department and seemingly needing only seasoning to become a top NFL quarterback.

"Did you guys hear about Claridge?" Hartman asked, sitting his six-foot-four frame on the bottom bench and pulling absently on his cock.

"Yeah," I answered, "how did you know?"

"Saw John this morning at the office. He said he was there."

Art Hartman and John Wilson, the strong safety, both lived in Lake Highlands, a nice middle-class suburb, and both worked for the same real estate agent. Hartman had made over twenty-six thousand dollars the previous spring on two industrial property deals. During the season he went to the office every morning before practice and every afternoon after.

"Anybody get arrested?" Maxwell asked.

"No. I don't think so." Art scratched his head. "But Wilson got his ass in a crack. His wife spent half the night at our house. She found lipstick on his shorts, can you believe that?"

"I didn't think he wore shorts."

"How you feelin', Seth?" Hartman looked back up at Seth, who was still on his back with his arm over his face.

"I tol' you once, kid, I feel fine," Maxwell replied without moving. "But all you young strong studs are beginnin' to make me feel my age."

"Which is sixty-one this morning," I piped in.

"You'll still be around long after I'm gone, chief," Hartman said, smiling.

"An' don't you ever forget it, kid." Maxwell sat up and smiled down at him.

There were those who were of the opinion that Hartman should have replaced Maxwell the start of the year and most certainly the next year. I didn't necessarily agree. I had a lot of confidence in Maxwell's head but it was hard to argue with Hartman's physical ability. He could throw farther, run faster, hit harder, and he never got hurt. He was the prototype of a professional football quarterback. Big, strong, and good-looking, his wife was his college sweetheart, his child came seven months after the wedding and weighed in at ten pounds. He had a three-bedroom brick home, two cars, and he belonged to the Society of Christian Athletes and the Oakridge Methodist Church. B.A. belonged to the Oakridge Methodist Church.

"How many times is that for Claridge?" Maxwell asked.

"Three or four, I think," Hartman interjected, being specific. "If you're counting totally naked. Partially naked I don't know." He smiled and shrugged.

"What else happened?" I asked Hartman.

"I dunno, I had to leave the office to show some property to a customer."

"Goddam, man," Maxwell responded. "What time do you get to the office?"

"Around six."

"Jeeeeesus," Maxwell and I said in unison. Maxwell fell back on the bench. "Mr. Businessman," he said.

Seth and I had both had enough heat and headed for the showers for a final cool-down.

"How's an old man like me s'posed to keep up with a kid like Hartman?" Maxwell asked.

"Just like everything else, man," I offered. "You gotta cheat."

Maxwell looked up from picking at an ingrown hair on his chest.

We finished our showers and stepped outside to dry off. Maxwell climbed onto the scales. The pointer moved to 217.

"Fuck," he moaned, shaking his head. "Explain that, will ya? I gained two pounds in the sauna."

I didn't even try.

Somebody changed the radio station and "the good music sound" of KBOX-FM filled the room. The equipment man must be back in his cage; he always played KBOX because it was B.A.'s favorite station. B.A. wasn't in the locker rooms ten minutes a day, but anytime he walked through and KBOX wasn't wafting around the lockers he went to the equipment man and demanded the reason. I spent a lot of time sneaking around the cage, changing the radio dial. It was great fun watching B.A. ask the sweating man why the team wasn't listening to good music. The equipment manager would nervously shift from foot to foot, shaking his head and saying it had been none of his doing.

Toweling off, I heard the front door slam and stuck my head into the locker room. It was Thomas Richardson. He was standing by the bulletin board. He saw me and waved.

"Did it get rough last night?" he asked.

"Is a pig's ass pork?"

"I figured it would." He reached into his coat pocket, pulled out a sheet of paper, and pinned it to the board.

I walked down to read the paper.

> MODERN MAN NO LONGER FEELS, HE MERELY REACTS.
>
> CREATIVITY HAS BEEN REPLACED BY CONFORMITY.
>
> LIFE HAS LOST ITS SPONTANEITY: WE ARE BEING MANIPULATED BY OUR MACHINES. THE INDIVIDUAL IS DEAD.

"Goddam. Who put that up there?" Maxwell stood behind me, drying his hair.

"Richardson."

"He is one crazy son of a bitch, all right."

"Don't you feel like you're being manipulated by a machine, Seth?" I asked, turning to face him.

"You bet, podnah," he replied, grinning and grabbing his cock and waving it at me. "This here machine, right here." He winced as his fingers rubbed against the wounds of the previous night's encounter. "I'm sorry, John Henry," he said, looking down. "I shore do treat you poorly."

I turned back and reread the paper the angry black man had stuck to the bulletin board just below Clinton Foote's notice that everybody had to wear coats and ties. I stared at the two pieces of paper for a long time, then turned back to Maxwell, who was digging in the crack of his ass with the towel.

"Can you think of anybody you ever loved?" I asked.

"Huh?" Maxwell was leaning to the side with one leg slightly raised to allow him better access to his rectum. "Goddam, I think I got piles." His eyes suddenly clicked to mine. "What did you say?"

"Loved somebody?" I asked again. "You know. Really loved. Not counting Martha and Duane."

Martha and Duane were Maxwell's parents. Maxwell being from west Texas, and raised a Baptist, he would automatically list his parents and two sisters as loved ones, unless I first ruled them out. He hardly liked them.

"How 'bout Billy Charlene and Norma Jean?"

I shook my head.

"Okay," he said. "Cherry Lane Rodent?"

"Cherry Lane? Sounds like a subdivision."

"You might call her that," Maxwell offered. "My first piece of pussy. She took a boy to the sand hills and brought home a man." He straightened up slightly and threw his shoulders back.

"Did you love her?"

"No. Shit no. That was a joke. I can't think of anybody."

He paused. "I used to think I loved my first wife, but I even doubt that now. No. I can't say I ever loved anybody."

"Me either."

I left Maxwell at the bulletin board, still reading and drying his hair.

There were a few pieces of mail in the top of my locker. A pencil-scrawled envelope was mixed in among the bills and nasty letters from the credit card companies.

Dear Phil Elliott

You are my favorit player and Dallas is my favorit teem. I think you are the best player in the hole world. Would you plese send me Billy Gill's autograph and pitcher.

Your friend
David Gerald Walker

ps—my sister says hi.

"Little Commie motherfucker," I said, putting the letter into Gill's locker.

My bare back squeaked and pulled against the blue cushion as the trainer worked my leg, trying to stretch out the troublesome right hamstring. Rand was standing at the foot of the wooden rubbing table, holding my ankle and knee and pushing the injured leg straight up and back into my chest. He increased the pressure until I signaled that the pain was no longer bearable. Then he replaced the leg flat on the table and kneaded the damaged muscle, after which he repeated the process, trying each time to increase the flexion. The whole thing hurt like hell.

"Uuuuuhnnn . . . fuck, Eddie," I moaned. "The son of a bitch is really sore."

The trainer dug his fingers into the torn tissues at the point where the leg and buttocks joined.

"You've got scar tissue in there like that," Rand said, holding up a clenched fist. "And scar tissue just don't stretch. Every time that leg stretches too far and you feel that sharp sting, it's tearing some more. Working your leg like this at least will keep it loose."

"Anything else I can do?"

"Just keep it warm, do these stretching exercises, and keep taking your pills," he said, taking hold of my leg again. "Now tell me if this hurts too much."

"Ahhhh," I groaned. "Motherfucker."

"Hey, Bubba." A white grin framed by the purple-black face of Delma Huddle loomed over me. "That ain't gonna make you no faster." He laughed his peculiar high-pitched giggle. His laughter subsided and he watched the trainer manipulating my leg. "Hamstring still botherin' you?"

"Sore as shit. But, if I ever get well, I'll make you a star."

Delma was a perennial All-Pro even though B.A. and Clinton Foote had attempted several times to squelch his nomination. They hoped to correct his "severe attitude problems and outrageous contract demands."

Early last season, B.A. had benched Huddle in favor of Donnie Daniels, the number one draft choice from Georgia Tech. After four consecutive losses B.A. suddenly noticed "a vastly improved performance level in practice sessions" and reinstated Delma.

According to B.A., Daniels had replaced Huddle because "Daniels is statistically the finest receiver in our camp." Daniels never left the bench again. He had believed what B.A. had said about him and was totally devastated by the demotion. He had often stopped me on the practice field to get my feelings on what he had done that had so suddenly snatched him from the road to glory. I tried to explain the political and economic ramifications behind the episode, but a twenty-two-year-old white All American from Georgia Tech just isn't ready for that kind of sports trust reality.

Daniels grew more and more bitter until finally, at the end of the season, he publicly demanded to be traded. He was immediately sent to Pittsburgh, as a warning to others about statements critical to the organization. The condition of the trade required that Daniels make the forty-man roster before Pittsburgh would have to fulfill their end of the agreement.

I met Daniels for a drink right after the trade had been announced. He seemed like the only survivor of a ten-car collision who was trying to explain how it had happened. Several times during the course of our conversation he had stopped to stare off into his disastrous past, thinking of all those glories that he had only tasted slightly.

Last August, Daniels's name showed up in six-point type on the waiver list, and Pittsburgh wasn't required to honor their end of the conditional trade.

Huddle, on the other hand, set a club record for yards per reception and was again named to the All-Pro team.

Huddle slapped me on my bare shoulder and walked over to the tape counter. With every muscle of his six-foot frame perfectly defined, he rippled when he walked. He grabbed a handful of chewable vitamin C tablets, and as he caught sight of a neat row of syringes lined along the top of the tape counter he shuddered. Thursday was the day for B-12 shots.

"No shots for me, Bubba," Huddle volunteered, nervously eyeing the syringes of cherry-red fluid.

Delma Huddle was the finest athlete I had ever met and I was constantly amazed by the ease with which he performed. With the possible exception of Thomas Richardson, no one else on the team had such an abundance of talent. The effortlessness with which Delma played often drew criticism and B.A. constantly considered Huddle a loafer.

Even though we were both wide receivers and therefore competitors, I conceded early in Huddle's first year that there was no contest. It was the only time in a profession of blind confidence and self-deception that I wasn't able to find, or create, a competitor's weakness on which to capitalize. The color of my skin was the only point in my favor.

Because Delma Huddle was indispensable to our offense, B.A. and Clinton Foote created elaborate schemes to convince him and the paying public that he wasn't. The enormity of Huddle's talent made most of the schemes obvious to everyone but sportswriters and fans, and they served only to irritate Delma. It was another example of B.A. and Clinton's technique to keep a player mentally off balance, and thus controllable, by means of strategically placed lies and half-truths. It is a difficult tactic to defend yourself against. If you never hear the truth how do you make any of those simple day-to-day decisions necessary to minimal physical and emotional survival? If any one thing can be false, it all can be false, and how do you tell the difference? Delma Huddle survived by never maintaining any continuous train of thought from one situation to another. Knowing that part of every situation was untrue or unreal, he saw no sense in trying to internalize any of it. As a person he had a definite sameness, but no continuity. Any interacting relationship had to begin and end in the same physical meeting to enjoy any hope of communication. He never carried over any assumptions. Experience rolled off him like water. Delma resisted acculturation as alien and untrue and survived on animal instincts. He was succeeding as a professional athlete.

"Hey, Bubba, did you hear Uncle Billy this morning?" Huddle asked, popping a vitamin C tablet in his mouth and crunching it up noisily. He walked to the table and picked up my unoccupied foot and began massaging it.

"No. But please don't stop. I think I love you."

"Claridge's mother sent a letter to the contest."

The contest was an invention of Carl Jones, the disc jockey, and it involved sending Uncle Billy Bunk a letter of twenty-five words or less picking your choice for the outstanding player of the next game and describing his future acts of glory. The letter that came closest to predicting what actually happened on Sunday won five free long-playing records.

"What did she write?"

I felt sorry for Claridge. His mother was a divorcee who had moved to Dallas when Claridge joined the club and would suffer a nervous collapse if she didn't talk to her "baby" at least once a day. She usually called the practice field. Claridge would turn red with rage at the falsetto cry, "Baby, your mommy's on the phone," and storm over to plead with her to leave him alone.

"I'm not saying anything, man," Huddle said. "If he don't know, I ain't gonna be the one to start it."

Delma Huddle and Alan Claridge had developed a solid friendship grounded in their respect for one another as great athletes and during practice they spent a lot of time together joking and laughing. Some of the players were contemptuous of the mixed friendship and referred to Claridge as being "queer for the nigger."

The importance of Claridge and Huddle to the team far outweighed any status held by their antagonists and thus kept the harassment from becoming more than an infrequent attempt by Meadows or Jo Bob to strike out in paranoia and frustration at something beyond their comprehension.

One time in the sauna I was listening to a conversation between Jo Bob, Tony Douglas the middle linebacker, O.W. Meadows, and a couple of others. Larry Costello was in his customary seat counting the sweat drops that plummeted off his nose. The conversation had wandered from black players asking white wives to dance at team parties to the infamous friendship. Meadows had just threatened to beat the shit out of Thomas Richardson if he ever spoke to his wife again.

"She knew better'n to tell me that black cocksucker had ast her to dance," the furious lineman had said. "I'd a killed the son of a bitch right there."

I sat silently in the heat, restraining any objections, feeling that a little touch of bigotry was better than massive contusions.

"I don't blame Huddle," Jo Bob said, commenting on Huddle and Claridge's friendship and antics. "I'd like to hang around with white guys too."

"Don't worry, Jo Bob," I said, unable to contain myself any longer, "someday you might get to."

Everything flashed white as Jo Bob's fist hit me behind the right ear and my head bounced off the cedar wall. I gripped my head with both hands, fighting to stay conscious. I squeezed my eyes shut against the pain. I kept them closed and dropped my head on my chest. The pain was insufferable. When I could move, I blindly pulled myself to my feet and started for Jo Bob; his foot caught me in the middle of the chest, sending me ass first into the door. Fortunately the door latch gave before my backbone did and I went sprawling into the hallway. I got back to my feet, stumbled to my locker, and threw up all over the blue carpet and my new kangaroo Pumas.

An ache settled behind my eyes that took several days to subside. Later that day I went to the trainers, saying I had taken a forearm in a blocking drill. When they assured me I wasn't going blind I considered myself lucky and took an oath to keep my mouth shut around people I didn't agree with. A pledge I kept until quite recently.

"Turn over." Eddie Rand slapped me on the ass to accent his injunction. I peeled myself up from the table top. My back had stuck to the vinyl.

Huddle, who had stopped massaging my foot, moved around to the head of the table. He locked his hands behind my neck and tried to pull my face toward his elastic-encased crotch; he was simultaneously making fucking motions with his hips.

I tightened my neck in resistance. A sharp ache at the base of my skull reminded me I was probably still a little high on mescaline. I was high on something all the time—codeine, booze, grass, speed, fear; in fact, I doubt that during a season I was ever in a normal state of mind, if there is such a thing as normal. After the season I went through withdrawal, sweating and walking most of the night for weeks, not really calming down until mid-March.

"Come on," Huddle pleaded, increasing the pressure on my neck.

"If I do, you won't respect me," I said, pulling back.

"Yes I will, honey," he replied. "I'll respect you more."

"Goddammit, Delma," Rand's voice cut into the game. "If there ain't nothing wrong with you, get the hell outta here."

"I'm trying to get what's wrong with me fixed right now," Huddle answered, making an exaggerated pelvic thrust at my face.

"You can get three years in this country for sodomy, boy," Seth Maxwell said, walking up to the table naked except for a towel hanging from his shoulder. He was the only man allowed in the training room without a clean jock. Nobody seemed to know why.

"More than that if you're a spade," I added.

The huge, pale, pimply cheeks of Maxwell's ass blotted out everything as he sat down next to my face and began talking to Huddle.

"Hey, Delma," Maxwell asked, "you gettin' any pussy?"

"Not like you, Bubba."

"Why, Delma," Maxwell continued, "if I had your women, I'd throw mine away. They all like them big dicks you guys got." Maxwell meant no offense.

Huddle fielded the remark with an ease that comes from a lifetime of reacting to unintentional insults.

"Bubba," Huddle responded, "if I had your dick, I'd throw mine away."

Laughing loudly at his own remark, Huddle tried to change the tenor of the conversation. I did it for him.

"Maxwell, you shithead," I said, "get your ass outta my face."

Maxwell took little notice of my remark. Huddle used it to escape out the door from the anxiety caused by people he liked but didn't understand, taking nothing with him but the slight pleasure that comes of casual human interaction.

Art Hartman walked in clothed in a clean supporter and T-shirt with WONDER WARTHOG silk-screened across the chest.

"Hey, guy," he said to Maxwell, putting his arms around Seth and kissing him lightly on the neck, "did you see what that Braniff stock did today?"

Maxwell nodded, grabbing the bicep of Hartman's passing arm with both hands. They barely circled the muscle.

"Goddam," Maxwell exclaimed to me. "Lookit that."

"Clean living and plenty of exercise, guy," Hartman said, flexing the muscle tight. "And an occasional piece of strange."

"The kid may be able to throw futher than ol' Seth," Maxwell said, winking at me, "but championships are won in bedrooms and bars. Everybody plays their way into this league but mos' guys fuck and drink their way out."

Maxwell stood up and the two men remained side by side with their arms around each other's waists. The training room was beginning to fill, as one by one the rest of the team began to arrive for the day's work.

"If you show Seth how to add ten yards to his deep passes,"

I said to Hartman, "maybe he'll rescue you from the dangers of premature ejaculation."

Seth and Hartman looked at each other quizzically, then frowned at me and unwound their arms. Maxwell slugged Art lightly on the arm as he walked over and climbed into a whirlpool, disappearing up to his neck.

"Everybody's reading that sheet Richardson put on the board," Maxwell said to me, his eyes still on his competition sitting in the whirlpool. His tone was grave and confidential. "Johnson ripped it down to show to B.A. He's certain you put it up."

Jim Johnson, the defensive coach, had never forgiven me for attending practice in a false beard, and he strongly resented my seemingly casual approach to a man's game. His ten years as a marine corps officer were not a point in my favor.

"What the fuck for?" I was amazed anyone had taken the time to read the paper.

"I dunno," Maxwell continued, "but he was really pissed."

"Jesus Christ. I—"

Delma Huddle stuck his grinning black head in the training room door. "I hate niggers," he screamed and was gone.

"Me too," I yelled back at the empty doorway.

"Stand up," Rand ordered, the rubdown finished.

I groaned as I got to my knees and pushed myself upright, the soles of my feet sinking unsteadily into the foam. The trainer set two elastic bandages on the table.

"Well," I said to Maxwell, who was picking his nose and watching Hartman in the whirlpool, "I didn't put it there, so I ain't gonna worry about it. Besides, what's the fucking problem?"

"I dunno," Maxwell answered, withdrawing his finger from the recesses of his nose and wiping it on the towel. "I'm jest passin' through on a load a turkeys." He turned and headed for the door.

"I didn't do anything," I hollered after him.

"What about my beer?" Rand interjected. "I don't know why I'm fixin' your legs."

"You ain't fixing them."

"Shut up and tell me how that feels."

The trainer encased both my legs in elastic tape and Ace Bandages from above my knees to my hips. He had criss-crossed the wraps around my waist so they would not slide down. I looked like a nude gunfighter. I sat down and extended my legs out over the end of the table, curling my toes back, tightening the tendons and ligaments in my ankles.

Slapping Vaseline onto the heels of both feet, Rand wound gauze around the feet and ankles and began to tape with a rote skill that comes from taping eighty ankles a day, six days a week, for sixteen years.

The trainers were responsible for the overall health of all player personnel. The problem was that their opinions carried little weight with management. The medical problems were constantly overruled by front-office tactical decisions, and there was no place for professional integrity. Each Sunday was its own problem that could only be solved satisfactorily by winning. If the trainers, highly qualified physical therapists, didn't finally bring their medical opinions into agreement with the current tactical needs of management, they would shortly find themselves administering enemas in the geriatrics ward at Parkland Hospital. As a result, a player who the trainers thought needed rest or even surgery often found himself shot full of Novocain facing a grinning Deacon Jones and the player was given the chance to exhibit the most desirable of traits—the ability to endure pain.

Trainers were technicians, line workers who repaired broken club property as it was conveyed slowly, but most certainly, to the scrap heap. The player who sat momentarily on the blue-padded tables to get taped, shot, rubbed, doped, shocked, burned, boiled, was numbed and sometimes, but not often, healed. Don't worry about health; after all the body belongs to the club. Deal in pain thresholds and analgesics, amphetamines and anesthesia. Short circuit that bothersome equipment that communicates pain, numb it, bind it, but get the property back to work. Pain is nothing more than the property perceiving the disintegration of its parts. Teach it the difference between pain and injury. If it is felt by the property it is pain. If it is felt by the corporation it is injury.

"Do you wanna pad on this?" Rand was thunking the lump

on my ankle that had permanently put me in cowboy boots.

I shook my head and wondered if the Japanese would replace trainers as they had replaced electronics workers.

"How about the knee?"

"Naw, it feels fine," I lied, adding more misinformation to the company's diagnostic bank. "I'll just wear an elastic sleeve."

"Fingers okay?"

I held up and flexed the two sausages that I had dislocated yesterday. They were still taped together.

"Back?" He continued down the list. "Do you wanna pad on it?"

"Naw." I didn't want to arouse interest by continuing to protect the smashed muscles and fractured short ribs. I would be careful in practice and try not to get hit. For games I would discreetly put the pad on myself.

"B-12 shot?"

"Yeah. Gimme two."

The needle hit me in the shoulder and I watched the red fluid disappear into my bicep. I immediately felt healthier.

"You better get a muscle-relaxant shot after workout," Rand ordered.

"Okay." I grimaced at the thought. Muscle-relaxant shots were like being bayoneted in the ass. But they kept my hamstrings and back from being crippling and I usually slept better on the nights I took them.

I walked back to my locker feeling that if the tape came loose I would just ooze out onto the floor.

John Wilson sat at the next locker and drank a twenty-cent canned soft drink from the machine that netted the equipment man 45 per cent. I took the can from him and washed down another Number Four codeine. I spread a towel on the floor and lay with my head inside my locker to wait for the meeting and steep in the heat of the analgesic.

I had slept some, had just gotten up, and was on the phone to Joanne, making plans to meet in New York. She was riding up with Emmett Hunter on the team plane.

Jim Johnson stepped in from the hall and called the meeting ten minutes early.

Hanging up without waiting for her good-bye, I bolted to my locker for my playbook and a pair of sweatpants. I raced down the hall.

Maxwell had saved me a seat and I quietly slid into the molded plastic cup and answered roll call. Jim Johnson finished the roll, glared at me momentarily, and then stepped away from the portable podium to make room for B.A. The coach was holding Richardson's quotation in his hand. Maxwell nudged me in the ribs.

"It's your ass," he grinned.

"I don't believe this," I mumbled.

"Did you say something?" B.A. stood at the podium looking down at me, without expression. His voice was iced.

"No, sir, just talking to myself."

"Maybe we would all like to hear what you've got to say," he pressed, his eyes glazed over and dead. I could feel the flush of guilt and anger rush into my face. My eyebrows pulled together and my mouth twitched.

God, I thought, now even I think I'm guilty.

"Did you say something else?"

"No, sir." I had tried to hit a note of humility and submission without sliding over into outright groveling. Instead I sounded guilty and pissed off.

"You always seem to think people want to hear what you have to say." B.A. held up the crumpled paper. "I suppose most of you have seen this?" He held the sheet up for the boys in the back. "Obviously there exists a player who seems to feel that the individual is more important than the team."

The gravity of B.A.'s tone frightened me. I had seen other players, maybe less talented or unfortunately black, disappear for transgressions as minor as this one.

". . . any man who puts himself above the team . . ."

The fear started to bubble slightly in my stomach. But I was still holding the card, since I knew who put the sheet up, and if things got much worse for me I was certain Richardson would step forward. At least, I hoped he would.

". . . no need for anyone who . . ."

The last time B.A. used *no need* Don Webster vanished.

Webster's disappearance covered one of B.A.'s larger perversions. It had been against Detroit in the championship game. With only seconds to play, no time-outs, and the ball fourth and goal on Detroit's five, Maxwell quickly called a roll out option to the right. The play required Alan Freeman, who substituted for Delma Huddle at split end on the goal line offense, to come down to a tight position and block Detroit's outside linebacker. This would allow Maxwell either the option run or pass to that side. As we broke the huddle, the clock ticking off the last few seconds, B.A. returned Delma Huddle to the game. No one knows why. Huddle, because of his relatively small size, never played on the goal line, didn't understand the play, and didn't stand much of a chance blocking a two-hundred-thirty-pound linebacker. The linebacker smothered Maxwell, who threw the ball away in desperation. Detroit intercepted and the game ended with the Detroit free safety jumping up and down in the end zone clutching the ball to his chest. Detroit won by seven.

In his postgame press conference B.A. made no mention of the final play, but did point out that three plays earlier Don Webster had jumped offside. That, B.A. reluctantly announced, cost us the game. Nobody thought to question B.A.'s premise that a five-yard penalty nullifying an incomplete pass was the deciding factor of the game.

For the next six months Webster was the star of every highlight film. Slow-motion shots of Webster jumping offside, telephoto shots of Webster jumping offside, isolated replays of Webster jumping offside, end zone shots of Webster jumping offside, learned comments of ex-pros over shots of Webster jumping offside, closeup shots of B.A. grimacing, supposedly, as Webster jumped offside. No need for Webster. The team has no need.

"We've got the biggest game of our careers coming up and this kind of talk . . ." He laid the sheet down and leaned forward over the podium. "Boys, I'm not a political man, you all know that. When I've got a problem I can find the answer in the Scriptures, but I'm concerned, as I'm sure you all are, about the trouble that is filling this great nation of ours. Drugs, permissiveness, lack of respect, violence. Some people believe it's part of a Communist plot. Now I don't necessarily agree, but when I find something like this on our bulletin board." B.A. scanned the room. "Well anyway, this kind of talk just doesn't belong here. We are a team and the man who did this–" he held the wrecked piece of paper high above his head, "–should have the guts to stand up and apologize to the team." B.A.'s face remained calm; his vacant eyes traveled the room, deftly avoiding the corner where I sat.

"B.A.," I said, sliding down in my seat, lowering my head, and alternating a sideways glance between the expectant head coach and the floor.

The vacuous face turned slightly in my direction and a sudden life leaped into his watery blue eyes. B.A. nodded and turned the assembly over to me to plead for forgiveness. He planned to forgive me. It was to be a morality play, a disciplining for the benefit of the whole squad.

"B.A. I'm not sure I understand what has happened here. I mean I read the paper and all." I hesitated, not at all sure what would come out of my mouth next what with all the Dexamyl and codeine floating around inside. "I mean, I read it and all . . ."

"You already said that," B.A. interrupted.

The men laughed nervously.

"I mean," I continued, unable to shut up, "I don't think it's all that bad in the first place but–"

"It's not up to you to judge what's good and bad here, mister," B.A. interrupted again.

"I'm sorry, I didn't mean to," I said, sitting back in my seat and repressing a smile as the solution to my problem popped into my head, "but when Seth and I arrived this morning, the thing was already up. I can't imagine who did it. Can you, Seth?"

Maxwell coughed and his chair skidded noisily on the tile floor. He shook his head and kept his eyes riveted on his stockinged feet.

Crow's-feet appeared at the corners of B.A.'s eyes as the

skin tightened over his brow ridges. He sensed it had all gone awry. He tried to detect collusion between Seth and me but it was hopeless. The good thing about B.A.'s bovine indifference toward the people around him was you could lie your ass off and he couldn't tell the difference. The only thing B.A. knew about the men who played for him were percentages and statistics, whether it was height and weight or results of psychological tests.

Once I involved Maxwell, the disciplining became complicated. If there was one person B.A. tried to understand and empathize with, it was his quarterback. They wanted the same things out of football, power and success. To reach their goals they both manipulated the team, differing only in technique. They both needed team success to assure them of personal triumph. So while they were ultimate adversaries for final power and control, they were also allied as masters against me and the rest of the players. They were co-conspirators, and B.A. knew Maxwell wouldn't let me or anyone else undermine the power structure they both needed. I knew that once I had involved Maxwell I was home free.

I turned around to smile at Jim Johnson. He glowered back at me and left the room, slamming the door. B.A. glanced at the departing defensive coach and then resumed speaking.

"Well," he said, wadding up the piece of paper, "I didn't call this meeting to have an open discussion of who might have done this. If no one else has anything to say, we'll consider the matter closed."

A feeling of relief rolled over me, leaving me weak but somehow elated.

"Okay," B.A. said, "we'll take a five-minute break."

Goddam, what a way to earn a living.

Alan Claridge plunged through the training room door and down the hall to the telephones. Someone had told him about his mother's letter. Thomas Richardson flashed me a big smile and Andy Crawford signaled me to meet him in the locker room. Along with Delma Huddle, Art Hartman, and Maxwell, we congregated in front of the equipment manager's cage. Nearby were a pile of footballs to be autographed. Maxwell picked up a felt-tip pen and a football and began signing. We had to sign fifty balls a week and got ten cents a signature. The club sold the balls to men's clubs, orphanages, and hospitals for twenty-five to fifty dollars a ball, the price increasing as our win-loss record improved. Each ball cost the club about six dollars, including signatures. I grabbed a pen and started earning my dimes.

"The police or somebody called B.A. last night," Claridge said. "He called us in this morning, really pissed, but we didn't have to pay no team fines or anything. Just damages."

"You left with Beaudreau's girl, right?" Crawford said to me.

"Uh-huh," I nodded, giving little attention to the question and continuing to sign.

"Beaudreau was really mad," Crawford elaborated, "screaming and crying, saying that you'd betrayed him."

"I'd betrayed him? I hardly know the asshole."

"Hey, man," Crawford said, "come on, he's a good guy."

"He's still an asshole." I was sick to death of sad little people who thought some bond was welded between us because they knew my height, weight, and jersey number. It was frightening to think that my life was woven into the lives of people like Beaudreau.

On the way back to the meeting I asked Maxwell what he thought of B.A.'s reaction to the incident at Rock City.

"I already heard it all," he said.

"When? I was there and I didn't know it all."

"B.A. came down here this morning around eleven or twelve and told me. I dunno . . . you were asleep or somethin'."

The assistant coaches had returned to the meeting room, singly and in pairs. B.A. came in alone, a suitable time behind the last assistant, and closed the door.

"Did he ask you anything about the paper?" I asked, my voice dropping to a whisper as B.A. reestablished himself behind the portable podium.

"Yes." Maxwell's whisper was barely audible.

"All right," B.A. instructed, "let's break up. Backs and ends stay here. Defense with coach Johnson. Linemen go with your coaches."

We had just finished seeing the New York kicking reel. Now we would divide up into our particular coteries and discuss the part we would each take in Sunday's game. The kicking film seemed to point up New York's biggest problem, organization. Twice as they lined up to punt only ten men were on the field, and once the center forgot to stay on the field for a field goal attempt. Their soccer-style kicker had a strong leg, but seldom got within field goal range or had the protection to get off a kick.

"Okay," B.A. said as soon as the room was cleared of everyone but quarterbacks, receivers, and running backs. "Take out pencil and paper. We're going to have a test. As soon as you finish you can get ready for workout."

Tests on the game plan were a regular part of B.A.'s coaching technique. They were a pain in the ass, but they assured him everyone had studied the plan and they made for at least one short meeting a week.

The mimeographed test questions were passed around and after a few scattered moans and pointless questions the room fell silent. The athletes bent to the task most had spent four years of college trying to avoid.

On the first page were the standard questions: List the depth chart of the New York defense. What is their blitz frequency on third and long? What is their favorite zone and in what field positions and down-yardage situations do they most frequently employ it? What players are replaced in short yardage situations? On the goal line? Against what formations will they shift to an odd defense? What are their tendencies against a split backfield? A set backfield? A triple wing? A double wing? A slot? What is your adjustment on a sixty-seven pass against a twenty-one roll zone? Safety zone? A thirty series defense?

I answered the questions as quickly as possible, marveling in spite of myself at the ingenious complexity of B.A.'s theory of multiple-offense football. It was devastating and unstoppable if properly executed. I breezed through the goal line and short yardage and arrived at the final question. It was essay. I giggled softly. The receivers had one question, the running backs another, the quarterbacks had to answer both.

"Seth. Seth." Art Hartman's whisper came softly from the seat behind me. "Number six. Is it a twenty or a thirty?"

Maxwell dropped his hand beside his chair and held out two fingers.

"Thanks."

Maxwell nodded.

I read my last question: Who do you plan to get deep on and how? List characteristics of backs you think can be beaten deep.

Hurrying to finish first, I quickly wrote:

"LHB Ely: looks into the backfield too much can be beaten with double move if qb will pump fake on first move i.e. zig out, out and go, square out and go, turn in and go, sideline and go. If he feels you going by him he will try and knock you off . . . is big and strong and can knock you down. try and get your shoulder down and into him when he tries to hit. He lays back but tries to cover everything. set him up with down and ins–square out and turn ins to get him coming up fast. qb is vital on the deep double move.
"RHB Waite: good speed but like Ely looks into backfield and is easily set up. zig out is good because of his fast close on down and in move. qb pump is important again. Also sharp breaks are important. He is slow to deep coverage on zone and is possible to run by him on safety zone.
"WS Lewis: best athlete but likes to force end runs and come up and hit. beat him deep with play action passes and run split routes between him and weakside cornerman.
"SS Morris: good, experienced ball player, smart competitor but small always strong safety. no speed . . . tight end could beat him deep on a 67 corner by releasing inside linebacker making short inside move and then back underneath flat to the corner. flanker must clear out deep to keep cornerback from dropping off and intercepting."

I quickly reread my answers. I had covered everything B.A. had mentioned during the week. The *i.e.* would irritate him, but beyond his pettiness and lack of empathy, B.A. was predictable and to that extent approached fairness.

I groaned out of my seat, careful not to straighten up too fast, and walked to the podium. B.A. had his eyes down, reading from the playbook. I leaned over and looked at the book. His eyes came up to my face.

"It's a good book," I said, smiling, "but everybody gets killed in the end."

His face seemed to get blanker. I slipped my test paper onto the podium.

"If that doesn't get me a scholarship," I said, already striding for the door, "I'll have to drop out of med school." The others were still finishing.

I went to the phone and called Lacota information and got the listing for John Caulder. I reached the number but there was no answer. Walking back to the training room, I met Maxwell coming out of the meeting.

"Hey, man," I asked, "how come you didn't cover for me with B.A. when you talked to him this morning?"

"He just said Johnson had this paper and was pissed. Besides, he told me he planned to use you quite a bit this Sunday."

My heart jumped.

"I talked him into letting me call for you from the field."

"Fantastic!!!" I yelled, not able to control the grin that spread across my face. My eyes were watering.

"So don't let me down," Maxwell instructed, at once becoming stern and paternal.

"I won't, man. Jesus I won't. Goddam. Too much."

I walked to the tape counter in the training room and grabbed a roll of flesh-colored half-inch tape to change the splint on the two fingers I had dislocated.

The adrenaline, triggered by the news about Sunday, mixed with the chemicals already washing around inside my body. It was more than I could comfortably handle. I tried splinting my fingers, getting the tape tangled and succeeding only in pulling all the hair off my knuckles.

B.A.'s decision to use me more on Sunday was easy to understand. I would play Sunday because we could cinch the division title, and New York at home was always tough. For his need to win B.A. was willing to risk slight damage to discipline. I was an optional accessory to his winning machine. Last week I had been hot; if I cooled off one degree I'd be out on my ass again.

At this point it didn't matter to me. I had known these things and had somehow managed to survive, powerless to control my own fate. It seemed that something like this happened every year, giving me just enough power to stay alive professionally.

And even if all the reasons for playing were a mass of fictions and personal contradictions, the thrill of playing was no less real and that thrill is indescribable. Doing something better than anyone else in front of millions of people. It is the highest I have ever been.

We were going through a last-minute polish of our goal line short yardage offense when the fight broke out. I had been standing behind the offensive huddle and had watched it building for several plays. Job Bob was working at right offensive tackle against Monroe White at left defensive end. Monroe, I'm sure, was still simmering over finding the toad in his helmet. The drill was supposed to be three-quarter speed for offensive polish but Monroe was moving that extra step faster, causing Jo Bob to be late on his blocks.

Maxwell called a straight dive wedge, a good play to get a yard, not much more. On the snap Monroe submarined on Jo Bob and the startled tackle fell sprawling on top of the rooting black man. The hole was plugged and Crawford got nowhere.

"Goddammit, Jo Bob," Jim Johnson screamed at the tired, sweating man as he scrambled to his feet, "you gonna let that guy push you all over this field. Maybe we oughta move him into your spot and let you be the wedge buster on the kick returns."

Jo Bob walked back to the huddle with his head down, swearing softly between tightly clenched teeth. It was late in the practice and tired, worn nerves were stretched to the breaking point.

"Okay, Jo Bob," Maxwell soothed in the huddle. "We'll get

that sandbagger this time. Green right dive forty-three on two."

It was a straight handoff and dive into the gap between guard and tackle. The tight end would block down on White to make him play pressure and fight away from the play. Jo Bob would drive him straight back or outside. On the snap Monroe drove straight into the gap and grabbed the ball carrier as soon as he got the ball. Jo Bob, anticipating an outside move, struck out into thin air and flopped helplessly on the ground.

"Jo Bob," Johnson's tone was painfully patronizing, "if you don't think you can do this drill, maybe we ought to go full speed."

Jo Bob's eyes were glazed. His nostrils flared as his body shook from almost uncontrollable fury. While Maxwell called the next play, Jo Bob stood straight up in the huddle and watched Monroe White, who glared back. Jo Bob clenched and unclenched his fists. I knew a fight was coming.

On the snap Jo Bob jumped up and hit Monroe on the side of the head with his forearm and the fight was on. Everyone stood shocked at the sights and sounds of these two giant, heavily padded men, flailing away at each other. The sounds of fists and forearms against helmets and face masks was almost deafening. It sounded like somebody hitting telephone poles with baseball bats. Johnson and B.A. exchanged grins, delighted at what they felt was an indication of the team's readiness to play.

After several moments B.A. nodded at Johnson and he moved toward the two men.

"Okay, you guys." The defensive coach stepped forward with the assurance of a drill instructor. "Let's break it up." He was smiling as he came between the two men. Jo Bob hit Johnson flush in the chest with a fist and he sat down, his eyes wide, gasping for breath. A cheer went up from the men assembled watching the fight.

Jo Bob jerked off his headgear and started swinging at White, who took the blows rather neatly on his forearm pads. He kicked at Jo Bob with his cleats, knocking out a hunk of flesh the size of a half dollar from Jo Bob's shin. Jo Bob threw his headgear at the black man. The helmet flew by White's ear and struck O.W. Meadows in the hand.

"Goddam you, Jo Bob, you dumb cocksucker," Meadows screamed, and pounced on the exhausted Jo Bob. They both fell in a heap on the ground. Johnson had regained his feet and breath and was trying to hold off White, who wanted to kick Jo Bob now that he was down.

"Come on, Monroe, come on now," Johnson tried to pacify the raging black man.

The giant defensive tackle tried to move around Johnson and the coach parried his move by stepping in front of him again and grabbing his arms. White shook free and turned on Johnson.

"Leave me alone, mothahfuckah," he screamed at the ex-marine. Johnson blanched white but stood his ground.

The whole team, most of whom were grinning at Johnson's predicament, were gathered around the struggling men. Meadows was sitting on Jo Bob's chest, cussing. Johnson had placed a hand in the middle of Monroe White's chest and was standing between him and the prostrate Jo Bob.

"Get yo' han's off me, mothahfuckah." Monroe tried again to move around the coach who courageously stood his ground.

"Just cool off, Monroe, I–" Johnson started to talk when suddenly the huge black man turned on him and grabbed his throat. Johnson looked like a doomed chicken, with his eyes bulging and his feet dangling in the air. The coach wrenched free and ran terrified through the crowd. The sight of a coach running for his life broke the tension and the field rocked with laughter. Johnson stopped running and looked back at the men. He turned red and walked on into the clubhouse. B.A. called practice and all of us went to shower, still giggling at the memory of the frightened coach, his shirt in tatters around his neck, running like a bandit from Monroe White.

In a codeine-inspired optimism I skipped the full ritual of my treatment, taking only ten minutes to soak the length of my legs in ice water. It hurt like a bitch but kept down any chance swelling.

"Do you wanna go for a beer?" Maxwell stood in front of the tub of ice water, naked except for his traditional towel over the shoulder. "Hartman and I are goin'. I thought I'd break the kid into the full responsibilities of quarterbacking." His voice dropped into the whiskey rasp.

"Have to pass, man," I said, moving my legs around in the water, the bone-deep ache occupying most of my consciousness. "But lemme use that towel." I stepped out of the tub.

"Okay," Maxwell said, "see you in the morning."

By 3:20 P.M. I was driving through the South Dallas ghetto, smoking a joint. I would be in Lacota by 4:00.

South Dallas blacks aren't a deprived ethnic group, they're a different civilization living in captivity. Just blocks from the phenomenal wealth of Elm and Commerce streets, South Dallas was a hyperbole. A grim joke on those who still believe we are all created equal. There isn't even a real struggle for equality. Equality with what? The white man? No, he's crazy. The blacks seemed to be waiting, watching, knowing they would always be getting fucked. They took solace in the dependability.

I pulled off the expressway at Forest Avenue and glided into a service station. A middle aged black man with protruding front teeth walked up to my open window.

"Fill 'er up?" he asked. I nodded and he eyed me suspiciously, then walked to the back of the car. After a suitable interval I heard the musical ding as the gas pumped into the car.

The attendant walked up beside me again, still peering into my face. I handed him my credit card. He studied it. "Ah knowed it. Ah knowed it was you," he said, his face shattering into a smile and his teeth seeming to move farther out of his mouth. "How you doin', Mistah El-yut?" He stuck his hand in through the window and we shook.

"Fine, fine," I said, grinning, caught up in his enthusiasm.

"I been watchin' you play fo' years," he said. "You sho' look a lot bigger than you do on the fiel'!"

"I am a lot bigger than I am on the field."

He laughed hard and stuck out his hand to be slapped. I responded rather clumsily.

"Hey, man," his voice softened and his eyes became serious, "can't you do nothin' 'bout that new stadium they's gonna build? I cain't 'ford no one-thousand-dollar bond." He pronounced the last words carefully.

"Me an' Gerald over there," he pointed to another black man sweating over a truck tire and several assorted tire tools, "an' a couple other cats been gettin' together every Sunday since you guys been here. We got just 'nuf money fo' fo' tickets in the end zone and chip in a quota' fo' gas. If they build that new stadium, I ain't gonna get to go."

"I don't know what to tell you, man. I feel like you do, but I just work for 'em. They don't listen to me."

"I can 'member," he began again, "when I could go to the Cotton Bowl on Sunday an' buy a ticket fo' a dolla' an' sit in the end zone. Now they wants six dolla' and I have to go all the way to the no'th side of town to get my ticket. Ev'ry year the price go up. Now they wants one thousand dollars befo' they even let me stand in line to buy a ticket."

"It's sorta like a dope habit, ain't it?" I offered. "They lower the price at first to get you interested, then once they got you hooked, boom, it's six bucks and risin'."

"You right, man," the black man replied. "Dat's jus' what they do. Boy, I don't know what we gonna do on Sunday, now. They won' even let us watch it on TV. Cain't you do nothin'?"

I shook my head.

A loud clunk signaled my tank was full. The attendant took my credit card to the small office, stopped to talk to Gerald, and pointed to my car. Gerald came over and extended his hand through the window.

"Jes' wanna say I met ya," Gerald said, sweat droplets running along the gouges the frown made in his face. He was a good-looking man.

"Hey, how are you?" I responded as we shook hands.

"You guys gonna play in that new stadium?" he asked.

"Ain't got no choice," I answered. "That is, if we want to play at all."

"It's a bitch, ain't it?" He frowned deeply and wiped the sweat off his face.

"Yeah, it's a bitch," I said, feeling quite foolish.

The buck-toothed fellow returned with my credit card and I signed the ticket. We all shook hands again and they wished me luck in New York.

Once through south Dallas I turned east and wound through the bucking, twisting hills that rolled toward the pine-tree country and Louisiana beyond. I always enjoyed the country outside Dallas. One minute you were crawling from light to light in a grimy ghetto and the next you were speeding through the rolling hills of north central Texas, watching cattle grazing or cotton growing. An expectant buzzard circled the black ribbon of asphalt. He was watching intently for a skunk or an armadillo to misstep and be served up on the roadside by the noisy steel monsters that raced back and forth.

A house cat stood in an open field and watched a cottontail flee across the road, the cat too smart to follow.

The horizon was clearly etched as the rolling black land met the clear blue sky; old abandoned farm buildings and an occasional naked oak or elm, its branches outlined against the blue like giant nerve endings, gave a forsaken feel to the landscape.

In the last few years it began to take more time to get to the farm country. Land that had been used to raise cattle and cotton was being changed to grow people. Huge signs announced YOUR DREAM in orange Day-Glo and three- to nine-acre ranchettes that could be financed for twenty years. House trailers and modular homes set on treeless plots, bordered by white Kentucky fences, could with a little imagination, $1,550 down, and a house trailer become a nine-acre Ponderosas. Everybody could be Ben Cartright.

But the land was still out there and not that hard to reach.

Sometimes I felt that knowledge was what kept me from going totally crazy in Dallas. Maybe. Someday. But lately that fantasy didn't seem to hold. How could I return to the land? I had never been there in the first place.

The tires of the Riviera began to hum as the car crossed an Army Corps of Engineers bridge. A manmade lake glimmered silver in the afternoon sun. One of the many government built lakes that had turned farmers into resort developers.

The steeple of the Lacota courthouse glowed an earth-red. I noticed three county sheriff cars parked on the square. I put out the joint I was smoking, and ate it.

A group of high school boys in faded Levi's and plaid shirts stood around a maroon GTO parked in front of the Rexall drugstore. Two of them wore new black Resistol hats with the Long Cattleman crease, dipped in front and back. They turned as I approached and then watched motionless as I stopped the brand-new Riviera at the corner. I could feel their eyes and felt like an intruder, strangely out of time and place. I turned slowly to the left, continuing around the square. As the car straightened out I pushed the accelerator enough to make the stock mufflers bubble and the low-profile tires squeak.

When I reached the gate leading to Charlotte's house, I noticed an orange Continental Mark III was blocking the drive. Red-and-white personalized license plates read: M FUNDS. The car belonged to Bob Beaudreau, and he was standing at the gate arguing with David Clarke.

"Just open the goddam gate." Beaudreau's raging face matched his red sport coat and slacks. White tassel-loafers cased his feet; his torso was bisected by a wide white belt.

"I told you, man, she don't want you up there." David's lips curled back in a mixture of fear and anger. Pushing his worn cowboy hat down over his forehead, he leaned back against the gate.

I walked to the front of the Lincoln and took a seat on the fender. Neither man seemed to notice.

"Goddam, don't that beat all." The bright-red fat man began

pacing nervously, his head down, talking into the ground. "A nigger cowboy tellin' me I can't see my own girl." He cocked his head back to look at his car. He didn't seem to see me.

"Just move on, man." David shoved his thumbs through the belt loops of his Levi's and hooked a rough-out boot over the bottom rail of the gate. "I don't want any trouble."

"If you don't want no trouble, then you better let me on through."

Suddenly, David grabbed Beaudreau by the lapels and shook him like a rag doll. "Look, you fat son of a bitch, you're lucky I don't kick the shit outta you." Beaudreau's face blanched. The anger drained away and was replaced by terror.

"You better not hit me." Beaudreau's lower lip quivered as he tried to hold a confident smile; it degenerated into a fearful sneer.

"I'll kick your teeth in, if you ever call me a nigger again. Now get the hell outta here before I change my mind." David shoved the frightened man backward and Beaudreau fell on his ass.

When he regained his feet and dusted himself off, Beaudreau turned to face me. "This is all your fault," he cried, pointing a shaking finger at me. Sweat had soaked through his jacket, making maroon half-circles under his arms. "You made a fool outta me last night. In front of everybody. That's what I get for being your friend."

"Beaudreau, you dumb cocksucker." I was enraged by his assumption that we had ever been friends. "I ain't your friend. I've never been your friend. I don't wanna be your friend. If you don't get outta here and leave these people alone, I'll kill you myself." I pushed the sobbing fat man toward his car.

Beaudreau turned the big Continental around and started back down the drive. When he had passed my car, he stopped, stepped out, and kicked the rear fender with a white foot. "Fucking pro-football player. Big man," he screamed at me. "Goddam asshole, that's what you are." He jumped back into the big orange Lincoln and roared away, spraying gravel all over my car.

"Jesus Christ." I shook my head.

"Sorry you had to get involved, but thanks." David took off his hat and wiped his forehead with his shirt sleeve.

"My life is filled with shitheads like that." I stared down the road into the settling dust. "They all watch too much television. . . . or maybe not enough."

"Sorry about locking you in last night," he said, putting his hand on my shoulder and smiling warmly. "I thought you were staying longer."

"So did I." The conversation struck me as strange. "I came to see Charlotte. Is she around?"

"Up at the house. Trying to decide whether to castrate a calf."

"Hope it's not anyone I know. Do you think she'd mind if I went up?"

"I can't say for her, but I don't," David said, "and I live here too."

I tried to fix a peculiar feeling I was getting. I studied the smiling black face to learn more. There didn't seem to be any more.

"Besides," he continued, "if she decides to save that calf a lot of anxiety and all-around wear and tear by cutting off his balls, I'll have to hold him. I could use a ride up to the house to hear the verdict." He paused. "Don't say anything to her about Beaudreau. It'll just upset her for no reason."

"No problem," I said. "Jump in."

He swung open the gate, then jumped into the front seat of the Buick. The gravel crunching and popping under the tires, we drove to the house.

"Does she do this often?" I asked.

"Do what?"

"Emasculate God's creatures." I shuddered involuntarily.

"What do you consider often?"

"I guess once is all I could stand."

As we approached the house I saw a small gray outbuilding. A Brangus calf stood in the middle of an attached corral.

"The condemned," David said, following my gaze.

"Jesus!" I said, feeling my testicles draw up into my throat.

Charlotte was sitting on the kitchen steps. David and I left the car and walked toward her. She watched us but made no sign of recognition. Next to her on the step lay a yellow bone-handled knife and a whetstone.

"Decide?" David asked.

"Yeah," she replied, her face grim. She turned to me and broke into a friendly smile. "Hi."

"Hello." I tried to control the muscles around my eyes and also to read more emotion into her greeting, but failed at both. The whole situation seemed so strange. I was glad to be there, although not particularly anxious to watch the calf's psychotherapy.

He will be a lot quieter, I thought. So will we all.

"Let's do it," she said, standing up and brushing off the seat of her tan corduroys. She turned to me. "You coming?"

"Why not? I'm an adult. I'm entitled to know."

I walked several steps behind, listening to a discussion of the nuances of gender conversion. I remembered a long-past fight with my ex-wife over whether or not to castrate our dog. "Fixed," she had said, like it was going to be a technological improvement. I was not swayed by her argument that the dog "didn't care." I tried to explain that just because a dog didn't *say* anything about his balls didn't mean they weren't of some concern to him. My logic eluded her and although I won the argument, she later used the incident in court as evidence of my sexual insecurity.

". . . calf fries . . ." was what I thought Charlotte said. I certainly hoped not, but anyway her voice brought my attention to the black calf, now slowly backing away from us.

David took a rope from around the gatepost.

"Somebody'll have to help me get this around him," he said, trying to back the calf into a corner of the corral. "I can't throw a loop."

Feeling silly and out of place, I ambled across the center of the pen to join David, who had cornered the calf behind the water trough. The young bull appeared to be four or five months old. As we stalked, it bolted directly at me.

Instinctively I dropped my shoulder, preparing to lock my

arms around the neck and hold on until David could get the rope on him. The tackle was perfectly executed, my shoulder hitting the calf in the brisket. I had expected a shock, but this was like tackling a '49 Hudson. Years of football training told me to hold on but my life instincts told me to let go. I let go and tumbled to a heap in the center of the corral.

I sat up, spitting out sand and cowshit, waiting for my nose to stop burning and my eyes to stop watering.

Except for a skinned bruise on the soft underside of my bicep, where the calf had stepped on me, and a numb cheekbone that had smacked into the animal's shoulder with enough force to break the leg of an NFL back, I felt surprisingly fit, and devastatingly foolish.

While David and Charlotte alternately laughed, inquired after my health, smirked at each other, and then burst into laughter again, I began to compose myself. Finally I stood up, slowly but grandly, and casually dusted myself off.

"The sun got in my eyes," I said, hitching up my pants.

Their renewed laughter brought a smile to my face that made my cheek hurt. I decided that calf needed his nuts cut off and I was just the man to do it.

Despite his claims to the contrary, David was a fair hand with a lariat and soon we had thrown and tied the calf. It lay struggling on its side with three legs bound. I was at its back with my knee on its neck, pulling on a rope rigged as a halter. Bending the head up and back, I tried to keep the animal immobile as Charlotte approached with the knife. I stared into a wild, rolling brown eye.

Milking the testicles into the top of the calf's scrotum, Charlotte grabbed the loose skin at the bottom of the sac and quickly cut it off.

"You didn't even say I love you," David grinned.

Jesus . . . Jesus, I thought, tightening my grip on the rope and watching the brown eye grow wilder.

Two large, milky-white blue-veined oblongs hung part way out of the gaping bloody hole that had been the bottom of the calf's scrotum. Charlotte took one of the oblongs in her palm and carefully, with the point of the knife, slit the thin white sheathing; out popped a pink gonad the size and shape of a hen's egg. It was still attached up inside by a cord the thickness of a lead pencil. Charlotte grabbed the pink testicle firmly, wrapped the cord a couple of turns around her index finger, then clenched her fist, and pulled as hard as she could. The calf lurched and made a frighteningly human groan as the cord tore loose with a pop somewhere inside. Eighteen inches of cord came away with the testicle.

"So much for foreplay," I said.

She quickly repeated the procedure on the remaining gonad, then sprayed a bright-purple disinfectant into the empty scrotum, pushed the loose edges back up inside and untied the calf. It lay motionless for a moment, then scrambled to its feet and trotted off to the other side of the corral seemingly undisturbed.

"Jesus—Jesus—Jesus—*Jesus*!!" I moaned. "JEEESUS!"

David and Charlotte both smiled back at me as I followed them, shaking my head and moaning nonsense to the Savior.

The recently liberated testicles, cords, and miscellaneous tissues were in Charlotte's hand. When we reached the house she tossed them at two cats who were sitting under the kitchen steps. I watched the cats sniff and paw at the balls. Then I followed the others into the house. Jesus.

The moon was up and we were sitting on the patio at the back of the house watching the shadows across the pasture. It was chilly and Charlotte had wrapped herself in a large Indian blanket. The plates from dinner were stacked beside her chair.

"I hope you didn't mind my coming. I tried to call."

I shifted uncomfortably in the canvas director's chair, trying to ease the pain in my back. The deadness in my right foot and the pins and needles in the leg reminded me that I had forgotten to ask the trainers what the cause could be.

"I'm glad you came," Charlotte replied. "It's been a nice evening."

Charlotte had cooked steaks outside while David and I had rolled joints and talked of Fuller, McLuhan, Cleaver, Nixon, Carlos Castaneda, and the upcoming New York game. The game was the only subject in which I was sufficiently versed to feel comfortable, although I found the others, with the exception of Nixon, profoundly more interesting.

After we ate David excused himself and returned to the bungalow to do some work.

Night sounds floated in from the shadows—an occasional night bird, dogs barking from distant farms and the rustling and snorting of animals in the nearby corrals and barn. Miles away a car door slammed. The wind picked up slightly and made a funny hissing sound as it eased through the needles of the big pine that rose above the patio. There were several gunshots. An owl hooted, its high-pitched "whoo" sounding like a Hollywood sound effect.

I fished a joint from my shirt pocket. We had run out of papers early in the evening and Charlotte had quickly solved the problem with unabashed pioneer spirit. I held up the exceptionally long joint and in the moonlight could make out the words SUPER TAMPAX. I snorted a small laugh and lit up, passing it to the slim hand reaching from beneath the blue-and-red Indian blanket.

"They sure make king-size joints," Charlotte observed.

"Enough to rival the legendary Austin torpedo, I would say."

Glowing brightly as she inhaled, the cigarette softly illuminated the dark depressions of her eyes. They were big, round shadows with a slight flash of light like catching a glimpse of the water at the bottom of a deep well.

My aching back and legs drew my attention and I shifted, searching a position that would strain as few nerves and muscles as possible.

"Nervous?" Charlotte asked, watching me fidget.

"No. Just sore."

"Do you want to go inside?"

"Not unless you do. This is fine." I made a sweeping gesture with my hand. "This here is a real fine universe."

I pulled the collar of my sheepskin coat up around my neck, burrowing my chin down inside. The sound of distant music and laughter stilled our Hollywood owl. There was a loud yell and a door slam and the night was silent again.

"That's the Bartlette kids," Charlotte said. "Their place is six miles that way." She pointed in the opposite direction from where I thought the sounds had come from. "The youngest son is engaged to a Mexican girl. It's causing quite a community crisis. He met her at Methodist Youth Fellowship."

I leaned back and smiled into the sky. The sky was filled with shining, flashing, changing little spots of light. They say you can never see more than five thousand stars with the naked eye. I didn't see one less. A meteor made a desperate try for Dallas but disappeared in a green-red blaze. I took the joint from Charlotte's outstretched hand, which immediately slithered back beneath the blanket.

"God, it's beautiful here," I said. I felt Charlotte turn to look at me. I took a long drag on the weed and turned to meet her gaze. "Would you please sleep with me again?" I asked.

Pulling the blanket up around her shoulders, she smiled, got to her feet and walked into the house.

"That's Tchaikovsky, isn't it?" I was lying naked across the bed, a pillow under my chin. *Swan Lake* drifted in from the den. It was one of the few pieces of classical music I knew.

"Did you see *The Music Lovers?*" Charlotte asked.

She was brushing her hair out and letting it fall down over her bare shoulders. She laid the brush down and arranged herself next to me on the bed with her arm resting lightly on my back. I could feel the warmth of her leg pressing against mine. Her fingernails scratched lazily on my arm, raising chills. She pushed her other hand up the nape of my neck, lifting my hair away, and sliding across my back she kissed me warmly on the shoulder. I could feel her breasts, the hard nipples brushing along my shoulder blades.

"It was a grand movie," she continued. "I loved Richard Chamberlain." She gently pushed me onto my back and kissed me wetly on the stomach.

We made love carefully and with few variations, often stopping to look into each other's eyes to try to read the feelings there. I watched her face and listened to her ragged breathing, trying to anticipate her climax. My back began to ache violently, distracting me enough to postpone my completion.

"Oh . . . oh . . ." was all she said, but she thrashed violently, gripping me tightly with her fingers and heels. As we ended, I was disconsolate, with a feeling of isolation.

"You know," I said. I was sitting propped up on several pillows, scratching Charlotte's head as she rested it on my stomach. "I have this theory. We all get this certain amount of energy each day and if we don't use it, it drives us crazy. Eats away the prefrontal lobe." I tapped my forehead.

"If we use too much energy we're exhausted, burned out. Too little energy use, insanity. We must reach a balance and that balancing mechanism, if you'll pardon the unscientific terminology, is fucking. Or, if you prefer, doin' it."

"I like doin' it better. It sounds warmer."

"Okay. Hunting used to be the way energy was balanced. A good hunt was a great combination of muscular and emotional energy. But now hunting just degenerates into butchery, which creates more energy rather than depleting it. Almost all human endeavor is that way. That surplus of energy is the cause of crimes of passion and spectator sports. Now fuck—ah—doin' it is the natural energy depleter and the savior of human sanity. When everybody gets laid enough, the world will be at peace and I won't have to play flanker." I paused momentarily for effect. "So my dear, if you'll just roll over."

"Gladly," Charlotte smiled. "If you think you can do anything with that." She pointed below my waist.

"How do you feel about a dove hunt instead?"

"How would you get their little legs apart?"

We both lay silently exhausted but too excited to sleep,

and after what seemed like several peaceful hours Charlotte sat up cross-legged on the bed.

"Are you happy?" she asked.

"I dunno."

"What do you mean you don't know?"

"Just that," I said, sliding up against the headboard and drawing my knees into a triangle. "I don't know what being happy is supposed to be. I always figured the secret to living was to find happiness. Do you agree?"

"Sure."

"Well, what is being happy? Is it freedom from being hungry and thirsty and having a roof over your head?"

"That's part of it."

"Then I'm partially happy. What else is there?"

"It's having somebody to love."

"I'm wrestling with that."

"But it's mostly having somebody that you can make happy," she continued, moving up to my feet and putting her chin on my knee. "Then their happiness is yours."

"How do they know they're happy?"

"Come on, Phillip, people just know."

"Well, I've lowered my sights some in the past years. Happiness would be nice and it's a swell goal, but all I want right now is to know. To know whether I'm happy or unhappy, it don't matter which, I just want to know which I am."

She dropped her eyes and I could see I had hurt her. I searched my mind for a kind thing to say.

"You've taken it personal, I'm sorry."

"Well, what am I supposed to think? You're in my bed telling me how unhappy you are." She was on the verge of tears.

"I don't expect you to understand but my confusion has nothing to do with you. My fear existed long before I met you. You've given me the only few minutes of peace I can remember. I feel safe in your bed. That's more than I can say for mine." I reached over and wiped a solitary tear from the end of her nose.

"Do you like it here?" she asked.

"Very much." I tried not to think about the long drive home and the flight to New York. "I could stay here forever. I could stick around and help you cut the balls off everything on the place. No offense to David."

"If you lived here," she continued, "it might not help your football career."

"Some career. Football's about to give up on me, I think."

"I don't mean necessarily to quit playing. I mean to quit thinking and feeling like that. Playing in the game seems the least offensive of all."

"What would I do? I'd have to do something. You don't want some crazy dope freak around doing nothing."

"I might. But there's a lot to do on a place like this. Run right, this place could make a good profit if we bought momma cows and really turned it into a ranch."

"Sounds like a lot of work."

"Well, it's up to you. I don't like what football makes you. You're a very mean man. I know, I just made love to you."

"Do you really want me to move out here?" It sounded interesting.

"Yes. You don't even have to work the ranch if you don't want." Her voice rose with excitement and her eyes began to sparkle. "I've got enough money to last until we learn to do without."

"Do without what?"

"Whatever is not worth suffering for," she continued. "That's my whole idea. We start off with everything we've learned to desire as twentieth-century children. All the perverse wants and needs that haunt this generation."

"Amazing."

"I mean it." She was becoming insistent. "I have plenty of money and you have a measure of success. Instead of starting with a one-room flat and slowly growing apart in pursuit of life in the seventies, we start with everything and whittle it down to each other. That's how we would live in this insane world."

"You mean start at the top and work our way to the bottom?"

"Sort of. And along the way if either of us wants out, out they go."

I was astonished by her logic. "I can't help but think I'm gonna have some real warm feelings for you before this is all over."

"Me too." Her arms wrapped around my waist and she snuggled her face into my chest.

FRIDAY

The morning was cool and crisp. The dew wet my boots as I walked to the car. The late fall sun was reassuringly warm as I guided the Buick through the front pasture toward the gate. Charlotte had looked beautiful on the kitchen steps, waving and telling me to come right back. I fought a melancholy premonition that told me not to leave but to stay there forever, raising cattle and watching the sun come up. First, though, I would have to deal with New York, Seth Maxwell, B.A., Clinton Foote, Conrad Hunter, fear, and me. Then I would stay there forever. I knew it the moment I stepped out the door, that was where I wanted to be. The new Brangus steer stared at me through the corral fence as I drove away.

The gate was open. As I drove through, a black fist shot out of the cottage window.

"Be cool, brother," David's voice rang out.

If I only could.

I waved and honked. What could I yell back? Power to the people?

I honked again as I turned onto the blacktop and sped toward the *Look* Magazine All American City.

The boarding gate was crowded with family, well wishers, and press people. Most of the team were milling around in the embarkation lounge drinking coffee and soft drinks served by brightly uniformed Braniff ground hostesses.

I had stopped by the house to change clothes and pick up some luggage, including my portable record player. I sat the record player down and looked around to see who else had arrived.

Art Hartman sat propped in the corner of the lounge. His head hung down on his chest and a gray 100X Resistol with a Fort Worth crease covered his eyes.

"Art?" I said, standing directly in front of him and bending down to try and look under the brim of his hundred-dollar hat.

"Uh." His body shook slightly from the effort of the grunt but he made no move to look up.

"Art?"

"Yeah . . . yeah." He raised his head slightly and pushed the hat back with his thumb. He was unshaven and peered up at me with one horribly bloodshot eye.

"God," I said. "What happened to you?"

"I spent a week with Maxwell, last night," he moaned, trying to sit straight up. He kept sliding back into a slump.

"We went out for a beer and met these two gals," he continued, smacking his lips and running his tongue along the insides of his cheeks as though his mouth were full of peanut butter. "They turned out to be married to guys that worked the night shift at Texas Instruments. Christ! What a night. Look at this." He pushed back the brim of his hat to reveal a scab the size of a postage stamp on his forehead.

"A fight?"

"Fight–" he snorted out a painful laugh, wincing at the throbbing in his skull. "She bit me."

"What'd you do? Try to rape her?"

"Me?" he exclaimed. "She raped me. God almighty, she couldn't get enough. She made so much noise her kids woke up."

"Jesus, Art, that's really second-rate."

"Don't I know it. You should see my back. I told Julia I'd been in a fight. I don't know if she believed me or not."

"What happened to Seth?"

"We left the gals about midnight and he took me to a country-and-western place down on Industrial. The next thing I knew it was three in the morning and he'd gone with the car. I had to get a cab home." He slid back down in the chair with a pitiful groan and pulled the hat back over his scarred forehead and eyes.

"Welcome to the NFL, Art," I said, and turned toward the girl with the beehive black hair and purple culottes who was serving soft drinks. I took a Coke and was walking to an unoccupied chair near the boarding door when "Scoop" Zolin stopped me for an interview.

Zolin worked for the morning paper and our team was his beat. His real name was Seymour Zolinzowsky and he was the worst reporter I had ever met. Maxwell and I had given him the name Scoop several years back, during the first year he traveled with us, because he was notorious for getting drunk before the game and missing the first three quarters. He would usually stumble into the press box about midway through the third quarter, pick up the play-by-play sheet, and begin to write his story. That year he won three national awards for outstanding sports journalism. A doper and drinker of huge proportions, Scoop was great fun but caused me much trouble. Often after a night with Scoop I would read the paper a couple of days later to find a full-page article of things I had babbled while in the throes of alcohol and cannabis hallucinations. If I didn't say anything interesting he would often make up quotes and attribute them to me.

"Leave me alone, Scoop," I said, as he approached. "I got enough troubles."

"The word around sports circles is that your legs are gone and you're over the hill," Scoop said, smiling, not put off in the least by my rebuff. "Do you care to comment?"

"Leave me alone, Scoop," I said, backing away.

"When questioned about his fading glory and rumors of ill health Elliott rebuffed this reporter with threats of physical violence and a warning to leave him alone, or else."

"I didn't say *or else.*"

"A little journalistic license. How many times I gotta tell you. I don't let the facts interfere with my style."

"Scoop, give me a break. What did I ever do to you?"

"Listen, man, I'm building you into a legend. Nobody gets the press coverage you get, except maybe Maxwell. I'm turning you into a personality."

"Yeah, with all the warmth, wit, and charm of a Lee Harvey Oswald. Jesus, Scoop, B.A. is still mad at me over that last article."

"Which article?"

"The one where you had me saying Larry Wilson was the ugliest man in football."

"Oh yeah, sorry about that. I took a funny little pill some Delta stewardess gave me before I wrote that one. But goddam, that was a great picture of you they used with the story."

"Jesus Christ. I have nothing further to say ever, and you can quote me."

"Okay. Okay, you don't have to get salty about it." He looked around the lounge. "Where's Maxwell?"

I shrugged and walked toward the gate. The plane was ready for boarding.

I closed my eyes, my mind freed by the white sound of the three 727 engines. I was sitting in the last seat of the tourist section. I like flying. It seems to be the only time I can really relax. At thirty thousand feet and surrounded by screaming jet engines and gasoline, I figure I can't be held responsible for anything that happens.

Maxwell sat sleeping next to me, smelling not unlike my grandfather in the terminal stages of alcoholism. Mumbling something about a girl who swallowed his cock, he had stumbled aboard just before takeoff, had fallen into the inside seat, and had gone to sleep against the bulkhead. Somehow, on Sunday, Maxwell would be as marvelous as was necessary to win.

Once Maxwell had told me that the only time he had any respect for himself was when he was on the field. When he was off the field, he was the biggest whore around, because he would do anything for anybody to get back on the field.

"Ah, but we're all whores, aren't we?" he had said, looking right at me. "I guess I should take some satisfaction in being the best."

I looked at the sleeping man, curled up, his back to me and his face buried in the tiny airline pillow. His sport coat was thrown carelessly over his shoulders. I pulled a plaid blanket from the overhead storage rack and covered him.

I lay back with my eyes closed and thought about how glad I was I had met Charlotte Caulder.

"Hi, Phil." Mary Jane Woodley, stewardess, stood in the aisle.

Last year on the drunken return from winning the division playoff, I had watched Mary Jane jack off Maxwell in the very same seats we occupied now.

Someone had donated twenty-five cases of cheap champagne for the victory flight and everyone got incredibly fucked up. Mary Jane and Maxwell were quite reserved compared to others. One guy was traded and another waived outright for the things they said and did in alcohol and amphetamine frenzies to Conrad Hunter and Clinton Foote.

It had been an amazing flight. Maxwell and I smoked several joints in the toilet and then drank ten or so tiny bottles of liquor apiece. Maxwell finally cornered Mary Jane in the galley and asked her to suck him off as indication of the friendship they had built up over the years she had been flying our charters. She said no, but he had already unzipped his fly and the shiny head of his stiff penis was peeking out from between the tails of his shirt. Mary Jane finally gave in and guided him to the seat, covered his lap with a blanket and brought him to climax with her thin white hands. She even bent down a couple of times to suck. It was all quite poignant.

After she finished with Seth, Mary Jane wiped her hands on the blanket and returned to the galley to fix steak sandwiches for Clinton Foote and several of the others riding in first class. I loved it all.

"Hello, Mary Jane, how are you?" I tried to be as friendly as possible because I liked Mary Jane and I could tell by her expression she was depressed.

"Not too good," she said, frowning. "I've got to go out with Emmett Hunter tonight. Why me? He brought Joanne with him. You suppose they're planning a scene?"

"If they are, be sure to call me." I grinned.

"I wouldn't go out with the fat motherfucker if I thought I wouldn't get dropped from the charters."

"You would."

"Yeah, I know," she said. "At least I'll get good and drunk."

"Too bad you have to do it," I said. "I wanted to take you out on the arm of the Statue of Liberty and show you my collection of Richard Nixon pornography."

I felt slightly responsible, because Joanne was leaving Emmett at loose ends tonight in order to meet me at a party given by a writer friend of hers from Fort Worth.

"Smuggle a lot of whiskey back for us on the return, will you please, Mary Jane?" I asked, indicating myself and the sleeping Maxwell.

"I'll try."

On return trips, players were allowed only two beers apiece, while there was an unlimited supply of liquor in the first-class section for the coaches, management, press, and wealthy middle-aged sports groupies. For years Mary Jane had smuggled the tiny bottles back to Maxwell and me. She had almost been fired over it once, telling her supervisor she'd taken the bottles for herself rather than reveal their true destination—the slightly enlarged livers of Seth Maxwell and

Phillip Elliott. Now most of the players brought their own bottles, but Maxwell and I had come to depend on Mary Jane. It was a ritual the three of us enjoyed.

"Bourbon for you and Cutty Sark for the King, right?" she finally smiled and started back up the aisle.

The curtain between the sections was open, and by leaning out of my seat, I could see Joanne Remington's finely turned leg sticking into the aisle of the first-class section.

Joanne had surreptitiously squeezed my shoulder as she made her way to the front after boarding up the ass of the 727. I had turned and momentarily met her gaze, then quickly shifted my eyes to Emmett Hunter, who was behind her. Emmett had his corpulence covered with a brass-buttoned, double-breasted red blazer, an iron-on team patch on the pocket. The patch looked as if it had come from the bottom of a box of cornflakes. The front-office personnel and all the hangers-on that rode in first class wore these patches. I could just see the black maids all over north Dallas swapping techniques on how to attach the ugly little pieces of blue cloth to $150 sport coats.

"Hidy, Emmett. How yew, Joanne? How ya'll doin'?" I had babbled, sounding like the opening of the "Buck Owens Show."

"Hello, Phillip. How are you?" Joanne had answered in a soft proper tone. She looked superb in a purple knit minidress, her breasts clearly outlined and swinging free against the clinging material. I could hear the blood pounding in my ears.

"Ready to get this here game won," I blurted out. Blah . . . blah . . . blah . . . I sounded like the complete fool.

They moved on down the aisle. Emmett nodded hello.

After my talk with Mary Jane, I had fallen asleep and was awakened by someone pulling on the lapel of my coat. It was Bill Needham, the team's business manager, who had been so upset by my ordering the large number of sandwiches and beer in Philadelphia. He was trying to slip an envelope into my inside coat pocket; I grabbed it out of his hand.

"Per diem?" I asked.

Needham nodded, startled by my awakening.

"Trying to slip it in without having to face me, huh." Needham was a nervous junior executive who caught shit from both sides of the fence. I loved to rag him. "How much this time?" I asked, as I ripped the envelope open to find two five- and two one-dollar bills. "Twelve bucks? For how many meals?" I looked up at Needham expectantly.

"Four," he said, his voice a whisper.

"Four. Jesus Christ. You guys are amazing. You know there ain't no way to eat four meals in a hotel in Manhattan for twelve bucks. It is incredible how far you assholes will go to scrounge every nickel out of us. I'll bet my sweet ass you and Clinton don't eat on any three bucks a meal."

"Now wait a minute, you can't—"

"Fuck you, Needham, leave me alone."

I closed my eyes and tried to go back to sleep.

The plane bounced into Kennedy and taxied to a deserted freight hangar where three chartered buses waited. Everybody jumped up as soon as the plane touched down and stood in the aisle jammed like cattle. I woke Maxwell, helped him down the ramp and to the back of the last bus in line. There he lapsed again into unconsciousness.

Everyone in my bus watched as Joanne climbed onto the bus in front. I couldn't help but smile at the remarks and heavy breathing. Emmett had boarded in front of her and Scoop Zolin was behind her. Scoop put his hand on Joanne's neatly outlined buttocks apparently to help her into the bus. (I don't really profess to understand the motivations for any of Scoop's actions.) Joanne turned around and slapped the shit out of him. Our bus rocked with laughter.

"Goddam," Tony Douglas exhaled, "I'd eat a mile of her shit just to get within an inch of her asshole." The frustration the big linebacker was building would probably cost some New York receiver his looks, or his knee cartilage, or both.

The bus crawled into the gray, grimy city amid cries and insults directed at the driver.

"Goddam, bussy!" Jo Bob screamed. The main antagonist, he was extremely vocal and obscene. B.A., Clinton, and Conrad Hunter had taken another bus. "We got from Dallas to New York faster'n you're gettin' us from the fucking airport into this goddam city. You better get your New York ass in gear."

Buddy Wilks, the team statistician, kicking expert, former-all-pro running back, and all-around flunky, glared back at Jo Bob. Buddy had been in a bad mood ever since the team had laughed him down on Wednesday when he tried to cover the kicking material.

"Fuck you, Buddy," Jo Bob shot back. "And suck that guy sittin' next to you."

Everyone laughed. Bill Needham, the business manager, who was sharing the seat with Wilks, was the constant object of much ridicule. No one seemed to know what Needham did except hand out per diem, arrange for buses to meet the planes, and make room assignments at the hotels. And since the buses were often late and the per diem was never enough, Needham caught a lot of shit.

"Goddam you, Needham, if the rooms are fucked up this week, I'm comin' down to sleep with you. And it'll be your night in the barrel," Jo Bob yelled and laughed while Needham squirmed uncomfortably in his seat.

As we crossed into Manhattan, Maxwell woke for the second time and stretched and looked out the window at the dingy skyline.

"This time I'm gonna whip 'er," Maxwell grunted, his voice in the characteristic whiskey rasp he uses when describing or anticipating some unusual sensual experience.

"Who?" I asked.

"Her," he replied, pointing out the window at the gray-black buildings outlined against the dirty brown sky. Various clouds of earth-colored smoke boiled up from around the buildings and slowly mingled in the sickly sky. I felt as if I were going underground.

"She's beat me too many times in the last five years," he

rasped, digging in his coat pocket and coming out with a cigarette. "Beat me to my knees, but not this time."

He pointed to the Empire State Building.

"See that?" he asked. "When I leave this here town, she's gonna be all mine. I'm gonna fuck her to dust."

"If anybody could do it, Seth . . ."

"You want part of it?" he continued, his gesture taking in all of Manhattan and parts of several other boroughs. "Which part?" His eyes were starting to glow, his spirits were rising; the city was having a visible effect on him.

"I don't know, man." I hesitated. "I'm sort of a country boy."

"Bullshit," he raved, "just name it, what do you want? Downtown . . . the Upper East Side is all mine . . . the Village . . . That's it—you can have the Village."

"Now you're talkin', pardner," I said. "Give me that Washington Square and all those sixteen-year-old girls trying to support a habit."

"You got it," Maxwell said, jumping to his feet and yelling to the front of the bus. "Take this man to Washington Square." He winced with pain, deep ravines digging in around his eyes. He grabbed his head with both hands and eased back into his seat and closed his eyes.

"Headache," was all he said.

He didn't open his eyes again until we reached the hotel. It was 7 P.M. eastern standard time.

The room keys were spread out on a table in the lobby. While I tried to edge through the crowd, Maxwell went to the desk to check for messages. We met by the elevator and exchanged prizes.

"Here's a message for you," he said. "I'll meet you in the room." I handed him my record player and records.

I went back across the lobby to the tobacco counter and bought a couple of long thin cigars. I liked to smoke cigars on the road, they relaxed me. The cigars turned out to be so old and dry I had to suck on one for several minutes before it would hold together long enough to light. I bought a *Times*, sat on a brown leather sofa, and read the message from Joanne. It instructed me to meet her at an address on Sutton Place at 9:30. She had signed the note "J."

I crumpled the note, thought fleetingly about eating it, then threw it in the silent butler at the end of the couch. It took three shots. I read the sports section of the *Times* and then caught the elevator to the eleventh floor.

Maxwell was lying in his shorts on one of the tiny twin beds. I nodded hello and threw the newspaper across his chest.

"They refer to you as a riverboat gambler," I said. "and to me as a lanky member of the receiving corps. I got an immediate mental image of a penis in a tin hat—don't ask me why."

I fell into bed, traditionally the one nearest the door. It was a deal we had; I answered the door and Maxwell got the phone.

"What you got planned?" I asked Maxwell, who was fingering himself through the fly of his shorts.

"Waitin' on a call from Hoot."

Hoot was an old friend of Maxwell's, who had moved to New York's Lower East Side about four years ago. Nobody seemed to know what Hoot did, but he always had a nice apartment and plenty of money. I thought he was a gangster and Maxwell had him pegged as a male prostitute, screwing rich old ladies from midtown.

"Hey, man," I asked, remembering. "What in God's name did you do to Hartman?"

"I took him honky-tonkin'."

"Well, he sure looked honky-tonked out at the airport."

Maxwell laughed a short raspy laugh.

"I tol' him quarterbackin' wasn't all that simple. I don' think that boy's gonna make it. I'll kill him with pussy and Cutty."

"Well," I announced, "I've got a party to go to—I guess I'll go to the bathroom and throw up." I got up, accompanied by my ever-present groan, and walked bent over into the bathroom.

It was an old-fashioned affair with white and black ceramic tiles and a cast-iron shower-tub combination. The plane ride always upset my system, besides making my joints and muscles stiff from all that sitting; a hot shower usually got me turned around, but not always.

The steam was billowing from behind the curtain; I stepped carefully into the tub. I have an inordinate fear of dying naked in a hotel bathroom, probably because I spend so much time in them feeling miserable.

"I think we're the only ones on this floor," Maxwell said, his voice coming closer. "Everybody I rode up with got off on nine." The curtain pulled back and he handed me a joint.

"Thanks." I handed it back after a long drag. "I needed that. Did Scoop see you yet?"

"What does that little cocksucker want?"

"I dunno, I just told him I wouldn't say anything he could print except 'no comment.'"

"That asshole wrote that the three biggest losers of all time were Joe Kuharich, Charles DeGaulle, and me."

"I didn't think DeGaulle was all that bad."

"Fuck you, second string. It'll be a cold day when I signal for you from the bench."

"Seth, Seth, let's not let personalities enter into this. You need me for the good of the team."

"It's too fucking hot in here."

The door closed and I was left alone with the hot water pounding on my neck, sending chills but not much relief through my body. I decided if I moved out to Charlotte's farm we would have to spend more time sleeping and less time philosophizing.

When I came back into the bedroom Maxwell was hanging up the phone.

"Hoot?"

"Yeah, he's sending a limousine for me. Wanna go?"

"No, thanks, I got something else going."

"Sutton Place?" He had read the message.

"Yeah."

"Be careful man," Maxwell cautioned. "Money's a dangerous thing for a country boy like you to go rubbing up against."

"I'll wear thick underwear." I absently picked some caked blood and big-city air from my nose. I lit another joint and offered it to Seth. He declined.

"The limo's s'posed to be here at nine." He opened his suitcase and fished out his playbook. "Might as well study a few things till then."

"Don't forget the wing square out and go," I reminded him.

"Yeah," he nodded. "Gill oughta do a helluva job on that one."

"Don't you wish."

The taxi ride took me through Central Park. I was sure it was the long way but I enjoyed the park. It was strange to watch the horse-drawn cabs clopping along while the automobiles careened wildly around them. You wouldn't see any horses in downtown Dallas.

It was 9:40 when the cab arrived at Sutton Place. I was met at the door by a uniformed doorman, who asked my name.

"No. No autographs please," I said, holding up my hands and backing away. The joints I had smoked, plus the cold night air, had effected my recovery. I felt fine.

"I just want your name, buddy," he said, creasing his face and holding up a clipboard, "if your name ain't on this list you don't get in."

"Phillip Elliott," I reported. "Lanky member of the receiving corps." I saluted stiffly while he ran his thumb down the side of his clipboard.

"Okay, fella," he said, opening the door and gesturing me inside with his head. I held the back of my hand beside my mouth and leaned toward the man so grandly bedecked in brass buttons, epaulets, braids, and chevrons.

"If I'm not out by midnight," I whispered loudly, "take the rest of the men and report back to Colonel Bowie." I darted quickly through the door.

Joanne was waiting at the elevator. She was wearing a mesh net minidress and thigh-length boots. I got closer and could see, as could anybody who cared to look, the pointed nipples of her unencumbered breasts; the only thing between her and the New York City autumn were flesh-colored bikini panties. The minidress was just a grid, a mere illusion. The woman was nude. A brown leather coat trimmed in chinchilla was thrown over her shoulder. She looked astoundingly beautiful and outrageously illegal.

I had reached her as the elevator arrived; we stepped on and started our ascent before we spoke.

"You look great," I complimented, "if a little obscene."

"Thanks. You do too. Only maybe not obscene enough."

"I'm trying to cut down."

"Where'd you get the coat?" she asked, rubbing a small hand on the sleeve of the leather trench coat and toying with its myriad buckles and belts. "Very fashionable."

"Neiman's gave it to Maxwell and he gave it to me. He's a cashmere man, you know." I held my arms out and did a full turn.

"Actually, I feel somewhat like a member of the KGB."

She didn't understand the reference but her confidence in my sense of humor triggered a short giggle. It irritated me that a shithead like Emmett Hunter was getting such a good deal. But I remained thankful for the timely appearance of Charlotte Caulder into my life and vowed not to meddle.

"Where the hell are we going anyway?" I asked. The lighted numbers flashing on and off above the door were already well into the twenties.

"To the top," she replied, her eyes sparkling with excitement. "All the way to the top. They're friends of Gary's."

"Gary being your writer friend from Cowtown?"

"Yes."

We rode in silence for about ten floors. I looked around the empty stainless-steel cubicle.

"Ahhhh," I said, opening my arms to embrace the elevator, "I'm sure gonna miss all this."

"What?"

"All this." I swept my hand around the elevator. "When you chose to marry, I took an oath of poverty. From now on I run pass patterns only for the good of mankind. Humanity's first flankerback. No, my good man, no, I won't contribute any money to the United Fund, I gave at the office. Two zig outs and a deep sideline. Ten percent of my deep routes are pledged to UNICEF."

Joanne laughed more at my elaborate gestures than at my dialogue; it pleased me. I like to make people laugh.

The elevator stopped and the doors glided back with a hiss, revealing a small foyer and carved wooden double doors. It resembled the entrance to the men's room of the Royal Knight Club back in Dallas.

I pulled on a gargoyle's head attached to a gold chain; I assumed it would summon somebody. If it didn't, I wasn't going to set foot inside the apartment. A gargoyle's head hanging from the ceiling with no utilitarian function was just too decadent; it reeked of ritual killers and liberal Republicans.

"Hello." A pleasant-looking gray-haired woman opened the door and greeted us. "I'm Margaret McKnight." She wore an orchid floor-length sleeveless gown; the neckline continued past her small breasts, revealing a large expanse of mottled tan skin.

The apartment was two stories high and had a wrought-iron spiral staircase that descended into the living room from a huge round hole in the ceiling. Groups of people clambered awkwardly up and down the stairs every now and then, seeming more awkward on the descent.

A tall, thin man, his shaggy hair gray-streaked, approached us. He wore wire-rimmed glasses and a tweed pinched-back coat.

"The sort of man who reads *Playboy*," I whispered to Joanne, "and doesn't look at the pictures." She stifled a laugh, making a sound like someone had stepped on a chicken. We were both smiling broadly when the man reached our corner.

"Hello, Joanne," he said. "It's so good to see you." He grabbed her shoulders and leaned forward rather clumsily to kiss her on the cheek; it landed just under her eye with his nose brushing up against her eyelid.

"Gary," Joanne said, reaching up to wipe a hint of blue eye shadow from the end of his nose, "this is Phillip Elliott."

We shook hands. His grip had a practiced firmness and I

considered dropping to my knees and screaming in agony. I decided against it.

"Gary Cassady, Phillip," he said, his face drawing into thought. "Phillip Elliott? . . . Oh yes, the football player. I've seen you play."

"That's strange," I replied. "I've always considered myself a very esoteric ball player."

He smiled politely and then described several instances when he had seen me perform on television. It quickly became apparent to me that he was talking about Willie Ellison of the Los Angeles Rams. Joanne didn't seem to notice, so I just kept smiling and nodding with great satisfaction at his recollections of superhuman effort and imperishable glory as if they were my own.

A short, stocky curly-haired man about fifty walked in from the foyer. Gary excused himself and joined several others to greet the man at the door.

"Who's that?" I asked.

"I'm not sure." Joanne shrugged. "A writer, I think."

"I just hope it's not Willie Ellison."

"Willie Ellison?"

"Just someone I used to be," I explained.

"Oh."

We stood silently for a time, watching the evening unfold. It was a leisurely cocktail party with people circulating from one group to another and people still ascending the spiral stairs and, after pauses of increasing duration, stumbling back down again, trying to look unruffled and in complete command of their faculties.

During the evening's course, I met a free-lance writer from Cleveland who had spent some time in a training camp with an NFL team. He was pleasant and knowledgeable about football and knew more players and statistics than I did. But it was apparent that he had not experienced the one thing that makes a professional football player—intense and constant fear. But how many people, aside from combat soldiers, advertising executives and actors, experience that kind of fear? Football players aren't people, who leave home to try and play football.

They are football players, who come home to try and play people.

The writer had never sat on a dormitory bed in training camp listening to those footsteps coming closer and realizing they could be for him, and would change his whole life. He had never spent nights wondering what his reaction would be to the inevitable end—surprise? Anger? Relief? Resignation? He didn't understand the total futility. One impossible situation leading only to another, the difficult succeeded by the more difficult. The past was worthless, the present anxious, and the future impossible. Experience his only commodity, all the player was doing was getting older.

While we talked I noticed the diminutive curly-haired writer circulating around the room. He glared at us constantly. It was becoming disconcerting.

Shortly, the football writer drifted away and Joanne and I were by ourselves. "Did you see that guy staring at us?" Joanne asked.

"Yes. He thinks we're too tall. I say . . . fuck him. . . . Let's go smoke this here marijuana cigarette I brought specifically to ease tension created by situations like these."

The doors to the foyer were open and we quietly slipped into the elevator, pushing all the buttons and sitting in a corner. I lit the joint and passed it to Joanne, who was sitting cross-legged in front of me—not a mean feat considering the minidress.

"Quit looking at my crotch, for God's sake."

"Just checking for signs of a hernia," I explained.

"Phillip, do you love me?" Joanne reached over and took my hand and gripped it tightly.

"Sorta, I guess."

"Sorta, I guess. What kind of answer is that?"

"The only kind I know how to give—when people I like seem to need the truth." I closed my other hand over hers and rubbed the back of her wrist with my thumb. "You gonna marry Emmett?"

"Are you offering an alternative?"

I shook my head.

"What can I offer? The best I had to give is already gone. On Sunday forty million will be glued to their televisions to escape themselves and their wretched lives. But where do I go to escape? They can believe the fantasy that fills the screen. I can't. I've seen this movie before and I know how it ends. And there's no future in it."

"I guess not," she sighed, squeezing my hand. "We have had some times, though, haven't we?"

I nodded, smiling, my eyes watering slightly. I lost partial control of my facial muscles and had to concentrate to keep my grin from becoming aberrant.

"I guess I'll marry Emmett for a while," she said, gazing blankly above my head. "You'll still come see me, won't you?"

"If I can."

We glided silently from floor to floor, sliding up and down the shaft, finishing the joint.

"Cheer up, Phillip," Joanne said, as we returned to the party. "Everybody gets married now and then."

It was past midnight when I heard Maxwell's unmistakable twang ricocheting in from the apartment foyer.

"Yes ma'am," he whined. "I'm just an ol' country boy in the big city."

Hoot was with him and when they entered the room the party for the first time had a focal point. They stood on the steps surveying the room and exchanged waves with people they apparently knew. Standing behind them, just inside the door, was a fat, dumpy-looking girl wearing Maxwell's cowboy hat. Several people approached to shake hands and exchange greetings. They remained on the steps for several minutes holding court.

The stubby curly-headed writer pushed his way through the crowd, extended his hand to Hoot, who in turn introduced him to Maxwell. The three immediately fell into an extended conversation and the crowd began to disperse. Maxwell and Hoot stepped down into the living room and the fat girl followed suit, staying a few feet to the rear. The short man guided them off to the side and shortly he and Maxwell were in deep discussion.

The stocky fellow suddenly stepped back from the group, bent slightly at the waist and extended his hands in front of him as if he were going to receive a snap from center. His head and shoulders jerked forward convulsively as he barked out silent signals. Then leaping into the air, he went through the exceedingly awkward motions of an imaginary jump pass. The move had all the grace and elegance of the death throes of a decapitated chicken. Maxwell and Hoot looked at each other quizzically, then at the man, and then back to each other. Hoot shrugged.

Maxwell noticed Joanne and me in the corner.

"Phillip . . . haa . . . haaaaaaa . . ." he bellowed, his voice deep and grating from the enormous quantities of alcohol he certainly had swallowed to get as drunk as he seemed. He pushed past the man who had just done the Johnny Lujack imitation and took long strides toward us. The man was furious at Maxwell's affront to his advice. He clenched his fists and leaned into a crouch. Before he could run and leap on Maxwell from behind, Hoot grabbed his arm and engaged him in talk.

Maxwell smiled and laughed as he ambled the length of the room. The brown suit he was wearing, another gift from Neiman-Marcus, fit perfectly, the pants legs stuffed into his alligator cowboy boots. The fat girl followed, wearing Seth's brown cowboy hat that was studded with turquoise and silver conchos.

"Phillip . . . ah . . . haa . . . haaaaaaa . . ." Maxwell roared. "Me and Hoot come to see ya . . . we was invited to the same party . . . haa . . . haaaa."

I couldn't help but smile at his antics: I reached out and we shook hands, smiling, laughing, and slapping each other on the back.

"Hey, man," I reminded him, "I thought you said money was dangerous."

"I did. I did," he admitted. "But that's fer you—as Amerka's guest that don't apply to this ol' boy.

"All I have to say," he whispered, leaning close, "in this town is I'm an ol' country boy, and the wimmin all wants ta fuck an' the men shits all over themselves . . . ahhh . . . haaaaa." He laughed like a goat.

"This here's my darlin'," Maxwell said, looking back over his shoulder trying to locate the girl in his hat. "Where are ya, darlin'?" The girl moved up beside him. "Here she is . . . ahh . . . haa . . . haaa. Darlin', say hello to these folks." The girl nodded.

Maxwell snatched his hat and put it on his head, setting it way to the back. "There a bathroom around here?"

"I think back there," I said.

"Come on, darlin'," he smiled at the fat girl, "le's see if you live up to yer reputation." He winked at me and ushered the girl back toward the hallway.

Hoot was still talking to the curly-haired writer, who glared at Maxwell as he walked across the room to the hall. Hoot finished the conversation and joined us; he was as drunk as Maxwell but more in control, or maybe more at ease.

"Hi, Hoot," I said.

Hoot was smoking a large cigar and wearing a gray Stetson Western hat with no crease. He was a tall, thick man topping six foot seven and weighing in excess of two hundred forty pounds. According to Maxwell, Hoot was good friends with Clinton Foote, our general manager, and on first-name basis with the league commissioner. Maxwell said that Hoot arranged girls and miscellaneous entertainment for the league brass and for top draft choices during the league wars.

"Mr. Elliott . . . how yew?" he said, removing his cigar as we shook hands. I turned and held my hand out toward Joanne.

"This is Joanne."

"Hidy, Miss Joanne," he greeted, tipping his hat to reveal a thick mop of straw-colored hair that easily covered his ears and collar.

Maxwell reentered the living room, his arm wrapped around his chubby companion. She was again wearing his hat. Their faces were sliced into teethy grins.

"It shore is a straaange life, but I loves it," Maxwell said as he approached. The girl laughed and then coughed and then cleared her throat. Maxwell gave her a sideways glance and grimaced at the sound.

Maxwell either hadn't noticed Joanne or it didn't register, because he said nothing to her.

"You were right, Hoot," Maxwell said. "I stood on the commode and watched in the mirror." The girl grinned and blushed.

Maxwell's hat was pushed down over her ears and all but covered her eyes.

The girl ran her tongue over her lips.

"C'mon," Maxwell said to me, his voice increasing in intensity, "we got a big black Cadillac and a big black driver and we're goin' honky-tonkin'." He grabbed our arms and started moving us toward the door.

"Darlin'," he said, stopping and turning to his chubby friend, "yer gonna have ta stay here." He reached over and plucked his hat from her head. "See that fella over thar." Maxwell pointed to the curly fellow who had demonstrated the jump pass. "He's a famous writer and ast me if he could meet ya. Just go over and introduce yourself and tell him I sent ya." He patted her on the head. Her face had fallen. "I'll call ya tomorrow."

Minutes later, we were downstairs heading for the limousine. The liveried chauffeur was polishing the hood when we came out of the building. The doorman tipped his hat to Maxwell, wishing him "good luck tomorrow."

"It's Sunday, general," Maxwell replied, "Sunday." He clambered into the back seat, banging his knee against a jump seat. We climbed in behind him and after a little jockeying for position, we were all comfortably situated.

I knew it was a mistake to travel around New York with Joanne. But it was too late to do anything, so I just got drunk and had a good time, as much of it as I remember.

First we went to an exclusive rather conservative discotheque and found Alan Claridge, his shirt unbuttoned to the waist and his fly open, dancing wildly with a forty-year-old woman in a gold lamé sheath dress. Andy Crawford was at a nearby table fondling someone else's date. Everyone in the place stopped momentarily to watch Maxwell walk to a table.

Claridge waved and began to pull off his shirt and unbuckle his belt.

"Crawford is here too," I told Maxwell. "I think we better get 'em back to the hotel. They seem to be in that mood."

Hoot instructed his driver to take Claridge and Crawford back to the hotel. Maxwell ushered them out, helping Claridge get his clothes back on, and told them he would meet them shortly at the hotel.

When Maxwell returned to the table, Hoot broke out some amyl nitrite and passed it around the table. We all sniffed deeply from the crushed capsule, then turned red and giggled insanely for several minutes. As we would start to come down Hoot would pop another capsule and the hysterics began again. Then Joanne leaped onto the table and screamed that nobody in the place, with the exception of us, was worth a shit. We had gone through a whole box when the headwaiter approached the table to tell us we would either have to stop throwing the exhausted capsules at the other patrons or leave.

A note arrived from a long table of people at the back of the room. They requested Seth to come and join them for a drink.

"Them folks wants ta drink with the King," Maxwell said, his voice in that peculiar rasp. "Who am I to disappoint 'em? I'm mere mortal flesh."

He got to his feet and ambled unsteadily across the dance floor toward the table of people, their heads all turned expectantly in his direction. A middle-aged man at one end of the long spread stood up to greet Seth. After a brief handshake, Seth pushed by the man and climbed on top of the table. Walking the length of the table, bending down to shake hands and introduce himself as "Martha and Duane's baby boy," Maxwell carefully stepped his alligator boots into every open-faced steak sandwich. Some of the people laughed nervously, but most just stared in stunned silence. Seth reached the end of the table and jumped down.

"Nice to meet ya'll," he said. "Ya'll ever in Dallas you be

sure ta come see me." He hopped back to our table on one foot.

"Now they kin tell their kids they met a star," Maxwell laughed, plopping down in his seat and cleaning his boots of A.1. Sauce with a napkin.

Hoot passed around a fresh amyl nitrite.

After the discotheque we stopped at a bar close to P. J. Clarke's. It was brightly decorated and had a live band. The customers, in costume, all stood around striking poses. The drinks cost $3.75 apiece. We ordered several rounds and finished Hoot's amyl nitrite, throwing the used capsules at a tall fellow in a purple ruffled shirt and a plumed hat. After several rounds of drinks (I lost count after five), we walked the check, running and leaping into the limousine and roaring away.

We ended up on the street in front of a place called Elaine's smoking twelve paper joints rolled by a friend of Hoot's.

I suggested trying some rolled in Tampax wrappers, but after being rudely rebuffed by several women in our search for Tampax, we gave up.

We headed back to the hotel around 5 A.M., dropped Joanne at the front and circled the block a couple of times before Maxwell and I stumbled out at the garage. While I said good night to the already unconscious Hoot, Maxwell sat on the curb and pulled off his alligator cowboy boots. He handed them to the driver.

"You're a goddam good nigger," Maxwell said. "Don't let nobody tell you different."

"Thank you, Mr. Maxwell." The black man smiled.

The big black car zoomed off into the dirty morning with Hoot asleep and drooling on himself in the back seat.

We slipped through the lobby and waited in front of the elevator for the door to open. When it did, we came face to face with coach Buddy Wilks. The former All-Pro running back was propped in the corner of the elevator. He was so drunk he could not move, his unseeing eyes wide open and filled with tears.

"Goddam fuckers," he mumbled, his tongue thick from alcohol. "Goddam fuckers."

"Hey, Buddy," Maxwell called and slapped him on the shoulder.

The coach cocked his head and attempted to focus on the quarterback.

". . . guys hate me, don'cha?" Buddy muttered, spittle running off his lip and onto his chin.

"Naw, Buddy," Maxwell soothed drunkenly, his hand still on the slobbering coach's shoulder, "we love you."

" . . . guys hate me . . . jealous . . . jealous fuckers." Wilks wiped his running nose with the back of his hand. Strings of mucus stretched out from his nose as his hand fell away

"B.A. too . . ." He slid slowly to the floor. "I'll show 'em . . . show 'em . . ."

The door opened at our floor and Seth and I staggered out. When the door closed, Buddy was lying on his side with his eyes closed.

SATURDAY

After two rings, I knew Maxwell wasn't keeping his end of the bargain and I answered the phone myself.

"It's ten o'clock. Good morning." I could tell by how fast the line went dead that she hadn't meant it.

The other bed was empty and I remembered that sometime during that ache-filled fog called sleep Maxwell had gotten up and gone to the bathroom. I moaned slowly to my feet. My hangover had increased my normal living pains tenfold. I shuffled to the bathroom, careful to keep my head lower than my shoulders to lessen the risk of blacking out.

I found Maxwell asleep by the commode, curled up on the bathmat and covered with towels. Blood was smeared on his lips and across his face. I despaired of standing and thumped down on the commode, holding my head. I nudged the unconscious form with my big toe, the only part of me not in terminal agony. Maxwell sat up quickly without opening his eyes. He pulled his knees to his chest and rested his head against them.

"Aaaaaaaahh, why did I ever leave Hudspeth County?" He wiped his hands across his mouth, licking his lips and tasting the blood. His eyes blinked open and he looked at the blood on his hand. "The ol' ulcer actin' up," he said.

"Jesus, do you think so?"

"I dunno. Anyway it's stopped." He looked around and tried to recognize his surroundings. He stared up at me. "Did I really eat the worm at the bottom of that bottle of mescal?"

I nodded.

"Aaggh." He spat on the floor a couple of times and then wiped his mouth with the back of his hand. "I feel like I've lived the whole of my life in Wichita Falls."

I wasn't sure what that meant, but from my memory of west Texas and the look of the white, blood-smeared, puffy-eyed face next to the commode, it couldn't have been good.

"That little man shit in my mouth again last night."

"Quit sleeping next to the toilet and maybe he won't." I held my cheeks with the palms of my hands and forced my eyes open. My eyelids felt like sandpaper. "Come on, the bus leaves at eleven."

We split a Dexamyl and I took a Number Four codeine. We dressed and went to have coffee. The morning toilet would have to wait until after workout.

I loved to walk through Yankee Stadium and look at the pictures of the sports immortals on the tunnel walls—Ruth, Gehrig, DiMaggio, Mantle. I wondered how many times they had felt as I did. Somehow, I felt closer to the greats when I was hung over.

The stadium was a ramshackle place, but I could feel the spirits in the rotting wood and stagnant water pools. Just as the new Dallas stadium would be ultramodern to the point of perversity, Yankee Stadium was a dead place, a thing of the past.

My locker was marked by a piece of white adhesive tape with my name written on it. Below my piece of tape was another bearing a different name, a remnant of the faded glory of last week's contest.

"Unitas," I said aloud. "Imagine that. Me an' ol' John sharing the same locker. Only in America. Unitas one day, feathers the next."

"What?" John Wilson, the safety man and real estate agent, looked up from emptying his equipment bag into the next locker.

"I'm a living example of the American Dream," I explained. "A man who, in any other time and place would be summarily executed, is allowed to share a locker with the fabled Johnny U."

"Terrific," Wilson responded, somewhat sardonically.

"Say," I asked him, "is your wife still pissed about the lipstick on your shorts?"

"What do you think?" He turned the bag upside-down and shook it into the locker.

"Tell her it's a mark from a Red Chinese laundry."

He threw a football shoe at me.

I stripped off my clothes, pulled on a supporter and a T-shirt and walked gingerly on the cold, damp concrete floor, back to the wooden tables near the showers. The area around the tables served as the training room.

"Can you rub me down, Eddie?" I asked. "I was mugged last night in Central Park. It left me pretty stiff."

"I hope you didn't try and run without warming up," the trainer shot back, keeping his eyes on the ankle he was taping. "That's a team fine." He looked up. "Let me finish taping. I don't wanna get analgesic all over my hands."

I walked back to my locker and emptied my bag into the metal cage. The workout would be short, mainly special teams, and I wasn't on any of them. I would get rubbed and wrapped, not taped. During the special-team drills I would jog around and try to loosen up, but do no full-speed running. The practice would last no more than forty-five minutes.

The trainer covered me with analgesic, rubbing my legs and back until I was on fire. When he finished wrapping my thighs and I had pulled on my sweats and warmup jacket, the locker room was empty.

As I climbed out of the dugout and ran to the back rank,

the team was forming up for calisthenics. Jim Johnson, the defensive coach, was lying in ambush watching for me, but I escaped the hundred-dollar fine by reaching the line before the exercises began. I returned his glare with a smile and the peace sign, and watched the veins pop out on his neck.

Maxwell and Tony Douglas led the drills. The big linebacker boomed out the cadence in his Mississippi drawl. We finished with ten jumping jacks and started to break into groups when Jim Johnson's marine corps drill-instructor voice halted everyone in midstride.

"Do 'em again," he screamed. "We're all supposed to count cadence together. Did you count, Elliott?"

He had me. I never counted. In fact, because of my back and legs, I was excused from most of the loosening-up drills. But I was trapped on the jumping jacks; I was supposed to do them and I was supposed to count. Counting together is good for team solidarity.

"You found me out, Jimmy," I said.

"We don't need a wise guy out here, Elliott," B.A. interjected. "If you can't do things with the team, get off the field."

I shut up and lowered my head.

"Okay. Everybody do 'em over," Johnson yelled. "You can thank Elliott for the extra work."

"Line it back up," Maxwell hollered, shaking his head at my getting caught. Douglas glared at me.

The ten jumping jacks were quickly dispatched, the cadence echoing loudly through the empty wooden stadium. When we broke into groups, I made a point of running past Johnson.

"I didn't count at all, sucker," I whispered to him loudly. "I just moved my lips."

"You son of a bitch!' He threw a football at me, just missing my head. I laughed and dodged down the field.

The practice went quickly. We were back in the locker room when B.A. announced that those who wanted to could ride the subway back to the hotel. The announcement seemed so strange that I laughed out loud. I was more surprised to find that Maxwell, Crawford, and I were the only ones to return on the bus.

The rest of Saturday was taken up with meetings and cat-naps. Maxwell took his understudy, Art Hartman, out with Hoot, saying he would return befrore the 11 P.M. curfew.

Joanne slipped up to the room around six, before her date with Emmett, and we screwed. It was pleasant, but seemed to lack much of its normal carefreeness. After she left, I decided that this trip marked the end. It no longer felt quite right. I wasn't sure why.

At eleven the trainers came around to hand out sleeping pills and take amphetamine requests for the morning. The butterflies were already stirring from their cocoons and were beginning to flap around. I tried to call Charlotte twice but got no answer.

I undressed, slipped into bed and studied my game plan to the sounds of the eleven o'clock news. My sideline adjustment against a roll zone was a turn in. *A building was blown up in Greenwich Village.* Against any shooting linebacker or safety blitz all but two of my routes automatically changed to quick down and ins. *Two policemen were shot from ambush while answering a disturbance call.* All wide receivers must pull up on deep routes against a three deep defense. *Two plastic bombs were found in suitcases in lockers in the International Terminal at Kennedy.* I closed my book and watched the weather forecast. Cloudy and cool for Sunday. Everything was in order.

It was 11:30 P.M. and Maxwell still wasn't back. He came in a half hour later.

"Bed check?" he asked, stepping inside.

"No. Not yet."

There was no bed check that night and we fell peacefully to sleep watching John Wayne slaughter the noble redman.

SUNDAY

Maxwell got the wake-up call after one ring. He groaned into the mouthpiece and then slammed the receiver back to its cradle.

"What time is it?" I asked, not moving my head from the pillow.

"Eight o'clock. Breakfast at eight-thirty, meeting at nine, nondenominational devotional at nine-thirty, Bullwinkle at ten. See, it all works out for those in the hands of the Lord."

Maxwell loved Bullwinkle Moose like he was kinfolks, and he worried whenever we played in a different time zone that team activity might be scheduled during "The Bullwinkle Show."

Seth crawled out of bed coughing and clearing great hunks of sludge from his breathing apparatus. He stumbled into the bathroom while I lay in bed and thought about my dream.

I had dreamt that I was late for the game and the bus had left without me. I couldn't find the stadium, although I could hear the noises of the game quite clearly. Finally I hitched a ride with Mickey Mantle, who told me Yankee Stadium was a nice place to visit, but he wouldn't want to live there. He dropped me at the stadium and disappeared. I started down the tunnel to the dressing rooms. The winding passages got very dark and I began to have difficulty keeping my eyes open. There were rats and spiders everywhere, but I could only glimpse them. Everything was dark and blurry. I kept running into giant spider webs, knocking hairy yellow-and-black spiders onto the back of my neck.

Then suddenly I was naked and standing in the dugout. The stadium was full and the game was in progress. I could see Rufus Brown, our clubhouse attendant, waving me to the other side of the field. He had my equipment and uniform. I started across the field and got caught up in the game. I was still naked. Maxwell threw me a pass but I wouldn't take my hands from covering myself. I was agonizingly embarrassed. The ball bounced off my face, breaking my nose. I could breathe again. I ground my jaw so hard from frustration and fear that all my teeth broke off. Then the tape around my thigh unwound and my leg fell off. I had the ball and I was crawling naked toward the end zone, still trying to hide by hugging my stomach to the ground. Then B.A. took me out of the game and told me to quit fooling around and made me sit alone on the bench. I was still naked and my nose was bleeding. Everyone was looking at me. . . .

"Come on, poot," Maxwell said, toweling off his freshly shaven face.

I jumped quickly out of bed and pulled on my pants.

"B.A. said we could wear turtlenecks, didn't he?"

"Yeah, but no love beads." He held one arm crooked over his head as he rolled on copious amounts of deodorant. It seemed peculiar, in light of the day's schedule.

The bulletin in the elevator listed Empire Rooms I and II as the locations for our meeting, pregame breakfast, and devotional. The rooms would also be used for much of the simple ankle and knee taping.

"MMMM . . . there's a delicious smell," I said, lifting my

nose and following it to the entrance of Empire I. "Eggs and analgesic. Just like Momma used to make."

I stopped at the doorway and checked out the tables set for breakfast. Most of the team was seated, waiting for the food.

Maxwell brushed past me into the room, singing. It was his favorite George Jones song.

> "*. . . a man come round today and said he'd haul*
> *my thangs away,*
> *If I didn't get my payment made by ten . . .*"

I stood in the entrance and surveyed the two rooms, waiting for Maxwell to choose what table he would grace while he took his pregame coffee and cigarettes. It was an important part of his game plan to choose the right table at which to smoke and drink coffee, tell jokes, and generally pump up the frightened men around him. The players he selected each Sunday were picked according to criteria known only to himself. We often split up at pregame meals because of my unpopularity with some of the men Maxwell chose.

The partition between I and II had been pushed back and the six breakfast tables were crowded into the front of Empire I. Near the partition several players in shirt sleeves and undershorts waited their turns to be taped.

My stomach began to churn as the endocrine glands redistributed vital juices for the coming contest. I yawned and stretched, suddenly feeling very tired, the first sign of nervous fear.

In Empire II, chairs, a blackboard, and B.A.'s ever-present portable podium were set up for the last-minute strategy review and the nondenominational team devotional.

Maxwell sat down with Jo Bob Williams, Tony Douglas, O.W. Meadows, and a couple of others. I walked to the nearest table and joined several blacks, including Delma Huddle and the wayward running back Thomas Richardson.

"Hey, Bubba," Huddle said, holding out his palm to be slapped. I obliged and the cold wetness of our palms made a soggy pop.

He was wearing a white silk shirt monogrammed on the cuff, a wide green tie, a light green cashmere coat, and boxer shorts. No shoes. No pants.

"Hey, man," he yelled at a rookie waiting by the partition for his turn to be taped. "I'm in front of you and don't let nobody in. Get me?" The rookie waved and nodded.

"How you feeling?" I asked Huddle, as I stood behind him to knead the muscles at the base of his neck. "Ready?"

"Yeah, Bubba. How 'bout you?" He reached back and tried to grab my balls. I jumped and he roared his high-pitched bursting laugh.

"I was ready there for a minute," I said, brushing my hand across the top of his woolly head and sitting down. My knee banged against a table leg and water spilled out of one of the metal pitchers.

"You ain't lettin' the Man get you down?"

I shook my head, a silent lie.

"Just settle down." Huddle smiled but his eyes remained serious. "How's the leg?"

"Feeling better," I reported, squeezing the quadricep of my right leg absently. "Gets to feeling too good they'll want to cut it off."

Huddle laughed again in his peculiar high-pitched giggle.

A heavyset waitress in a dirty white smock set a plate of scrambled eggs and steaks in the middle of our table. The traditional pregame meal was precooked steak and powdered eggs, proven to be among the worst foods a man can put in his stomach before extensive physical activity. They just lie there and putrefy, pregame fear having shifted the blood from the stomach to other parts of the body.

"Look at that, Bubba," Huddle said, pointing to a plate of food. The scrambled eggs were a light green. Hotel kitchens put food coloring in the powdered eggs to make them look yellow. Green isn't too far removed on the color spectrum. In Pittsburgh, the hotel dyed our eggs so yellow that Huddle donned sunglasses to eat them.

The sweating waitress delivered the green eggs to each

table, receiving treatment at the hands of Jo Bob and others similar to the harassing served up to the bus driver on the way in from the airport.

"Hey, lady," Jo Bob yelled, "was the chicken ready to lay these or did you go in after 'em? They don't look ripe to me."

The waitress kept her jaws clenched but moved her lips silently. Every so often she paused to wipe rivulets of sweat from her nose and forehead.

"Don't sweat in the scrambled eggs, Momma," Jo Bob sang out, stringing the words together like a song title. Several people across the room laughed.

When the last plate of eggs was deposited, there were murmurs and grumblings, but shortly the emerald eggs were consumed. They would lie quietly until the body could get around to digesting them. Or they would sit uneasily waiting for that incredibly tense moment just before game time when they would spout all over the locker room floor and any bystanders.

It was 9 A.M. I took the first of my day's dosage of codeine. I would take another at eleven and a third just before game time. Huddle watched me swallow the pills.

"Codeine?" he asked.

I nodded.

"Doesn't it make you sleepy?" Huddle asked, his eyes fixed on my face.

"No. Actually I feel pretty alert, just numb."

"You remember Jake?" Huddle asked.

I nodded again. Jacob Jacobs was a black running back who had come to Dallas in the middle sixties. When we got him he had been around nine years and was pretty beat up, but he still played hard if not too well.

"Jake used to take codeine and hearts," Huddle confided. "It made him feel nineteen and untouchable. He'd take five of each. He said it put ten panes of glass between him and everything else. The only thing was it made his eyes burn."

"Jesus, how strong were the hearts?" Hearts were Dexedrine or Dexamyl tablets.

"He didn't say. I think they were greenies, but I dunno. I don' mess with that shit, man."

"You were born perfect," I pointed out. "Some of us need to constantly make alterations or we don't make it." I smiled and threw my shoulders back. "I guess I'll have to try Jake's formula. I may have ten more years in me if I can just master the chemistry of this game."

"You shore are weird, Bubba."

"Hey," I said, the time just registering. "I thought we were meeting at nine."

"The Man has a special speaker for the devotional," Huddle explained, "and he can't get here till nine for breakfast."

"Who is it?"

Huddle's face opened into a ridiculous smile.

"Oh shit," I groaned. "Doctor Tom?"

Huddle toasted me with his coffee cup and nodded.

Doctor Tom Bennett was an enigmatic figure who had materialized in our training camp three years ago and had been haunting me ever since. Nattily dressed in cardigan sweaters and duck-billed golf hats he wandered around the dorm and was everybody's pal. He was a Doctor of Divinity and B.A. had invited him to address a team meeting on the miracles of God, Christ, salvation, and faith.

Using himself as an example, Doctor Tom explained the pitfalls of a lack of faith in the power of the Lord. He recounted how during his early ministry his modicum of faith caused him to be saddled with a tiny worthless congregation in northern Washington. Doctor Tom soon realized that to make it big he needed greater faith. He immediately got some. Rewards weren't long in coming. Soon our Doctor Tom commanded a large, wealthy congregation in Florida where he successfully led his flock in their struggle for salvation and security in the face of universal cynicism and ever-spiraling inflation. In return Doctor Tom received great personal satisfaction and a small percentage of a large ocean-front real estate deal.

Once a wealthy man, Doctor Tom set out to fulfill the bargain he had made with the Lord. In an even swap with God for salvation and its Puritan ethic ramifications, Doctor Tom swore an oath to the Lord Almighty on the blood of the crucified Christ that he would carry the mantle of Christianity without recompense to a congregation that desperately needed his divine guidance. He chose the National Football League.

B.A. and Doctor Tom became fast friends, Doctor Tom wanting to hang around football players and B.A. wanting to hang around God. B.A. took to wearing cardigan sweaters and golf hats and inviting Doctor Tom to give inspirational messages before important contests.

The Doc had tried several times to get me to attend the devotionals. In the first categorical rebuff, I explained there were other places God was needed more than in a hotel in Minneapolis, listening to some pompous fool refer to him as The Big Coach in the Sky. After that Doctor Tom took a chummier approach, directing the talk to young girls and drinking.

I always made it a point to talk as profanely as possible around the Doc. I would raise my eyebrows and wink at him, after making loud senseless denials of anything resembling a God, and I would always point out what a sucker Jesus was.

But in all fairness I must admit the Doc was a pretty good sport and quite fast on his feet. He had rescued me more than once when I was set upon in the middle of my mindless tirade by one or more of the larger and more pious members of the team.

B.A. stood up at the head table, a fragment of green egg in the corner of his mouth, and announced that Doctor Tom's schedule had required a slight shuffling on our part and that the meeting would begin at nine thirty-five with the devotional at ten.

I looked over at Maxwell, obviously struggling over the merits of Doctor Tom and the devotional versus the eternal verities of Bullwinkle and His Friends.

At ten o'clock, as the meeting ended, I walked out in my usual negative response to B.A.'s invitation "to those who would like to stay and hear the message." I gave the Doc a smile and a short wave as I crossed in front of the portable podium. Maxwell fell into step next to me.

"Jesus," Maxwell moaned, once we were in the hallway, "he really looked pissed."

"He'll probably let Art Hartman lead the Lord's Prayer. First, loss of grace, next, loss of position. It's a universal pattern, that's why the Commies are doomed."

Seth Maxwell walked to the elevator, his head down. "Why do I punish myself like this?" he asked himself over and over.

After "The Bullwinkle Show" I packed up, grabbed my record player, and caught a cab to the stadium. Maxwell stayed in the room and read the Sunday paper. He would ride out on the team bus at eleven thirty.

Because of serious injuries and the complexity of their treatment, nine players, myself included, were required to arrive at the stadium early so the trainers and team doctor could have enough time to effect repairs. A tenth player, Gino Machado, recently acquired from the Rams, came out early just to take his amphetamines and "get ready to kick ass." Machado would sit by his locker, his legs shaking uncontrollably from the speed surging through his brain, and talk like a top-forty disc jockey to anyone within earshot. I spent hours listening to him describe sex acts, fist fights, and ball games. His lips were white from constant nervous licking, his mouth stretched open from time to time in a grotesque, compulsive yawn, and his eyes rolled while he clenched and unclenched his fists. Every now and then, gripping his shoulders with his hands, he would hug himself and bend double as if trying to slow himself down. In the early season Texas heat, the trainers often had to pack Machado in ice after a game to cool down his incredibly overheated body.

On the first day of camp Machado took twenty milligrams of Dexamyl to run "B.A.'s Mile." The linemen had to finish the four laps around the track in six minutes and thirty seconds to prove they had come to camp in condition. Gino took four hearts before he left the locker room. He went blind on the third lap and fell down six times before he crossed the finish line. It took him over eight minutes but he finished. He lay in the dummy shack while everyone else went to lunch. He was still there when we returned for the afternoon workout.

The cab to the stadium took me through Central Park.

"You afraid you ain't gonna get a seat?" the driver asked. "You're goin' to the stadium pretty early."

"Yeah," I replied. "I know."

"I went to see them bums last week, when the Colts was here," he continued, alternating his attention between the road and the back seat. "The Giants stink. They ain't hadda good team since they got rid of Huff an' all them guys—remember? How can they run a football team and be so stupid?"

"The same way they run everything else, I guess."

"Well, them Texas boys'll kick their ass, I'll tell ya. I got twenty bucks on it."

"Invest your winnings in real estate," I advised.

Two cabs, doors open and trunk lids up, were parked at the player's entrance to Yankee Stadium. The trainers were unloading bags of tape and medication.

"Phil, grab a couple of these bags," Eddie Rand ordered as I stepped away from my cab.

"Sure." I shifted my flight bag to my left hand, tucked my record player up under my arm, and grabbed two black medical kits from the cluster stacked behind the cabs.

I started down the ramp toward the uniformed guard defending the entrance. As the distance closed between us he began to eye me nervously for some identification.

"Player," I said casually, looking him straight in the eye. He waved me past.

Just act like you belong. It was the advice my older brother had given me to get me into bars before my twenty-first birthday. It was the only thing he ever said that made sense. An All-American in high school and college, he graduated with honors and became a successful high school coach. Last spring he quit his job, left his wife and three girls and ran off with the senior-class valedictorian. She came back after three weeks. No one has heard from him since.

Instead of heading down the tunnel to the locker room, I turned up one of the ramps leading into the stadium seats. I walked down ten rows and sat. The ground crew was removing the tarpaulin covering the patches of green and brown that made up the playing field.

In a far corner of the stadium a high school band was countermarching to the shallow sounds of "Raindrops Keep Fallin' on My Head" done in march time. The band members were in full uniform but wore coats and sweaters against the damp morning chill. A row of shiny silver sousaphones executed the gyrations of a routine that seemed to combine the techniques of a marine close-order drill team with the intricate moves of Smokey Robinson and the Miracles.

Several rows in front of me a television-camera crew was setting up. The camera operator was talking into his headset to the director in the mobile van, discussing just what America was going to see today.

Near the New York bench three men stood in a semicircle, chatting and pointing to different parts of the playing field. One of the men was Frank Gifford. I didn't recognize the other two.

I sat for several minutes trying to imagine how I would look and feel down there on the field in a few short hours.

Two concessionaires in aprons and tricornered paper hats walked up and stood two rows in front of me. They surveyed the field.

"Hey—" the shorter of the two, a man in his forties, nudged his companion, "—that's Frank Gifford over there."

"Where?"

"There, the guy in the trench coat." The shorter man leaned over and let his friend sight down his arm and out his pointing finger.

"Oh yeah," the taller responded. "Hey—hey—Frank . . . Frank Gifford." Both men waved and called frantically.

Gifford heard his name and turned toward the sound.

"Hey, Frank," the shorter man shouted, "we need you out there today. Whattaya say? Huh?"

The man who for more than a decade had lived this city's

football fantasies waved back and returned to his conversation.

"What a great guy," the tall man said, as they turned back toward the tunnel entrance. "Just a great guy."

His partner seemed equally excited but a serious look chilled his eyes as the two passed me.

"You know," the taller huckster began, "somebody told me that he wears a hairpiece. Do you believe that?"

"Frank Gifford? Are you kidding?"

"I didn't believe it either."

"Not Frank Gifford."

They disappeared down the ramp.

I ran my eyes up and down the field, trying to fathom its condition. It looked soft, but I couldn't really tell anything until I got on it. I considered mud cleats, deciding to wait until after the pregame warmup before making up my mind. Combination baseball and football fields like Yankee Stadium were difficult to gauge during wet weather, some parts being wet and soggy, others dry and quite hard. It had something to do with the drainage being set up for baseball.

Mud cleats, helpful on wet, loose ground because of their excessive length, were a danger in dry areas for the same reason. In Cleveland I sprained an ankle by hitting the dry clay of the infield at full speed wearing mud cleats. Suddenly the consideration of which cleats to wear struck me as foolish. I wasn't even sure I would get into the game, let alone cover all areas of the field.

Standing up, I felt a stitch in my back. I remained in the aisle for several minutes, rotating my trunk and rubbing my back, trying to work out the muscle spasm.

They say you should quit when you still hurt on Sunday from last Sunday. I wasn't sure I wasn't still hurting from exhibition season. I entered the tunnel and began winding my way through the catacombs to the dressing room.

Clusters of men in paper hats and change aprons stood around talking and laughing. Rubbing their hands together against the morning chill, some of the men nodded hello, but most just stopped what they were doing and stared at me as I passed.

"Where the hell have you been?" Eddie Rand screamed as I entered the dressing room. "You've got all the flesh-colored tape."

"Sorry, Eddie," I said, tossing the medical bags on top of a blue equipment trunk. I walked to my locker and sat down.

My nervous system was beginning to take over, trying to get my body and mind into the right chemical balance to survive the afternoon with a minimal amount of damage, whether it was to be a physical beating on the field or mental degeneration on the bench. I was becoming extremely tired and wanted to lie down and pull a blanket over my head. Stretching and yawning, I stood up and began to undress.

Hopping from foot to foot because of the cold concrete against my bare feet, I checked around to see who else had arrived. Tony Douglas stood naked on one of the wooden tables, the trainer tightly strapping the inside of the linebacker's right knee. The knee was missing both inside and outside cartilage, and the medial ligament had been totally reconstructed with tissue from his thigh. Without elastic tape, Tony wouldn't be able to set foot on the field. It was a great invention. I have been making it on elastic tape—and codeine—for years.

Gino Machado was sitting on a towel, leaning back against an equipment trunk. By the look of his eyes and his tapping feet, he was already well into his day's dosage of Dexamyl. We exchanged silent waves, though we were not more than twenty feet apart.

I walked to my locker to sort my equipment, already neatly arrayed according to tradition by the equipment manager. Shoulder pads turned upside-down on the top shelf of the metal cage, with my newly polished helmet sitting in the neck hole. Hanging from hooks inside the locker were my game pants and jersey.

On the floor of the locker were neatly shined and newly laced game shoes and a tidy stack of miscellaneous knee, thigh, forearm, elbow, and hip pads. The hip and knee pads were squares of half-inch sponge rubber. The thigh pads were quarter-inch thicknesses of molded white plastic. I made the pads myself and if I was injured in a spot protected by my homemade pads I could be fined as much as five hundred dollars. But they were lighter, more maneuverable pieces of equipment. As injuries slowed me, I made it up by cutting down on the weight of my pads, either paring them down or discarding them altogether. If things kept up as they had been, I would soon be hitting the old gridiron stark naked.

"Phil," Eddie Rand yelled, "you ready?"

"Yeah."

With practiced efficiency he quickly taped my ankles, locking my left and leaving my right free. He used a base of elastic tape to allow more flexibility, then put the final straps on with white adhesive tape for extra support. He finished the second ankle and slapped the bottom of my foot. I rolled over on my stomach and he began spreading analgesic on the backs of my legs. Lifting my shirt, he rubbed the hot cinnamon into my back. At the end of the rubdown he slapped my ass and I immediately stood up on the table while he wrapped both thighs with Ace Bandages to retain heat and give additional bracing. When he finished, I stepped down, pulled a new elastic knee brace over my right knee, grabbed a roll of white tape and walked to my locker.

I dug inside my coat and grabbed a cigar and lit it. I turned on my portable stereo and began sorting through my phonograph records, looking for one that, in addition to the various tapes, wraps, balms, drugs, and chemicals normally produced by the organs of my body under stress, might put me in an advantageous psychosomatic condition in which to endure the afternoon. I selected Country Joe and the Fish.

"Gimme an F . . ."

I turned my game pants inside out and inserted the knee and thigh pads into their respective pockets and turned the pants right side out again. The thigh pads were in the wrong pockets; it often happened because turning the pants inside out disoriented my already stricken mind. I changed the pads and pulled the pants on and slid my game jersey over my head.

"Be the first one on your block
To have your boy come home in a box . . ."

The silver game pants had a satin front, but the backs of the legs were made of an elastic fabric similar to that used in ski pants. The pants fit snugly, like a glove, giving a strangely secure feeling, like being hugged by an old friend. They also gave my damaged legs the feeling or illusion of additional support.

"Whoopee we're all gonna die . . ."

I rummaged through the pads in the bottom of my locker and found the thin piece of molded plastic I had made to protect my crushed back. I slipped it into place beneath my jersey, securing it quickly with tape. No sense letting anybody see me do it. Country Joe and his pals blasted into the first of "The Streets of Your Town" as I spread a towel on the floor and lay down, my head resting on a pile of elbow pads.

"As I walk around the streets of your town
And try not to bring myself down . . ."

I stared up at the ceiling and listened to the other people in the dressing room: trainers, teammates, equipment men, lower-echelon stadium maintenance people chattering nervously about a variety of topics ranging from the coming game to "nigger pussy" to "The Carol Burnett Show." Joe McDonald and the Fish tinned out of the cheap speakers.

"The tears of the insane
bounce like bullets off my brain . . ."

I closed my eyes and tried to rest, the chemicals in my blood flashing on my eyelids images of pass patterns, defensive backs, wobbly passes, angry linebackers, and Charlotte Caulder.

I finished the cigar and the record started over. Sitting up, I pulled on my blue-and-white striped knee socks and taped them at the tops of my calves. I folded two strips of white adhesive tape in half lengthwise, leaving the sticky side out, and wrapped them around my legs just above the ankles. Then I drew my wool sweat socks on and up over the tape, squeezing them tightly against the strips with my hands. The tape would anchor the socks neatly in place and keep them from falling down during the course of the game; not a necessity but a definite plus for one who wants to look well groomed in front of fifty-six thousand attending people and untold millions of hypnotics watching at home. Nothing is more unsightly than sweat socks sliding down and bunching around one's ankles.

"New York City good-bye
New York City good-bye
Good-bye New York City . . ."

The outside door banged open and shut and a rush of frothing athletes, thinly disguised in suits and sport coats, came crashing into the dressing room. The stream of players so neatly dressed and carrying attaché cases looked like five o'clock at State Farm Mutual.

The sights and sounds of my arriving teammates increased my anxiety. One thirty P.M. eastern standard time steadily approached. My mind wandered over the game plan checking to be sure I recalled all the adjustments that made B.A.'s multiple offense so deadly.

"Normal people rush through the dawn
with their normal people faces on . . ."

I shut off the record player before B.A. sent an assistant over with a directive, but the music still bounced around in my skull, mixing with roll-zone tendencies, man-to-man coverages, and the anticipation of good-looking women in the stands within eyeshot of the field.

"Kickers, quarterbacks, and receivers on the field in fifteen minutes."

Sliding the kangaroo game shoes around my tape-encased feet, I carefully laced one. I pushed the lace through the patented heel-lock strap that ran across my Achilles tendon and tugged the strings until the strap pulled taut along the top of my heel and the shoe closed snugly around my foot. I repeated the process with the other shoe, stood up and stamped a couple of times to seat the shoes, and then clacked back to the training tables. The conspicuous click and added height of the cleats further increased my awareness of the coming kickoff.

"Goddam, Doc," John Wilson moaned. He was standing at one end of a wooden table grimacing while the team doctor probed the point of his right hip with a three-inch needle. Wilson had a hip pointer.

The needle slid easily into a roll of flesh at the top of the afflicted hip. The doctor moved the stainless-steel spine around, changing the angle of insertion five or six times and simultaneously pumping in several cubic centimeters of Novocain. He succeeded in deadening a large portion of the muscle.

Alongside the doctor, the trainer lined up a row of syringes filled with local anesthesia. Several nervous players waiting their turns milled around behind Wilson.

"How's it feel?" the doctor asked the scowling safety man.

Wilson, keeping one hand on his hip and the other on the table for balance, flexed from the waist like a ballet dancer.

"Fine," Wilson nodded. "I can't feel a thing."

"Good," the doctor said. "Next." He reached out to take a prepared syringe from the trainer and caught sight of me standing to one side watching. "How about it?" He held up the syringe.

"No thanks, Doc," I said, recalling my previous bout with his needle. "I'm trying to quit."

The last time he tried to block my back with Novocain he had used three syringes of the opiate and I made it only halfway through warmup before collapsing. I rubbed the spot absently, feeling the dead skin and sore muscles beneath.

I watched while the doctor quickly jammed another needle into Monroe White's thigh. Monroe sported a slight cut under his eye, a result of his short and furious fight with Jo Bob during Thursday's practice. I turned to leave.

"Phil," the doctor called, "wait a minute." He handed the used needle to the trainer and grabbed me by the arm, walking me into a corner. His eyes were on Monroe White, limping out toward the lockers. "Goddam goldbrickin' nigger."

"What?" I had heard what he said.

"That White," he said, pointing at the wide black back as it moved back into the dressing area. "He ain't hurt, just like all them niggers. Only place you can't hurt 'em is in the head."

I nodded.

"Listen," the doctor leaned close, "I don't think there's anything bad wrong with your leg. I know it hurts you but there ain't nothing worse you can do to it by playin' on it."

"That's what you said about my back."

"You're playing, ain't ya? Anyway I overheard the coaches talkin' and they're beginning to think you're doggin' it. Now you and I know better, but that's what they're saying, so go out and show 'em something today."

"Okay, Doc." I nodded, keeping my eyes fixed on the floor. He slapped me on the shoulder and walked back and grabbed a new needle. As I walked away he was shoving the shiny stainless-steel point into the top of Jo Bob Williams's shoulder. Jo Bob winced and screamed in pain.

I hopped up and sat on top of one of the equipment trunks and watched the eye blinking, jaw working, and lip licking that indicated several of my teammates were beginning to feel the effects of their amphetamines. O.W. Meadows was sitting on the floor rolling his head and jerking his shoulders, trying to loosen the speed-tightened neck muscles. Tony Douglas was sitting next to him rubbing his hands together as if they were cold. Both men's eyes were glassy.

Conrad Hunter walked in from outside, his cheeks rosy from the cold. He was smiling with anticipation. At his side was his friend, advisor, and constant companion Monsignor Twill of the Sacred Heart Catholic Church. The two men circulated rapidly around the room, slapping players on the back and giving smiles and words of encouragement. They missed me and continued to the training area, Monsignor Twill digging a Coca-Cola out of one of the ice chests and guzzling it down in one long swallow. Hot pipes, the sign of a long night of drinking.

Maxwell was sitting by his locker looking absently around the room, his mind already out in the stadium dealing with mud, wind, blitzes, zones, his teammates, and B.A.

I wandered into the bathroom to pee. All the commode stalls were closed. A row of stockinged feet with jockstraps and silver football pants hanging around the ankles testified to the effect of fear on the bowels. From the moment the team arrived at a stadium until we assembled for the pregame supplications, the commodes were occupied. The nauseating sounds and smell kept all but the most desperate at a safe distance. I held my breath, feeling the rise of panic as the capacity of my lungs threatened to be outstripped by the size of my bladder.

I clattered back into the dressing area and was hailed by Gino Machado.

"Elliott, gimme a hand."

Machado was trying to wind some tape around his forearm to secure a plastic forearm pad.

"Wind it for me, will ya?" he ordered, breathing heavy. He ground his teeth and tapped his toes rapidly.

"Tighter," he moaned, his huge pupils burning a hole in me. "Come on, asshole. Tighter."

"Jesus, Gino," I argued, "you're gonna get gangrene."

"Don't worry about it, fuckhead," he shot back. "Just wrap it tighter."

I complied, wrapping the tape so tightly around his forearm and pad that the veins on the back of his hand stood out half an inch. I hoped his fucking fingers fell off.

"Okay! First group on the field."

I fell in step next to Maxwell. We followed the tunnel to the dugout, both of us carrying blue warmup jackets over our shoulders.

"How you feelin'?" I inquired nervously, not really interested in how he felt.

"Awright," he answered absently, not bothering to look at

me. "B.A. gave me shit on the bus about walking out of the devotional."

"Did you explain to him about Bullwinkle?"

Maxwell gave me a blank stare, his lips curling with a hint of disgust. He shook his head.

Reaching the dugout, we stepped over a pool of stagnant water and up onto the field. It was chilly and we both slipped our jackets on, then broke into a jog. There was a scattering of applause among the fans already in their seats. Maxwell was a New York favorite.

When we reached our bench, Doctor Tom Bennett was standing there holding a ball.

"Missed you boys at the devotional this morning," Doctor Tom sang out, tossing me the ball with the commissioner's autograph on it.

"We were getting head from the maid in the linen closet," I answered, gathering in the ball. Doctor Tom laughed good-naturedly and nodded.

Throwing the ball back and forth, Maxwell and I slowly backed away from each other to a distance of about fifteen yards, where we stood and played catch, Maxwell loosening up his arm while I practiced different catches.

The sounds of cadence numbers and the heavy thunk of foot against ball filled the stadium as the kicking specialists worked out, getting the wind and range from different parts of the field. Vendors were already hawking and the public address system kept crackling on and off.

The field was soft where we stood, but one of the kickers said the infield and the ground inside the twenties was pretty hard. I decided against mud cleats.

The assembled fans began to cheer and boo simultaneously as the Giant specialists, quarterbacks, and receivers took the field. Tarkenton and Maxwell exchanged waves and Bobby Joe Putnam, a wide receiver, trotted over to shake hands. Bobby Joe had gone to Texas Tech.

"Howdy, Seth. Phil," Bobby Joe said. "How ya'll doin'?"

"Passable, Bobby Joe. How 'bout yerself?" Maxwell answered. We started a game of three-cornered catch.

"How's the new coach?" Maxwell asked. The New York team had fired their coach at the start of the regular season and the owner had hired the new coach from his team "family." An ex-player and all-round nice guy, the new coach was having great difficulty winning any games.

"He's a good guy," Bobby Joe responded, tossing me the ball. "You know, dumb like most of 'em and scared to death of Jerele."

Jerele Sanford Davis was the owner of the New York franchise and ruled it with an iron hand. Tyrannical and religious, Davis ran his team by the same principles that ruled Conrad Hunter. He differed from Hunter by not giving his coaching and management personnel as wide a latitude in running the team as Conrad did.

I tossed the ball to Seth.

"You know what Leon did the day Jerele announced he was the new coach?" Bobby Joe asked, giggling. "He called a meeting of the team, Jerele was there too, and stood up in the front and told us he wasn't gonna be a hard ass and from Sunday night to Wednesday we could drink and chase pussy as much as we wanted. That's exactly what he said, we could drink and chase pussy as much as we wanted."

"Sounds like my kinda coach," Maxwell interjected, zinging the ball to Bobby Joe. It bounced off his hands.

"Goddam, Seth." Bobby Joe complained, shaking his hands and bending down to pick up the ball, "no wonder you get so many drops." Bobby Joe threw the ball to me as hard as he could.

"Hey. What the fuck are we playing," I asked, rubbing my palm where the laces had hit, "burn out?"

"Anyway," Bobby Joe continued his story, "Jerele stood up at the back of the room and said that was bullshit. Nobody on his team was drinking or chasing pussy ever. Leon retracted his statement."

Seth shot the ball to Bobby Joe again.

"Goddammit, Seth. Cut that shit out. The fate of New York rests on these babies." Bobby Joe held out his hands for inspection.

"The fingers look a little stubby to me, Seth," I said. "What do you think?"

"Looks like the forepaws on a momma 'coon," Seth drawled. "Probably can't catch but if he does he runs to the nearest stream and washes the ball."

Seth and I laughed insanely, while Bobby Joe stood glaring good-naturedly at us. Finally we recovered enough to resume our game of catch and Bobby started another story about his new coach.

"After we lost to the Jets," he went on, "Leon came in and tol' us that the reason we lost was that nobody was sittin' in the right place on the bench. Now he's painted numbers on the bench and we all have assigned seats. Can you believe that?"

"Yes," Maxwell and I said together.

Bobby Joe threw the ball ten feet over my head, wished us good luck, and trotted, laughing, back to the end zone where his teammates had assembled.

"Nice guy," I said, watching Bobby Joe jogging to the end of the field.

"There ain't no nice guys," Maxwell answered, sounding foolishly like Leo Durocher.

The rest of our team was coming out of the dugout and running onto the field. They passed Seth and me, and began breaking into ranks for exercises. Seth jogged to the front to lead, while I walked slowly to the twenty-yard line, where the other members of my file would shortly assemble.

I could feel Jim Johnson glaring at me from somewhere in the press box as I sauntered to my assigned position and began to stretch my aching legs and back. The soreness wasn't acute, the nerves dulled somewhat by the codeine, but they still seemed unusually painful. I decided to increase my codeine dosage when we went to the lockers for the ritual.

Maxwell led us quickly through exercises, finishing with the usual ten jumping jacks. I started to count, then caught myself and remained silent for the rest of the drill.

We broke into passing groups. The temperature was in the high forties and it took a while for everybody but the speed freaks to warm up. But soon we were running deep routes and Maxwell was hitting with amazing efficiency.

"Phil," Maxwell ordered, "gimme a deep square in. I'll drop it right on the six."

He called the snap number, backed up ten yards, and planted, gathering himself to throw. I drove at John Wilson full speed, moving slightly inside, forcing Wilson to adjust his outside position. He showed no sign of favoring his recently anesthetized hip. By fifteen yards downfield I had moved a couple of yards inside and Wilson had turned, ready to run deep. I broke the pattern off square inside and simply ran away from the defender. The ball came on a straight line, between linebackers, never getting more than six feet off the ground. I took it in the chest, feeling the solid thunk. It had traveled better than twenty-five yards in the air, slamming into the left side of my chest, right on the six of my jersey numeral 86.

"Great shot!" I exclaimed, charged with the thrill of a perfectly executed play.

Maxwell couldn't do it again on a bet. But that was Maxwell's secret. He always knew when he could do it.

After we ran a few team plays, B.A. herded us back into the dressing room for the final prekickoff preparations and pep talk. Inside, everybody moved around nervously, a few guys puffing on cigarettes, a couple of last-minute bowel movements. Finally, B.A. called us all together.

"Okay, listen up," B.A. droned. "Don't forget to take your helmets off during the national anthem. And it wouldn't hurt some of you guys to sing."

We used to stay in the locker room until after "The Star Spangled Banner," then would come player introductions, toss of the coin and all that. But now the national anthem was last and we got typed instructions from the commissioner on how to stand and on what we should not do, such as picking our noses, or scratching our nuts. I tried to do at least one at every game.

It was part of the television package, the cameras moving

with deliberate slowness down rows of players, faces contorted with fear, speed, and attempts at remembering the words.

> *". . . Uncle Sam needs your help again*
> *He's got himself in a terrible jam*
> *Way down yonder in Vietnam . . ."*

The Blue Angels fly by, while Anita Bryant smiles. Flags waving, color guards standing, and men sitting in their living rooms trying not to raise their beer cans until the end, usually starting toward their lips on "home of the brave."

> *". . . There ain't no time to wonder why*
> *Whoopee we're all gonna die . . ."*

Sometimes when we were all lined up, neatly in a row, helmets on our hips, I would have to fight the urge to put my arms around the men flanking me and do a fast series of high kicks.

"And Phil," B.A. called, his eyes searching me out. My heart accelerated at the sound of my name. "You stay close. I may need you to run plays."

I glanced at Billy Gill and watched his face fall. B.A. hadn't bothered to tell him. It was okay with me, I couldn't stand Gill.

"Okay, boys. Let's bow our heads," B.A. ordered.

Immediately half of the team fell to one knee, resting the bridges of their noses on curled fingers in a classical meditative pose. The rest remained sitting or standing with heads bowed and eyes closed.

"Well, boys," Monsignor Twill's voice bounced around the silent concrete room. "This morning you heard Doctor Tom Bennett, now how about a word from the competition?"

A titter of laughter flitted through the ranks.

"Dear Lord, please be with these boys as they go out today to do battle." The priest was dressed in the standard black smock and he seemed to glide around the room as if on roller skates. He had his eyes closed and his head raised. His face seemed to glow. Every now and then as he floated around the room, he would squeeze one eye open to plot his course and to avoid stumbling over one of the kneelers.

I looked at B.A. He had his eyes closed, his hands clasped, his head bowed, and his hat on. His pants legs were rolled up a couple of turns to reveal crepe-soled shoes and white sweat socks. I wasn't sure whether it was the cold or emotion, but his cheeks were flushed.

The prayer thanked the Good Lord for giving us the chance to play football in the United States of America, and asked his protection, reminding him that none of us care about winning or about ourselves (a little reverse psychology on the old Master Workman). I almost laughed at the mention of our sound minds and bodies. Finally the Monsignor blessed the whole Hunter family and invited us to join in the Lord's Prayer.

I kept my eyes open, looking around, to make sure I didn't get caught not praying. A curl of smoke ascended from behind an equipment trunk. It was Maxwell sitting on the floor, smoking a cigarette and watching the smoke drift aimlessly upward into the maze of concrete supports and electrical conduits.

". . . the kingdom and the power and the glory forever. Aaamen."

The supplicants rose to their feet and broke into a long animal roar, preparing for battle, as the Monsignor had so eloquently put it.

"Let's kill those cocksuckers!" Tony Douglas screamed, leaping up from his knees. He caught himself and glanced sideways at the Monsignor, who was standing near him. "Sorry, Monsignor."

"That's all right, Tony," the Monsignor replied. "I know how you feel."

"Okay," B.A. yelled. "Defensive team out first." We had lost the coin toss, so the defense would be introduced.

The starting players elbowed their way to the front of the

crowd milling by the door. When O.W. Meadows reached the door he jerked it open and the team filed out and down the tunnel to the dugout entrance.

A fat bald man with bad breath and a walkie-talkie lined up the defensive starters according to the list he had on his clipboard. He belched loudly, then said something into the walkie-talkie. Moments later an electronic voice introduced our starting team to a chorus of boos.

After the introductions the rest of us climbed up through the dugout and trotted to the bench to join the wild-eyed defense, already busily banging the shit out of each other in a last-minute frenzy to ready themselves.

Maxwell picked up a ball and waved me behind the bench, where we played catch during the fraudulent coin toss. As the crowd roared over New York's good fortune, the public address system announced that a National Guard unit from New Jersey would guard the colors and a nightclub singer from Stamford, Connecticut, would sing the national anthem. I thought momentarily about Charlotte and the late John Caulder.

While the teams lined up on the sidelines for the anthem, Maxwell and I stayed behind the bench. I began to toss the ball nervously from hand to hand, dropping it twice. I couldn't remember any of the plays, and I was beginning to regret not wearing mud cleats. The field would certainly get soggier as the day progressed.

I dropped the ball again and when I bent to pick it up, a twinge of pain in my lower back reminded me I had forgotten my codeine. I panicked and walked several strides toward the rigid trainers (standing like seabees on parade in their white duck pants and shirts) before I realized the crowd was only at "ramparts' red glare." I was the only person in the stadium not at attention. I flinched and expected the color guard to open fire on me at any moment. I continued on to the end of the bench and stood behind the trainers, waiting for the anthem to end.

There was a general uneasiness in the stands as the crowd

finished a full line ahead of the Stamford songster. The noise of the crowd erased the last four words from his lips and threw countless beer drinkers across the country out of sync.

I smiled at the confusion, scored two codeine, washed them down with Gatorade and went back to our game of catch.

The team was huddling on the sidelines, the coach giving last-minute encouragement, and everybody stacking their hands on top of other guys. It was a tradition I avoided since discovering in high school that the coach said the same thing every week.

"Hey, man," I said, tossing the ball to Maxwell, "have a good one."

"Uh-huh," he responded, tossing the ball back.

The crowd bellowed as our kicker bore down on the ball, the roar increasing as the ball sailed through the air. It sounded as if they were surprised he hit it. They apparently knew about our kicker. The sounds of the crowd, although having a definite pattern, don't seem to coincide with their wishes. The clamor rose again as the New York receiver caught the ball and moved upfield. The noise reached its peak as our coverage team knocked the shit out of him.

As the eleven men on the New York offense huddled in the middle of the field, I watched the other twenty-nine men walk to the bench to find their numbers and sit down. I pointed this out to Maxwell. He didn't seem interested.

On first down, New York ran an unsuccessful trap for a loss of two yards. Maxwell quit playing catch, picked up his helmet, and walked to the sideline. I moved close to B.A. by the phone table and watched O.W. Meadows bat away a second down pass. On third, New York lost two on a draw when the back fumbled the handoff in the backfield. The crowd booed their offense to the bench.

New York lined up to punt. Alan Claridge and Delma Huddle were back to receive as Bobby Joe Putnam lofted the ball from his twenty-five. Alan caught it and started back upfield. He was turning the corner, trying to get behind his blocking wall, when a New York tackler hit him head on. The ball popped straight up, hanging in the air an eternity, and then dropping straight into the arms of another New York player. He looked around startled and then ran the thirty yards to our end zone unmolested. B.A. threw his hat down and glared Claridge to the bench.

After the official time-out to sell beer and shaving lotion, the crowd settled down. B.A. put his hat back on, and New York kicked off. The kick was short and Huddle raced forward to grab it. Misjudging his stride and the condition of the field, he overran the ball, tried to stop, and slipped down. The ball bounced off his shoulder. New York recovered on our nineteen. B.A. hit himself in the forehead with the palm of his hand and walked to the phone table. He picked up a headset and screamed at one of the assistants in the press box.

New York quickly lined up at scrimmage, snapped the ball, and ran a reverse, handing off to the split end. Nineteen yards later the split end slammed the ball onto the end zone grass. He was so excited, he raced to the bench and leaped on Tarkenton's back. They both fell in a heap on the sidelines. New York 14-Dallas 0.

Maxwell stood at the far end of our bench. He stared at the scoreboard. The kickoff went out of the end zone and Maxwell walked slowly toward the forming huddle.

"Elliott." B.A. called me to his side as the huddle broke. He put his arm around my shoulder and leaned close to my ear, ready to send me in with instructions.

Stepping quickly under the center, Maxwell went on a quick count, not bothering to set the line. He caught the defense in the middle of a shift. Both backs faked into the line, while Maxwell kept and rolled to the weak side, laying the ball out in front of Delma Huddle five yards behind the New York secondary. Delma stepped out of bounds on the five.

Seeing the completion, B.A. pushed me away and strode down the sideline yelling encouragement.

A dive play didn't fool anybody. On second and goal, a picture pass over the middle hit Billy Gill in the face and fell harmlessly to the ground. Maxwell had barely gotten the ball off ahead of a blitz and sat on the ground watching Gill walk back to the huddle.

I could tell by the third down formation it would be another pass to Gill. It was like Maxwell to come right back to a receiver who had just dropped a pass. He did it for me often enough. I tried not to hope Gill would drop the difficult outside throw, but I did, and he did.

The field goal team passed Gill and Maxwell as they left the field. Gill extended his arms to show Seth how far he thought the ball was off target.

The field goal was blocked and New York recovered on their own fourteen.

Tarkenton was unsuccessful in moving the Giants the first two downs, and on third and nine his deep post was intercepted by safetyman John Wilson and returned to the New York twenty.

Maxwell took the offense back on the field, turning back to yell at B.A. and point at me. The first play was a strongside pitch to Andy Crawford trying to sweep the end. Morris, New York's strong safety, came up fast behind his linebacker and quickly forced the play, dodging the tackle's block and stopping Crawford at the line of scrimmage.

"Elliott. Elliott." B.A. was motioning for me. "Get in there and tell Seth to watch for a sara blitz."

Gill saw me coming, dropped his head, and trotted off the field. Neither of us said a word as we passed.

I stepped into the circle of heavily breathing men. Maxwell was down on one knee looking up at me expectantly.

"All he said was to watch for that strongside blitz." I shrugged.

"Okay," he said. "Fire ninety T pull pass. Wing zig out."

It was a good call, faking the fullback into the line while Crawford flared wide from the halfback spot with the tackle pulling and leading, faking a run. If Morris, the strong safety, forced the run fake, I would be man to man against Ely, the cornerback. Ely's tendency to look constantly into the backfield should set him up perfectly for Maxwell's pump fake on the inside move of the zig out.

Schmidt, the center, snapped the ball. The tackle, the two backs, and Maxwell executed their fakes, forcing the strongside linebacker and safety to play the run and leaving me one on one against Ely.

I drove down hard slightly to the cornerback's inside, making him adjust his outside position. He was inching in, afraid of the quick-breaking post route. The play fake had robbed him of any inside help. At six yards I made my inside break. Ely went with me driving strong toward me trying to close the distance between us. He was covering the quick post well. I swiveled my head looking into our backfield. Maxwell brought the ball up high and made a strong pump fake at me. I planted my left foot and drove back outside, passing under Ely, still covering the inside move.

"Goddammit," Ely said as I slid beneath him and headed at a forty-five-degree angle for the sideline.

As he released the ball, Maxwell was hit from the blind side and the pass took off. I turned quickly back to my left, diving for the ball as it wobbled toward the ground. I caught it with my right hand and bounced into the end zone on my head and left shoulder. Sitting up, I checked for flags. Seeing the official with his hands up, I slowly got to my feet and started toward the bench, where Maxwell stood smiling with his hands on his hips.

B.A. would leave me in until I made a mistake. I would try not to make any.

The defense held New York again on the next series, and, after a fair catch by Delma Huddle, we took over on our thirty-five.

There was an official television time-out as we were forming our huddle on the twenty-five. Maxwell stood back on the twenty alone looking toward the other end zone. The rest of us milled around giving each other encouragement. The whistle blew and Schmidt, the center, raised his hands and called the huddle on him. We were all waiting expectantly when Maxwell stepped back into the circle. He was singing.

"It wasn't God that made honky-tonk angels . . . I shoulda knowed that you'd never make a wiiiife . . ." He stopped, looked around the huddle smiling, and called a play.

During that series of downs Maxwell was superb, mixing

his passes and runs, and in ten plays completed the drive with an audible pass to Delma Huddle. The split end stole the ball from the hands of Davey Waite, New York's right cornerback, for fifteen yards and the score. I had two catches during the drive, for eight and fifteen yards. The fifteen yarder was a good catch, going over the top of two defenders. Both catches were third downs. I was having a good day.

We went to the locker room tied 14-14.

The tops of the equipment trunks were covered with cans of Coca-Cola and Dr. Pepper. The Cokes were disappearing quickly. As far as I knew, Maxwell, Jo Bob, and O.W. Meadows were the only Dr. Pepper drinkers.

I sat in front of my locker wiping the sweat from my eyes and trying to catch my breath. Ever since I had been benched, I had trouble getting my second wind. Sometimes I thought it was conditioning, other times panic.

Several players were sprawled around the floor smoking cigarettes and coughing. Maxwell sat down next to me with a lighted cigarette and a Dr. Pepper.

"All I need now is a moon pie," he said, grinning and dropping his voice to a rasp, "and halftime would be hog heaven." He was confident and it was contagious. I felt my spirits rise.

On the blackboard was a list of the first half Giant defenses. B.A. and Jim Johnson were standing beside the board studying them and listing the offensive formations we would use the second half to penetrate those defenses.

Our defense was huddled in the back of the dressing room considering the most systematic way to stop Tarkenton's scrambling. Except for that and the one end around, the New York offense had been powerless.

Over by the wooden tables, the trainers were patching a hole in the bridge of Jo Bob's nose. His helmet had smashed down and gouged out a quarter-sized hunk of flesh from between his eyes. Red rivulets had been running down both sides of his nose since the start of the second quarter. It looked as if he was crying blood. The doctor was bent over John Wilson, shooting his hip full of Novocain again. Three or four others were waiting their turn for treatment, blood pouring from torn flesh and joints swelling as body fluids pumped out of mutilated vessels.

The cigarette smoke began to get thick and I moved back to the showers to get some air. I took two more codeine.

Halftime was just long enough for muscles and ligaments to stiffen, while America sat and watched Dick Butkus shave without water. Many teams lost their momentum at the half, slowed by too many cigarettes and too much advice.

I watched O.W. Meadows down two fifteen-milligram Dexamyl Spansules. The pills wouldn't start working until the fourth quarter and maybe not until after the game. Dexamyl Spansules were one reason why Meadows never shut up all the way home after a road game. Spurred on by a goodly amount of bootlegged liquor, he would babble incredible shit at the top of his lungs about his personal philosophy of life, which fell somewhere between Spartacus and the Marquis de Sade.

I walked nervously into the bathroom and met John Wilson as he came out wiping his hands on the front of his silver pants.

"Pissed all over 'em," he said, holding the hands out for my inspection.

Most of the team was up and milling around. The coaches were still next to the blackboard talking over last-minute strategy that would be forgotten as soon as we hit the field.

Alan Claridge lay face down on a table while the doctor probed and prodded his right hamstring. Finding the knot, the doctor held his thumb on it and reached for a syringe. He drove the needle deep into Claridge's leg, moved it around, and emptied the syringe into the muscle. Repeating the procedure twice more, he deadened a large portion of the hamstring. If Claridge reinjured the leg in the second half, he wouldn't know until it was too late, but with luck he would finish the game with little problem.

The referee stuck his head in the door and signaled five minutes remaining in the halftime. As he opened the door, I could hear the distant strains of "Raindrops Keep Fallin' on

My Head." I hoped everything was going off like clockwork for the boys with the sousaphones.

"Okay, listen up," B.A. said, walking to the middle of the room. "We've had some bad breaks out there, but we've come back and it's a brand-new game. We receive this half, so let's take it to 'em. The same team that started the game starts the second half."

Since Gill was the only starter on the bench, it would have been easier just to tell him and me. But B.A. didn't believe in dealing in personalities.

The crowd was back from the hot dog stands and America had returned safely, if somewhat confused, from CBS Control, when we took the field for the second half. The shadow of the stadium had moved almost halfway across the playing field, adding a dimension of time to the vacuum of fear. It was beginning to get cold and the sky was a fast-darkening gray.

The third quarter went quickly, with me alternating my attention from the field to the clock, hoping New York would get out ahead and I would get back into the game. The shadow steadily moved across the yardlines.

The Giants didn't move in the third quarter and Gill played a steady game, catching a nice turn in and a difficult sideline. I waited vainly for a signal from B.A. to carry in a play. Feeling powerless as my fate was being decided by twenty-two other men, I sat silently hating football, B.A., Conrad Hunter, Maxwell, my teammates, and the color guard from New Jersey. I could do nothing but wait and wish bad luck on my own team.

Near the end of the third quarter, Crawford fumbled a pitchout and my spirits rose. The Giants recovered on our thirty-five. Three plays later our defense had pushed them back to the forty. I could feel B.A.'s eyes searching me out as the ball hit the crossbar and bounced over. New York 17-Dallas 14.

"Elliott."

That familiar cry, a cloud of dust, and a hearty hi-ho.

I turned my smile into a grimace and walked quickly to his side, trying my best to look as dedicated as I felt.

"Go in for Gill on the next series," he said, never taking his eyes off the field.

"Yes, sir," I said, immediately changing my allegiances and looking for Maxwell to discuss how we could salvage a victory. He was at the phones talking to a coach in the press box. His face was ashen and he was talking rapidly.

"Goddammit," he shouted into the phone, "I haven't had time to throw a deep zig out all day, maybe that's why they ain't coverin' it. Fuck you, don't tell me, you cocksucker, tell your fuckin' lineman."

Slamming down the earphones, Maxwell took a cup of water from one of the trainers. Looking over the rim of the cup, he watched me approach. The cup came away from his face.

"You in?" he asked, his breath coming in gasps. I nodded.

"Good. I wanna try and run wide and I want you cracking back on Whitman."

That news took the edge off the thrill of playing. It wasn't the fear of hitting the 235-pound linebacker, although that was substantial. It was the fear of missing him. If I missed and Maxwell didn't run me off the field, B.A. certainly would. The only way I could be sure of making the block was to spear him with my head; for me, it was the surest of open field blocks. I would dive headfirst at his knees, making it next to impossible to miss. The drawback was that I wouldn't have any control over where I took the blow—head, face, neck, back. It all depended on whether Whitman saw me sneaking back down the line at him and what kind of evasive technique he used if he did.

I watched Claridge bring the kickoff out from three yards deep in the end zone. Reaching the twenty-yard line, he suddenly straightened up and grabbed the back of his leg. He went rigid and as he fell forward Bobby Joe Putnam hit him full speed flush in the face with his headgear.

Seeing the ball torn loose elated me for an instant. Then

guilt washed over me as I realized I was back in the game and had changed sides. I felt as if I had wished the fumble. I felt no better when Tarkenton scrambled to the five on the first play from scrimmage and the quarter ended.

The fourth quarter started. We were trailing 17-14 and New York had the ball, first and goal, on our five. Tarkenton tried to roll out, was trapped, and reversed his field back to the twenty-five, dancing around our exhausted defensive linemen for a full thirty seconds, finally making it back to the ten. New York was penalized for holding the next two plays in a row, and on second and goal from the forty Meadows trapped Tarkenton back at the New York forty-five. The next play we were called for pass interference and New York took the five-yard penalty and automatic first down.

They stayed on the ground the remainder of the drive, pushing out three first downs, getting the final yards on fourth down each time. They stalled on our eighteen and settled for a field goal. New York 20-Dallas 14.

I moved around the sidelines to loosen up, waiting for the network to return the slightly altered television audience so New York could kick off. Several people were standing over Claridge, who was stretched out face down on the bench. The doctor was digging his fingers in the hamstring he had anesthetized at halftime.

"See," the doctor said, "feel this. The hole? I can put my four fingers in it. It's torn pretty bad."

Claridge had his face turned away, into the back of the bench. He appeared to be in great pain, mumbling and crying apologies for the fumble. I knelt down next to him and put my hand on his shoulder. I shook him gently. I was going to explain that New York only got a field goal and we would get that back this series. I was again amazed at how quickly the team spirit possessed me when I was in the game.

Claridge turned to me; he was covered with blood. His double bar mask was shattered and his face was swollen and discolored a purplish-black. It seemed lopsided, twisted into a grotesque scowl, the running blood continually changing the expression. His nose was smashed flat and split open as if someone had sliced the length of it with a razor. The white cartilage shone brightly from the red-black maw that had been his nose. His eyes were wide and bright but seemed sightless. He tried to say something, raising his hand, but it was lost in a gurgle as black blood poured from his mouth.

"Goddam," I screamed. "Goddam, somebody get over here and fix his face!"

Claridge had apparently gotten off the field under his own power and collapsed on the bench. Face down was the only way he could keep from strangling on the blood. I held his head up slightly, gripping his headgear through the earholes.

My cries brought several people and directed the doctor's attention from one end of Claridge to the other.

"Did he bite his tongue?" The doctor shoved a finger into Claridge's mouth and searched for his tongue, making sure he hadn't bitten it off or swallowed it. "We'd better get him to a hospital."

"What happened?" B.A. was peering over the huddle around Claridge.

"Smashed up his nose pretty bad," the doctor said. "Better take him to the hospital."

"Oh." B.A. nodded, and turned back to the field.

The crowd noises indicated America had returned to her living room and New York was about to kick off. Backing away from the mutilated man, I heard the kick but couldn't take my eyes off the black blood running through the slats in the bench and into the damp sand below.

The ball sailed out of the end zone and I walked slowly alongside Maxwell to the huddle at the ten-yard line.

"Jesus," I said, recalling the face that didn't resemble Claridge and the pitiful mindless eyes, "did you see Claridge's face?"

"I ain't got time to worry about that shit," he said, his mouth drawn and his eyes tired. "If you can't take it . . ." He broke into a trot and hurried to the huddle before he finished.

I followed a few steps behind.

The men in the huddle were tired and openly hostile to

each other, the day's frustrations pushing several to the breaking point. The spirit and attitude had degenerated markedly from the first half.

"Goddammit, Andy. Hold onto the fuckin' ball this time."

"Fuck you, Schmidt. You just snap the ball, I'll take care of myself."

"All right, quiet down," Maxwell instructed angrily, kneeling into the huddle. "I'm the only one that talks in this huddle. All you guys shut up unless I ask you somethin'."

I looked around the huddle at the battered, bruised, and exhausted men, some already worrying about mistakes they would have to explain next Tuesday. Scared to death and angry, it would be a miracle if they could even get off on the same count, let alone outthink, outmaneuver, and outmuscle the men of similar talent across the line.

The shadows of the stadium had covered the field, adding further gloom to an already dismal afternoon.

"All right," Maxwell ordered. "Red right dive forty-one G pull. On two."

It was a simple trap up the middle. Jo Bob Williams jumped offsides. We walked back five yards.

"Goddammit, Jo Bob, pay attention to the count."

"Shove it up your ass, Schmidt. Who died and left you in charge?"

"Okay, I'm telling you guys," Maxwell shouted. "You better shut the fuck up in my huddle."

The huddle was silent as the quarterback scanned the grimy, sweaty faces. The gouge in Jo Bob's nose had opened up again and the blood was running into his mouth, turning his lips shiny red. He licked them nervously.

"Okay, Brown right dive forty-nine G take. On three."

It was a pitchout with a guard lead, coming off a fullback slant fake over the tackle. We ran it from a set backfield and the key block was our tight end against their defensive end Deyer. Deyer made the tackle for a two-yard loss.

"Jesus Christ," Crawford yelled, straightening his helmet as he regained his feet. "What the fuck is goin' on?" He wobbled back to the huddle, spitting out grass and mud.

"Sorry, Andy."

"Fuckin' sorry ain't gonna get it."

"Come on. Knock it off—"

"All right," Maxwell screamed. "This is the last time I'm gonna say it. Shut the fuck up in my huddle."

"If the dumb cocksuckers would do their jobs." Bill Schmidt, the center, was talking. Because he was a member of the original expansion family and worked for Conrad Hunter personally in the off season, Schmidt considered himself a player-coach and the leader of the offensive line.

"Shut your mouth, Schmidt," Maxwell ordered, "or you're off the field."

"Bullshit, I am," Schmidt shot back, glaring at the quarterback.

Maxwell looked up, shocked, and returned Schmidt's gaze thoughtfully for a few seconds, then shook his head and stepped from the huddle. He walked in measured steps to the referee and then on to the sidelines.

The official signaled a Dallas time-out. The huddle dissolved into a group of pointless men, pulling off their helmets and kneeling down, or standing and looking around aimlessly, waiting for Maxwell to return. Nobody said a word. I looked over at Delma Huddle and he flashed a big smile and gave me the thumbs up sign. I smiled back. Looking up into the stands at the mass of gray dots that were faces, perched atop flashes of colors that expressed their egos, I suddenly realized how peculiar we must look. I thought of Al Capp shmoos paying six dollars a head to watch and scream while trained mice scurried around in panic.

Eddie Rand, his whites smudged and bloodied at the end of a long day, started out on the field with towels and water. Maxwell stopped him and sent him back to the sidelines.

B.A. walked a few steps onto the field to meet with Maxwell. Neither man looked at the other, Maxwell had turned almost away from his coach and seemed to be staring out at the milling, disorganized rabble that was his command. B.A. was looking down to one end zone and the scoreboard. The stadium band broke into a halting "Tea for Two Cha Cha." Maxwell suddenly whirled around and pointed his finger directly into B.A.'s face. The coach dropped his head momentarily, then nodded and turned back to the bench. Maxwell returned to the huddle.

"Schmidt," he said, matter-of-factly, "you're out."

Marion Konklin, a backup guard who doubled at center only in practice, lumbered onto the field.

Schmidt stared at Maxwell with pure animal hatred. Maxwell turned his back and stepped into the huddle already forming around Konklin. The veteran center turned and walked rapidly to the sidelines, throwing his helmet into a crowd of his teammates. The row of players lining the sidelines opened up slightly to dodge the helmet and let Schmidt pass, then closed as the furious man disappeared.

"All right, goddammit," Maxwell ordered. "This time we go. I wanted you out here, Konklin. Don't lemme down. You know what to do on a draw delay trap?"

It was third and thirteen.

"I'm not sure."

Several players coughed and moved uneasily.

"Just set for pass. Then fire out and get the middle linebacker. It's no sweat," Maxwell reassured the frightened substitute.

The whistle blew, signaling time back in.

"All right. Red right draw delay trap on two. Got it Marion? On two."

Maxwell stepped up behind Konklin and patted him reassuringly on the hip. The terrified center nearly leaped into New York's secondary. Maxwell shouted out the defensive alignment, set the line, and stood scanning the linebackers and deep backs. The middle linebacker moved up into the line showing blitz. I watched Maxwell as he considered an audible against the blitz. Konklin's legs started shaking slightly. Maxwell decided against the audible. Konklin would certainly miss it. Maxwell was gambling the linebacker was faking.

By the time Maxwell called the second hut, Konklin's legs were shaking noticeably. He slammed the ball up into Maxwell's hands and shot into the middle linebacker. He forgot about waiting to show pass set. It couldn't have worked better if it had been executed correctly. The straight power block caught the linebacker guessing. He had been expecting a pass or at least a pass set. The block caught him totally unprepared and he went right over backward with Konklin on top of him. Crawford carried for fourteen and the first down.

"That's a start. That's a start," Maxwell chattered confidently, clapping his hands and smiling broadly. He slipped into a heavy Texas drawl. "We're gonna run an' tho' this ball rat down thar thoats."

The huddle formed around Konklin, who was smiling broadly as everyone congratulated him. The energy was returning.

"All right. All right." Maxwell knelt back into the huddle. "Fire draw forty-one Y zig out on two. Now come on, you guys. I didn't leave them sand hills jest to come to the big city an' git beat." The huddle broke with a low grunt.

Maxwell hit Delma going out of bounds on the New York thirty-five. They had two men on him when he caught the ball.

The sound waves from fifty thousand diaphragms blew through our bodies. It was innervating. My stomach started to churn violently. I needed to evacuate; the pressure was intense. I farted and felt better.

"Who the hell did that?"

"Goddam."

The huddle started to break up as players fanned at the air in front of their faces and scowled with disgust.

"All right you guys. Get back in here," Maxwell ordered. "Jesus, who did that?" He looked around the huddle. I looked accusingly at Crawford next to me. "Okay," Maxwell began again. "Red right freeze protection. Wing out at six yards. You linemen on the strongside cut block to get their hands down."

I took long strides heading for Ely's outside shoulder forcing him back. On my fourth step I made a rounded cut with no fake and drove hard for the sideline. The ball was in the air when I looked back. I grabbed it and put it away quickly. I planted my right foot, dropped my shoulder, and turned upfield. Ely drilled me in the chest with his headgear and knocked me flat on my back at the twenty-five. The back of my head slammed into the ground, making my nose burn and my eyes water. The roof of my mouth hurt.

"All right. All right. Green right pitch twenty-nine wing T pull. On two."

My heart jumped and my mouth went dry at the call. I would have to crack back on Whitman, the outside linebacker on the right-hand side. Crawford would try to get outside of my block with the help of the strongside tackle.

Whitman moved toward the sideline in a low crouch, stringing the play out and watching Andy and the leading tackle. At the last second he felt me coming back down the line at him. I dove headlong as he turned. He tried to jump the block and his knees caught me in the forehead and the side of the neck. We went down in a jumble of arms and legs, my shoulder went numb, and a hot burn shot up my neck and into the back of my head. The play gained eight yards.

"All right. All right. Here we go." Maxwell looked up at me. I was shrugging my shoulders and rolling my neck, trying to ease the sting. "You okay?" he asked.

"Yeah, I'm fine."

"All right. All right. Here we go. Red right freeze. Wing out and go. You guys cut block just like the out but tie 'em up an' gimme some more time."

Just before the snap Ely moved up close to the line and played me tight, bumping me as I sprinted off the line. He covered the out move I had beaten him on earlier. I took three hard strides to the sideline, looking back for the ball, then planted hard and turned upfield past him.

"Son of a bitch!" he yelled when he realized Maxwell's pump was a fake and his interception had dissolved.

I caught the ball on the five and ran it into the end zone. Dallas 21-New York 20.

Our defense kept New York bottled up inside their own twenty and after a long punt by Bobby Joe Putnam we took over on our own thirty-five. There were less than two minutes to play.

An I formation tackle slant was good for three yards and we

were huddling up for the second and seven situation when Billy Gill raced in from the sidelines. He slapped me on the shoulder and delivered a play to Seth.

B.A. waved me to his side when I reached the bench. He put his arm around me, keeping his eyes on the field as our huddle broke and the team lined up to run the play. It was a draw delay trap. The fullback made it to the line of scrimmage.

It was third and ten.

"Tell him to roll weakside and hit Delma on a sideline. Or run with it himself."

I turned and raced to the already forming huddle.

I repeated the order, leaning into the huddle.

"Okay," Maxwell nodded. "Green left. Roll right Y sideline at twelve. Okay, Delma?"

"You get it there, Bubba, and I'll catch it."

The Giants rolled up into a zone against Delma. He dodged the cornerman's cut block and curled out to the sideline in front of the deep covering safety. Maxwell dropped the ball right in the hole to him. Delma dodged the fast-closing deep man and was cutting across the grain heading down the middle for the end zone. The middle linebacker made a desperate dive and hooked his arm. The ball popped free. Lewis, the Giant free safety, scooped up the crazily bouncing ball and returned it to our twenty. Gogolak kicked his third field goal of the day with fifteen seconds to play.

New York 23-Dallas 21

The locker room was almost deserted. The equipment man was finishing packing the soiled and bloody uniforms into the blue trunks and was making a last-minute check of the lockers. He found Jo Bob's headgear. "Goddam Williams," he grumbled. "He'd ferget his ass if he wasn't always on it."

An aged black stadium custodian swept the used tape and gauze, the disposable syringes and needles, and the discarded paper cups and drink cans into a pile in the center of the room.

The last sportswriter had just left after listening to B.A. "reluctantly" place the blame on several players, most notably Delma Huddle and Alan Claridge.

The last bus to the airport was outside the stadium, its exhaust blowing white in the cold New York twilight. The first bus was well on its way to Kennedy.

The trainer had just given me a muscle-relaxant shot, had rubbed down and rewrapped my legs, and had strapped my arm to my chest. The taping gave protective support to the shoulder that had collided with Whitman.

I heard the sound of running water in the shower room. I pulled my coat on over my shoulders and walked back to investigate. Seth Maxwell was sitting in a steel folding chair, his head on his chest and a steady stream of water pounding on the back of his neck. His ankles were still taped. Every now and then he rotated his right arm at the shoulder and flexed his fingers. I watched him silently for several minutes. Finally I broke in.

"Hey, man, the last bus goes in about twenty minutes."

"Okay, okay," he responded instantly. "Throw me some tape cutters."

I borrowed cutters from the trainers and tossed them to Maxwell. He quickly sliced off the tape and slammed the water-soaked bandages against the shower floor.

"Cocksucker. Cocksucker," he shouted, punctuating the epithets by whacking the tape on the wet tile. "Cocksucker!"

"Shit," I said, smiling and trying to adjust my taped shoulder comfortably. "The way it went today, I'm surprised you hit the floor."

I ducked aside and the tape cutters clanged on the wall behind my head.

"That's more like it," I said, wincing slightly. Dodging the cutters had made my shoulder throb. I pushed up on my tightly bound forearm. "Come on, get dressed and let's find someplace to get high."

The trainers were taking their showers when we left the locker room. In the tunnel, the equipment man was loading the trunks into the back of an air-freight van for transport to Kennedy, where an orange Braniff 727 with a galley full of dry chicken sandwiches and eighty warm beers sat waiting.

"I sure could use me a Cutty and water," Maxwell rasped,

his hands thrust deep in the pockets of his brown cashmere coat. His hair was slicked back and still slightly wet from his shower. Little beads of perspiration dotted his forehead.

"I mentioned it to Mary Jane on the way up. I'm sure she'll have us something."

The leather trench coat started slipping off my taped shoulder. I tried to pull it back on with my free hand but the twisting motion sent hot pains into my head. Maxwell noticed my struggle, grabbed the coat and reseated it on my shoulder.

As we reached the exit to the parking lot Maxwell went past and started up the ramp to the stadium seats. I followed, after making sure the bus was still waiting.

"We don't have much time," I called, as Maxwell disappeared into the stadium.

The covered seats were in such deep shadows that I had to stop for a moment to let my eyes adjust before I located Maxwell. He was sitting on the aisle four rows in front of me.

"You got a joint?" he asked.

There was a determination, a destructiveness, in his voice. He kept his eyes fixed on the field, almost totally lost in darkness. It looked cold and barren in the gray city dusk.

"Yeah, I think so. But we'll have to hurry." My caution drew a look of distaste.

"Sometimes I wonder about your manhood," he said.

The insult puzzled me, but I avoided his eyes and dug in my pocket for a joint. As long as I played well I was seldom upset by a loss. I looked at winning or losing as someone else's benefit, distantly removed from my daily struggles for existence. Maxwell took losses to heart, regardless of his personal performance.

I lit the joint and inhaled deeply; it made my shoulder hurt. I leaned over and passed to Maxwell, at the same time looking around the stadium for the police I knew were hiding behind every pillar. Maxwell pushed his cowboy hat down over his eyes, propped his feet on the seat in front, took a long, loud drag, and passed back to me. We smoked the whole joint in silence. Finally Maxwell stood up and flicked the glowing roach away.

"Well," he said, starting back down the ramp to the waiting bus, "she whipped me again."

Mary Jane had reserved the same seats for us and had filled the seat-back pouches with tiny bottles of Cutty Sark and Jack Daniels. It took over an hour to get clearance out of New York and during the wait we consumed eight bottles apiece. I took two more codeine pills and Maxwell took one. The combination of codeine, marijuana, booze, and the heavy drone of the jet engines put Maxwell to sleep and me into a trance.

A short but furious pillow fight erupted between some members of the defense and several men who hadn't played in the course of the afternoon. As the tiny airline pillows sailed back and forth, it looked like a Michigan snow storm. A heavy-throated, official-sounding voice quoted some obscure FAA regulation over the intercom and brought the fight to a halt, although every now and then a white square would hum through the air and land with a thump.

Some players were up and moving around. Distinctive bulges and flashes of white under their clothing identified the wounded. My shoulder had become numb and I sat pleasantly stoned.

Alan Claridge, stitched up and sedated, arrived semiconscious by ambulance just before we taxied into line for takeoff. The doctor suggested placing him in the first-class section where he would have more room but his constant gagging and spitting blood disgusted Conrad Hunter's wife. He was carried back to the tourist section, both his eyes swollen shut. There were seventeen stitches in his lip.

I recalled B.A.'s postgame locker room press conference. "Undoubtedly," he had said, standing by the wooden taping tables, "the two fumbles by Claridge and Huddle were costly. Nevertheless, that's no excuse for our all-around sloppy play."

B.A. would probably place Claridge on injured waivers for the remainder of the season, making certain to state it had no bearing on his performance against New York. He was merely a damaged part being replaced. And he was right, that was what was so infuriating. He was always right, analytically, scientifically, technically and psychocybernetically right. Football was technology and he was a master technician.

Andy Crawford sat across the aisle in his undershorts, ice packed on his right thigh to keep down the swelling of a bruise. He had been leg-whipped, just above the knee, in the first half. The Novocain had worn off John Wilson's hip, making it so painful he couldn't sit. He spent the entire flight in the aisle, watching Jo Bob and Tony Douglas play gin. Jo Bob set down his cards and, with great pain, made his way toward me and the bathroom beyond. As he passed he smiled weakly and congratulated my play. It was always surprising how sedate and friendly Jo Bob was after a game. I am sure it is the same principle that recommends masturbating circus lions to exhaustion before setting foot in their cages. The postgame Jo Bob was as calm and affable as the Dreyfus Lion after a couple of good whackoffs.

"Everything all right?" Mary Jane Woodley slipped into the row of seats behind Maxwell and me.

The question was directed at me, but her attention seemed to be on the sleeping quarterback. Leaning on the back of his seat, she was looking wistfully at her fingers as they trailed gently through his thick brown hair.

"As good as can be expected, the quadruple amputee replied trying to rise and shake hands," I said. "Thanks for the drinks."

She didn't reply and I looked back to see if she had heard me. Her eyes were still focused on the top of Maxwell's head as she combed the hair away from his eyes with her red-brown fingernails.

"How's he feeling?" she asked.

"Okay, I guess," I answered, without really considering the question. Besides, I never knew how Maxwell really felt. "A little depressed . . . and really smashed," I added, to give her something to work with.

"He played a great game," she said, disappointed but not surprised by the thought that Maxwell was despondent.

"We didn't win," I pointed out.

"Does it matter that much?"

"To him it does."

"Not to you?" She seemed surprised.

"A little, I suppose. Mostly I'm just trying to survive." I was a little embarrassed by the drama in my statement.

"I'm just trying to get the job," I explained. "He worries about getting it done right, or what he thinks is right."

I paused for a minute and watched her fooling absently with his hair.

"You really like him, don't you?" I observed.

"I really do," she said, keeping her eyes on Maxwell. There was a tone of hopelessness in her voice.

"Why?"

"Because he's a man," she said. "What I thought all men were supposed to be like."

"What about me?" I asked with mock indignity.

"*You*," she said, turning to look at me and smiling wryly. "You. You're what men really are. Like you said, just trying to survive."

I started to protest, but she was approximately right and my defense could, at best, be termed extenuating circumstances.

"I brung ya a drank." Seymour Scoop Zolinzowsky stood in the aisle in front of me holding out a styrofoam cup with the club insignia silk-screened on the side.

"What is it?" I asked, making no move to accept the drink.

"Vodka and Alka-Seltzer. They didn't have no tonic water." Scoop was weaving perceptibly and his face was ruddy. He called it his amphetamine flush.

I waved the drink off, not only nauseated by the idea of vodka and Alka-Seltzer but also knowing there were strings attached to almost any outright gift from this newspaperman.

"How 'bout you?" Scoop offered the drink to Mary Jane, who had stepped into the aisle and was trying to edge by him to get to the front. She shook her head and he stepped aside and bowed, waving her by with a flourish. He turned back to me.

"Well, what happened?" He tried vainly to focus his eyes on me.

"No comment, Scoop."

"Come on man, quit movin' and tell me what happened. I missed the whole goddam thing."

"Didn't you even go to the game?" I was astonished that even Scoop would fail to attend at least part of the game.

"I went awright, I jus' don't 'member any of it." Suddenly he fell to the floor as if he had been struck dead by the hand of God. I leaned over to look at him. "Did you see that guy push me?" he said as he grabbed onto my chair arm and pulled himself rather shakily to his feet.

The seat in front of me was empty, so Scoop pushed the seat back forward until it lay flat, then crawled up on it and assumed the lotus position.

"C'mon man, tell me what happened."

"We lost."

"Good," he said, nodding his head, then looking around absently. "I forgot my pencil 'n pad. You gotta pencil 'n pad?" I shook my head. "Never min', I'll 'member." He winked at me and tapped the side of his head. He offered me a drink from his cup. I leaned forward and peered into it. It looked like vodka and Alka-Seltzer. I shook my head and waved it away.

"Say," Scoop said, snapping his fingers soundlessly, "did the nigger really lose the game?" I winced at the volume that he used on the word *nigger.*

"What nigger?" I asked, too loudly. I looked around but didn't see any black faces or glaring eyes.

"I dunno," he continued, reeling and almost falling backward off the seat. "Clinton jes' said that the dumb nigger dropped the ball."

"I don't know anything about that."

Down the aisle Monsignor Twill made his way rather clumsily from first class back to tourist. He was quite drunk, as he always was on return flights, and stopped by various players to offer his condolences and pat them on the shoulder. Twice as he leaned over to talk to players the plane hit light air pockets and he sprawled into their laps. When he reached us, Scoop had noticed my gaze and was also watching him.

"I can't stan' drunks," Scoop said, as the Monsignor came to a halt beside us. The Monsignor was noticeably offended by the remark.

"Don't mind him, Father," I soothed. "He's upset by the loss."

"I can understand your feelings, Seymour," the Monsignor said, "but that is still no reason to be disrespectful."

"Don't call me Seymour."

"Should I call you Mr. Zolinzowsky?" The Monsignor straightened up, angry at Scoop's abrupt and rude manner. Scoop didn't answer and the Monsignor tried to calm himself and right the situation. "Isn't that a Polish name?"

"Why do you wanna know?" Scoop demanded, taking a long swig of his drink. "You selling bowling shirts?"

The Monsignor glared momentarily at Scoop, then shifted his eyes to me as if expecting an explanation. I shrugged. He shook his head and turned around to tell Andy Crawford he played a great game and he hoped the leg wasn't too long in healing because "we" needed him next week. Then he moved on down the aisle and disappeared into one of the two rest rooms.

"I hate Catholics," Scoop said.

"I thought you were Catholic."

"Tha's what I hate 'bout 'em."

Art Hartman slid into the seat next to Scoop.

"Hey, guys." He smiled. "Played a great game, Phil."

Scoop perked up at the comment.

"He did?" the reporter asked, grabbing at his ear for the nonexistent pencil. He turned to Hartman. "You gotta pencil 'n pad?" Hartman shook his head and then looked at me. His eyes wide, he rolled them in the direction of Scoop. I smiled and nodded.

"I gotta go talk to the losin' coach," Scoop announced, sliding from the seat back to a kneeling position on the floor. As he pulled himself upright, he sloshed his drink all over his hand. He saluted Hartman and me and moved back up toward the front.

"That oughta be a great interview," Hartman observed.

Scoop missed the doorway between sections by about six inches and banged his shoulder into the bulkhead. Backing away, the determined newsman made another run and shot through into first class only slightly scathed.

"How's the King feeling?" Hartman asked, looking around the seat at the sleeping Maxwell.

"Older, I think."

"He'll never get any older."

"That an observation or a complaint?"

"Just a statement, guy. I don't need him to grow old before I get that job. I'll get it when I deserve it."

"Some people thought you deserved it this year."

"Well, it just didn't work out."

"Doesn't that piss you off?"

"Naw." He shook his head. "I'd like to have started this year but B.A. doesn't think I'm ready and I can see his point. I need seasoning. And listen, guy, I love that man," he said, looking at the unconscious quarterback. "He's one of the best in the business. He's taught me a lot. We're good friends."

"You really believe that?"

"Sure, our friendship has nothing to do with competition on the field. We respect each other. When I'm playing, I work my butt off to beat him out, to take that job, but when we step off the field we're still friends."

"Don't you think you're better than he is?"

The question stopped the former All American and he chewed thoughtfully on his upper lip, his eyes squeezing into slits. He thought for a long time.

"Well," he finally said, hesitantly, "that's hard to say. I mean sure I think I'm better than he is. I have to if I ever hope to win the job. But it's B.A.'s decision as to who starts."

"What if B.A. makes the wrong decision. Or the right one and you don't start?"

"That won't happen."

"Why not?"

"Cause it just won't. I concentrate. I follow directions. I work hard. When my chance comes I'll be ready."

"What if it doesn't come?"

"It will come. It has to. I mean if I do everything right, it just has to."

"What if Maxwell's better than you?"

"He's not."

"Then why aren't you playing?'

"Look, I told you, that's B.A.'s decision. I wouldn't have done some of the things Maxwell did today and when my chance comes that'll be the difference between us."

"If you say so," I said, leaning back in my seat and closing my eyes.

"Whattaya mean by that? We lost, didn't we?"

"I don't think the loss was his fault."

"It's always the quarterback's fault when you lose."

"Okay," I said, pushing my feet against the floor, feeling the strangely delicious ache in the muscles. "If you say so." I dug my head into the seat back and fell asleep.

In a dream I was transported to the playing field at the Los Angeles Coliseum. The dream had something to do with being able to throw a football through an old tire. I don't know what the contest was, but I remember that I was scared to death that I couldn't do it. The guy in front of me had just missed and they were carrying him toward the tunnel. The crowd was yelling so loud I woke up. I opened my eyes to hear the sounds of an argument between O.W. Meadows and Jim Johnson. Apparently one, and most likely both, of the Dexamyl Spansules the giant defensive tackle had taken at halftime were beginning to work. The argument was typical postgame behavior for Meadows; he didn't quite grasp the chemistry of time capsules. Standing, screaming at Johnson and inspired by thirty milligrams of Dexedrine and Miltown, he gave vent to a new theory of football that had begun to take shape in his normally fallow brain.

Meadows's gestures were strangely exaggerated by the ice pack secured to his elbow with Ace Bandages and elastic tape. The elbow had been hyperextended in the second half. I was still in a dreamlike state, watching the ice bag wave in the air. I pictured the gruesome mechanics of Meadows's hyperextension. He had been knocked to the ground early in the third period and had extended his right arm to cushion the fall. His palm had dug into the soft ground and he had locked the elbow for support when the ball carrier slammed into the joint from the backside. The blow forced the bones the wrong way; ligaments and muscles stretched and tore. The two primary bones rode grinding over each other. For an instant the elbow dislocated, leaving a huge hole where the elbow point used to be. Somehow the remnants of the muscles and ligaments held and the bones popped back into place with a resounding snap.

He had run off the field, the injured arm hanging limply at his side, and had sat out the rest of that series while the doctor and trainers checked the arm and taped it into a half-flexed position. He returned to action the next series and finished the game.

Tomorrow he would go to the hospital and get x-rayed for breaks. Tonight he was high on speed, adrenaline, codeine, and alcohol. He was feeling no pain if one could judge by the ease with which he whipped the arm around to add force to his argument with Johnson.

The defensive coach had the good sense to know that Meadows was too stoned to give obedience to the social nuances of player-coach relationships and might well use physical force to make his point. This left Johnson in a difficult position. Meadows was becoming louder and more specific in his theorizing, dealing generally with the idea that responsibility for losing in the final seconds to an inferior team fell entirely on the coaching staff. Johnson had several choices: he could continue to suffer insults at the hands of this Hercules and have his reputation as a man, already seriously damaged by the Jo Bob-Monroe White fight deteriorate further, or he could stand his ground and confront Meadows physically. He tried for a third alternative.

"Shit," Meadows was screaming. "You never give us anything to take into a game but fucking facts. I'm sick of goddam tendencies. It's a goddam business for you but it's still s'pose' to be a sport to us."

"You're a professional," Johnson protested. "You should—"

"Professional my ass," Meadows interrupted. "You mean under contract! Goddam, I'll work harder than anybody to win. But man, when I'm dead tired in the fourth quarter, winning's got to mean more than just money. I can make money selling real estate."

"You're hired to do a job. If—"

"Job! Job!" Meadows screamed into Johnson's face. "I don't want no fucking job, I wanna play football. If I wanted a job I'd go to work for Texas Instruments, you asshole! I want some feelings, some fucking team spirit."

Johnson's jaws tightened, but he remained calm out of respect for Meadows's size and rage.

"Listen," Johnson continued, "this ain't high school, you don't have to love each other or us to play."

"That's what I mean, you cocksucker," Meadows raged. "Every time I try and call it a business you say it's a game and every time I say it should be a game you call it a business. You and B.A. and the rest want us to be eleven total strangers out there thinkin' we was a team."

Johnson's eyes darted around the cabin. He knew he was in danger and only wanted out.

"Well, I'll tell you this." Meadows wagged his finger in the coach's face, his arm wobbling from the imbalance of the ice pack. "You and B.A. and all the rest are chickenshit cocksuckers, who couldn't really play and feel this game at all. Oh sure, you'll win, but what'll it mean? Just numbers on a scoreboard. Well, that ain't enough for me."

Meadows stood in the aisle, his face purple, clenching and unclenching his fists. His breath was coming in heavy gasps.

"I don't have to take this from you or anybody else," Johnson yelled and turned to leave.

"Oh, yes you do, you cocksucker," Meadows bellowed, grabbing the front of the coach's short-sleeved shirt. There was a loud rip and the front of Johnson's shirt split open. His clip-on tie came away in Meadows's hand as the coach quickly fled to the first-class section to tell B.A. about the episode.

Johnson had lost two shirts and most of his self-respect in a few short days. It was a tough business.

"Chickenshit cocksuckers," Meadows screamed at the retreating figure. "Coaches are chickenshit cocksuckers. . . ."

Waving Johnson's tie around the cabin, he screamed at his teammates, "You're all chickenshit cocksuckers!!"

I knew I was. I couldn't speak for the others.

I closed my eyes and sang a few lines from a Dylan song. The jet engines drowned the words from all ears but mine.

> *". . . Some speak of the future*
> *My love she speaks softly*
> *She knows there's no success like failure*
> *And failure's no success at all . . ."*

The big 727 banked sharply and brought me out of my alcohol-and-codeine fog. I straightened up in my seat. I could see the lights of Dallas through the window. I shook Maxwell's shoulder gently.

We started losing altitude as we approached Love Field from the south, flying directly over downtown. I could see the flying red horse that someone had told me used to be the tallest point in town. Now it was dwarfed by bank buildings and insurance towers and, of course, the CRH Building, which tonight spelled out a reminder that Christmas wasn't too far off.

The pilot sighted down Lemmon Avenue and we skimmed the tops of franchised pizza parlors, hamburger stands, sandwich shops, beauty parlors, and car lots.

A large crowd of fans and friends was waiting when the plane pulled to the gate at the end of the Braniff terminal. As we filed down the ramp and across the concrete apron, Maxwell and I split off to avoid the crowd. Moving along the outside of the building, we made it to the baggage-claim area. We had finished off the remaining six bottles in the seat-back pouches and were very drunk. Brushing past the baggage handlers, we climbed through an open bay into the terminal buildings, arriving simultaneously with the luggage off Continental 917 from Lubbock.

"How ya'll doin'?" Maxwell hollered, waving and smiling at the startled people as we climbed over their bags and jumped to the floor. Shaking hands on the way, the quarterback walked, with some difficulty, to Valet Parking to claim his car. I followed several feet behind, striding stiffly and frowning, trying my best to look like an FBI agent.

"You played a fine game out there today, Seth," the Valet attendant was saying as I stepped up with my stub in my hand. "Too bad that boy couldn't hold onto the ball."

"Jest wasn't in the cards," Maxwell explained.

"Well, when I played . . ." the attendant continued, stamping Maxwell's parking ticket and scribbling on it with a ballpoint pen. "That'll be seven fifty. When I played, if a boy fumbled like that he had to take five laps right then, during the game. You know what I mean?"

The attendant picked up his phone and called down to the lot.

"Number five four six eight. Blue Cadillac convertible, I think. That right, Seth?"

Maxwell nodded.

By now a line of people were behind us waiting to retrieve their machines. I handed my stub to the attendant as soon as he set down the receiver. A well-dressed man, who appeared in his middle forties or fifties, grabbed Seth on the shoulder.

"Seth?" the man said, smiling and shoving his hand into Seth's. "Harlen Quaid. From Tyler. We've got a couple of friends in common." His eyes twinkled with excitement.

"Oh yeah." Maxwell struggled to be courteous. His smile showed signs of strain.

"Yep." The man beamed. "Bibby and Gordon Mercer. I saw 'em just yesterday before I left Tyler. I had to come down here for a board meeting. I'm in the oil business."

Bibby and Gordon Mercer were the parents of Francie Mercer, Seth's first wife.

"Why that's real fine," Maxwell said, slipping more and

more into his Texas twang as he tried to figure out what this man wanted, if anything. "How's ol' Bibby and Gordon doin'?"

"Jes' fine." The man was beside himself with excitement. His smile split his face open. "Saw Francie, too. An' the little boy. Looks jest like you." The man's smile widened, which seemed physically impossible.

Seth's eyes clouded with pain. He opened his mouth to speak but no words came. His smile collapsed. His eyes flicked around the people assembled watching him and waiting for their cars.

"Hey, man," I said to the oil tycoon from Tyler, "why don't you fuck off before they send you back to east Texas in a sponge."

An ambivalence crept into the man's expression but the grin remained stubbornly on his face as he tried to decide who I was and what I meant.

"I ain't joking, motherfucker." I was almost yelling. "Get the fuck out of here." I pointed aimlessly back up toward the main section of the terminal building. "Now!" I screamed.

The man looked at me and then at Seth, who had leaned against the Valet Parking counter and didn't look at all well.

"There's no need to get violent," the man protested, nervously fingering the knot of his tie. His smile remained strangely intact, although the glitter had left his eyes. "Seth and I were just . . ." His eyes suddenly became angry and he tightened his lips into a scowl. "Who are you anyway?" he demanded.

Maxwell's car pulled up in front. Seth was still leaning against the counter, his face white. I pointed to the car and gave him a slight push in its direction. He stumbled toward it, bending perceptibly in the middle. I turned around and kicked the man, Harlen Quaid, as hard as I could in the shins. I followed Seth outside.

As my car pulled behind the Cadillac, I walked to the driver's side of Maxwell's blue convertible. Seth was sitting on the seat, his head and feet still outside. He was doubled up with stomach cramps and trying to throw up.

With the help of the parking attendants, I got Maxwell into my car, returned the Cadillac to the lot, and drove him home. The ride to his house was punctuated by several stops for his stomach to disgorge itself of what seemed like gallons of a reddish-brown whiskey-smelling foam. By the time we had reached the rows of thirty-five-thousand-dollar boxes in far north Dallas, he was feeling much better and invited me to stop by his apartment for a joint.

When it seemed as though I had gone so far north that the next hill would fall away to reveal the Red River, Maxwell told me to turn right, and we were immediately lost in a jungle of apartments. The architecture ranged from Spanish to Swedish, with one set of units that might be described as early Maginot Line. Seth had just moved to these apartments and wasn't too familiar with the layout, but he soon recognized a yellow MG that belonged to one of his neighbors ("She only likes to suck cocks—and she swallows it"), and I pulled in next to it. I wanted to go see the neighbor but he insisted on just smoking a joint.

We were met at the door by Seth's friend, roommate, and constant companion, a black unclipped standard poodle named Billy Wayne. The dog's size and friendliness made entering the apartment a constant problem. He would leap joyfully at any visitor, driving his forepaws into their genitals. Billy Wayne was the only thing Maxwell retained from his now-defunct marriage to Judith Ann.

"Goddammit, Billy Wayne," Maxwell yelled, "giddown."

The dog danced around us with his tongue out, wagging his whole body, his nails clicking noisily on the tile floor.

While Maxwell changed his clothes I pulled off my coat, readjusted my shoulder, and moved around the apartment poking into cupboards and closets. It was a typical north Dallas $175-a-month one-bedroom furnished apartment. The furniture was early orthodontist and already showed signs of wear, although the whole complex was less than six months old. There were large stains on the red deep-pile living room carpeting and a couple of heaps of dried poodle shit scattered around.

The drawers and shelves in the kitchen were practically

bare. Three monogrammed glasses from a service station giveaway sat dirty and molding in the sink. A Budweiser can opener lay on the drainboard. I couldn't find any glasses or plates. The refrigerator held nine cans of Coors and a half-empty bottle of apple wine. The whole place reeked of rotting food, stale cigarettes, and beer.

A cardboard box that had once held a dishwasher lay wedged in the corner of the breakfast nook. It was filled with trophies, plaques, government citations, autographed footballs, loving cups, and game balls. I rummaged through the results of a lifetime of hard work and dedication; two All American awards, a College All Star Game autographed ball, no fewer than five game balls awarded by his teammates in Dallas, three awards for Professional Athlete of the Year (two cups and a wall plaque), three Pro-Bowl and All-Pro selections and innumerable citations and rewards for jobs done outstandingly well. For all this metal, plastic, and rubber millions of Americans would give their right arm and both testicles (if we are to believe recent surveys about football and sexual sublimation).

"How 'bout that dope?" Maxwell walked into the kitchen, holding a foil package of antacid tablets. He tore the package open, popped the tablets into his mouth and crunched them up noisily, impatient for their promised relief.

"Aaahh," he moaned happily, rolling his eyes. "With Rolaids and cigarettes, I'm indestructible." He boosted himself onto the countertop and waited nervously while I fished a joint out of my shirt pocket.

Lighting the joint and inhaling deeply, I was almost struck unconscious by the stabbing throbs of an alcohol headache. Holding my breath increased the pounding to the point where I expected a loud pop inside my skull and everything to go black. I endured and passed to Maxwell. From somewhere in the recesses of my ravaged brain, I recalled an early doping maxim bequeathed to me by a friend now doing two to life in Huntsville for possession: no matter what happens, he had said, always pass the joint first. Unlike most of the rules by which I have tried somewhat unsuccessfully to get my ship safely into port, that rule given to me by a man who must now be enduring unspeakable assaults on his integrity has held up against time and the Texas sun. What else can I say?

As Maxwell snatched the joint from my outstretched fingers he noticed the rather large red blotches that spotted my forearm.

"What's that?" he asked.

I didn't know and held up both arms for further inspection. They were covered with them. I unbuttoned my shirt and found my stomach and chest covered also.

"Looks like I O.D.'d on the codeine and booze," I decided.

Maxwell had changed clothes and was wearing an old pair of faded Levi's and a red silk Western shirt coated with sequin wagon wheels and cactus plants. The front of the shirt, the two flap pockets, and the cuffs were riveted with white mother-of-pearl snaps. He was barefoot and looked like Porter Wagoner at the beach.

I considered driving out to Charlotte's; I was anxious to see her, but the headache and my overall physical condition dissuaded me. I would get a good sleep and drive out in the morning.

While we smoked the joint, I reflected on the day's work. I was pleased by my performance. Although we had lost, I had a total of five passes for two touchdowns, had not missed an assignment that I could recall, and had made several key blocks. It had been hard and frustrating, but things were looking up. I made a mental note to be more agreeable with the staff and my teammates. It couldn't hurt to bend a little.

"You played a helluva game today," I said, offering Maxwell the joint. He waved it away, inserted a Winston between his lips, lit it, and dragged deeply, throwing his head back as he exhaled.

"Not good enough," he said. He looked emptily at his bare feet. He stuck the tip of his tongue out and picked a piece of tobacco off the end. "Not good *e*nough." He accented the *E* heavily.

"You can't take the blame, man," I argued. "There were

a lotta mistakes out there. Christ, look at Claridge and Huddle. Besides, you and I both know we'll win the division. Shit, nobody can touch us—"

"That don't matter," Maxwell retorted. "My job is to win. Nothin' else is good enough."

"You and that Vince Lombardi no-second-place shit," I harangued. "You sound like Art Hartman." Maxwell's head came up at the mention of his competitor's name.

"You know," he said, "I used to think that that kid had it all." He shook his head and looked at the floor. "But he don't. He's got the size and the arm. He's conscientious and he works hard." Seth brought his eyes up to meet mine. "But he's simple, too simple. I'll get him. He just don't understand what it's all about." Maxwell paused and a smile trickled from cheek to cheek. "You know what I mean?"

I nodded.

"He thinks that he is destined to be number one," Maxwell said. A note of amazement edged his voice. "When I win he really seems pleased. He never seems to worry about it."

"He's a team man."

"I'm a team man," Maxwell said. "He just ain't on my team. Besides, a man that don't worry, don't win. And as long as I win for them they need me."

"Well, you can believe all that sport shit if you want to," I said. "But we're not the team, man, they are. B.A. and Conrad Hunter and Clinton Foote, and all those front office cocksuckers, they're the team. We're just the fucking equipment to be listed along with the shoulder pads and headgear and jockstraps. This is first and foremost a business, with antitrust exemptions, tax breaks, and depreciations. And all the first and tens, all the last-second touchdowns, and ninety-five-yard passes, are just items on a ledger to be weighed along with the cost of precooked steak and green eggs. People don't talk about football teams anymore, they talk about football systems, and the control long ago moved off the field. Tell me who looks more pathetic against our defense than Johnny Unitas."

"He looked pretty bad," Maxwell admitted grudgingly. "But—"

"But nothing. He looked bad because B.A. had got old Johnny U. and Johnny U.'s system logged in those computer banks downtown and he knows what old high-tops is gonna do before old high-tops knows it."

"So?"

"So, everything you think is so swell and wonderful and unduplicatable about you as a quarterback B.A. has on a tape downtown ready to be pumped into the next guy like he was pulling on headgear."

"You're wrong," Maxwell argued, "dead wrong. You're just pissed off because you can't get the starting job. And if you don't quit goofing off pretty soon you'll never get it."

"Probably so," I said, shaking my head slowly and wondering whatever possessed me to start the argument. "But what can I do? I'm too used to seeing myself on a list—a six-foot-four-inch two-hundred-fifteen-pound flankerback, right alongside the six and seven-eighths helmets and the size thirteen shoes. No, man, I *FEEL* like a piece of equipment. I *know* I'm a piece of equipment."

We both fell silent.

"Ya know," Maxwell began, "you just don't understand. You let things bother you too much. I learned a long time ago, you can't let things bother you."

"How do you keep from it?" I knelt down to rub on Billy Wayne, who had come over and was licking the back of my hand.

"It's easy, man. You just don't. When I was about six or seven, I don't remember too clear, my folks took me to the doctor to have my tonsils out. Only they didn't tell me what was goin' on . . . just that we was goin' to the doctor. It was a plan they'd worked out with the doctor to keep me from raisin' too much hell.

"Well, anyway," Maxwell continued, "I knew somethin' was up by the way my folks acted in the car, so by the time we got to the doctor's office, I was scared shitless, but I didn't let on. You know what I mean?"

I agreed, my mind swimming back twenty-odd years to a small doctor's office in Michigan.

"But even when they laid me out on the table I never let on I was scared. Even when they put the mask over my face and tol' me to count backwards from ten, I knew they didn't think I could make it but I held my breath and counted real fast and got to zero just before everything went black."

"Do you know what I'm sayin'?" he continued. "Let 'em do what they want, I just keep foolin' 'em."

"Jesus," I said, finally. "That's almost the same thing that happened to me, except I thought they were killing me and I screamed bloody murder from start to finish."

"They still took your tonsils out, didn't they?"

I nodded.

"Well, that's my point. It don't do no good to fight. What you gotta do is fool 'em. I been foolin' 'em ever since."

"Yeah, man," I protested, "but if you spend all your time pretending you're something else, that's what you are—something else.

"That's what I love about sports, man," I continued, trying to explain. "There is a basic reality where it is just me and the job to be done, the game and all its skills. And the reward wasn't what other people thought or how much they paid me but how I felt at the moment I was exhibiting my special skill. How I felt about me. That's what's true. That's what I loved. All the rest is just a matter of opinion."

Maxwell's eyes brightened slightly and he nodded his head.

"I know what you're saying," he admitted. "I guess that's why we all start playing in the first place."

I nodded and smiled, pleased that we had an understanding.

"You still feel that way?" I asked, not really certain of my own answer.

"I dunno anymore, man. Back before we won it all, I used to always feel that way. Hell, there was hardly any other reason to play, you remember that. I used to fight with B.A. all the time, just like you do now. Shit," he laughed, "I not only wouldn't call the plays he sent in, I ran the guys that brought 'em in off the field. But, I do know this. B.A. is the winning side, and I may not have the fun that I used to, but I sure win a lot more and that's good enough for me.

"It's tougher now; maybe that's the price of winning," he conceded. "Now, it's all sort of mixed up with statistics, incentive money, and how much money I get if I win the division or lead the league. I still play for the thrill, but winning has its responsibilities and it gets a little confusing."

"You're totally obsessed with winning," I pointed out. "Don't you think that's wrong?"

"No. If you don't win, what's the sense of playing?"

"The game man," I argued. "The game. Not the end, the winning or losing, but the means: the game. That's the reason —the game, only the game."

"Well, all I know is what I have to do statistically to keep playing and that's what I try and do each week. If I enjoy playing, that's great, but I need those numbers first and have to do whatever is necessary to get 'em."

"It takes away a lot of the fun."

"What's fun?"

We fell silent while I continued to pat on Billy Wayne and think about what Seth had just said. Finally, I stood up and began to organize myself to leave.

"I guess it's whose opinion is the most important to you," I said. "I don't know whether it's really my keen judgment I respect or if I'm swayed by the fact that I'm the only one who thinks I'm any good."

Maxwell seemed no longer interested and called Billy Wayne to his side and they resumed their play. I picked up my coat and threw it over my shoulder.

"See you tomorrow or Tuesday," I called, heading for the door.

"Right," he answered without looking up. He was holding Billy Wayne's curly black head and looking into his brown eyes. He was whispering something to the dog but it was too soft for me to hear.

The wind was picking up as I walked slowly to the car, my head tilted back, searching vainly for the supernova I knew

I would never see. If I can just get to zero before everything goes black.

The house looked dark and uninviting as I stopped the Riviera at the front curb. I let the engine idle and listened to Mick Jagger grind through "Jig-saw Puzzle."

I thought of the incredible confusion I had come through in just seven short days. My career had moved out of peril into an area of relative security and possible success. I always felt I had the ability to be a great receiver and now it could be working out. B.A. would have difficulty denying my performance today. The day seemed almost surreal. My legs and back still hurt, but I had a new energy, a force, that helped me endure and overcome the debilitating effects of constant pain. Amazingly I no longer worried about the pain, I accepted it.

I knew that all the good somehow started with Charlotte, a change she had made, a shift in perspective. All the ingredients were there and she helped me sort them out. Since we met I was somehow different, less myself, but more myself. My stomach turned over warmly as I thought about her and I became at once excited and optimistic. There was something magical about her. Even away from her I felt her presence in my thinking, in my feelings about living. Yet, I could not recall her face, could not conjure an image of her in my mind. I knew all her adjectives, I knew she was beautiful and desirable but I could not picture her. Instead I saw only her name in block sans serif type and it gave me chills. Instantly, irreconcilable and confusing thoughts made perfect sense.

The smell of her remained constantly in my head, although I have no idea where it came from, my nose being less than sensitive. I wanted to bury my face in the hollow of her neck and hide in her long hair.

> "*. . . And me I wait so patiently*
> *With my woman on the floor*
> *Just trying to work this jigsaw puzzle*
> *Before it rains anymore. . . .*"

MONDAY

When the phone rang at 10 A.M. I thought I was still in New York and let it ring several times before I even opened my eyes.

"Coach Quinlan would like to see you in his office at eleven this morning." It was Ruth, B.A.'s secretary.

"Is this a recording?" I asked sleepily.

"What?"

"Nothing, Ruth, tell him I'll be there as soon as I get my heart started."

"What?"

"Never mind, Ruth. I'll be there." I hung up and made a mental note to have the phone ripped out and melted down for sunglass frames.

I had some difficulty getting out of bed. My shoulder had stiffened during the night and coupled with my other aches and pains made sitting upright a test of concentration and desire. My knee had filled with fluid and I had trouble straightening it. Finally I got to my feet by rolling off the mattress and onto the floor.

I shuffled into the bathroom amazed, as I was every Monday, by how much pain I was feeling. By the time I had soaked sufficiently, being careful to keep my knee elevated and out of the hot water to avoid further swelling, cleared my sinuses of dried blood and mucus, and otherwise effected enough of a recovery to walk upright, it was a quarter to eleven. I made the twenty-minute drive in fifteen and was standing anxiously at the reception desk at eleven exactly. B.A. made me wait another twenty minutes and, after thumbing through the only magazine, *A Guide to High School Coaches in Idaho,* I struck up a conversation with the new receptionist, a pretty, proper, black girl (not too dark).

"How are you?" I said, cleverly using my standard opening.

"Fine," she said, keeping her face buried in the book she was reading, *Mandingo,* the story of a slave-breeding farm in the 1800's.

"Have you gotten to the part where the master boils the high-yellow buck down to soup and bones for screwing his wife?'

There was no answer. I am strangely encouraged by people who ignore or discount me. I plunged right on with the lopsided conversation. I had difficulty disguising my eagerness. "How about the scene where the master catches his daughter in carnal knowledge of a Kikuyu in a cornfield and cuts the cheek of his ass off with a hoe? . . . Wait a minute, that was another book."

The phone rang. She picked it up, listened a moment, and then replaced the receiver.

"You can go in now." She never looked up.

As I walked down the hallway toward B.A.'s office, I noticed all the other offices were either empty or had their doors closed. I encountered no one in the halls and on reaching my destination had decided, as many Hollywood Indian scouts did just before they took an arrow in the throat, that it was just too quiet. Ruth solemnly opened the door to the head coach's inner sanctum and I fell among a war party of pin-striped Apaches.

B.A. sat regally at one end of his oval desk. Arranged around the desk and in various parts of the large room were an alarming number of club and league officials. There was an empty seat opposite B.A. and he motioned for me to take it. As I moved slowly toward him I looked into the several faces that just stared blankly, and grimly, back at me. I seated myself. I recognized all of the assembly with the exception of a stocky man with close-cropped, thinning hair. He appeared to be in his midforties and, in contrast to the other men, was dressed quite gaudily in an ill-fitting brown-and-yellow-checked wool sport coat.

In an effort to assess what was happening, I studied the faces at the desk. The head coach was flanked by Conrad Hunter on his right and Clinton Foote on his left. In the awkward silence, I could hear the distinctive tapping of Clinton's foot. He was loaded on amphetamines for a long day. On Foote's left sat Ray March, who was in charge of internal affairs and security for the league. March was a ten-year veteran of the FBI. All were also ex-FBI agents. Their primary responsibilities consisted of surveillance of player personnel and investigations of improper conduct.

B.A. shuffled noisily and awkwardly through several stacks of paper arrayed on his desk. Finally he selected one and held it out with both hands, studying it intently. His face was deeply furrowed and he licked his lips several times before trying to speak.

"Phil," he said, his eyes riveted to the paper, "where were you last Tuesday until approximately eight A.M. Wednesday morning?" He never raised his eyes.

"What?" I would be an outstanding witness.

"On Tuesday night of this past week," B.A. repeated. The paper was still in his hands but his eyes wandered absently down to the table top. He still hadn't looked at me. "Where were you?"

I continued to survey the room, noticing the conspicuous absence of Emmett Hunter. His place had been taken by a fellow named O'Malley, the team attorney and long-time family friend of the Hunters. He was an odious, fat, red-faced man, who always appeared to be holding his breath. His round cheeks, pink from alcohol-shattered blood vessels, and his heavy eyebrows all but concealed his eyes.

"I don't remember where I was," I said, half-truthfully, though I was pretty sure. One thing for certain, they knew where I had been and they weren't happy about it. "Why do you want to know?"

"Answer the question," Clinton Foote interjected with a glare, exercising the general manager's universal preemptive rights. I hoped the trainers hadn't given him a big Dexamyl Spansule; it would make him difficult, if not impossible, to deal with.

"What's this all about?" I asked, looking from face to face. "What am I supposed to have done?"

"You better answer, young fella." Ray March sounded like my high school principal when he discovered I had written *fuck* on the door to the girls' washroom. I grinned at the comparison, further heightening the tension.

"You obviously have the answers," I said. "Why else would I be here?"

"They want to hear your side before they make any decisions," B.A. offered. He had attempted compassion and impartiality. He landed somewhere near irony.

"Yeah," I observed, "that's why we're all here looking so grim."

"You'd best answer." Clinton Foote tried to make cooperation sound like a wise business decision. The thumping of his foot was deafening. I knew I was in big trouble.

I lowered my eyes to the table and shook my head, taking the only remaining refuge—insentience. The room was silent.

"Mr. Rindquist." Clinton Foote finally broke the silence.

The stocky stranger moved quickly across the room and took a standing position directly behind B.A. From where I sat the two men appeared in tandem, B.A.'s perfectly tanned and manicured head centered in Rindquist's overhanging, slightly untidy belly. Rindquist had a craggy, corrugated face and thick, heavy hands. His narrow, furtive eyes barely revealed their color, light magenta. He was a violent-looking man.

"My name is George Rindquist. I'm a vice officer with the Dallas police. During my off-duty hours I work for Mr. March here, checking out reports of player misconduct."

I watched Clinton Foote's head bobbing rhythmically with the modulations of Rindquist's gravelly voice. The speech was rehearsed.

"Several weeks ago I was requested by Mr. March here to take up investigative surveillance of one Phillip Elliott, an employee of the Dallas franchise."

I suddenly remembered Rindquist's face and grating voice. He had called, months back, and convinced me to make a gratis appearance at a fund-raising banquet for the families of two patrolmen killed in an automobile accident. I met him and sat next to him during the banquet. So much for community service.

". . . I followed the suspect from the time I was contacted by Mr. March's office up to and including Friday morning last when the suspect boarded a plane allegedly bound for New York."

"Anything to say?" Clinton Foote inquired.

"The plane did arrive in New York," I offered. The general manager's eyes blazed and there was a momentary uneasiness as he fought to control his temper.

"Please continue, Mr. Rindquist," Clinton said. Picking up a pencil, he began drumming on his yellow note pad. I dropped my eyes from his gaze and shook my head.

"I will read from my log of the past week." Rindquist spoke with the careful diction of an experienced witness. Pulling a stenographer's notebook from his coat pocket, he began reading. "On Monday at eight o'clock in the morning I picked up the suspect and followed him to Fort Worth via the Dallas-Fort Worth Turnpike. Arriving in FW—that's Fort Worth—the suspect proceeded across town to a Big Boy Restaurant near the old Weatherford Highway where he met several other adult males—"

"Excuse me," I interrupted, automatically raising my hand. "Did you happen to recognize any of the other adult males?"

"I did not."

"Well," I pressed, "was there anything distinctive about those men? You know, size, weight, color."

"No," Rindquist answered quickly, his eyes jumping nervously from me to Clinton Foote.

"What's this all about?" Clinton angrily asked.

"I was just trying to establish the reliability of the witness," I answered, snatching the phrase from an old Perry Mason show.

"This isn't a court of law," Foote announced. "Go on, George."

"The three adult males and the suspect transferred several shotguns and various types of hunting equipment into the back of a pickup truck. When the truck was loaded the suspect climbed into the back and the remaining men climbed into the cab and headed out west on the old Weatherford Highway. I assumed they were going hunting and didn't follow for fear of being discovered."

"We wouldn't want you to be discovered, would we," I said.

"Shut up," Clinton Foote shouted, slamming the flat of his hand on the table, his face puffed and red.

"I waited in the parking lot of the restaurant until they returned later that afternoon." Rindquist paused and looked from March to Clinton, both of whom glanced at each other and then at me. I shrugged my shoulders.

"After leaving FW—that's Fort Worth—the suspect returned to Dallas and drove directly to The Apartments on Maple Avenue, where a party was in progress. I again kept my distance—"

"What apartment was the party in?" I asked.

"You oughta know," the cop shot back, "you were there." His retort brought a murmur of laughter.

"Yeah," I said, "but you got it all written down. You're paid to know."

"Well, I don't," he replied angrily.

"Mr. Elliott," Ray March interrupted, placing his hand gently on Clinton Foote's arm as the general manager was about to leap to his feet in rage. "Must we remind you again, this is not a court of law. Mr. Rindquist is giving us the information he thinks is important to your case."

I closed my eyes and nodded my head, letting it sink slowly to my chest.

"Go ahead, George," March instructed.

The officer continued his story, carefully avoiding any particulars on the party and recognizing none of those present with the exception of myself.

"At one point in the evening the suspect was observed in the outward physical appearances of smoking marijuana with another unidentified male companion." He had delicately failed to recognize Seth Maxwell, the singularly most identifiable face in Texas sports history.

"How do you mean outward physical appearances?" Clinton posed the question without raising his eyes from the table.

"Well," Rindquist elaborated, "the physical act of marijuana smoking differs considerably from the actions of normal cigarette smoking."

The unmistakable accent on *normal* was aggravating, but I remained unresponsive.

"Marijuana smokers," Rindquist pronounced the words with the same distaste he would have if discussing niggers, lepers, or meskins, "cup the cigarette, or joint, in their hands, taking short puffs and holding their breath. It makes the smoking action very jerky in appearance and easy to identify. That was the manner in which the suspect was smoking."

There was a short lull while everyone in the room waited for me to offer something more, a defense or an admission. I just slowly shook my head, my lips twisted into a wry smile. I could feel the world crumbling but could do nothing to stop or even slow the process.

"Shortly after observing the suspect smoking marijuana—" Rindquist began again.

I leaped to my feet and pointed a finger at the policeman. "Do you know it was marijuana, you fat son of a bitch? Do you have any proof? You lousy . . ." My voice and energy trailed off as I was unable to conceptualize a proper insult. I fell back into my seat, exhausted.

"Look, boy!!" the policeman yelled back at me and started toward me with his fists clenched. He caught himself and stopped, looking around the office for reassurance. Ray March came to the officer's assistance.

"We understand fully, Mr. Elliott," March's voice was authoritative and his statement was carefully and impassionately structured, "that Mr. Rindquist's remark is merely an assumption on his part. But in all fairness you must understand that we hired Mr. Rindquist because of our immense respect for his abilities and judgments as an experienced peace officer."

"Why didn't you just have him shoot me and be done with it?"

"You can be flippant if you wish, Mr. Elliott, but the charges against you are serious. And lame attempts at humor can only be regarded in terms of consequences. Please continue, George."

The policeman's eyes moved from me to Clinton Foote, who gave him a tight smile and a short affirmative nod.

"As I said," Rindquist looked down at his notebook, "shortly after observing the suspect smoking marijuana, I broke off surveillance for the night, picking him up again the next afternoon, Tuesday, as he left the north Dallas practice field. He proceeded downtown to the CRH Building, where he remained for approximately two hours. After leaving the CRH Building he proceeded north on Central Expressway to Loop Twelve where he turned east and proceeded to the Twin Towers Apartments, where he remained the night."

"Do you know in which apartment Mr. Elliott spent the night?" Clinton leaned forward and glared at me, then leaned back and crossed his legs. His foot was wagging nervously.

"Yes sir, I do. Twenty-five forty." Rindquist didn't bother to check his notes. "The apartment is occupied by—"

"There's no need to discuss the occupancy of the apartment," O'Malley said. The Hunter family attorney spoke for the first time. "It's not important to the case being discussed here."

A look of perplexity passed across Rindquist's face, his lips still pursed to say *Joanne.* His speaking pace slowed perceptibly as he stumbled on, confused by the interruption. "He spends the night there often." Rindquist's eyes flitted back and forth from Foote to March to O'Malley, trying to determine if he had made a mistake.

"You are really a bunch of sleazy cocksuckers," I said, feeling appreciably better as the insult rebounded around the room and seemed to fit everyone perfectly, including me.

"At about midnight," Rindquist continued, ignoring my anger, and picking up his old rhythm, "—I left the Twin Towers and drove to the suspect's house where I effected a search of the premises, finding several pill bottles and a quantity of obscene literature."

"And twenty bucks," I added.

I was again ignored.

The number and variety of officials present was a pretty good indicator of impending doom and I realized the folly of any attempted defense and began to build an ending, a climax. I swallowed hard and laid a hand on my chest trying to calm my heart. When I leaned back in my seat I could see it pounding against the shirt tightly drawn over my chest.

"The following night . . ." Rindquist was boiling on to the conclusion, proud that he had done his part before I turned to ax murders. The assumptions were already drawn, inferences already allowed, and punishment already decided, I knew that now. All that remained was animation to make it plausible. ". . . I again picked up the suspect as he left the practice field and followed him to the house of one Harvey Le Roi Belding, a suspected user and dealer in narcotics and a known campus agitator and political revolutionary."

"A real Che Guevara," I muttered.

"While the suspect was inside I searched his car. In the glove compartment I found and photographed two marijuana cigarettes. You have the photographs."

Clinton Foote held up two Polaroid prints for the assembled officials to verify. His hand shook noticeably.

The detective rounded out the remainder of my week, covering the fight at Rock City, again unable to identify anyone else present with the exception of Charlotte. He followed us to Lacota and then picked me up again after Thursday's practice and tailed me back to Charlotte's. He was careful to point out "her peculiar relationship with a nigra boy."

"Well," I said, breaking into a short, bursting laugh, "I'm sure glad you're all doing this to me. For a while there I thought I was getting paranoid."

Clinton Foote took his eyes momentarily from Rindquist to glare at me. Nobody else seemed to have heard.

Rindquist wrapped up with my boarding the 727 "allegedly bound for New York" and quickly returned to his seat. Clinton looked at Rindquist and gestured toward the door with his eyes. The policeman bounded out the door.

"Thank you, George," Clinton said to the closing door and then turned to his attention to me. "Anything to say?"

"Well," I started slowly, clearing my throat, "I'd like to thank all the little people who made this possible."

Clinton Foote exploded. I can't say that I blamed him.

"Who in Great God's Hell do you think you are?" Clinton screamed. He jumped to his feet. His face was purple with rage. "A goddam broken-down football player. You guys are a dime a dozen. Do you think you're here because by some divine intervention you deserve to be here? Do you? Huh?"

I was stunned by his passion and pulled back into my chair. I said nothing.

"You're here because we let you on," he continued to bluster, pointing around the room at the assembled officials. "We let you on, no other reason. We don't owe you, you owe us, and there are sixty million fans out there who agree with me." He pointed out the window at the Dallas skyline.

"That's something you'll have to work out with them," I said. I had calmed some after his first outburst and tried to argue.

"What?" His head swiveled back from the window, his face a mixture of surprise and fury. A thin smile controlled his lips.

"Okay. You're so goddam cocky. We gave you a good job, paid you," he looked down and dug through a sheaf of papers on the desk and pulled out a Standard Player's Contract, apparently mine, "good money. Go out and try and earn as much out there." He pointed back to the window. "You'll find nobody gives a fat rat's ass who you were or how many zig outs you can run."

I just looked up at the fuming man and smiled.

He held the contract up for my inspection. "Well, if you could read this, which I doubt," he had me there, I never could read a whole contract, that was why they made them so long and involved, "you would see that we own you and you check with us when you want to do something, we don't check with you." He shook the contract in my face. "That's why we pay you all that money. It ain't for your good looks and charm."

Ray March reached up and grabbed Clinton's arm. Clinton pulled away, then looked at March, who signaled him to calm down and be seated. Clinton stared back at me for a moment.

"Oh, all right," he said, and sat down.

"Do you have anything to say that is pertinent?" March asked me.

I shook my head.

B.A. nodded and began digging through the papers in front of him. He selected one and stared at it blankly. It was the same disarming technique that Clinton used when negotiating contracts, acting as if there were information on the paper that diminished his opponent's position.

"Phil," the coach began slowly, "you've been up here for conferences with me several times in the years you've been with the club, haven't you?"

I nodded.

"What did we talk about those times?"

"Different things, mostly your reasons for benching me. You benched me three times, or so, a year."

"Did I tell you why I was benching you?"

"Well, you usually said it was maturity. I either lacked it or had too much, I don't recall."

"Maturity," B.A. mouthed the word carefully. He remained

silent for several seconds, gazing at the piece of paper. "I think you're a good receiver, Phil," he began again. "You probably have the best hands in football today. You're a good football player, but so is everybody else on this club. That's why you're all here. And football is other things besides ability. It's dedication and it's discipline. You must give something back to the sport, you can't always be taking."

"B.A.," I said, "I can barely stand up, can't breathe through my nose, and haven't slept more than three hours at a stretch in over two years, all from leaving pieces of me scattered on playing fields from here to Cleveland. Isn't that giving something back?"

"That's not what I mean," he protested. "You must live by the rules that have been built up over the years by people who love the game and sacrificed for it. You just can't come in here and disregard those traditions and change what you want."

"That's really funny, B.A.," I interrupted. "You people change everything, a game becomes a corporate enterprise for one thing—money. Look at you all," I pointed around the room, "pinstripe suits, hundred-dollar shoes, and razor cuts. And now you tell me I've got to be Bronko Nagurski."

B.A. frowned and shook his head. He scanned the paper, his forehead furrowed in thought. Finally he looked up.

"You think you're so smart," he said. "I've heard all those tired arguments about professional football corrupting and I don't believe 'em. And furthermore, I know about you." He dug into the stacks of papers and came up with several sheets of psychological tests that had been administered to me and the rest of the team. He held up one of the papers and read from it.

"You're a high achiever who is totally self-reliant. You have no close friends or loved ones. You need nothing but yourself. You are dangerous to organization for the same reason you are desirable. As a high achiever you tend to be violently frustrated and will, if not controlled, destroy that which frustrates you." He put down the paper. "Don't you see? We must have a way to control people like you."

"How about a frontal lobotomy?"

"You refuse to understand," he continued. "You resent my coldness, my logical approach to problems. Well, I have a job to do and I can do it best without my personal feelings being involved. But *you* can't. You refuse to submit to the rules."

"Don't you see?" I was beginning to crack. I saw no escape from the inevitable. "You control my life, but don't feel any need to become involved with me as a person. Don't you understand how frightening that is for me? To have absolutely no human rapport with the people who, as he said," I pointed at Clinton Foote, "own me. You own me but you don't want to get involved with me. What the fuck does that mean?"

B.A.'s face remained unresponsive.

"I fully understand your objections to the way I run this team," he said dispassionately. "I just don't agree with you. You have a job to do and you should do it. Your personal life is something else. We have a difference of opinion and you refuse to keep it out of your work. Well, I'm in the business of winning football games, not clearing troubled consciences. I can't have you constantly questioning my authority. I don't care if you like me, but I insist you respect me."

"B.A., you can't order people to respect you. As a man who wins football games you don't have a peer, but you seem to think that qualifies you as an exceptional human being full of personal and Godly grace." I stopped for a moment to catch my breath and control my voice, which had been rising markedly as I spoke.

"You think that there is something wrong with winning and I won't tolerate that." B.A. pointed a finger at me, his face masking the emotion that was obvious in his voice. "Winning is *the* most important thing. The sacrifice and responsibility that must be shouldered in order to win are what make men. It's what makes this country the greatest in the world. Feared and respected. Sticking to the rules and winning. You're just not willing to pay the price."

"If the price is thinking like you, then I won't pay it. But if you think it's *merely* a difference of opinion you're a very silly man." I sank back in my seat, suddenly worn out from a battle that hadn't even taken place. I knew it was hopeless to argue, but I had to do something.

"Well," B.A. answered, his voice calm and his eyes frosted, "you make your existential quests on somebody else's time. The issue is simple. People must, and I mean must, submit to control at some level. You refuse. So, you must leave." He looked down and began sorting and stacking the piles of papers in front of him. He placed the papers in a manila file folder and laid them back on the desk. He kept his eyes down and leaned back in his chair. Nobody moved until he finished.

Ray March pulled a folded paper from his inside coat pocket. He studied the paper carefully, then looked at me.

"When the commissioner was first made aware of the charges against you—"

"Charges?" I interrupted. "I haven't heard any charges. Just the week's calendar of a fat voyeur."

"Mr. Elliott, you continually seem to think this is some sort of court proceeding. We are not concerned with semantics or strict interpretation of the law. There is no record being kept. What we are concerned with is conduct unbecoming professional football. That is what you stand accused of, and I might add, pretty well convicted of."

"You still haven't said what the conduct was," I insisted.

"Smoking marijuana for one," March said.

"What else?"

"The girl," March replied, looking apologetically down the table at Conrad Hunter.

Hunter never looked up from the pencil he was twirling between his thumb and forefinger.

"The girl? She's not even married." I knew it was hopeless.

A long pause followed, as the officials exchanged weary glances; tired to the bone with the charade, they wanted it ended. The chilling realization of what was to come crashed down on me. My chest constricted and I lost control of my breathing.

"Listen," I pleaded, inhaling deeply and trying to collect myself, "listen, there has got to be more to it than this. I'm truly sorry if I caused anyone any difficulty. But goddam, the girl wasn't even engaged until last week. And the marijuana, I mean, Christ, I take stronger shit than that just to get on the field. You people give it to me. We all know marijuana is hardly—"

"Marijuana is against the law," Clinton Foote interrupted.

"Oh come on," I moaned. "You know plenty of guys in this league who use it, and LSD and mescaline." I was pleading. "That kid in Boston said he played a game on it. And the girl. You got guys on this team screwing each other's wives. And each other—"

"We're not concerned with other people's behavior," March interjected, "only yours has come to light." His face was drawn into a frown. I was becoming tiresome.

"Why are you doing this to me?" I begged. "It's not what you say. I know. And you know I know. What is it? You could be wrong."

"We're not wrong!" Clinton Foote leaped to his feet. My contract was crumpled in his hand. He had lost patience with his own charade and was anxious to have it ended. "You were seen doing these things and according to the Standard Player's Contract the commissioner has the right to suspend you, which he has already done as of eight o'clock this morning." He tore the contract into pieces and wadded them into a ball. He dropped it in front of him on the table. His voice turned soft and a smile contradicted the look in his eyes.

"You're on the street, fella." The general manager sat down and looked around the room, pleased with his performance.

O'Malley the lawyer unwadded the crumpled, shredded contract and sorted the pieces, then he slid a legal-sized paper across the table to me.

"Sign this if you would, Mr. Elliott. It's a release absolving us from any further responsibility for you. We would like to get this all done as quietly as possible for all concerned." The fat lawyer smiled slightly. "You wouldn't want all this to become public."

"Clinton, you can't do that," I protested.

"It's already done." Clinton tapped his pencil lightly against the edge of the desk, then he stopped and pointed the eraser end at me. "And I would advise you that Mr. Rindquist already has an extensive police file on you. If I were you I'd vanish."

"Goddammit, I haven't done anything that half the guys, management included, haven't done and you know it. It's my legs, isn't it? You don't want to pay my contract."

"Mr. Elliott," March's indifference was agonizing, "I'm sorry that you feel that you have been treated unfairly, but you should have considered your actions more carefully." His eyes fell back to the paper.

"When the commissioner was first made aware of the charges against you, the first concern of his office was to make sure your rights were protected. When the commissioner was satisfied that your protection was guaranteed, he authorized an investigation and collection of facts . . ."

March droned on, but I shut him out, squeezing my eyes closed and fighting the flood of emotion that surged behind my eyelids. I sank submissively in my seat and exhaled loudly, regaining control and beginning to think clearly again.

". . . the commissioner has asked me to make a statement on his behalf."

The ex-FBI man began reading.

"As commissioner it is my duty to preside over and guarantee the integrity of the league from attacks from inside as well as outside our structure. This case, as all cases, has been judged solely on its merits. It is not the position of the commissioner's office that criminal action by legal authorities be initiated before we consider a person's behavior detrimental to the well-being of the game. It is, in fact, desirable from the standpoint of the good name of professional football that undesirables be weeded out and removed from out of our midst with as little public notice . . ."

I quit fighting and accepted the insanity of the situation. The whole affair seemed morosely funny. Sitting there trying to talk to men who purposely deceived themselves. Like so many people, they weren't concerned with the truth. They wanted an arrangement of facts that coincided with their present needs and wishes. And because they were powerful, it was relatively easy for them to rearrange the stuff of daily experience to correspond with their current views and desires. Once they rearranged it all, they attacked the situation with a moral zeal and believed they were doing the right and just thing. And maybe they were. They wanted me out of football with no legal claims and this meeting had been arranged to convince me of the futility of a legal fight. I signed the release and pushed it back to O'Malley. The fat man smiled and nodded.

"You may feel that your personal rights have been abridged since judgment was passed before you were allowed to speak in your own defense. As commissioner, I must point out that you are in a position of privilege, giving you certain responsibilities to your employers and the public. You violated this privilege and cannot expect the same rights and protections as an ordinary citizen. It is my considered opinion that your insidious behavior is detrimental to professional football and all those principles and values that we hold inviolable. . . ."

Suddenly a great weight lifted from my mind, a mental tightness releasing, a runaway concentration relaxing. I felt myself opening and I saw this room as if for the first time. I was no longer fighting, trying to control these things and people around me. I was just observing them. The game was finally over. I would no longer fear defeat and failure. I had been trapped on a technicality that explained the ultimate pointlessness of the life I had been living. The game wasn't on the field, it never had been. It was here. I hadn't been beaten and I hadn't quit. I had been disqualified. I had forgotten to sign my scorecard, but that still didn't mean I hadn't shot a sixty-seven and broken the course record. It just meant that if I did they wouldn't accept it and ultimately that was their problem. Because the only part of the game that is real is me and only I can judge. It was over. I didn't have to compete for the right to exist. From now on I would just be. I would leave this office, ride down the elevator, and walk to the parking lot and crank up my car. I would race to Lacota and see if Charlotte wanted to be with me. I was free.

"You are as of nine A.M. eastern standard time suspended indefinitely from performing as a professional football player. Your Standard Player's Contract is hereby declared null and void and you are advised that this office rules that no further disbursements of contractual monies or benefits accrued will be made by the Dallas club."

Actually it wasn't me they were after in the first place. It was my three-year contract that had to be dealt with. I was just a necessary prop. They had no further need of my presence. Once the commission had ruled and the appropriate officials were convened to notify me, I ceased to exist. There was little chance to reincarnate myself through the courts. The meeting was designed to point that out clearly to me. I wondered why they went to all the trouble; if anybody in the world knew how really worthless the Standard Player's Contract was to the standard player it was this group of men. They could terminate a player for anything and just say not good enough. Who was going to argue? My only choice was acceptance. I wouldn't cut much of a figure in court and only a true believer would file a civil suit in Texas against a government-protected monopoly.

Ray March finished reading and looked up as I pushed my chair back and started for the door without saying a word. I pulled the door open and turned back to look at this room full of men who lived their lives manipulating other men like cattle and who hoped someday to be able to dictate a directive like the one just delivered to me. I smiled at them, shook my head, and stepped through the door.

"It's signed by the commissioner," March yelled after me.

There was a low-pressure area somewhere in the Panhandle near Amarillo and the air was rushing out of Dallas west at about thirty-five miles an hour. The wind blew my jacket open as I stepped out into the parking lot of the North Dallas Towers.

The cold December wind was startling, but its omnipotent

violence was reassuring as it roared around the concrete building. There was a change coming, I could feel it in the air.

I put my head down and headed into the bluster and toward my car. I was leaning to unlock the car door when Maxwell's blue convertible pulled next to me.

"Hey, Seth."

He rolled down the electric window on the passenger side without moving from his position behind the wheel. His right arm was draped across the wheel, his hand hanging limp from the wrist. His eyes were hidden behind wraparound sunglasses. He stared straight out the windshield and said nothing.

"You recovered from last night?" I asked, not sure how to begin the conversation.

He looked over at me and nodded. I walked over, leaned against the right-hand door, and looked through the open window. We were silent while I ran my eyes absently over the blue and white leather interior. Maxwell turned back to stare out the windshield again.

"What happened?" he finally asked, still looking straight ahead. "I heard you met with B.A. this morning."

"Yeah," I said, trying to decide what he was doing at the office on Monday. "He didn't make me a starter."

"I know that. What did you say?" He seemed irritated.

"About what?'

"You know. About everything."

"What are you talking about?" I asked. "You don't know what happened up there this morning."

"Did you say anything about me?"

"What about you? Christ man, Hunter and B.A. and Foote and that guy March from the commissioner's gestapo. They were all up there. They suspended me for good." I paused to wait for a reaction from Maxwell. There was none.

"How did you know I'd be here?"

He ignored the question and continued to look straight ahead. He frowned and scratched the back of his neck. "Thanks for not saying anything about me."

He put the big Cadillac in gear. The transmission clunked and the car started to ease away.

"Hey," I yelled, stepping back as he pulled out, "how did you know I'd be here? Seth! How did you know?"

The big convertible roared onto the access road and quickly slipped into the northbound stream of traffic.

"Son of a bitch," I said softly, as the huge automobile disappeared.

I started my car and pulled onto Mockingbird, leaving the North Dallas Towers behind, and aimed toward home, my mind a jumble of thoughts. I was saddened and guilt-ridden but also lighthearted, almost excited, and felt nowhere near the great pain I would have expected over my sudden fall from grace. I guess it's like B.A. said, football teaches you to overcome adversity. I must be cranking up to overcome.

Football had been my refuge from the fear of loneliness and worthlessness. But now I was beginning to see what Charlotte meant. I must have a value to myself and that has to come from inside, not from achievements in the world.

I turned off Mockingbird and cruised through the wealthy and highly restricted township of Highland Park. On the street and in the driveways I passed parked cars that cost my whole salary. It was reassuring to think of Mr. Businessman's Rolls Royce or Mercedes in terms of how many bone-shattering blows I would have had to endure to earn it. In terms of ripped ligaments, shredded muscles, and lacerated skin, it put in perspective where I had really been and what an imaginary ephemeral thing I had just lost. I wasn't their equal. I was merely their entertainment.

The reverend's Cadillac was idling roughly in the drive when I reached home. Johnny would be inside singing hymns and emptying ash trays. Ash trays were all she cleaned on Mondays. It didn't take her long as I never smoked tobacco and I ate all my roaches.

I shut off the Riviera and headed up the walk to my house.

The front door was open slightly. It resisted my push and made a loud scratching noise against the hardwood floor of the living room. Sometimes in damp weather the door warped so badly I couldn't get it locked. Up until the appearance of

Mr. Rindquist, I had never worried about it. Now I was glad to be moving.

When I walked in, Johnny was bent over the fireplace emptying an ash tray onto the hearth.

"Hidy, Mr. Phil," she said, looking back over her shoulder. Two gum wrappers floated lazily to the concrete. "How's you feelin' tiday?"

"Fine, Johnny," I replied, without thinking, "just fine." The truthfulness of my answer surprised me. I did feel fine, I felt more than fine, I felt excited, anticipatory. It was a new game and I couldn't deny the thrill of it.

I knew I would lament the way it had all gone, but it would be a bittersweet regret, not pit-of-the-stomach remorse. I had been a good football player and had worked hard on the field; I would rue some of my tactics but I was satisfied; I played because I was good and they couldn't take that from me. It would be enough.

"Johnny, I won't be needing you anymore. I'm moving."

"Oh." Johnny's face wrinkled into thought for a moment, then she smiled brightly. "That's awright. Mr. Andy and Mr. Claridge wants me to come work fo' them in they new house. I was wantin' to talk to you 'bout it tiday."

"Well, that's fine, Johnny," I replied. "Tell them you can start today. And Johnny—" I dug some crumpled bills out of my pocket, "—here's fifty dollars. I want to buy the center page in your church program again. But try and remember this time how my name is spelled."

"Why, thank you, Mistah Phil. An ahm shore the rev'ren'll be rat pleased. Thank you. Thank you." She smiled widely and began untying her apron.

I wandered back to my bedroom to decide what to take and what to leave behind.

I sat on the bed and looked around the room, thinking about the sleepless nights I had spent there, some because the aches were too great to allow any rest, others because the fear had crept to the back of my throat and waited for me to close my eyes. I had lived in terror of its all ending, but now that it had, except for a slight melancholy ache and some momentary confusion, I felt great. It made all those fears that still floated near the ceiling and hung from the walls seem foolish, pointless; the nights I lay in bed and cried wolf to myself. I could recall few good times inside these bedroom walls; an occasional girl who passed through my life in one night looking for something I didn't have or had misplaced. Mostly it had been a place where I would finally retreat to let my mind and body heal.

I pulled an old suitcase from beneath the bed, gathered up three pairs of Levi's and several sweaters, and carried it to the car.

I returned to the house and unplugged the color television and placed it on the bed. I decided to leave the old Voice of Music stereo that had played everything from The Brothers Four to the Rolling Stones. I wrote a note to my landlord, enclosed a month's rent, and told him he could have anything left in the house. I picked up the color television and walked out to the car. I stopped to attach my landlord's letter to the mailbox.

"Mr. Phil."

I finished loading everything into the back seat of the Riviera and turned to face Johnny, calling me from the reverend's car as it backed from my driveway.

"Yeah, Johnny," I answered, impatient to be on my way.

"Uncle Billy Bunk sent that tape back."

The aged Cadillac bumped into the street.

"What tape?" I asked.

"You know," Johnny replied, "the one me an' mah sistah an' the rev'ren' here recorded about you."

I nodded that I recalled the tape. A loud metallic clunk from beneath the car signaled the shift from reverse to drive.

"Well," Johnny continued, leaning out the window and calling back to me as they moved off down the street, slowly picking up speed, "Uncle Billy says they couldn't use it. He said you was . . ."

The reverend had nursed the clunking, smoking car up to

speed and out of earshot. The last of Johnny's statement was lost in a cloud of blue vapor.

"I should think not," I said aloud. "I should think not."

I folded my arms on the car roof and rested my chin on them. I gazed vacantly at the ramshackle house across the street; the rot of age already had consumed the front steps and part of the porch. The collapsing house was occupied by a creaky old man I had seen only a couple of times as he shuffled hopefully to his mailbox only to find it empty. I stared at the house and the unkempt lawn for a long time, wishing I had been a better neighbor to the old man.

"Well, old man," I said to the dying house, "I guess this means neither of us will get a phone call from the President."

I climbed into the front seat, adjusted the steering wheel, pushed *Sweetheart of the Rodeo* into the tape deck and pulled away from the curb. I never even looked to see if the front door was closed.

I smoked a joint, pointed the car east and smashed down on the accelerator. Once on the highway, I kept the needle on ninety. The speed was exhilarating. Combined with marijuana and the Byrds at full volume it was near hallucinogenic.

> "*. . . I don't care how many letters they sent*
> *The morning came and the morning went.*
> *Pick up your money and pack up your tent*
> *You ain't goin' nowhere . . .*"

I was on the two-lane stretch, about twenty miles from Lacota, the central Texas hills rolling by. As I roared along the concrete strip, cattle looked up lazily from their grazing and children ran down to fence lines to wave. Charlotte would be expecting me sometime today. Standing in the yard in a loose-fitting Western shirt with her breasts thrust forward and her hands jammed in the hip pockets of her jeans, she would break into that even, gentle smile that came more from her eyes than her lips. We would go right to bed. Or maybe just there on the cold grass and show that poor Brangus steer what he missed.

". . . Buy me a flute
And a gun that shoots
Strap yourself to a tree with roots
Cause you ain't goin' nowhere . . ."

That the front gate was open didn't even register in my excitement to get to Charlotte. I reached the house and pulled up behind Bob Beaudreau's Continental Mark III with the personalized M FUNDS license plates. He was probably inside pleading with her to take him back. I would beat his ass if he even looked sideways.

The door on the driver's side had been left open and the sound of the still running engine blended eerily with the high-pitched buzz that signaled the keys were in the ignition. I reached inside and switched off the motor, taking out the keys and laying them on the seat.

Instantly it was silent and I strained to hear some clue as to what was happening. My mind jumped at a masochistic flicker of finding them in bed together, but I knew it was false.

The two cats were resting lazily in the sand beneath the kitchen steps. They looked up hungrily at the sound of my foot on the bottom stair, expecting another set of calf testicles.

The house was quiet as I moved from the kitchen down the hallway toward the den. My confusion was rapidly building. Maybe they weren't even in the house. I should have checked the barn.

I felt excited, almost lighthearted, as my adrenal cortex reacted to the tension. I stepped around the corner and down into the den.

Bob Beaudreau was sitting on the couch, alone. He was dressed neatly in a light blue suit and a wide red-and-blue-striped tie. He watched calmly as I entered the room.

"I thought I heard somebody," he said, crossing his legs. Large dark brown stains covered his trousers. "They're in the bedroom," he added, pointing down the hall and then using his finger to scratch his cheek.

Lying on a magazine atop the low coffee table in front of

the couch was Beaudreau's fat blue steel .357 Magnum. He had placed it on a magazine to keep it from scratching the tabletop.

They were just shredded pieces of brown and white flesh. Lumps of nothing. The bullets hadn't hit solidly anywhere, just knocked off hunks of meat and bone.

Charlotte must have died instantly from a bullet that hit her in the cheek and tore off the side of her head back to her ear. Another slug had hit her breast, bursting it like a balloon, leaving a ragged, bloody flap of skin hanging from her chest.

David must have bled to death, a huge red-black path followed him to the corner where he was grotesquely huddled. One of his hands was almost blown off at the wrist and was twisted palm up in a silent gesture. Two giant trenches had been ripped out of his back and buttocks.

"I caught 'em in bed early this mornin'," Beaudreau explained, his voice calm while his wild eyes searched my face. He started to giggle. "I'll bet you didn't know she was fucking the nigger."

I walked over and picked up the gun and stood in front of him.

"You thought you'd tricked me," he said, looking up at me and trying to control his giggle. His white tassled loafers were soaked with blood and had turned a bright auburn color. "The both of you—having a big laugh. Well, the joke's on you." He broke into a short high-pitched giggle, then stopped as suddenly as he started and narrowed his eyes. "I tried to be your friend," he cried, pointing a finger at my face. "I liked you."

I raised the gun and aimed right into his face. His expression never changed. I turned my head as I pulled the trigger, because I knew he would splatter some.

"It's empty," he said.

The hammer slammed into the spent cartridge with a pointless click. The frustration ripped through me like an electric shock. I lunged across the low table, lifting the gun over my head like a club. My foot caught and I fell on top of him. He began squealing like a pig and tried to crawl away from me. I swung at his head with the gun and hit him a glancing blow on the forehead with the barrel. The sight gouged a chunk out of his brow just below the hairline and the blood ran down into his right eye.

"Stop it," he screamed, rubbing his hand over his eye and looking at the blood that came away on his fingers. He started to scramble off the couch away from me. "You're crazy!"

I swung at him with all my strength, the weight of the gun adding a murderous velocity to the blow. I hit him just behind the right ear as he was trying to stand. Somehow my index finger had gotten between the trigger guard and his skull. I felt the finger shatter. Beaudreau went down in a heap on the floor. My hand had gone numb and the gun flew across the room when I tried to hit him again.

I started kicking him while he lay whimpering on the floor. I wanted to kick him to death, but he was too fat and had curled up in a ball.

I picked up the coffee table, but my broken finger wouldn't hold and the table slipped to the floor. I grabbed it again and tried to crush his skull with it, but I couldn't grip it tightly enough to get a good swing. It bounced off the side of his head and out of my hands.

"Fight, you son of a bitch!" I screamed at the huddled man. I stood over him crying and hitting him with my good fist. "Fight, goddam you."

I ran into the kitchen to get a knife. My chest started to close and I couldn't breathe. I started to sob uncontrollably. I sank to the kitchen floor and threw up.

I lay in the kitchen for a long time. Suddenly Beaudreau appeared in the doorway. He was straightening his tie and smoothing out his coat. Blood was still running from the cut over his eye and the shoulder of his coat was caked with blood from the wound behind his ear. The gun was stuck in his belt.

Beaudreau stared at me lying on the floor, then shook his head and walked over to the wall phone.

"Man," he said, lifting the receiver and starting to dial, "you're crazy."

It was dark by the time the sheriff's deputies had finished their investigation. Beaudreau had been led away, his face still bleeding, and the bodies had been taken to the white and colored funeral homes in Lacota.

After they had finished questioning me and one of the ambulance drivers had taped my finger, I went out and sat in the barn. I didn't cry, I didn't even think, I just sat there. The Brangus steer eyed me curiously from a nearby stall.

The sheriff's car was the only one left in the yard, besides the Riviera, when I returned from the barn. The sheriff was standing, fat and brown, with his alligator-booted foot on the bumper of his Ford.

"That boy a frien' a yern?"

"Nope."

"Well, we found a lotta marywana in the gal's room, and what with him findin' her with the nigger. If he jest buy hisself a good lawyer he'll probably be all right." The sheriff's face wrinkled into a thoughtful frown. "Pretty girl like that," he said, shaking his head. "How could she do it?"

The sheriff dropped his foot from the bumper and walked around to the driver's side of the Ford. "Be seein' ya," he said with a short wave.

He wadded himself behind the wheel and started the car. Instantly the night was ablaze with his red and blue flashers. He started to pull away and then stopped, reminded of something. He rolled down his window.

"Hey," he yelled at me, "good luck next Sunday."

He roared off down the gravel road. I heard the tires squeal as he hit the main road and stomped on the gas. The whine of his siren hung in the damp night air. When the siren faded, there was no sound at all.

I walked over and leaned against the corner of the corral. I looked out over the silent rolling pasture and waited, listening for sounds of life in the distance.